The Human Face of the Israel - Palestine Conflict

AIA PUBLISHING

David Kerr

'This novelised account of the Arab/Israeli conflict that followed the creation of Israel after the Holocaust is one of the best I've read. Even-handed in its telling of a desperate situation, it is full of human stories, both joyful and tragic. It is gripping, shocking and heartbreaking, yet at the same time full of love. Though hard-hitting, this is a very readable story, and it is a clear and affecting account of a complex situation. The experiences of all sides are shown with humanity and compassion. Highly recommended.' Barbara Scott Emmett – author of *Delirium: The Rimbaud Delusion*.

'*Wall of Tears* has many levels—political, historical, inter-personal, social, national, religious and driven by the author's style. The Jewish/Muslim animosity is graphically and emotionally portrayed. A well-researched novel—a seminal book.' Dr Rob McMurdo – Psychiatrist.

'Many books and novels have been written on the Palestinian-Israeli situation. Most of them focus on the mega picture of "Palestinians" and "Israelis" and few go to the depth of understanding the deep personal aspects that influence the collective. In his novel, *Wall of Tears*, David Kerr, takes us to the core, to the point of pain and trauma, that in it and through it, a healed and true understanding of peace can be envisioned.' Sami Awad – Executive Director, Holy Land Trust, Bethlehem, West Bank.

'The writer demonstrates a profound ability to empathise with both Jews who live with the trauma of the Holocaust and traumatised Palestinians who have been dispossessed. The book ought to be widely read by all who enjoy reading about characters of integrity.' Dr John Reid – Theologian.

Dedicated to Chris, my wife,
who shares my passion for the
Holy Land and its peoples.

Israel and Disputed Palestinian Territories
LEBANON
Tyre
Banias Springs
SYRIA
GOLAN
Haifa
Nazareth
Sea of Galilee
WEST BANK
Tel Aviv
Ramallah
Amman
Jericho
Jerusalem
Bethlehem
JORDAN
Hebron
Dead Sea
GAZA
Masada
Beersheba
NEGEV DESERT
EGYPT
0 10 20 30 40 50 60 km
0   10   20   30   40 mi
Eilat

Foreword

*'The love of liberty is the love of others;
the love of power is the love of ourselves.'*
William Hazlitt

The American Novelist William Faulkner wrote, 'The past isn't dead; it isn't even past.' The sand and soil of the land the Jews call Israel and the Arabs, Palestine, may cover much of the physical remains of these proud peoples. However, the struggle of their fierce sibling rivalry is as much alive today as it was in the days of Isaac and Ishmael.

My purpose in writing this novel is to promote the stories of Israelis and Palestinians I have met on my visits to Israel/Palestine or acquired through research into the historical events in the Holy Land since 1948. Many of the scenes were created around historical events used as a backdrop for the novel. While I have used stories from research and interviews, the characters are fictional, except for recognisable public figures who were associated with this period, such as David Ben-Gurion and others.

My aim is to highlight the impact of trauma on Holocaust survivors and the trauma experienced by Palestinian Arabs, dispossessed of their homes in the formation of the State of Israel. My plea is for you to come to my offering with an open mind. The more I read and listen to current conversations on both sides of the conflict, the more insight I gain as to the complexity of the issues. Human nature often demands black or white; one is right and the other wrong. That is lazy thinking. The real task is to try to understand the dynamics of the system that drives the conflict.

My endeavour is to be vigilant in understanding, valuing and maintaining respect for both Israelis and Palestinians, many of whom have become friends and contributed to the stories in this book.

Readers will undoubtedly find variations in 'the truth' as they have read or experienced it. As former US President Harry S. Truman said, 'No two historians ever agree on what happened, and the damn thing is they both think they're telling the truth.'

To prescribe a remedy to heal this ancient wound would be arrogant. By highlighting relationships where transformation from hatred to acceptance and reconciliation has taken place, my longing is to create hope for the future.

Glossary of Terms

Aufseherinnen – female SS guards.

Auschwitz-Birkenau – joint extermination camps created in Poland by the Nazis.

Bar Mitzvah – ceremony of a Jewish boy who has reached the age of thirteen and is regarded as ready to observe religious precepts and eligible to take part in public worship.

Beta Israel – a term used to describe Ethiopian Jews.

Copa – name for a 'privileged prisoner' elevated to the status of a guard in Auschwitz.

Diaspora – Jews living outside Israel.

Eretz Israel – the greatest expanse of land that matches the original biblical Israel. 'Land of Israel' ('eretz' meaning land).

Fatah – formerly the Palestinian National Liberation Movement, is a Palestinian nationalist social democratic political party and the largest faction of the confederated multi-party Palestine Liberation Organisation (PLO).

Fellaheen – (plural) farmers or agricultural labourers. The word derives from the Arabic word for 'ploughman.'

Haganah – 'defence.' A Jewish paramilitary organisation created by the British during the British Mandate of Palestine.

Hamas – a Palestinian Sunni-Islamist fundamentalist organisation founded in 1987 to free Palestine.

Hasidim – an orthodox spiritual revivalist movement that emerged in Eastern Europe in the 18th century.

Hava Nagila – Jewish folk song traditionally sung at Jewish celebrations.

Husseinis – Palestinian Arab Muslim nationalists who trace their origins to the grandson of Muhammed.

IDF – Israel Defence Force.

Intifada – Arabic, 'shake', 'shaking' or 'shake off.' Palestinian attempt to shake off Israeli power and gain independence.

Irgun – a right-wing Zionist organisation founded in 1931, disbanded in 1948.

Gakhlits – a Yiddish word for new immigrant recruit going to Palestine – 'scum of the earth.'

Jilbab – any long and loose-fit coat or garment worn by some Muslim women.

Keffiyeh – head scarf worn by Arab males.

Kippah – also referred to as a 'skullcap' worn by orthodox Jewish males.

Lake Kinneret – Sea of Galilee.

Mitzvah – 'a command,' usually a charitable or beneficial act.

Mufti – a Muslim legal expert who is empowered to give rulings on religious matters.

Muslim Brotherhood – a right-wing Sunni Islamist organisation founded in Egypt in 1928.

Nashashibis – influential Palestinian family based in Jerusalem since 1500s.

Palestinian Islamic Jihad (PIJ) – Muslim organisation founded in 1981, committed to the 'liberation of Palestine.'

PLO – 'Palestine Liberation Organisation: founded in 1964 with the purpose of the liberation of Palestine.'

Shabbat – 'the Sabbath.' Jewish holy day of rest.

Shadchen – Jewish matchmaker.

Shema – the Shema is the central prayer in the Jewish prayer book taken from Deuteronomy 6:1.

Shin Bet – Israeli Security Agency.

Shoah – 'catastrophe.' Used by Jews to refer to the Holocaust.

UNSCOP – The United Nations Special Committee on Palestine appointed by the UN General Assembly in May 1947; an Anglo-American committee set up to investigate the Arab-Israeli conflict and recommend whether British involvement should continue.

Wailing Wall – the holiest site for Jews in Israel, which became known as the 'Western Wall' after Jerusalem was captured by the Israelis in the Six Day War.

Yad Vashem – Israel's official memorial to the victims of the Holocaust.

Yishuv – the resident collection of Jews committed to the national movement of establishing an independent state in Palestine.

Yizor – memorial books.

Yom Kippur – Day of Atonement; holiest day of the year in Judaism. The central themes are atonement and repentance.

Part One

Chapter One

February 1973
Uri

'What are those birds called, Papa? ... PAPA! What are those birds called?'

'Eh … huh … they're swifts. They come here every year at this time from Africa to nest. They've done it for hundreds, maybe thousands of years. They're strong fliers.'

'That's amazing. They must feel it's safe to build their nests here.'

The small black birds dart around the Wall in the warm afternoon sunlight, feasting on insects swarming above the masses crowding the open courtyard in front of the sandstone Wall. I see dozens of cracks and openings between the large blocks of stone where the birds are making their nests.

All my family are here. I'm the oldest—eight-and-a-half years old. Yesterday we travelled for hours by bus from our kibbutz in the north of Israel to be here at the Wailing Wall in Old Jerusalem. Rabbi Yousef told me it's called that because Orthodox Jews cry for all the suffering that has taken place here. We now call it the Western Wall.

I'm so excited to be here. Papa fidgets with his bag as I say, 'The swifts must feel safe. Our people haven't always found this a safe place, though, have they? I remember you saying that the Romans destroyed Jerusalem and killed many Jews, and that many countries have invaded us.' I glance at Papa but he's not listening. 'Papa, have you been to the Wall before?'

'Ah … no … we've not been able to come here until six years ago, after we captured Jerusalem in the Six Day War, after you were born.'

'Why?'

'Our Arab neighbours, the Jordanians, stopped us, even though they signed an agreement to allow the Jewish people to come here.'

I like hearing about history and Papa is sometimes happy to tell me. 'I'm glad those soldiers are here,' I say, watching the men and women in army uniforms standing in groups. 'I feel safe because they have guns.'

'They're always here. Sometimes there's trouble from terrorists …'

'Stop pointing, Sabella,' my mother, whom I call Ima, says gently to my sister. Four Orthodox Jews stride past in their funny black hats, talking among themselves.

I frown. 'Papa, why have people been so cruel?'

'Oh, Uri, it's … so … complicated.' Papa sighs. 'Jerusalem is a very special place for so many different kinds of people.

Nations have fought over it for centuries. The Western Wall is the holiest place in Israel—in the world for us Jews.'

'Why is that, Papa?'

'This is the Western Wall of the temple built by Herod. The Ark of the Covenant was closer to this wall than any of the other walls in the temple.' (Note 1)

Ima interrupts: 'Ah, Leah, there you are.' Leah, Ima's friend, appears beside me. We stayed with Leah and her husband, Issur, last night in the Jewish quarter. They're old people and have two sons who went to America to live.

'Are you enjoying your first visit to the Wall, Uri?' Leah says.

'Yes, it's exciting. I love the birds.' She smiles. 'They come here every year around February. It's a sign spring is just around the corner.'

Ima turns to Papa. 'Abdiel, Sachi is getting restless. I think I'll go for a walk with the children. Do you want to come with me too, Uri?'

'Papa, can I stay with you, please … please?'

'Um … okay,' Papa mumbles.

I'm puzzled. Does he really want me to stay?

'Abby,' Ima asks, 'are you feeling alright? You seem as though you're somewhere else.'

Papa shrugs.

'*You* wanted to come here?' Ima's voice has a question mark.

Papa is silent.

Leah says, 'I'll come with you Maya.'

Ima bends down and lays Abraham gently in the pram. Leah takes Sabella and Sachi's hands and walks towards the

Dung Gate. My gaze follows them, their colourful headscarves still easy to see among the growing number of people.

I turn back to look at the Wall. My chest is getting cold, but the sun feels warm on my back. The place where we stand gives us a good view of what's happening. The stone pavement slopes down gradually to the Wall where hundreds of worshippers are gathering, most in black coats and trousers, some with funny black hats. Most of the men wear a Kippah, like Papa and me. At the Wall the men sway backwards and forwards as they say their prayers. Rabbi Yousef calls it 'bobbing' or 'davening.' He says it's moving forward to God. Now I hear a group of worshippers starting to sing. The tassels of their prayer shawls swing from under the bottom of their coats.

'They're so happy, Papa.'

'They're singing praises to God. They're very happy to be at the Wall, now, after many years, they're able to worship.'

The group of singing worshippers makes a long line and moves forward as they sing and dance.

'Can we go closer to the Wall?' I ask.

'Yes. We need to go and wash at the font over there.' Papa points to a small stone stand to our left.

Today is Friday, a special day at the Wall. Shabbat starts at sundown; in an hour's time, many Jews in Jerusalem come to the Wall to worship. They go back to their homes afterwards and have a special meal. We walk to the basin as the singing group makes a circle, singing, clapping, dancing and jumping.

I smile at the sight. 'I love this, Papa.'

Papa turns on the tap. 'Watch what I do.' He puts his left-hand under the tap, catches the water and tips it into his right-hand, then pours it from his right hand back into his left. He does this seven times. I know this is like a spiritual washing before we go near the Wall. But Papa's hand is shaking. Is he nervous?

I do what Papa does, and then we slowly walk towards the Wall. Papa has lived in Israel for twenty-five years since he came to Israel by boat in 1948 but he's never been to the Wall before. During the war, he was in a concentration camp in Poland, but he doesn't talk about it. Ima told me not to ask him questions. She said, 'Your father may tell you when he's ready. It was a terrible time for him and also for me.'

We stop a short distance from the Wall. More groups sing and dance around us. The sun shines from a blue sky without a cloud to hide it. The sounds and smell of people crowding around me is so different from life in the kibbutz.

'This is wonderful. I'll never forget this, Papa. Why are there pieces of paper stuck in the Wall?'

'They're the prayers of worshippers. They believe they're closer to God here and that God will more likely hear and answer their prayer. In 1967, after we won the Six Day War, our people could pray here for the first time. One of our famous leaders, Moshe Dayan, squeezed his prayer into the Wall. Apparently it was "for a lasting peace to descend on Israel."'

'I've read about Moshe Dayan and what he did in the war.'

'I'm glad you like learning about our history,' replies Papa. He frowns and looks worried, though.

I want to touch the Wall like the other boys and men are doing and say a prayer, but there are too many people. I know Papa wants to make a prayer too. Many times I've heard him say how he looks forward to the day when he can pray at the Wall. Papa has been to Jerusalem twice since my birth, but he's never come here. Ima used to say to him, 'Abdiel, why don't you go? You've waited so long.' And he always replied, 'Yes, I will, but not just yet.'

I look up at Papa. 'Are you excited Papa?' He says nothing, just looks serious, stares at the Wall and stands very straight. His back is usually slightly rounded from the many hours he bent over when he made shoes and boots. At the kibbutz he spends most of his time looking after fruit trees. That's why his face is so tanned. His chin pokes forward on his face a little and his left ear is … kind of … twisted—from some accident, I think. I like the way he speaks—slowly. He's the same height as most other men and not fat, because he works so hard.

I point to the Wall where two men have left after walking backwards for a few steps, which is being respectful to God— Papa says you don't turn your back on God. 'Papa, there's a space there for us, *there*.'

Papa doesn't move, and his face is hard. It seems like he's a long way away. His body starts shaking, and he grips my hand so tightly it hurts. *What's wrong with Papa?* I want to go to the Wall but I want Papa with me. *Why won't you go?*

His head tilts forward, and a single silent tear runs down his cheek.

'Papa. Why are you crying?' My heart beats fast. What's happening to him? I've never seen Papa cry—ever.

He takes a deep breath and straightens his body, but stares at his feet, carefully examining the stone pavement. 'You go, Uri. I'll wait for you here.' He gasps—his voice is heavy.

'No Papa. I'm not going without you.'

I stand beside him for what seems like a long time as worshippers press their hands against the limestone—many bobbing energetically and chanting—the dancers and singers behind us continue their noisy worship.

Finally, Papa says with a deep sigh, 'Sorry, Uri, maybe next time.'

I feel sad inside but don't think it's right to ask Papa questions. I've never seen him like this before. Maybe I'll ask Ima. We turn and walk back up the slope. Long shadows cover the pavement as the sun sinks behind the old stone houses repaired after the war. Shabbat is ready to begin.

'There you are, Abdiel.' It's Issur. He's come from an appointment he said he needed to go to this afternoon. 'I wanted to let you know that Maya and the children have gone back to our place with Leah for the meal. Do you want to stay longer or do you want to come back now?'

'Thanks, Issur, I believe we're ready to walk back,' Papa says, breathing more easily.

As we climb the steps, I turn around for one last look at the sea of black and white, chanting, singing and dancing. So much fun and joy—yet Papa so heavy with sadness that he could've burst into a flood of tears. I won't ask him now, but one day I will. I want to know. I'll never forget that tear.

~

1: The Ark of the Covenant was described in the Old Testament as a gold covered wooden chest with a cover lid containing the two stone tablets of the Ten Commandments. It also contained Aaron's Rod and a pot of manna.

Chapter Two

February 1973

'Are you feeling okay, Abby?' Ima turns her head to search Papa's face as he drives the kibbutz car back north to Atak.

'I'm fine, just a little tired,' he replies, shrugging his shoulders.

'Our precocious Uri seemed very subdued last night—not his usual self,' Ima whispers.

I sit on the backseat of the car and can't stop thinking about Papa not going to pray at the Wall. *What caused that big tear to roll down his cheek?* Today he seems quiet except when us kids fight. Then he gets angry. Squeezing us three kids together in the backseat for a long time isn't good, but we're lucky to be on an excursion together at all.

It's rare for birthparents to take their children away from the kibbutz for an outing, but the council gave us permission because Ima had a long depression after I went into the children's house. Most kids have little contact with their birthparents. I guess I'm fortunate in that way.

Papa stops the car three times for Ima to feed and change Abraham before we arrive back at our kibbutz late in the afternoon. I head for the children's house and am allowed to play with the other children before dinner. Sometimes I go down to friends in the settlement and play with Ghazi and

Aalia. Their parents, Omar and Sabah, are Palestinian Arabs and good friends of my parents. They have two younger children. Our favourite game is hidings—we can't go outside the orchard, but sometimes Ghazi cheats and hides in the corn when it's tall.

My favourite place is Banias Springs, up in the Golan. Our people couldn't go there until after I was born in 1965, too dangerous. We're going there to celebrate my ninth birthday in August. Can't wait. A little further north is Mt Nebo where you can see the whole land of Israel. This is where Moses viewed the Promised Land.

~

The day has finally come, and I'm so excited. We run from the truck to the stream that bubbles over smooth stones.

'Don't get into the water yet. Wait for me,' I hear Ima call.

Papa lifts Abraham onto his shoulders and walks up beside me. 'You can change into your swimmers now.'

Minutes later I'm splashing Sabella and Sachi.

'Stop it Uri,' they scream, but I think they like it. The cold clear water gives me goose bumps. It comes out of a rock like magic. We walk up the stream a little way and see Pan's Temple carved in the side of the mountain. They say it's thousands of years old—goes back to Canaanite times. My other favourite thing to do is climb to the top of the hill. It's very stony, but when you reach the top, you can see over the countryside, see the green bushes and trees growing beside the stream that runs down into the Jordan River. You can look down over Pan's Temple and think about what the ancient people did there. There are secret caves that we play in. They're cool inside where we hide from the sun. I love this place … my favourite place in Israel.

We sit under the trees and have my party—chicken, shawarma, pita bread, falafel, lemonade, and of course, a chocolate cake. Ima's a good cook and didn't have to ask what I wanted!

'Can I have one more swim before we leave?' I plead as Ima and Papa pack up the plates. The girls have already changed and are chasing a butterfly along the edge of the stream. I'm glad to be free to explore.

'Don't go too far away. We need to leave soon,' Papa says.

Minutes later I'm floating gently over the coloured rocks while the stream sings to me. As it turns through a bend, the low, soft branches of a tree stroke my face. *This is what heaven will be like.* Further I float, staring at the blue cloudless sky. Suddenly two soldiers lift me out of the water and sit me on the bank. My heart is racing as I catch my breath. They have guns, and no smiles.

'Where are your parents?' asks the soldier with stripes on the top of the upper arm of his shirt.

'Back there.' I point.

'You need to go back to them now. We'll walk with you.'

What are soldiers doing here? Am I in trouble? I had no idea I'd floated so far downstream. I stand and we follow the dirt track beside the stream. A short while later, I spot Ima and Papa with my sisters and brother loading the truck.

Ima and Papa frown when they see the soldiers. 'Has he been up to mischief?' Papa asks.

'Not at all,' says the soldier with the stripes. 'We're taking precautionary steps. We don't want to alarm you, but we advise you to leave the area and return to your home. We don't believe there's any immediate danger, though—it's only a precaution.'

'Thank you, sergeant, we're just about to leave,' Papa replies.

'What's going on?' Ima asks Papa as we drive off.

'No idea. I suppose they know something we don't. Maybe they're being careful, maybe overcautious. Egypt's been threatening to attack for ages. I think Sadat's all noise and no action. Let's check the news when we get back.'

'I hope that didn't spoil your fun, Uri?' Ima says with a frown.

'No way; I'll never forget today.'

We're almost home, and Papa hasn't said a word. 'Are you okay Abby? Ima asks.

'I'm just tired,' Papa says, shrugging his shoulders.

'Did the soldiers upset you?'

'No! I tell you I'm just tired.' Irritation creeps into Papa's voice.

Ima lets out a big sigh. 'Why don't you continue with your diary? You said that really helped you.'

'I don't have time to write in any diary. It takes me all my time to do the weekly newsletter.' Papa shifts in his seat and pushes harder on the accelerator.

'Oh, Abby, please slow down. I didn't mean to upset you. I'm just trying to be helpful.'

Papa slows the truck and remains silent.

Nobody says a word until we arrive back at the kibbutz. I get out of the car, wondering about Papa's diary. I didn't know he had a diary. He's a very good writer, and I think he really enjoys it. Everyone in the kibbutz loves reading his newsletters. Papa is good at speaking and writing English. He can also speak and write Polish, German and Yiddish. I think I need to find his diary. Maybe it'll help me find the answer to the tear.

Two weeks have passed since I heard about Papa's diary, and today I've managed to sneak away from the children's games and enter Papa and Ima's room. The most likely place to find it is on a shelf in an old wardrobe, above where his clothes hang. Ima is in the kitchen helping prepare dinner and Papa is in the orchard. I quickly move the wooden chair from the corner and stand on it. The top shelf has a few old woollen jumpers, some magazines, copies of the kibbutz newsletter and an old brown suitcase. I move the chair so I can more easily reach the suitcase. It isn't too heavy, so I gently lift it down and lay it on the floor. I can hardly wait to open it.

Click, click go the locks, and I lift the lid. It smells very old. I think it hasn't been opened for a long time. An old dark dress, which I imagine belongs to Ima, lies inside. It smells bad. Underneath is a prayer shawl. I didn't know Papa had one! I've never seen him wear it. There's also a black kippah, an old copy of the Torah and two books, which I think are German. The only other thing is an old black writing book with a thick cardboard cover that has scratches and marks on it.

It's old and smells funny. Is this the diary? I open it. A number of pages have been ripped out of the front. The first page is in Papa's handwriting and at the top he has written, *Thursday, 10th July, 1947, Sète France.*

My heart leaps. I can hardly believe it. This is it! The writing is neat, but the page is yellowish. I can still read it, though. I sit on the floor resting my back against the bed.

I stood motionless and stared at the grey, amorphous mass of hundreds of children, most of them orphans, huddled together on the wharf in the French port of Sète. I suspect this pathetic image will sear my brain and remain with me forever. The children clung together, and not from cold—it was a warm summer afternoon. Like small fish in the ocean or animals in the field, they've learnt there is security in numbers. They know who to trust and not to trust.

Multiple layers of ragged clothes hung from their emaciated bodies. It's easier to wear clothes than carry them. Risking clothes to a carry-bag that could be lost or stolen is not an option. Most clutched a small object—a doll, a toy, a photograph, some link with their past. Deep in their pockets, pieces of mouldy bread provide emotional comfort. It is never eaten. Whispers with coded meaning—secret eye movements—have helped them survive their brutality. They do not have to speak to relate their story. Their lifeless eyes say it all—full of suffering and unspeakable violence: parents executed before their eyes; childhood friends whose skulls were crushed with rifle butts or who had suicided by throwing their frail bodies into the electrified barb wire; men and women torn apart by savage security dogs.

Tears fill my eyes, and I feel bad reading this. Should I be reading it? This is terrible. What if Ima or Papa catch me? But I can't help myself. I pause for a moment … I must read on.

Here are the survivors, who in their two-year-long flight through Europe bought and sold gold teeth from the dead, rings, eggs, and condoms.

I wonder what a condom is.

They lived, breathed and moved as one body. Some of the piercing blue and brown eyes staring from emotionless faces gave a hint of hope—the boat before them. All eyes were united in a fury against the God of their forefathers who has abandoned them. They will remain silent for years, sometimes for the reminder of their lives—their children will never hear their stories.

My heart races. Papa doesn't want me to know about his story. He doesn't want *anybody* to know what happened to him. My hand shakes. But if I stop reading, I may never know about the tear.

Someone signalled from the bridge for the children to board. Quietly the ragged mass formed a line. The children mounted the gangplank, clutching any remaining possessions from their past—their sole belongings. The adults followed, many stumbling and slipping. A small number of crew scrutinized the possessions of every passenger. Rage and anguish overcame many who had to forsake their precious possessions when they exceeded the 'permitted' allowance.

Then a voice sounded from the upper deck. It was Shmuel Roseman, chairman of the Refugee Committee. He proclaimed with great emotion, 'Today we are boarding the ship, the ship that is the battle of the Jewish people.'

Friday 11th July.

I found it hard to sleep last night. Yesterday I searched the faces of the masses, looking for my brother Daniel and

Maya, but no sign. I combed every corner of the compound during our long days at the camp in Marseilles without success. News they had survived the camps came from a UN worker, but they couldn't be located now. The three of us escaped the Nazi onslaught in our village in North Poland. I can't understand the hatred of our neighbours and local residents, tearing apart our quilts and pillows and scattering them in the street. A Polish priest who knew my parents saw what was happening and arranged for us to escape. We made it to Brussels before being discovered and then joined the masses in the cattle trucks for Auschwitz. The terrible news of my parent's death in Auschwitz came to me from a neighbour. Two Poles informed the Nazis of the kind priest's action. The priest and my parents were executed.

My grandparents were shot! I sit dumbfounded. Was this the reason for my Papa's sadness? I'm feeling guilty reading, but I can't help but turn the next page.

The ferry, President Warfield, is the result of secret negotiations by Haganah.[Note 1] *I heard this morning that the British had sunk many boats trying to enter Palestine.*[Note 2] *I'm anxious about this flimsy boat getting us to Haifa, especially if we're attacked by the British.*

Some time during the morning, a young, well-built, olive-skinned man in kakhi **shorts** *and shirt appeared at the railing near the bridge.*

'That's Yossi Harel.' The words crackled from an old, bearded man standing beside me. 'He's in charge of the operation, a good man to have as commander. Tough,

determined, compassionate—if anyone can get us to Palestine, he will. I was on board the Abba Berdichev with about 800 from the camps last November when it sailed with the Knesset Israel to Palestine. We got smashed up in the Adriatic, but the Knesset Israel rescued us. Yossi was in charge. The conditions were terrible, though. Nearly 4000 bodies crammed together.'

*'Clearly you **didn't** make it that time,' I said. 'What happened?'*

'A British destroyer ordered us to go to Cyprus,' the old man continued, 'but Yossi ignored them. We headed to Palestine but three British destroyers blocked our way. Yossi refused to budge, and the Brits escorted us into Haifa harbour. That's when all hell broke loose. The British Navy attacked us with batons, rifles and tear gas. They killed two of us, but we wounded many British sailors. They forced us off the boat at Haifa into holding camps and then packed us off to Cyprus. I was one of the lucky ones who managed to sneak back to France. I hope I make it this time.'

I like the old man with his withered face obscured by his ragged white beard. He told me that Yossi is in his late twenties and was chosen to head the operation because he's daring, yet level headed—an amazing tactician—and has a passion for sailing. He joined the Haganah when he was fifteen and trained with a British military unit commanded by a Captain called Orde Wingate.

The old man became silent after giving me that information. His eyes glazed over and he seemed lost in his own world. Wherever he went in his mind, it was probably better than here. We were squashed into a tiny space on the second of the four decks surrounded by the odour of unwashed bodies and stale breath.

An hour after boarding yesterday, an anxious wave of murmuring had swept the ship. The French authorities had gone back on their promise and banned the ship from exiting the harbour. They'd caved-in to the British. Unbelievable! The French commanded us to leave the ship. Yossi thought for a few minutes, and then he gave orders to burn all our documents and passports. We threw them into large metal bins where they were burned. Yossi said that no one was to leave the ship. Two British destroyers were sighted lying in wait outside the port, and Yossi said he'd heard that the British were intent on teaching the Jews a lesson.

However, later, under the cover of darkness, without a harbour pilot and after a 'generous' provision of alcohol resulted in two drunk French customs officers, our President Warfield crept quietly out of the harbour. It wasn't a clean escape. Our terrified captain bumped the sides of the harbour, and a sandbank seized the hull, which required dangerous manoeuvring for an hour, thrusting back and forth to break its grip. Eventually, however, our ghostly vessel finally made its way into calm open water.

Oh no! The dinner gong sounds, and I know I must run quickly to the dining hall. I put the diary back into the suitcase. My mind searches for an excuse if someone asks me where I was.

The hall is filled with clashing plates and noisy voices. After I collect my meal, the only seats left are beside one of the older boys who help organise the children's games before dinner. Just my luck!

'Didn't see you this afternoon, Uri?'

'Oh … I was feeling very tired and needed to rest,' I said with fake confidence.

'Is everything all right?'

'Yeah. I just didn't sleep too well last night,' I lied.

Fortunately he didn't ask any more questions and shovelled chicken and vegetables into his mouth faster than anyone I've seen. I'm glad he didn't want to talk. It gave me time to think. When could I get back to the diary? I couldn't keep on slipping out of the games time. The adults would start asking questions. It seemed clear to me that Papa didn't want me to know about his past, but I don't understand why. If Ima found out, would she tell Papa or not? But I didn't want to risk anyone finding out my secret search.

Then I have a brilliant idea. Every so often, the adults meet for games or a movie in the hall at the end of Shabbat. Next Saturday night something special is happening. During our free time, before bed, I could sneak back into Papa and Ima's room and read more from the diary.

~

The days couldn't go quick enough, but now I'm back in my parent's room, holding Papa's diary in my hand. My heart thumps as I turn the pages and find the next day …

Saturday 12th July.

We heard from the ship's radio that the British were furious that the President Warfield had slipped through their fingers, and this morning two British destroyers appeared out of nowhere.

Life has developed its own rhythm on board. The Hasidim maintain their exclusive space and time for their prayers, as do the regular Orthodox and the ultra-orthodox. People come up on the deck to escape the claustrophobia and the stale air below. Men, women and children weep and rejoice. We shower, eat the simple food prepared in the cramped kitchens and drink water. Endless lines wait patiently at lavatories, as do the sick, who are eventually treated by doctors.

I joined the floating taskforce and performed my duties in the kitchen, as well as scrubbing decks and cleaning toilets, but I still found time to spend many hours reading in the library. Young people organise debates, play music, sing and dance. A choir has been formed; a newspaper is printed daily. The atmosphere is bittersweet. Celebration at escaping the horrors of Europe, but the threat of deep water and British destroyers replace the electrified barbed wire of the camps, causing more fear and frustration. We refer to our ship as the 'The Floating Auschwitz.'

Sunday 13th July.

It's three days since we've left Sète, and one of the pregnant refugees collapsed. She gave birth to a son, but is unwell. Though the two midwives did the best they could, she's lost a lot of blood. This morning disputes among the refugees ran high, and Yossi had to intervene and deal with their grievances.

I feel anxious for Papa and what the destroyers might do. This is amazing. Why didn't Papa want us to know about this? I turn the page …

Monday 14th July.

The woman who gave birth died today. Yossi buried her at sea, wrapping her body in canvas and the Zionist flag. Her body, tied to the chains of the anchor, slid with hardly a splash into the water. She survived the camps and the flight across Europe only to die at the gates of Palestine—so sad. The baby remains alive, but there is no milk, so he's fed on pineapple juice. (Note 3)

I mingled spellbound amongst the mix of creatures, sad, sorrowful, yet sometimes bursting with life, and I watched a woman lying on the ship's iron floor longing for death.

'I just want to die,' she said over and over.

I continued to search the decks for Daniel and Maya, moving amongst the mass of desperados, meeting orphaned children. Their eyes are sad, but there are glimmers of hope. I spoke with a frail Polish woman in her fifties who had adopted six Jewish children to save them from an extermination camp. She narrowly avoided death when the Nazis learnt of her actions. She was tipped off, and nuns hid her in the basement of a church, then she later escaped to a safer hideout in central France. She was one of the fortunate few. The Nazis executed anyone hiding Jews on the spot or pushed them onto the cattle trucks to join Jews in the gas chambers.

We passed Malta, and another two British destroyers joined our escort, making four in total. We must be very important to have so many ships keeping their eyes on us. We trained harder today, expecting an attack.

Tuesday 15th July.

Political and literary debates dominate the attention of many of the young people, but they turn into shouting matches. One discussion, termed 'a trial,' argued on the subject of the value of cynicism. Other topics were whether suicide is an ideal choice; the merits of 'ethics versus etiquette,' and whether 'man made history' or 'history made man.' The Marxists among them seem to be the most vocal. I love their energy and passion. To witness the sharpness of their mind and the strength of their voice after mind-numbing incarceration is wonderful to behold.

One young intellectual yelled out the number tattooed on his arm whenever anyone asked him for his name. He said he was now just a number, and his name had been taken away forever. The crude scratching and ink of the tattooist is more than skin deep; it has seared his soul.

I know it's getting late and I should leave the room … but I can't stop reading …

Wednesday 16th July.

As the days progress, tensions grow. Yossi was called on to intervene in a number of disputes, but generally people are tolerant, especially given the cramped conditions. Tensions have escalated from the religious Jews. Yossi didn't interfere with their prayers on deck, but he didn't give in to their demands for a kosher kitchen and no cooking on the Sabbath. Yossi tried to gather them together for prayers, but they refused and split up into their separate groups—the Hasidim and their opponents the Misnagdim, the regular Orthodox and the ultra-orthodox.

I befriended a young couple who met on the ship. He's a painter and spent hours today sketching her slender figure in various poses. Her smile when she viewed the completed work briefly covered the pain she carries. I watched him conduct some sort of ceremony to divorce himself from his dead fiancée and then commit himself to his new-found love. As part of the spontaneous ritual, an old woman gave him a piece of candy hidden in the hem of her dress. Two young men from his hometown gave up their small corner of the ship, and the newly betrothed couple entered the enclosure. A neighbour stretched a string across the front and hung socks and shirts on it to enclose the space, enabling them to complete their betrothal.

I hear the sound of footsteps and wriggle under the bed. They stop outside the door. My heart is racing. Have Ima and Papa come back early? The door opens and the light goes off. A familiar voice says, 'They left the light on.'

I wait until I can no longer hear them, then I fumble in a drawer for Papa's torch. The light is good. I open a new page. Maybe a few more minutes and then I must leave.

Thursday 17th July

Land crept nearer today and our mood lifted. Eyes strained to see the uneven coastline. I stood on deck, squashed between two middle-aged men. One I had seen regularly cleaning the decks. The constant motion of the ship disturbs the equilibrium of many non-seafaring souls, and sometimes they don't make it to the railing in time. The vomit has to be cleaned up quickly, and when it happened today, the bald-headed man standing beside me was quick to spring into action.

His name is Levi. He said it's not far to go and he's ready for a fight. He doesn't think the British will wait for us to land—they'll try and stop us at sea even though that doesn't comply with international law.

We had a name-change today—four men fixed a sign to the railing: 'Exodus from Europe 47' painted in bold white letters. A cheer went up. I love it—a proud moment.

Suddenly, in the afternoon, the ship swung due north and sailed towards Gaza. The word went out to prepare for action. Groups of fighters moved to strategic spots on the ship. They came armed with tin cans from the kitchen, steam vents and keys for the ropes fastened to the ship's huge rafts. The plan is to release them and throw them onto British sailors that attempt to board our ship.

The British destroyers maintained their escort; one in front, another behind, port and starboard. Darkness fell, bringing with it a long night of waiting. Everyone is tense.

Friday 18th July.

At 2 a.m., far from the territorial waters of Palestine, one of the destroyers drew near and flooded us with the glare of searchlights. An officer's voice crackled from a loudhailer instructing the ship to come to a halt. Yossi's plan snapped into place. Masses of passengers rushed to the decks from below. Everyone knew his or her place and task. The ship didn't stop; instead the ship's wheel spun, and we turned to the open sea.

Undeterred, the British commenced their assault on the high seas rather than risk a fight on land. Two other ships appeared. I crouched inside the cabin door on the upper deck, my heart pounding as I gripped a club in my right hand. One of the British ships drew alongside with ropes and ladders at the ready.

It was a hopeless battle. Five model C destroyers and one cruiser against the wreck of an old riverboat, packed to the hilt with homeless civilians. One of the destroyers rammed the Exodus with a splintering crash. It trembled; beams collapsed, bunk beds crashed, people screamed and were thrown onto the deck, and British sailors stormed the ship. The destroyer's powerful sirens shattered people's eardrums. I saw three British invaders manage to make it to the pilot bridge.

Some of the young people wounded the sailors. Some even grabbed and tossed the intruders into the sea. An

American volunteer who worked on the ship was hit by the butt of a rifle and collapsed, dead on the spot. The fighting grew more intense. Shots were fired and teargas canisters released.

Yossi yelled, 'People in the camps fought in order to die with dignity. Here, gentlemen, you are fighting for your lives.'

My club connected with the arm of a marine when he attempted to pull himself over the railing. The sailor screamed in pain and fell into the water. My orders were to patrol the starboard. I swung my weapon again when a wave of British marines clambered over the ship's side. They fell back, cursing, into the water. Clubs, metal bars, screws and bolts, bottles, oil, coal dust and tomatoes were the only weapons we could muster in our defence.

About half way through the battle, a rifle butt hit my head, and I fell to my knees. The British sailor gave me a solid kick to my ribs, sending me writhing to the deck, twisting in agony. I lay still for a moment, and then with great effort, dragged my body under a raft. I shivered in fear while rifle shots exploded, and the cries and screams from my fellow fugitives filled my ears. I thought to myself, 'I survived Auschwitz on land, but will I survive Auschwitz at sea?'

The fighting persisted and the battering continued. In international waters off the coast of Gaza, the Exodus failed. People slipped on the oil poured on the decks as a defence. People bled. The sides of the ship began to split. Angry British soldiers covered in the garbage and black *coal dust hurled at them, vented their fury on the refugees who were fighting for their lives.*

The battle lasted around three hours and left the ship precariously afloat. At five in the morning, the British pushed hard to finish the battle. I heard more gunshots, and more bullets hit more people. The British rammed the ship again and again, and more marines poured over the side of the ship.

The strategy and tactics of the British were superior and finally our ship was taken. It listed so dangerously that people staggered like drunkards, trying to stand upright. Yossi surveyed the devastation of the ship and the state of the bloodied people entrusted to his care. With an expression showing his heavy heart and lucid mind, he gave the order to stop the fighting. The remains of the battered Exodus flying the Zionist flag limped into Haifa harbour. I heard that three refugees were killed and twenty-eight seriously wounded.

I can hardly believe what I'm reading. I'm shocked to know Papa was in such a huge fight. He's lucky to be alive! I turn the page, and a cutting from a newspaper falls onto the floor. The top part has been torn off. The paper is very fragile, and I have to handle it carefully.

... little did the wretched community on board the Exodus know that all the traffic had stopped in Tel Aviv and every city in Palestine. In every kibbutz and settlement, the entire Jewish nation listened to the plight of their fellow countrymen on radio. As the refugees disembarked and commenced loading onto the three

deportation ships lying in wait in the harbour, another terrible scene erupted. Terrified people jumped into the sea while British police boats circled the ship. The patience of the British was again tested to the limit. Refugees were fired on with live ammunition, struck with batons. Women fainted, children trampled, men screamed in fear and rage. The British used their batons with contempt and herded the unfortunate masses onto their boats with swinging batons and fixed bayonets. Now the eyes of the defeated filled with tears, their hearts broken and without hope.

Some Jewish leaders were disappointed that Yossi Harel, the commander, had surrendered. Yossi replied, 'I didn't accept the command to convert refugees into fighters and certainly not take wounded survivors of the Holocaust just so they could die enroute from Netanya to Haifa, nor play with their lives over something we already proved. Leaving Europe was itself resistance.'

The disembarkation of the Exodus, including dozens of the injured took place with Judge Sandstrom and Yugoslav Vladamir Simitch, a UNSCOP member looking on. Beside them stood an array of international journalists. They had been 'invited' to the port by Jewish Agency Political Department's Director, Moshe Shertok. Sandstrom and Simitch spent two hours on the pier and spoke with passengers. They came away shaken. Simitch was heard to say, 'It's the best possible evidence we have.'

The following day the two men reported what they had seen to other committee members of UNSCOP. The full committee also heard the testimony of an American cleric,

Papa went back to Germany! I never knew that. I feel very angry at the British for what they did to Papa and our people. Why hasn't Papa told me about this? He's a hero.

I realise how late it is and tear myself away from the diary, placing it back under the old dress and the prayer shawl in the suitcase. I creep along the pathway in the darkness to the children's house, wondering how any of these things might have caused Papa's sadness at the Wall. How would I ever know?

~

5th September 1973

We are sitting at the breakfast table in the dining hall, and Jonathan, a senior member of the kibbutz, asks us to be silent for a minute. He clears his throat and says in a sad voice, 'On this day twelve months ago, eleven of our athletes were killed by the Black September terrorist group at the Munich Olympics. We will never forget them and all the victims of terrorists who have attacked our people.'

We bow our heads.

'Thank you, children.'

We had been allowed to watch some of the Olympics on our television, but we didn't see the attack. We were shocked to hear that some people hated us so much that they want to kill us.

We're much quieter than usual as we eat breakfast this morning.

~

The following weekend I sit playing with Ghazi who has come up to challenge me to a game of chequers on the floor of the games room. His mother and father have brought sweet cakes and baklava to have with coffee. Papa tells them about the soldiers at Banias Springs and their warning.

Ghazi's father, Omar, looks serious. 'Every week there're more and more terrorist attacks. It's not looking good,' he says.

I like Omar. He's a Palestinian Arab and a good man— kind and a good friend of Papa and Ima. His wife, Sabah is a nice lady. I know our soldiers give them a hard time, but they still like us. I want to know more about how they came to live near us, but Papa said when I'm older. There's so much I want to know: why so many countries helped Hitler kill my people and put Papa and Ima in concentration camps; why we have to fight for land that belonged to Jewish people going back to King David, and the question that won't go away is why Papa was so emotional at the Wall. Every day I think about it. Papa is such a strong man, so whatever it is must be big, very big.

Papa's boat trip was scary, but I can't see anything that could be connected with the Wall. It has to be something to do with the Wall. I know Papa wanted to go there, like most of my people, but when he had the chance he held back. Something in his memory ... I must find out.

~

1. The British set up and trained the Haganah during the period of the Mandate to assist in providing law and order in Palestine. The Haganah turned on Britain when the growing number of Jewish refugees exceeded the restrictions Britain imposed to satisfy the demands of Palestinians.

The converted American ferry *President Warfield,* (renamed by Mossad, the Israeli Secret Service, *Exodus from Europe – 1947*) would transport 4,500 refugees to Israel. Since August 1946, the British had returned captured illegal immigrants to Europe. They were getting tough on the 'illegal boat people' in Europe. Britain's MI6 unleashed a violent campaign of sabotage against Haganah's ships in European ports. They had sunk the *Vrisi* in Genoa harbour the previous night, and anxiety ran high as the immigrants crowded onto the wharf in Sète.

The Haganah, dressed as British soldiers, using British trucks, may have fooled the eyes of onlookers, but the British tracked their every move, and were ready to teach the Jews a lesson they would never forget.

2. The *USS President Warfield* was an old American riverboat, 330 feet long, made of steel, built in 1928, licensed to carry 400 passengers and fifty-eight crew. Its conversion to a troop carrier for transportation on the Normandy coast in World War I raised its capacity to 1028 persons. The Haganah refitted the worn-out vessel to transport 4,500 people to Palestine.

In 1942 a German submarine had attacked the vessel resulting in its decommission in September 1945. Its buyers, the Weston Trading Company, a front for the Haganah, rescued the craft from the wreckers who had paid $8,000 to the US Navy, describing it as 'a matchbox splintered by a nutcracker.' The wreckers charged Haganah $50,000, and the 'wreck' required a further $130,000 to ensure it was seaworthy and could accommodate the refugees. Even then, a storm flooded the engine room at sea and threatened the safety of the vessel.

3. The baby died months later in Haifa.

4. Content for this chapter has been gleaned from *Commander of the Exodus,* by Yoram Kaniuk, (New York: Grove Press, 1999), *The Jewish Virtual Library, 1948: A History of the First Arab-Israeli War,* by Benny Morris (New Haven and London: Yale University Press, 2008).

Chapter Three

A mixture of pride and fury filled the hearts of the Jewish refugees. Many sat nursing their depression, staring at the strands of barbed wire stretched between the wooden posts of Camp Poppendorf. It's not the high razor wire fences of Auschwitz, charged with high voltage electricity, but combined with patrolling British guards, it makes the cruel statement that illegal immigrants are not welcome in the local Austrian community or anywhere else in the world. Not a single place exists for us outside the prison. Europe has slammed its doors shut to Jewish refugees. America too, while sympathetic, keeps its gates firmly closed.

We've survived the spontaneous collective hunger-strike on the Exodus in France; survived the brutal British batons and the powerful water cannons in the forced removal from the ship in Hamburg; survived the long train journey from Hamburg to Poppendorf and the truck ride to the camp. Now, in Poppendorf Camp, Austria, we wait, around 2,500 shattered souls. The remaining 2,000 of the Exodus community languish in a camp at Lübeck. Our efforts to reach Palestine, crushed, liberated but not free. Freed from barbed wire and Nazi guards in Germany, only to be replaced with barbed wire and

British guards in Germany. British violence, indifference and insensitivity replace Hitler's violence of extermination.

Two days later I have my chance to sneak back to Papa and Ima's room in the late afternoon. My heart races as I reach up and lower the suitcase onto the floor. The diary is in my hand, and I turn the pages quickly. There are no dates on the pages now, just 'August'. Papa's writing is neater.

My upper left arm still hurts from the swinging baton of the British marine who struck me twice on the Exodus. We were all united in our stand against the order to disembark at Hamburg, but the strength of the water canons was no match for our struggling bodies, weakened by the hunger-strike in Sète. Now life is about waiting ... waiting for what?

The camp has the capacity to hold around 1,000 inmates, but the emaciated bodies squeezed into tents and corrugated-iron huts are probably more than twice that many. The huts are like living in a huge iron drum, cut in half and secured to the ground. The cold easily penetrates the uninsulated walls, and every survivor is dreading winter. Ten circular tents in the middle of the camp surrounded by two fences of barbed wire is a special enclosure for troublemakers.

It's now day three in our new 'temporary home.' A dazed, eerie silence blankets the camp. Inmates sit and stare at the wire. Others sprawl in the welcome shade of a few trees lining the perimeter of the camp. The most severely affected wander chalked-faced, ghostlike, gaping, in a trance.

The children remained glued together during the first two days, huddled beside one of the large corrugated-iron huts. Now they creep through the camp in small groups, hand in hand, wandering aimlessly among the large trees towering over their drab quarters. They peer through the barbed wire at the British soldiers who regard them with indifference. I stink of the delousing powder pumped under my clothing by a masked nurse as I entered the camp. The thorough dusting of every survivor entering the compound left us coughing and spluttering. We retreated from the hospital room looking like refugees from a snowstorm.

Arrival at the camp was tense. The classification process demanded by the British met with stiff resistance. Many of us refused to be part of the humiliating process. The British screening was to identify our country of origin. Nearly everyone responded 'Palestine', which frustrated the British officers. Every one of us from the Exodus carried a certificate provided by the Jewish leadership. It read:

'The holder of this, No. #### is a Maapil of Exodus 1947, he or she was brought by force to Germany from Haifa and is in exile on his way back to Eretz Israel.' Issued in exile camp Poppendorf.

Our photo was mounted inside the certificate. I see it as a statement of defiance that gives a small seed of stubborn hope to a people without a home. The other reason for the screening is to 'weed out' agitators. The incarceration of fifty of the 'difficult' refugees, including sixteen leaders and several women in an old warehouse in Hamburg, brought fierce protests from us. The reports were that they slept on the bare floor and were under heavy guard.

We are very hungry and protested through the Red Cross to the authorities. The Red Cross say 1800 calories a day is inadequate. The British are unsympathetic. They say our continuing hostility is 'simply a show for the world press.' Around one-hundred refugees are now on a hunger-strike.

The conditions of the camp are deplorable with limited food and water, poor showering and washing facilities. Rooms shuttered against the sun are cold and bleak. Most wander like lost sheep around the dusty grounds of our drab and lifeless prison. Washing hung from makeshift clotheslines is guarded by the owner. Stealing is an act of survival, well-developed in Auschwitz and other camps. Nothing is left unattended. Faint rays of the sun struggle through broken cloud on a windless day. Not much hope of dry clothes today.

Day 4

I met a new arrival at the camp today. He was sent from an American camp to Poppendorf as punishment for forming a protest group to challenge the practice of inmates being forced to work.

In their defence, the American guards had said, 'Why sit around all day when you can do something productive?'

He'd replied, 'And work to rebuild the German economy! Work to help these evil bastards who killed and abused us for years? Not likely!'

I agree.

He told me the US camp is much better—better conditions, more food. They're given biscuits, chocolates, cigarettes ... not as strict, too.

He said, 'I can't understand how we have been the problem, scattered throughout the world. We don't have 'a land' or an army. We are not as other peoples, attached to their home soil, organised, with powerful armies. We are sand, scattered throughout the world.'

I like him. His name is Simon, and he's from Hungary.

We watched two boys fighting over some bread.

Simon said, 'I'd like to see these British bastards survive on our rations. They walk around like stuffed pigs.'

The British added German guards to patrol the fence! Would you believe it? German guards! What are they thinking? Apparently there aren't enough British. The children were very angry about it. They threw rocks at them and called them names. The guards just moved away and ignored them. I don't know how to help these kids.

I saw a young boy sitting alone on the ground, drawing stick figures in the dust. I sat down beside him and asked who they are. With one quick swipe of his hand, he wiped *out the figures, leapt to his feet and ran away. The children have forgotten how to play. They've forgotten how to laugh and smile. Their dull eyes reflect hopelessness. I feel so sad.*

I think about that young boy, and tears fill my eyes. I wonder who looked after him?

Day 5

I met a woman, Leah from Chęciny only fifteen kilometres away from my home-town Kielce.

She tried to return to her home after being in Ravensbrück. She went back and knocked on the door, and found that strangers had moved in. They told her to go away. She stayed with a friend for three nights and then the violence happened. A mob of Polish soldiers, police and a violent pack from the town murdered forty-two of our people and injured over forty others. She hid with a friend in a barn overnight, and the next day walked through the countryside and found Russian troops. They helped her get to Germany and to Poppendorf. The Polish authorities were mostly responsible for confiscating Jewish property. Homes were ransacked. Most of our people who lived there would be too scared to go back.

Simon asked what caused the outbreak.

Leah told him about the undercurrent of hatred that's been there for years. And then the vile rumour of Jews drinking the blood of Christians as part of their ritual … so wrong. Leah burst into tears. She said we've nowhere to go. Our own townspeople don't want us. Europe doesn't want us. America, Australia, New Zealand, Canada, nobody wants us!

Suddenly a scream pierced the air. I'll never forget it. It came from a young woman running from behind one of the huts. Leah and Simon leapt to their feet as the slender figure of the woman ran towards us.

She gasped, 'How could they do it? He's in the camp with me! I can't believe it! I want to get out of here. What can I do?' The words tumbled from her trembling lips. She said a German guard is inside the camp. He was a guard at Ravensbrück and was responsible for a group of the Aufseherinnen—female SS guards. He never raped or killed any of the women, though. He wasn't violent like 'The Hyena' or 'The Beast.'

An olive-skinned man in his thirties strode towards us. The insignia on his cap identified him as one of the Jewish camp police. He came to check if there was a problem. The young woman explained sighting the German guard. The camp policeman informed us that there are six former German guards here. The British thought it was a good idea to help the Jews by reversing the German's position. Let the abusers serve their victims ... give the Germans a taste of their own medicine ... humiliate them.

I said there'll be a special place in hell for them.

The young woman nodded and her body shook. She said she felt like she was being abused again. The Jewish

The door opened before I knew what was happening. I must have been so engrossed in reading that I didn't hear footsteps.

'Uri,' Ima says, 'what are you doing … oh … you've found Papa's diary!'

'I'm sorry, Ima. I really want to know about Papa and you … how you met; how you came to Israel.'

Ima stood still, breathing heavily. After a long pause and a sigh, she says, 'I can understand you wanting to know.' She fidgets with her apron and looks back out the door. 'But Papa would not be pleased with you reading his diary.'

'Why? It's so interesting. I had no idea …'

'I don't think he wants his children to know how bad it was. He's trying to protect you.'

I'm feeling frustrated. 'I think I'm old enough now to know about grown-up things.'

Ima's smile is sad. 'You're growing up … and Papa and I are very proud of you. But there are some things Papa doesn't want to speak about …'

'But he doesn't have to tell me; I can read about them,' I protest.

Ima reaches forward, takes the diary out of my hand and places it back in the suitcase. 'I won't mention a word to your Papa about this.'

'Why are pages torn out of the diary?'

'I don't know. They would've been when he was in Auschwitz.'

'Do you know when we went to the Western Wall, Papa was upset. I saw him cry. Why?'

'I knew he was upset that day, but he didn't know what it was. Your Papa doesn't say much when he's troubled.'

'He doesn't say much anytime!'

'Now Uri, that's enough. He'll be here soon, so you need to leave.'

'I don't even know how you and Papa met.'

Ima can see my frustration. As she closes the cupboard door, she lets out a big sigh and thinks for a moment. 'I'll tell you about how we met when you're older.'

'How much older?'

Ima pauses. 'When you're preparing for your Bar Mitzvah.'

'Do you promise?'

'Yes, I promise, and I'll try to encourage Papa to join in.'

'Can I ask one more question … please?'

'If you're quick.'

'Why were the British angry with our people?'

Ima frowned. 'It's complex. The British wanted to create a Jewish State and had control over Palestine for many years and our people were tired of being occupied. Also, they didn't want to upset the Arabs who also lived in Palestine. The Arabs were concerned about the large numbers of our people immigrating … now run along.'

I hug Ima and hurry towards the children's house. A mixture of feelings churns inside me. In one way I'm glad Ima caught me reading the diary; she now knows how important it is for me to know about Papa and whatever secret he's hiding.

But I'm frustrated that I have to wait. I'll not be able to read any more of the diary. All I have to do now is wait, wait, wait.

~

I know Papa and Ima miss me because I sleep in the children's house. We can visit parents sometimes between four o'clock in the afternoon and eight o'clock at night. But there's no room to sleep with them, even if we were allowed. Their room is small and just fits their bed. Papa is sometimes strange because he likes me working beside him—like in the orchard—but he says very little. He doesn't seem to know what to say.

We have jobs to do and little time to play. We study hard in the schoolhouse. I have a good teacher. Her name is Bina. She has long hair, blue eyes and is very pretty. Rabbi Yousef helps me, too. He's very funny and knows lots of things. Bina and the Rabbi say I'm a good student. They want me to grow up to help make Israel a strong nation. My favourite subjects are mathematics and science. Maybe one day I'll be a scientist.

All the children help with jobs. The worst one for me is picking olives because the leaves are dusty with insecticides and afterwards I feel sick in my stomach. My favourite is climbing the ladder to pick pears. I have a ring-shaped thing the pear has to fit through so I know it's right to pull off the tree. A big canvas bag hangs from my shoulders and covers the front of my shorts. We also have oranges and lemons, grapefruit, almonds, corn and wheat, horses and cows. They say we're lucky to have good black soil because the crops grow well. I don't like it in the summer when the soil is hot and gets into my socks.

One favourite fun-thing is shower time. All the boys and girls under nine-years old line up without clothes on in the shower room and one of the women hoses us with water. The girls squeal the loudest. We call her the 'Gestapo Woman.'

Chapter Four

'We will have to face the reality that Israel is neither innocent, nor redemptive. And that in its creation, and expansion; we as Jews, have caused what we historically have suffered; a refugee population in Diaspora.' – Martin Buber, Jewish Philosopher, March 1949. [Note 1]

Bina, my teacher, is teaching us about the early days of our nation. Whenever the past is raised, I prick up my ears. Any clues about what happened to my parents, especially Papa, are important.

The small classroom has many photos of tanks and planes pinned up on the wall, and a large map of Israel hangs beside the chalkboard. Bina has gone to a lot of trouble.

'Now children,' she says, 'the 1948 War was called 'The First Palestinian War' by the Arab world and 'The Disaster' Naqba by the Palestinians who lived in Palestine. Our people called it 'The War of Independence,' 'The War of Liberation,' or 'The War of Establishment.' It had two stages. The first was a civil war, beginning on 30th November 1947 and ending on 14th May 1948. Then came a conventional war, beginning when the armies of the surrounding Arab states invaded Palestine on 15th May 1948 ending in July 1949. The civil war between Palestine's Jewish and Arab communities was a guerrilla war. Arab volunteers from the wider Arab world joined their Palestinian brothers against the Jews.'

A girl who had recently moved into the kibbutz, puts up her hand.

'Yes, Mina,' Bina says, 'you have a question?'

'What's a guerrilla war?' Mina asks.

'Guerrilla war is when fighters attack in small groups and then hide. There's no enemy lines because the enemies come out from hiding and attack, and then they go back into hiding. The weapons can be anything: bottles filled with petrol; firebombs; guns; anything.'

'Is that what happened here in Atak?' asked an older boy, who often played practical jokes on the girls.

'Yes. I'll come to that later. A conventional war is fighting between two sides using conventional weapons, guns, tanks and planes. It's more open and clear where the two sides are fighting.'

Atak was attacked by guerrillas? I didn't know that!

Bina continues, 'The conventional war ended officially in July 1949, but the fighting stopped in January 1949. Armies of Syria, Egypt, Transjordan and Iraq, with groups from other Arab countries, attacked our new nation. Now, the Atak community had lived on high alert from the end of November when the Arabs had the upper hand and the Haganah were on the defensive. Continuous, small-scale guerrilla fighting was made against towns and there were constant ambushes along the roads. Arabs attacked Jewish settlements, and the Haganah fought back. There were no front lines, no armies moving back and forth, no pitched battles and no territory captured.'

'That must have been very scary,' I said.

'Yes, Uri. Every kibbutz had a safe room, like the one we have today. When the siren sounded, everyone would run and hide inside. In April, the Haganah went on the attack, and by the middle of May, they had crushed the Palestinians. The second stage involved major campaigns and battles, and resulted in us capturing territory. At the end, the Jews held territory with clear front lines, with the areas beyond it under Arab control. The Jewish people kept the area recommended by the United Nations but also sixty per cent of what was recommended for a Palestinian state. It included Jaffa and Lydda, the Galilee, parts of the Negev in the south, and a wide strip along the road from Tel Aviv to Jerusalem and parts of what is now called the West Bank. Now, for homework, I want you to research which parts of the West Bank came under Jewish control and who took control of Gaza.'

~

I seek out the Rabbi to see if he can tell me more. He's always happy to talk about the past, and we love him. 'Yousef,' I say, 'Bina mentioned in school today there was an attack on our Kibbutz just after Papa and Ima arrived. Do you remember it?' The other children who were hanging around him run off at my question, leaving him all to myself. 'Were you and Papa involved?'

'We certainly were,' he replies.

My interest grows. Here's more of Papa's story I've not heard. 'Can you tell me about it?'

'It's an important part of our kibbutz history. For sure.'

Yousef is a great storyteller. He makes them so interesting. He's so knowledgeable and will tell you exactly how it was—well, I think so. We sit down in the shade of a tree on an old wooden bench.

Yousef looks up into the sky and pauses for a moment. 'Well, Uri, where do I start? It was in August 1948. Chaos and uncertainty gripped Palestine in the dying months of the mandate—when the British were still in control. British troops weren't always fair in the way they treated Arabs or Jews. They confiscated arms from both Haganah and Arab militia.'

'I would've like to have been a Haganah fighter,' I say.

He nods and smiles at me as if he isn't surprised. 'They were fierce warriors—well trained by the British … but back to the story. In February a British patrol disarmed Haganah men at a roadblock in Jerusalem and arrested its members. All men were later released unharmed into the hands of an Arab mob who hung them and mutilated their bodies.'

'Oh, that's terrible.'

'It certainly was. A fortnight later, British troops disarmed and butchered a group of Haganah fighters. Jewish retaliation was swift, blowing up a British troop train, killing twenty-eight soldiers and wounding dozens more. [Note 2] The report sent shock waves throughout the countryside. How would the British react? Additional security was given to us at Kibbutz Atak.'

'What did the kibbutz get?'

'Guns and two Haganah fighters. Our kibbutzniks and others joined with Jews throughout the land when David Ben-Gurion, effectively the prime minister, declared the new State of Israel on 14th May 1948. I said to the community at Atak at the time that Ben-Gurion was not concerned about the Palestinian Arabs. His fear was the Arab nations on the borders of Palestine, who could freely buy arms and train armies. His strategy was to mobilise forces to strategic points on the southern border with Egypt, Gaza, and the West Bank, open to a Jordanian and Syrian offensive, and in the north, an attack from Lebanon.'

'How did you know these things?'

'I have contacts, Uri. Tension gripped the New Israel. But we were always optimistic. I knew there'd been underground arms production. Some of our skilled tradesmen had created two and three-inch mortars, Sten machineguns, grenades, and bullets from tools and machinery smuggled in from outside Israel. Under agricultural sheds and buildings scattered throughout the country, a secret industry flourished. One ammunition factory was underneath a kibbutz in Ayalon.'

'Where's that?'

'A short distance south of Tel Aviv on the coast. Beneath the laundromat, teams secretly worked every day on manufacturing bullets. They tested their work at a makeshift firing range when the laundromat's equipment was operating to cover the sound of the explosions. The Brits had no idea what was going on. Our men provided a free service to their military. Their uniforms were always pressed and spotless!'

I laugh. 'That's so funny. It was good the British never found out what was going on.'

'Yes, the people concerned would have been executed.'

'But what about the attack on Atak?'

The Rabbi clears his throat and strokes his beard. 'We heard that Arab militia were coming up from the south. Then the word went out to all the men to be ready to move.'

'Did you have any training?'

Yousef shakes his head. 'Not much. Your father and I watched the spotter plane fly low over the kibbutz. The command from the leader of the band of Haganah fighters came to be ready to move in ten minutes. Your Ima didn't want to let your father go, but he insisted. I remember her saying, "Abby, I'm so scared. Please … please stay safe. Don't try to be a hero." She was crying.'

'Poor Ima.'

'Minutes later the command was given to move. There were advanced parties of Haganah at three points on the southern side where we believed the attack would come. We were to provide backup if there were casualties. We crept forward. About half-an-hour later, the signal came to remain silent, and our group of fifteen "rookies" inched forward to an area amongst the trees where one of the advanced parties of the Haganah had set up a machine gun post.'

'Were you scared?'

'Yes, we all were.'

I lean forward, feeling my heart beat faster.

'A three-inch mortar sat in place with shells neatly stacked a few metres behind. The position was strategically placed on high ground, at the edge of an open field. I became more anxious as time dragged on. An hour passed without any sign of Arab fighters. I held the rifle in my hand, and I was shaking.'

'Did you learn to shoot?'

'We were only allowed to fire two rounds at a makeshift target.'

'Did you hit the target?'

'I did, both times. It was a miracle.' Yousef chuckled. 'Only fifty rounds of ammunition were given to every kibbutz. Anyway, your father and I lay in the grass. The sun was blazing between the branches of a cypress tree. Perspiration drenched our shirts. We fought the flies … then … suddenly, the engine

of the spotter plane roared overhead and minutes later ...'
Yousef paused.

'What happened next? Go on!'

'Our leader, a Haganah, said that around forty men with only light arms were about 500 metres away and moving up on our eastern side. He selected a group of the Haganah to fan out to the eastern flank. Fifteen minutes crept by, maybe twenty minutes. Then the sound of gunfire brought a sudden flood of adrenalin. We braced ourselves for our first taste of combat. I won't forget the words of our leader: "Only fire if you have a clear target."'

I feel so scared for Papa and Yousef. I can hardly sit still.

'The Arab fighters crouched down and moved across an area covered in low bushes. We could see their red headscarfs moving. Maybe twenty crept forward. The first mortar shell exploded, and our leader said, "Nobody move." I had no choice. I was frozen to the spot.' Yousef's expression grew even more serious. 'Five minutes passed; still no movement. Our leader told us to spread out and crawl towards the enemy. He said, "Take care; they could be foxing." I glanced at your Papa as we elbowed our way forward. Our bodies were trembling.' Yousef paused to brush an annoying fly from his face.

I plead for him to continue. 'Go on, what happened next?'

'Every five metres or so, the leader lifted his head and checked for movement from the Arab fighters. Bodies lay motionless in the grass. Then we came to the first body. I felt sick. Shrapnel from the mortar had partially shattered his face. "He's only a teenager!" your Papa said. We crawled on. But, Uri, it was weird. The sight and smell of death was no stranger to us. In the camps it had been a terrible but normal part of life. But here in Israel, on the edge of our kibbutz, our safe-haven, we both wanted to run.'

He pauses again, shaking his head. His eyes are growing moist. I can see these memories are hard for him to share, and I feel honoured that he is willing to tell me.

'I was thinking,' he continues, "*How many are dead? What if some are alive?*" I gripped my rifle and pushed my face into the grass. I could hear moaning, and then … an agonising voice screamed in Arabic. I looked up and saw the leader and two Haganah standing upright, guns levelled ready to fire. The leader said, "Watch for any movement," and we moved forward. I stood up beside your Papa, steadied myself and staggered forward. Bloodied bodies were strewn throughout the undergrowth. Those who weren't dead, wailed continuously. They were all so young. The sound of their cries was awful.'

He takes a deep breath and lets it out slowly, as if willing himself to continue with the story, 'A single mortar shell had done all that was necessary to stop them. The Haganah had killed some Arab fighters in the opening volley, and others were badly injured. The remaining members of the group fled south and were chased by the Haganah.' Yousef took a deep breath and thought for a moment. 'I felt like being sick, but your Papa vomited onto the grass.'

'Oh, no! It must have been terrible for him and you.' I could understand why Papa wouldn't want me to hear some of these things. I feel very sad for Papa, Yousef and the men at Atak.

Yousef glances at me. 'These are not pleasant stories, Uri, but I believe you young people need to hear them. We have been reunited with our land at a great cost. There's been much suffering, and it will continue. You must be ready for it. You have a strong body and mind, and I believe you will be a leader one day.'

'Do you think so? I don't feel like a leader.'

He turns and looks me straight in the eye. 'You will, Uri, mark my words.'

I'm puzzled. So many thoughts swim in my head, but I think this is the right time to ask Yousef the question that hangs in my mind. 'When we visited Jerusalem recently and went to the Wall, Papa was very upset. His body was shaking, and I thought he was going to burst into tears. He fought so hard not to cry, but I saw a tear. It upset me to see him so upset. Why was he like that?'

Yousef stroked his beard again and shook his head slowly. 'It could be many things. I don't imagine it was anything to do with the attack on our kibbutz.'

'What about when he came to Israel on the Exodus and all the fighting and being taken back to Germany and Austria?'

A quick smile passed across Yousef's face, and then he became serious again. 'Ima told me you found his diary. He wouldn't be happy to know you were reading it.'

'Nobody tells me anything,' I protested. 'Well, except you,' I added quickly.

'I really don't know what might have been the trigger—the memory of a person, or a place, perhaps. There's been so much happening for him and for all of us. Auschwitz, the Exodus, Poppendorf Camp, the Six Day War, the Yom Kippur War … just to name a few. It might be that he was missing your Uncle Daniel. Maybe he always thought his brother would be standing with him at the Wall. But I'm only guessing.'

'I feel sad to know so many bad things have happened to him and you. I want to help him.'

'Bless you, Uri. You have a strong heart. I believe he'll tell you whatever is troubling him at some time in the future, when he feels it's safe.'

'Will that help him?'

'Yes, it may. I pray for him regularly. Respect and care for him.'

'I try to … sometimes he seems far away when I'm with him.'

'I know, but that doesn't mean he doesn't love you.'

We sit in silence for a minute watching a wheelbarrow of vegetables being wheeled towards the kitchen.

'Why were the British so terrible to smash *The Exodus?*' I ask.

'They were trying to teach us a lesson. They were tired of trying to please the Arabs and the Jews, and when the Haganah organised the breakout of fighters in Acre and the British officers were hanged, that really made them angry.'

'I don't know about that,' I replied. 'Can I read about it?'

'You certainly can. You'll hear about it later in your history class. It helped change world opinion and opened up the way for us to return to our homeland.'

'Thank you, Yousef.'

Yousef smiled and touched my shoulder. 'Only too glad to be your guide, but no more reading your Papa's diary … and I won't tell him what I know.'

'I love you, Yousef.'

He smiled. 'One day you'll be part of the New Israel. You *will* be a leader.'

~

1. Martin Buber, Jewish Philosopher, addressed Prime Minister Ben Gurion on the moral character of the State of Israel with reference to the Arab refugees in March 1949. David Liepert, *Muslim, Christian and Jew,* Toronto: Faith of Life Publishing, 2010.

2. Benny Morris, *1948: A History of the First Arab-Israeli War*, New Haven and London: Yale University Press, 2008, p. 81.

Chapter Five

March 1948, Kibbutz Atak
Abdiel and Maya

Kibbutz Atak had a photo of Chaim Shalom Halevi on the wall of the dining hall. His passion for Zionism and *Eretz Israel* had grown after he left Europe and entered into the 'Promised Land' in the 1920's. And it grew further after World War II when the world closed its doors to the thousands of Jews who survived the Holocaust, thus creating the necessity of desperate measures from a desperate people. His powerful influence, combined with the efforts of David Ben-Gurion and other Zionists, defined the 'New Man' essential for the establishment of a Jewish state. The vision was its creation, regardless of economic logic. Halevi turned his back on the bourgeoisie ways of living in the Diaspora. In a letter to his parents he defined the type of sacrifice required to create the new resilient community which Abdiel and thousands of refugees willingly embraced:

> *At every step and inch we must push ourselves past our limits, sacrifice ourselves, do without. The country is unique. It loves only those who bind themselves to it with all their heart and soul. Only someone who comes without looking back, who burns behind him all the bridges leading to Constantsa and Trieste and Marseilles—the*

ports from which European immigrants departed—only he puts down roots, and gains a foothold in the country. The country needs soldiers. There is a war ahead of us, long and hard against the Arabs and the English, against the sea and the rivers, the mountains and the valleys, the cold and the heat, the sand and the desert, the rocks and the boulders, a war that may go on for perhaps hundreds of years. May my grandchildren be privileged to see its end. (Note 1)

~

'Abby; it's 6 a.m.,' Maya exclaimed with concern.

Abdiel rolled over and muttered, 'I'm so tired.'

'You should've gone to bed earlier,' Maya replied with little sympathy.

Abdiel made a half-conscious effort to sit up, but flopped back onto the old mattress. He yawned, then, with a sigh, dragged himself from the bed. 'I'll grab a bite and get the tractor down to the first row to meet the others.'

Abdiel dragged on his well-worn trousers and grey shirt and headed for the dining hall. He grabbed the first item of food within easy reach: a piece of goat's cheese lovingly created by Anna, the best cheese maker in the kibbutz; two slices of bread, and a banana. His shoe repairing skills weren't in great demand, and so he'd found his way into caring for the ever-growing number of fruit trees. Now, he had fifteen minutes to move the tractor into the position where he'd finished last night. Abdiel's efforts to enrich the soil with fertilizers, and the construction of an effective irrigation system, would hopefully reap the rewards the collective needed.

Abdiel and Maya loved the north. The Galilee, relaxing, with natural springs, sprawling forests, groves of olive and citrus trees and rows of pomegranates, refreshed their parched spirits. In the south, Judea crouched in the sun like a striped tiger, dangerous, tense with vitality, sullen and dispassionate with age. Jerusalem, perched high on its ridge, contained the inflammable atmosphere of three religions.

The two lovers passionately embraced the fundamental values of their new community: frugality, equality and the rejection of private property.

Abdiel fired-up the overworked tractor and chugged past the workshop, the tired engine enjoying the gentle slope of the path to the orchard. A fresh-faced kibbutznik greeted Abdiel with a smile as he cut the engine at the end of a row of orange trees.

'You're a little late this morning,' she teased.

Abdiel avoided her gaze and replied with a hint of guilt, 'Hard to get out of bed after a long day yesterday.'

In spite of his fatigue, Abdiel found working in the orchards and vegetable gardens cleansed his spirit of some of the stains of his traumatic past. The presence of Rabbi Yousef, whom he'd met in Poppendorf, was another bright light. His lively wit and ability to relate to people was remarkable. Children loved him. Yousef had gladly performed the marriage ceremony for Abdiel and Maya in the grounds of the kibbutz on a cool afternoon a week earlier. Yousef's slight figure, greying beard and rimless glasses made him easy to spot in the grounds of Kibbutz Atak. The previous day, Abdiel had been throwing a ball to one of the young boys before dinner when the Rabbi had appeared.

The young lad had said to the Rabbi, 'Rabbi, why do you always answer a question with a question?'

'Why shouldn't I?' Yousef replied with a grin.

The boy laughed. 'Rabbi, what has a face, two hands but no arms or legs?'

'Don't know.'

'A clock.'

'Hah, good one. Very clever.'

The Rabbi's great gift of sprinkling friendship and joy wherever he went brought pleasure to the community. Another gift was his ability to tap into the current state of affairs. Yousef spent time in Haifa and other local villages, coordinating religious classes for youth. Not every kibbutz welcomed a Rabbi. Some 'pure Zionist' collectives were founded on imported Stalinist principles from Europe, devoid of any 'divine necessity.' Kibbutz Atak, north east of Haifa, was secular with a touch of the sacred. Abdiel, shaped by his Jewish faith as a child, had more than the edges blurred by the horror of the Holocaust. The *Shoah* had almost extinguished from him any sense of the divine. Yet, Abdiel quietly admired the Rabbi's faith, which was real and had survived the pain and torture of the camps.

'He that can't endure the bad, will not live to see the good,' was one of Yousef's sayings. 'Now we're tasting the good.'

After a morning in the field, lunch consisted of freshly baked bread, tomatoes and cucumbers with a little cheese. The workers ate heartily and drank the cool water collected from a local spring. Not every collective was fortunate to have such a provision.

Maya appeared with apples delivered from a kibbutz further north. 'I've heard the army will call soon and prepare us for fighting,' she commented, handing Abdiel a piece of fruit.

'I knew that would happen soon,' Abdiel replied. 'Rabbi Yousef mentioned last night there's the threat of armed Arab groups coming in from Lebanon.'

The afternoon crept on for Abdiel. His mind played with a conversation he'd had with the Rabbi the previous evening, reignited by Maya's comment over lunch. At first he'd been overwhelmed with the thrill of his new home: freedom, clean air, fresh food, safety and a comfortable bed. Winter in Israel was a vast improvement on winter in Europe. Now a cloud threatened to cover the sun. While the UN had defined the boundaries for the partition of the new State of Israel, Arab nations didn't accept the division and neither did Jewish Prime Minister David Ben-Gurion. The British were withdrawing, and the tension was mounting. Members of the Haganah would soon be present, training the men and fortifying the kibbutz.

In spite of his wandering thoughts, Abdiel managed to finish his designated duties, then showered and presented himself for kitchen jobs at the appointed hour.

After dinner he rose from the table and spotted the Rabbi sneaking into the hall through a back door. 'Shalom, Abby,' came his tired voice.

'Shalom, Rabbi; you're late.'

'It's been a long day,' Yousef replied.

'There's a meal set aside for you.'

'Thanks, Abby.'

Abdiel disappeared into the kitchen and returned with a plate of chicken and salad.

'Thank you,' Yousef said. 'Can you join me or do you need to go?'

'Love to talk.'

The Rabbi picked up his knife and fork and, before he commenced eating, said, 'The military will be here tomorrow to start the training. Hope you're ready for a crash course in combat?'

'We all, us youth, *have* to take the training.' Abdiel sighed. 'I'm okay about it.'

'You're a little distracted,' the Rabbi said.

Abdiel hesitated and shifted position on his chair. 'When will the fighting ever finish? Ever since I was born, it's been a struggle. Poland, Auschwitz ... the camps ... and now here! We arrive ... the UN, the world, has created a home for us, and now we have to fight.' He shook his head. 'When will it ever end?'

'Abby. It's not easy. I know you struggle. I struggle—we all struggle. Yet the lower a person feels, the closer he comes to his true state and to the Creator.'

'I've had some low points in my life, and I've never felt more distant from my Creator as I do now!' Abdiel confessed.

The Rabbi nodded. 'I'll pray you'll find the path. Don't let your anger rule you, Abby. Once you enter the path, the Creator assures us of success if the directions of our goals are correct.'

Abdiel leaned back on his chair and muttered, 'I envy you. You're so positive and peaceful.'

'I can assure you, I'm very human.'

Abdiel became aware of Maya, who moved to his side. 'Hope I'm not interrupting the conversation.'

'You're welcome to join us,' Yousef said.

'Let's move to more comfortable seats,' she suggested.

The company of three left the basic surroundings of the dining hall—floorboards, laminated tables, wooden chairs—and moved to the lounge room.

As they sunk into the lounge chairs, Abdiel said, 'What are the chances of us losing a war with the Arabs?'

Yousef took a moment to consider, then replied, 'Well, England thinks the Arabs would win. They think the Jews won't be able to cope with an Arab offensive. They expect we'll be tossed out of Palestine unless we can strike some deal with the Arabs. I suspect they're relying on Arab and Jewish negotiating skills to prevail.'

'So on paper, the Arabs would win,' Abdiel replied.

'Yes. They enjoy a population ratio of two to one over Jews and cover more of the surface of Palestine than we do. They also have the high ground and the Jews the lowlands. Another advantage for the Arabs is they have neighbouring states, which can supply them with volunteers and safe-havens. Jewish immigrants … well their back-up is hundreds and thousands of miles away in Europe, and they're no longer safe-havens!'

'There's nowhere to run for us here; it's a long way to swim to Africa,' Abdiel observed with a groan.

'Exactly, but we have better trained military, manpower, weapons, morale and motivation. The Haganah, trained by the British military, really, they're a formidable force. We have a greater sense of national unity—we still have our divisions, of course, but the Arabs' loyalties lie with their family, clan village and sometimes their region. Arab society has greater divisions along social and religious lines than we have. There's a huge rift amongst the better educated that goes back to the 1920s between the Husseinis and Nashashibis. That falling out between them during 1936 – 1947 was like a civil war and left them impoverished, both politically and militarily in Palestine. There're millions of dollars flowing from Jews in America to support us. The Arabs aren't so generous, and so … I believe Israel will win the war.'

Maya smiled at Yousef. 'I love to hear you talk like this … it's so comforting; you remain so calm.'

Abdiel said, 'I hope you're right. You're knowledgeable about these matters.'

Yousef placed his hand on Abdiel's shoulder. 'We've a strong community here in our kibbutz, in Palestine and throughout the world … and God is with us.'

A bird flapping its wings outside caught the attention of the trio for a moment and distracted further comment, until Yousef asked, 'No word about the whereabouts of your brother yet?'

'Nothing at all,' Abdiel replied with a sigh. 'He was spotted after Auschwitz, but … no sign since. The British Red Cross will let me know if they hear anything.'

Yousef sighed. 'It's terrible, not knowing. I don't have any family left, except for an uncle and aunt somewhere in the US. I pray you'll be reunited. It'll be a matter of time.'

Silence allowed each to their own thoughts until Yousef stood and looked towards the door. 'Please excuse me. I need to complete some writing before bed. I'll see you tomorrow.'

'Good night, Yousef,' Abdiel and Maya replied in unison.

'We could have an early night.' Maya, with a glint in her eye, reached out and rested her hand on Abdiel's knee.

'I'll need to if I'm going to be involved in war games tomorrow.'

'I wasn't thinking of your war games.' She grinned. 'I had *other* games in mind.'

Abdiel smiled and placed his hand on hers. 'You talked me into it; let's go.'

They followed the path down to their small room, paused to stare at the stars in the southern sky and then entered their safe-haven.

~

1.   Tom Segev, *One Palestine Complete*, London: Abacus, 2001, p. 262.

Chapter Six

Uri

Yesterday I crept back into Papa and Ima's room only to discover the diary wasn't in the old suitcase. Ima must have hidden it. I felt guilty because I promised Ima and Yousef I wouldn't look again, but I can't help my mind—it wants to know. I lie awake at night thinking about the tear at the Wall. Maybe if I know what the problem is, I could help Papa. But nobody knows, which makes it more fascinating. I wish I could stop thinking about it, but I can't.

I've heard that this Saturday night after Shabbat, the adults are going to watch a movie. Special times like this happen every so often. I overheard one of the men say, 'My cousin was one of the inmates. I can't wait to see it; it helped change world opinion.'

The man he was speaking to said, 'And it explains why the British gave the Exodus such a hard time. I don't know how Abdiel and the others survived.'

My ears burned when I heard those words, so I started to plan how I could see the movie. Anything to do with Papa and the past is important to me—especially around that time. The movie may give me some clues. Usually children aren't allowed to see the movies after Shabbat; us kids go straight to the children's house and to bed. But I have a plan. On Saturday afternoon I'm going to sneak into the back of the hall where the movie will be shown and make a hiding place, then when the lights go out after the movie starts, I'll creep in. I'm very excited.

~

Most of the children are asleep. Good. I creep out of my bunk and sneak across the grass towards the hall. The night is cool, and I shiver as I climb a tree and hide in the branches. Five minutes pass, and then the lights are switched off. With my heart racing, I make my way to the door of the hall. The title of the film is on the screen—*Breakout*. The credits roll on and music fills the room. Five paces take me to the secret place I made from boxes stacked along the back wall, and I settle onto my box seat. Nobody has seen me.

The screen is high enough for me to see over the rows of heads. I spot Papa and Ima sitting in the second row. The date '28th April 1947' flashes on the screen.

The movie opens in Acre prison near Haifa, on the coast in the middle of an old Arab town where no Jews lived. I've heard that it was the most highly guarded fortress in Israel. The movie shows thick walls surrounding an ancient, solid building, and there's a moat on two sides. It looks like a terrible place.

The next scene shows a British captain sitting in his office with two officers, talking about the riots. They talk about the prisoners—members of the Jewish resistance and Arabs who'd rioted against the British in Palestine—and moan about how ungrateful both the Arabs and Jews are.

'After all that England's done for them!' one of the officers says in disgust.

'The problem was we tried to please both the Arabs and the Jews,' the captain said. 'It was never going to work.'

Then the scene changes to inside the prison walls. A man in Arab clothes named Fahim hears something in the oil storeroom through the south wall of the prison. Faint sounds of women's voices come in from the street outside the wall. A clock shows just after 3 p.m. The doors of the cells are open and the prisoners are having exercise time. Fahim looks around as if seeking someone, spots his target and walks over to him. A voice tells us that the man is the most senior of the Irgun prisoners, a militant group, that had broken away from the Haganah, the Jewish resistance movement.

'Eitan. Have news,' Fahim says. 'In oil storeroom today. Heard women's voices through wall.'

'Yah!' Eitan's eyes dart from side-to-side. 'That means the south wall must be on a street or alley in the Old City. Good location for an escape. Well done, Fahim. Don't mention it to anyone.' Eitan Livni's eyes gleamed with excitement.

We then see a note passing through many hands and ending up in Irgun headquarters. A new date appears; it's a week later, and a Jewish man named Amichai, Irgun chief operations officer, tours the Old City of Acre disguised as an Arab.

A day later in a house in Haifa, a senior Irgun addresses a small number of the underground group. 'A break-in through the south wall into the oil storeroom is possible,' he says. 'But it will mean the prisoners will need to get from their cells to the storeroom on their own.'

'The doors at the end of the passageways will be locked,' says another man.

'Correct, so we'll need to get explosives in. Ari that will be your job. Start working on it now.'

The scene moves back to the prison. In the yard we see Eitan Livni, an Irgun fighter, and watch someone hand him a cigarette. Then the prisoners return to their cells. Exercise time is over. Back in his cell, Livni removes a piece of paper rolled up inside the cigarette.

Mission approved. You will receive goods tomorrow.

A broad grin crosses Livni's unshaven face.

Next we see guards examining a parcel of goodies and declaring it safe, and then a young Jewish man called Rafael opening it. It's from his parents. The story continues with a man talking to Rafael's parents, Calev and Adina, about 'goodies' for their son. The man makes sure they understand the risk. If they're caught it's imprisonment or execution. The couple agree to play their part.

'We've never taken a risk like this before,' Adina says as the man leaves.

'Yes, but Amichai is relying on us to do our part for the cause,' Calev replies. 'And I'll do anything if it means Rafael can get out of that place.'

The next scene shows Ari, a member of the Haganah, placing small sticks of gelignite at the bottom of a jar of thick strawberry jam. He then creates a thin false layer at the bottom of the tin of olive oil and places fuses and detonators in it.

The movie cuts to Calev and Adina sitting outside their home on the outskirts of Haifa enjoying the spring air after their evening meal. Without a sound, a dark figure carrying a small bag steps out of the darkness. 'A present for Rafael for your visit tomorrow,' the man says, then he disappears before they can reply.

Next we see Calev and Adina waiting at the gate of Acre Prison. They look worried, and I feel really nervous for them.

'Take some deep breaths and relax. Don't forget to smile,' Calev whispers to his wife.

Adina nods, takes a deep breath and manages a small smile.

Calev's fist bangs on the old iron door, and a moment later a face appears at the grill.

The heavy door creaks open, and the guard signals them to enter. After a brief body search, the guard leads them down a dark corridor to the next locked door. A second guard releases the lock, and then Calev and Adina stand in a small room beside a desk.

A British sergeant enters. 'More rations for your boy?' he asks with a cheeky grin.

'Yes, strawberry jam and some of my olive oil,' Rafael's mother replies with a smile.

'Our food's not good enough?' The sergeant chuckles; he seems to be in a good mood. 'Let's have a look at it.'

Adina takes a deep breath and hands over the jar and the large tin of oil for examination.

My heart beats fast as I watch the sergeant unscrew the lid of the strawberry jam and insert a finger. 'Hmm, it's a bit lumpy at the bottom.'

The movie shows Adina's gaze freeze on the sergeant for a moment. 'Oh,' she says with a smile, 'it didn't gel properly, unfortunately. It's not my best effort.'

The sergeant pauses. Adina doesn't look at Calev but keeps her composure, taking deep breaths.

'It's a better brew than I'd make.' The sergeant places the jar on the small wooden table. 'So this is your olive oil. Did you press it yourself?'

'Yes, we have a small number of trees and a winepress. I love the process.'

The sergeant unscrews the lid and pokes in a long stick to check the level. Ari's effort to reduce the false cavity to less than one centimetre has paid off.

'All's good, through you go.'

I realise that I've been holding my breath, and I let out a gasp. Luckily everyone in the hall is so caught up watching the film they don't hear me.

Both Calev and Adina look so cool and relaxed as they go through the next door. Any sign of the tension I think they must be feeling would raise suspicion.

The sergeant watches Adina hand over the 'goodies' to Rafael.

'Nothing like mother's cooking when you're away from home,' he jokes to a nearby guard.

The box I'm sitting on suddenly becomes uncomfortable, and I stand up, taking care not to disturb any of the boxes. 'Sunday 4th May 1947 – early afternoon' shows up on the screen, and the events of that day unfold before me. Information—such as the numbers of people involved, who people are and when things happened—shows on the screen at different points or is told to us by a narrator.

It starts with a convoy heading from Shuni, a former Crusader fortress, towards Acre, carrying a group of Irgun fighters dressed in British Engineering Corps uniforms with their hair cut in 'English style.' Three wear Arab clothing. All are armed and ready to put their plan into action. The command jeep leading the convoy contains the commander, Dov Cohen. He sits beside the driver dressed as a British captain. A three-ton military truck, two military vans with

British camouflage colours and two civilian vans follow. When the convoy reaches Acre, the two military vans enter the market while the truck waits at the gate.

The so-called engineering unit enters the Turkish bathhouse to supposedly mend the telephone lines. Ladders are removed from one of the vehicles and placed against the roof of the adjacent wall. Dov Cohen, the unit commander, helps his deputy, Yehuda Apiryon, haul up the explosives and fix them to the windows of the prison. Two blocking squads scatter mines along the routes leading to the site of the break-in.

Inside the prison, Eitan and the forty-one prisoners he chose to escape with him, wait nervously. A narrator's voice tells us that Irgun headquarters decided to free only a quarter of the 163 Jewish prisoners held in the prison because it would be difficult to find hiding places for a large number.

At 3 p.m. the cell doors open for afternoon exercise. Eitan and the other escapees remain in their cells while the remaining prisoners go out into the courtyard to enjoy the spring sunshine. An hour later, Eitan organises his men into three groups.

At 4.22 p.m. an explosion—so loud I nearly jump out of my skin—shakes the south wall of the fortress, creating a gaping hole. In the courtyard, the prisoners who aren't supposed to escape create a diversion, while outside the prison, the three men disguised as Arabs, now in position north of Acre, fire a mortar at the nearby British army camp. At the same time, the command jeep stops at the petrol station at the entrance to the new town, lays anti-vehicle mines and sets fire to the station.

Back in the prison, the noise of the explosion signals the first group of escapees to leap from their cells and run down the corridor to the hole in the wall, but a group of Arab prisoners run in panic out of their cells and block their progress.

'Get out of the way,' Eitan screams.

Thirteen frantic fugitives push their way through the scrambling mass. The first to reach the gate in the corridor attaches the gelignite to the lock on the metal door and lights the fuse. The lock shatters into a thousand pieces, and the door flies open. The second gate receives the same treatment.

A second explosion signals action from the second group. Inmates spill kerosene mixed with oil onto the passageway and ignite it, blocking the advance of any prison guards.

The third group throws grenades at the guards on the roof, then flee. Amidst the dust and rubble, smoke and fire, explosions and screams, forty-one Jewish prisoners make their way to freedom.

Everyone in the hall claps and shouts.

The movie continues with the captain cursing about how explosives had entered his prison and how the Jewish prisoners had escaped—no one had ever done it before. While forty-one prisoners escaped, some were later recaptured and others killed in the fighting.

Irgun leaders decide to capture two British officers and trade them for three Jewish fighters they'd captured. Irgun tell the British that they will hang the British officers if the Brits execute their fighters. The British ignore them, though, and hang the three Irgun fighters in Acre prison. It's a terrible scene and I have to look away.

Then the following day, the British find their two officers hanging in a eucalyptus grove near Netanya. While they're being cut down, a booby trap on their bodies goes off, injuring a British officer. The voice on the movie tells us that this made headline news around the world and that 'it helped to create favour for the establishment of a Jewish state'. (Note 1)

It's getting near the end of the movie, and I don't want to risk being caught. Everyone is still watching the screen, so I tiptoe from my cubbyhouse of boxes to the door and run across the grass to the children's house.

It takes me hours to go off to sleep. I can't stop thinking about the movie. The hanging of the two fighters stays in my mind for ages—I can still see their faces. Ugh! But what about Papa and his tear? My mind goes back over the movie, and I can't make any link. I can understand how upset and angry the British were in having their officers killed, and maybe that's why they were so brutal in attacking Papa's ship and taking him to the camp in Poppendorf. But there's no other clues … I have to keep looking.

~

1. Some content drawn from *The Jewish Virtual Library.*

Part Two

Chapter Seven

April 1948
Omar and Sabah

Omar stared at the rows of olive trees grounded in the rich soil, sloping down to the small stream that provided life for his land in northern Palestine. A mixture of mauve and white anemones carpeted the lower slopes of the hillside. Spring had signalled their colourful awakening, bringing joy to the bees and the small Arab community. The fragrance of Damascus roses hung on silent air.

A passion for the land had seized him ever since he thrust his hands into the rich soil. A love affair, instilled from his father and his father's father. On the western side of Omar's 'patch of paradise,' as he called it, nestled a mix of lemon and orange trees, guarded by a row of fig trees. Two mature goats provided fresh milk and cheese for his small household. The large stone house he called home had provided comfort and shelter for four generations of his family. Two of his brothers had headed for Europe after completing their education.

Ishmael, the youngest brother, had remained and, like Omar, was committed to preserving the rich agricultural heritage of his forefathers. Ishmael and Gila shared the old family home with Omar and Sabah.

Omar wandered into the kitchen where his new wife, Sabah was preparing baklava. Her dark brown eyes smiled. 'I hope you're hungry.'

'Yes, my dear. It's been a long day. My arms are complaining, holding the sprayer for hours—reaching up to the top of the orange trees …'

'Poor, Omar.' Sabah removed her hands from the sticky mixture, wiped them clean on a towel and held her husband's shoulders with her delicate wrists. Lips pouted, she kissed him playfully on the lips. Omar returned her gentle kiss and squeezed her bottom.

'Oh! You don't seem *too* tired.' She grinned.

Omar smiled and poured himself a lemonade while Sabah returned to her baklava.

Sabah and Omar had known each other since they were children. They'd grown up in the local village where they'd laughed and played with the other Arab children. Their bond had resembled that of a caring brother and sister until they reached puberty when hormones changed their shape and the connection between them.

Two weeks earlier, on the second anniversary of his father's premature death, Omar had visited his father's grave. A massive heart attack had wrenched him from his beloved family. Omar remembered it as if it were yesterday: the men washing his lifeless body, dressing it in white cloth, carrying it to the humble mosque in the village for prayers and then placing it in the earth. Omar's grief was still great, and deep sighs accompanied any thought of that sadness. The death of his mother, twelve months prior to his father's passing, compounded his grief. Her long, slow fight against the cancer that finally claimed her life was tenacious, but the disease had won. Omar loved his parents and was intent on recreating for his own family the safe and caring environment they had achieved. 'May Allah give us many children to love,' was his constant prayer.

Ishmael and Gila breezed in through the backdoor with six eggs collected from the fowls that scratch for food around the family home.

Sabah smiled. 'You've timed it well.' She turned to her husband. 'Omar, we're ready.'

Omar brought to the old wooden table a jug of Erk Soos—a refreshing drink made from extracts of the liquorice plant mixed with water—and added it to the evening meal Sabah had laid out: chicken roasted with a fig and pistachio couscous stuffing and basted with a spicy lemon marinade which kept the meat deliciously moist; a bowl of leafy salad with fresh oranges which helped to balance the spiciness; a large bowl of *Fasoliyyeh bi z-zayt*—green beans lightly covered with olive oil and coriander bread—and a plate heaped with pita bread.

'We thank God who has brought this blessing to our possession; may He keep this blessing spread among us at all time.' Omar's prayer was the signal for Sabah's meal, prepared with love and care, to be shared among the grateful.

As they ate, they discussed the emerging crop of citrus, and the need for increased irrigation and servicing the old tractor.

Gila stood slowly, her face white with nausea. 'Please excuse me. I love the food but my stomach is not well.'

Sabah reached out and placed her hand on Gila's. 'I'm sorry your baby still makes it difficult for you. Please go and rest.'

Gila nodded. 'I'll be so glad when this stage is over,' she said, then retreated to the bedroom at the rear of the house. Omar and Sabah had agreed that the coolest room in their home was best for a pregnant mother who would soon carry her baby through a hot Palestinian summer.

Omar smiled. 'I love the chicken … I love it all.'

Sabah beamed, and her eyes sparkled to hear the response she longed for. Pleasing her husband was important to her.

'That goes for me, too,' Ishmael added, reaching for his water pipe. He moved to the sofa and ignited his sole source of evening pleasure. Omar joined him while Sabah busied herself clearing the table. Ishmael relaxed, drew long slow breaths on the pipe, then handed it to Omar. Part of the pleasure of this ritual for Ishmael was sharing it with his brother. In the heat of the workday, the focus was often on what needed to be done on the farm. The evening ritual provided a space to reflect, dream, laugh and sometimes cry.

'I hear the Jewish fighters are pushing our people out of Ramallah and Lydda,' Ishmael said. 'There've been threats. Do you think we're safe here?' A characteristic twist of his mouth accompanied Ishmael's question, as it always did when he posed a question of significance. He waited, his quick, dark eyes searching for a response from his companion.

While Ishmael's tanned face displayed his feelings openly to the world, Omar's poker face disguised his internal world. Sabah's careful observation of her husband had given her insight, however. She knew from his eyes the state of his being.

'His eyes are the windows to his soul,' she'd whispered to Gila when she'd first been married.

Omar thought for a minute. He never hurried his responses. 'We've a good relationship with our Jewish brothers here, as you know. We're family—have been for many, many years. I don't believe that'll change.'

'It may not be up to our Jewish brothers here.' Ishmael's voice strengthened. 'The Irgun militia are strong. Their voice is growing louder in Palestine, and they have weapons from Europe and the US. They'll have their way …'

Omar offered his brother the pipe and then motioned dismissively with his hand, saying, 'Allah will protect us. Our Jewish brothers will stand with us.'

After that they sat in silence for a few minutes. Heavy white smoke hung above their heads, a visible symbol of their friendship—their brotherhood.

Talk about the farm followed until Omar said, 'I think I'll turn in. Hope you and Gila sleep well.'

'Thanks, and may your dreams be pleasant,' Ishmael responded with a smile.

Omar entered the bedroom to find Sabah curled up under a sheet. He grinned, 'You don't waste time, do you?'

Sabah's eyes invited him to her side as she seductively pulled the sheet to her waist revealing her breasts. 'Are you tired?' she asked, placing her hands behind her head.

'Not that tired,' Omar replied with growing enthusiasm. He removed his shirt, slid onto the bed beside her and lowered the sheet.

Her eyes fixed on his gentle smile as he observed her slim, olive nakedness. Her smooth, long, dark hair, hidden from the gaze of other men in public was now on full display, lying gently over her breasts. 'I'm so blessed to have such a beautiful wife,' he whispered as he lowered his head.

She turned on her side to face him and ran her left hand through Omar's trimmed black beard. Then she placed both her hands behind his head and pulled him firmly towards her. Her passion rose as she kissed his eager lips. 'I've married a very handsome man, a man I love deeply. I want to be with him forever.'

The moon, beaming through the open window, was the sole witness to their lovemaking. It also observed the dark forces gathering, not too far distant to the south of their peaceful Palestinian community.

~

Late April 1948

'Jewish soldiers are coming ... soldiers ... they're coming ...' the boy said gasping for breath.

Omar stood on the top of a ladder leaning against the side of the barn and stared down at the startled face of young Hirsh, who'd run from the village, ten minutes away. His family often helped Omar when fruit-picking took over his life. Omar had laughed, groaned and sweated together over many years with Hirsh's family.

'Father and the other men are in the square talking,' the ten-year-old cried. 'They want you to come. Now!'

Omar climbed down the ladder, recalling his conversation with Ishmael two days earlier.

Ten minutes later, he entered the village square. Familiar faces, men in work clothes, robes and *keffiyehs,* spoke in hushed tones.

Imad, the carpenter, spoke to Omar, his tense voice reflecting his anxiety: 'Have you heard the news?'

'Only what Hirsh said, that the soldiers are coming. What are they coming for?'

'Reconnaissance,' Burhan interjected his reply. 'They're doing a survey of the north, and we're to provide accommodation.'

Without hesitation, Omar said, 'We'll welcome them and offer our best help.'

Even though Omar was in his mid-twenties, he was well respected in the village, even by men twice his age—both Arab and Jew. Omar had responded well to the education offered in the local school. His quick mind, high intelligence and wisdom beyond his years marked him as a leader.

Conversations continued, speculating on what 'reconnaissance' meant. Were the Zionists searching to establish a new settlement for some of the thousands of Jews who had streamed into Palestine in the last year? Men argued about where that space might be found.

'The natural place for a settlement is on the slopes on the southern side of the hills,' one of the men pointed out.

'But where would I take my goats?' Burhan asked.

Azhar, the oldest member of the community, raised his sinewy hand and the chatter ceased. His hands had tilled the soil so long they had absorbed its colour. 'As Omar has said, we'll offer them help. We've worked together for many years, and we can find ways to work with any new Jewish brothers who may wish to settle here. We join together with our Jewish families here at harvest—they help us—and there's no reason for that to change. When they come, let's have a feast ... let's welcome them.'

Azhar's strong, measured words spoke to the hearts of his people. His tanned and weather-beaten face, straggly grey beard and flowing robes gave him the aura of a prophet. His words were sufficient. Men nodded in agreement. 'We'll let everyone know when they arrive,' Azhar assured the men as they dispersed.

They didn't have to wait long. The following day, twelve Jewish soldiers entered the village. News of their arrival spread like a bushfire driven by wind.

'We're not here to harm you,' the leader said, speaking calmly. 'You're safe with us. We'll protect you.' His confidence soothed those with troubled gazes fixed on the guns slung casually across the shoulders of his men. 'We're here to do a survey. Don't be afraid.'

Omar, along with two other men and a number of women, took responsibility for organising the welcome feast of lamb and goat on the spit, chicken, rice dishes, stuffed vegetables, peppers, and a vast array of spices and Palestinian dishes of meat and chicken. Preparation included *Tamr Hindi*, a sour chilled drink, and *Jellab* created from rosewater. Also baklava, sugared almonds, date pastries, an array of fresh fruit, and the list went on.

The soldiers wandered through the village, occasionally stopping to chat among themselves. The children, kicking a football, followed the Jews at a distance. The afternoon progressed; long shadows stretched across the dusty village square, and the delicious smell of slow-cooked lamb and goat drew the soldiers back to the generous villagers, who'd been busy creating their offering. Soon olives were offered with cheeses and nuts. Grape juice was poured into beautiful goblets fashioned from olive wood and offered to the visitors. Men performed their carving skills, slicing meat and passing it to the Israelis. Plates were piled high with fresh pickings from the farms. The sound of flutes, lyres, zithers and drums filled the air with celebration and joy. This is the way Arabs welcome their guests, and Omar's village provided their best, giving their produce, time and energy to the men who were there to protect them.

'The soldiers keep to themselves,' Burhan observed.

'Look at the children,' Imad added. 'They're trying to talk with them, but it's clear they don't want to socialise.'

'They'll soften up. The night is still young,' Omar said.

Dancing replaced eating, and the oil lamps seemed to flicker in time with bodies and colourful costumes moving to the hypnotic music. The soldiers sat together, sharing a water pipe, enjoying the welcoming festivities, but they resisted any invitation to dance, content to watch and relax with a pipe.

The moon had risen high in the evening sky when the captain announced to Azhar, 'Thank you for your hospitality. We have enjoyed your food and your welcome. We need to turn in now.'

Azhar called to each family who had volunteered to take guests. Six families led two soldiers to their homes and made them comfortable for the night. The remaining villagers removed the remnants of the feast from the tables, extinguished the lamps and returned to their homes.

'You'll take our bed,' Sabah said to the captain of the soldiers and his companion.

He rewarded Sabah's efforts with a smile of approval. The beautiful woven carpets, the tapestries and the colourful bed covers reflected many hours of Sabah's passion for perfection. Her eye for detail and colour was well regarded in the village and now by the young Israeli captain. His manner had become more relaxed as the evening had worn on. His handsome face and blue eyes had caught the attention of the young women in the village, but Sabah experienced discomfort about a hesitancy she found in his manner. She provided him with a basin and pitcher of water to remove the dust of the day, then she retired with Omar to the back room and prepared their bedding.

'What do you make of them?' she asked.

Omar removed his shirt and hung it over a chair. 'Oh, I don't know. They didn't say much. We tried, our men … um, to talk, but they wanted to stay together. They seem pleasant enough. They repeated that they're here to protect us and to survey the land.'

Sabah changed into a lace gown and rearranged the pillows. 'Protect us from what?' she asked.

'That's what I asked, but they didn't reply, and I wasn't prepared to push them. I don't know; maybe it's some of the militant splinter groups causing trouble. There's a lot of confusion in the country. Things are changing.'

'Something isn't right,' Sabah responded as she slid under the covers.

'We've lived with the Jews for … forever. We're brothers.'

'I know, I know; you always say that Omar, but I have this strange feeling.'

Omar raised his hands in frustration. 'Let's get some sleep.'

'You've worked so hard, my darling. You deserve a good sleep.' Sabah's soft hand stroked his face.

He responded with a forced smile and closed his eyes.

The next morning, the captain and his offsider rose early, and Sabah soon had flatbread with olive oil, *za'atar*, olives, tomatoes, small cucumbers and boiled eggs on the table.

'You make good coffee,' the captain said.

Sabah smiled at the compliment and offered him more bread.

'No thanks. I won't be able to move,' he said with a laugh.

Omar noticed that the captain seemed more relaxed. 'Did you sleep well?' he inquired.

'Very well, thank you,' came the polite reply. 'You've made this a very comfortable place.'

'We love this house. It's been in our family for generations.'

'The olive trees are old.'

'Yes, they were planted by my family many years ago. They give the best fruit in the land … oh … but maybe I'm biased,' Omar said with a laugh.

'Your figs are coming on.'

'We can start picking them in a few weeks. Please come back and have some.' The captain appeared in good spirits so Omar slipped in a pointed question. 'What happens next?'

'We report back to the chief … not sure what happens from here.' The young captain turned to Sabah and Omar. 'Thank you for your kindness. You're good hosts. We'll do whatever we can to protect you.'

Omar took the plunge. His relationship with the Israeli seemed secure. 'Why do we need protection?'

The captain paused for a moment before speaking, 'As you know, this is a time of great change in Palestine. There're armed groups of Jews causing concern for us … taking the law into their own hands. In other parts of Palestine—especially along the eastern side—your countrymen are frustrated with the number of immigrants. We want to make sure the land is secure for everyone.'

'We're grateful for your protection,' Omar said without hesitation.

'The rest of our team are meeting with us in fifteen minutes in the square so we need to push off. Thanks again, *tus bih 'ala khayr.*'

'*Tus bih 'ala khayr,*' Omar repeated. The captain and his aide hastened towards their jeep without looking back.

Omar smiled. 'I told you everything is well.'

'Let's wait and see,' Sabah said, retreating into the house. 'The captain's mate said very few words. It seemed he was … play acting …'

'Maybe he's shy … I don't know. I like the captain. I think he's a good man.'

'Let's wait and see.'

~

A week later, the captain returned to the village. This time the number of soldiers had increased to forty. Within thirty minutes, most of the villagers had gathered in the square where twelve of the Jewish contingent had previously experienced the best of Arab hospitality.

The captain seemed uneasy and his soldiers reluctant to make eye contact with the people. The captain raised his hand to quieten the murmuring. '*Sabahul khayr.* You're in grave danger. You must leave immediately and hide in the hills. We will protect your village. You've nothing to fear as long as you stay in the hills. I'll send my men to collect you when it's safe to return. However, I must urge you … leave now.'

A gasp erupted from the people, and they stared at each other in disbelief. Sabah took Omar's hand and looked at him without saying a word. Omar felt her eyes boring into him. He avoided her gaze and stared at the ground. His heart was racing, his mind exploding with a thousand questions.

'Captain. What's the threat?'

'I can't give you details. The information I have is very grave. Please trust me. You're in danger. You must leave the village *now* and hide in the hills.'

'How long are we going to be there?' Azhar's strong voice cut through the babble.

'Perhaps up to a week,' the captain responded.

'What do we need to take?' Azhar asked, his voice shaking.

'Whatever you need for a brief time. You've little time left, so move now. We can only guarantee your safety if you move quickly to the hills. Go; go *now,*' the captain shouted. 'We'll protect your homes.'

Some villagers ran, others walked quickly; a few, still reeling from shock, stood motionless.

'Why can't they protect us in the village?' Sabah asked. 'What do we take?' But nobody could answer that question. Every thought and effort was directed to what they might need for their temporary exile.

Soon a line of frantic humanity snaked its way across the valley into the wooded hills: old people stumbled along the path; parents and young people carried a few belongings; and children led goats and carried chickens. They hurried, the words of the captain ringing in their ears, 'We can only guarantee your safety if you move quickly to the hills.'

'Can we trust the captain?' Imad the carpenter asked.

'I believe so,' Omar replied frowning. 'The captain is anxious and concerned for us.'

'We've no other choice but to do what he says,' Azhar said. 'We've lived here in peace for years, and there's no reason why it shouldn't continue.'

Two hours later, the weary villagers reached the forest canopy. Each family claimed a portion of the uneven rocky ground among the shelter of the trees. The children's faces reflected their excitement—to them this was a *real* adventure. Parents organised children, concerned about how they would manage. Children helped grandparents remove stones and arrange foliage for their bedding.

'It'll only be for a few days,' said one mother, trying to comfort her elderly father. Two small children clung to the fold of her *Jilbab*. Her rhythmic rocking soon closed the eyes of the baby resting in her arms.

By nightfall movement had ceased. Bodies exhausted from the physical effort of the unexpected evacuation had taken its toll. The only sounds came from an occasional bird rustling in the trees or the whimper of a child.

The morning sun roused the refugees. Figs, tomatoes, cucumbers and pita bread soon filled complaining stomachs. Waterbags delivered cool, life-giving refreshment to thirsty mouths. Suddenly, the sound of truck engines alerted them to movement on the dusty road leading into their village. All eyes turned to the valley.

'I've seen at least ten trucks going in this morning. Wonder what they're doing?' an elderly woman said.

'Hopefully they're protecting our homes,' a voice replied.

'Allah will keep us safe,' another added.

Omar and Sabah helped teachers gather the children for lessons and then walked to the edge of the tree-line and stared at the village.

'I can hear voices, laughter and … it sounds like crashing. What's going on?' Omar asked with a frown. 'I might sneak down to the olive grove and have a closer look.'

Sabah released her hand from his and grabbed his arm.

'You know what the soldiers said,' she protested.

'I'm only going to the edge of the grove.'

'Omar, if the soldiers see you, there'll be trouble. It's not worth the risk. Please … let's go back to the others.'

Omar sighed and turned back, kicking a small rock in frustration.

Sabah took his hand.

'I suppose you're right,' Omar muttered. 'But I don't know what all the noise is about.'

'We'll find out soon enough. It's dangerous disobeying the captain's instructions. As you know, there's strife in Jerusalem and other parts of Palestine. The soldiers are only doing their duty. Allah is good; he'll protect us and our homes.'

They reached the edge of their campsite, strewn with baggage and belongings, and heard the voices of children singing.

'They seem happy enough,' Omar said.

'They're amazing. Keeping them occupied is a good thing,' Sabah smiled.

A relieved Omar shrugged off his frustration, pleased he hadn't indulged his curiosity.

'I can't believe this weather,' Sabah's friend, wife of the carpenter said. 'It's so mild. No sign of rain. Allah be praised!'

'What'll we do if it does rain?' an elderly voice asked.

'It's not going to rain,' Sabah replied, searching the sky.

'It might by the end of the week, but I'm sure we'll be back in our homes by then,' Omar said.

The fourth day dawned with a heavy grey cloud blanketing the region. The refugees shivered as the chill from a light rain seeped into their tired bodies. Small shelters erected from branches and foliage provided inadequate shelter. Supplies of food ran out, and every family foraged for food in the hills. No word came from the captain, but military trucks continued to move in and out of the village.

'We can't keep going on like this!' Azhar growled, his face gaunt. 'The older people are suffering. Young children are becoming restless. We've no food except for what we can scrounge.'

'But what can we do? It's clear it's not safe for us to return.' The question came from Azhar's close friend, Hamil, a well-recognised figure in the village. His weather-beaten, wrinkled face deceived most villagers about his real age.

'I think we should send some of the men down and see if it's safe to return,' Omar said. 'I'm happy to go.' He arched his back and crossed his arms to ease the stiffness from sleeping on the ground.

'Let's give them a little more time,' Azhar replied, stroking his beard.

'How much more time?' Imad fumed. 'My baby is sick. We need to go back.'
His eyes looked like those of a big gentle animal, pleading.

Azhar nodded and thought for a moment. 'Three more days, then we go. Allah will protect us.'

Murmuring followed, but the general consensus was taken to delay any movement towards the village.

Chapter Eight

May 1948

Omar lay motionless, listening to the sounds of dawn. Insects buzzed in frantic activity; a lark called and crickets sang. The agony of unanswered questions had robbed him of sleep. He gazed into a cloudless sky, waiting for the sun. Three more days had passed without the appearance of the captain or any Jewish soldiers—the longest days of their forced exile. Tensions were running high, even amongst friends. The agony of fleeing their homes, deprivation of sleep from lying on rocky ground, lack of food, herding children, and the uncertainty of the future became an explosive cocktail for rebellion. On the last day of waiting, the community restrained four men from making their way to the village.

'We'll do this together. We must take care to think it through.' Azhar's voice was calm and firm. 'Our investigation should be done with respect, not in anger. We don't know what's going on in the village. We mustn't be hasty.'

A long discussion followed, and the community chose six men, three middle-aged and three younger.

'A good balance between brain and brawn,' one woman quipped.

Badri was a successful businessman and negotiator, who'd done well in producing garments for the region. Karam, the shoemaker, had a mind as steady as his hand. His good friend, Hanif, well experienced in local politics, was keen to be involved. Omar and Iyad an energetic goat keeper, and Imad, the carpenter, provided a youthful balance.

After breakfast, the villagers gathered to wish the party of six well in their effort to assess the safety of their village.

Sabah gave Omar a long hug and kissed him firmly. 'Allah is with you, my love,' she whispered.

The carpenter waved to his wife, who was busy leading her class in activities. He didn't want to interrupt.

'May Allah protect you, my brothers,' Azhar offered as the company of six left the anxious assembly.

The men set off at a brisk pace, eager to find answers to questions that had plagued the community for the last twelve days. An hour later, their heart rate increased as they entered the outskirts of the village. An eerie stillness hung in the air. No sound of voices or vehicles.

'It's like a ghost town,' Hanif said.

'The place is empty,' Badri exclaimed with surprise. 'Where are the soldiers?'

'Look at this!' Karam cried, pointing to the general store.

Iyad ran to the open door. 'It's been ransacked,' he shouted. 'Look at this. Furniture broken, sacks of flour and sugar gone. There's nothing left! Falah will be furious!'

Open-mouthed, they continued their nervous exploration. Shop after shop had been looted, remaining contents vandalised. Homes had suffered the same fate; mattresses torn open, tables and chairs broken, curtains shredded—the evidence of an orgy of pillage.

'They've taken everything of value,' Badri cried. 'They promised to protect our homes.'

Then it happened. Imad, the carpenter, came to his workshop joined to his home. His energy and creativity were evident in every item that came from his workbench. Love fashioned the furniture that customers craved, and he embraced his two young children every afternoon as he walked through the door of his simple home. His tools were like paintbrushes to an artist, handled with great skill, carefully sharpened and treated with care. He ran to the door of his workshop, stood motionless, then steadied himself, gripping the doorposts.

'My tools are gone,' he gasped. He ran to his safe at the rear of his workplace. 'It's gone … all my money … gone.' His voice quivered. 'I've worked so hard for so long …'

A sound from outside alerted the shattered men, who stood together sharing Imad's devastation. The six villagers stepped into the street, trembling. Four Israeli soldiers walked towards them, rifles slung casually over their shoulders.

'Where's the captain?' Badri asked, breathing deeply, trying to swallow his nervous anger.

'He's not here. What are you doing here? You were told to wait in the hills.'

'Who's in charge?' Badri asked with greater firmness.

'That doesn't concern you. Leave – *now.*' The young soldier took the gun from his shoulder and gripped it firmly with both hands.

'You promised … you promised to protect our homes. They've been looted, our possessions broken. You've betrayed us.' Karam's words cut the air like a knife.

Unmoved, the young Jew motioned with his rifle to the men to return the way they'd come. 'Leave now. This is no longer your land. Get out. Leave, *now.*'

Imad's passion was not confined to his work. His sense of justice was sharper than his tools. Imad was a strong man, often going to the hills to cut down trees for the furniture he produced in the village. Sometimes he engaged his body before his brain, and this was one of those occasions. A large rock sat at the doorway of his workshop—a silent sentinel. Its colour, shape and size had caught Imad's eye years earlier when he stumbled over it in a field. Not only was it pleasant to the eye but also it kept the door of his workshop open. Unable to contain himself, he reached down, seized the rock with his right-hand and shouted, 'This is our land; you've betrayed us.'

'Imad, stop!' Omar screamed.

Rage blinded Imad's accuracy. The rock flew past the soldier's head. Four clicks sounded and safety catches released.

'No!' Badri screamed. 'Don't shoot!'

The rifles exploded in unison. Imad's chest blew open, and he fell to the ground, dead. The five villagers froze, staring in horror at the broken body of their dear friend.

'He's dead ... he's dead,' Omar stuttered in disbelief.

The soldiers raised their rifles. Instantly, the five dropped to their knees, hands raised.

'We'll go; we'll go. Don't shoot,' Badri pleaded.

The soldier in command signalled with his rifle. The five staggered to their feet with raised arms and walked backwards while the soldiers continued to level their weapons at them.

'We're going,' Badri repeated, shaking.

'Go and don't come back, ever,' the soldier hissed.

'Please, can we take the body of our friend and give him a proper burial?' Omar asked.

The young Israeli thought for a moment and then without saying a word, motioned with his rifle. The five shocked survivors of the bloodshed sprang to life and with trembling hands lifted Imad's lifeless body from the widening pool of blood. Each stared into the stricken, white faces of their comrades as they raised the shattered body to their shoulders. They nodded to the soldiers, who maintained their aggressive stance with rifles at the ready, and crept away from their aggressors, the only sound their shoes treading softly on the dusty road. Blood dripped onto the ground, leaving an ugly trail of evidence of Jewish violence. Imad's blood drenched their clothes, but no discomfort, no complaint came from their lips. He was their brother. Each shared Imad's pain. Now they shared his blood. A strange feeling stirred, loyalty, comradeship—a sacred privilege.

Omar and Iyad led the grief-stricken procession, the weight of the body supported on their shoulders. Badri and Karam took up the rear of the procession, and Hanif supported the bloodied body between them. No one looked over their shoulder. They felt the eyes and guns at their backs.

Badri wished they would pull the trigger. What was there to live for now? His beloved home had gone, his land confiscated. Thoughts flooded his tortured mind as the rhythm of their feet marched towards the open fields. The sudden shock and the agonising sorrow of losing his friend allowed no room for him and his traumatised companions to feel the grief of losing their village, their homes, their fields, to which they would never return.

~

The community soon spotted the pathetic figures climbing the hill with leaden footsteps. Men and women ran screaming and wailing from the trees towards the silent, bloodied group. The tears of the five bearers ran unrestrained, mingled with blood.

Imad's wife flung herself hysterically onto his body. The procession stopped, explanations were given and the chaos of emotions continued until Dirar, their religious leader, gave instructions for preparing the body for burial. Imad's wife washed the body five times and shrouded it. Ritual demanded three washings, but Imad's flesh was so badly stained it required more. Once clean and prepared, they covered the body in a white sheet. Two women provided three, large white sheets. They placed the body on top of the sheets, left hand lying on his chest. His right-hand rested on his left-hand—a position of prayer. Imad's wife and two women folded the sheets over his body, first the right side and then the left, until all three sheets wrapped the body.

Men secured the shrouded body with ropes, one tied above the head, two tied around the body and one below the feet. Funeral prayers were said, and then the men accompanied the body to the gravesite at the edge of the forest. They lowered the body into the grave and placed a layer of stones on top to prevent direct contact between the body and the soil. Each man filed past and placed three handfuls of soil into the grave. Then they filled the grave and placed a small stone on top.

Omar in a solemn voice said, 'I'd like to have used the rock he threw at the soldier.'

Tears flowed long into the night for the death of one of their favourite sons.

The following morning, after the edge of their grief had lifted, the exiles debated their future.

'Of course we can't stay here,' Badir said. 'We must move. Maybe our brothers in Harin will help us.' Harin rested in a valley, a day's walk to the south.

'Today we prepare,' they decided. 'Tomorrow we walk.'

The following day, under a cloudless sky, two hundred tired, hungry, grief-stricken souls trudged with aching limbs to a destination of hope. A fresh morning led to a warm spring day. The only respite to lift the refugees' spirits was the chaos of colour: vast stretches of red anemones; blue lupines; and the whites of the iris and narcissus. The visual feast took the edge off their agony, but it ended half an hour before they reached Harin. Goat herds had removed most of the vegetation that struggled to survive in the fierce, rocky ground.

The elders of Harin gave them a restrained welcome. Men and women ceased their tasks and stared in silence as the wave of weary exiles flowed into their village. Some of the women made coffee; children brought jugs of water.

'Salam, **Azhar.** We heard about what happened in your village … and you can't go back?' The words came with feeling from a softly spoken elder.

'That's true. We've nowhere to go' **Azhar** replied, **shaking his head.**

'Let's drink coffee.' The elder's wife pointed to a seat shaded by a large fig tree and offered figs and dates with coffee. Azhar accepted them gratefully.

'You can rest here for a day or two,' the elder said, 'but as you know, we've limited room. We can't manage all your people. I know we've been friends for a long-time but … we need to be practical. The soldiers came last week, and we offered our fruit and supplies, including many goats.' He waved his hands in despair. 'I'm not sure how our people will manage this summer. I'm so sad for what happened to you and your people. Your land is more fertile than ours; I suspect that's why they didn't want it.'

'I understand,' Azhar responded in a lifeless voice. 'We'll make camp for two days and think what we might do.'

Omar and Sabah rested under a large cypress tree beside the dusty road with the small number of survivors of their village. The late morning sun had sapped any reserves of energy they'd regained from a restless sleep in the rough. Their path of uncertainty took them east from their beloved village. Some of the villagers headed for Syria and Jordan. Most of the older men and their wives, including Badri, Karan, Hanif and Azhar found their way into small Arab communities.

'We're too tired to go on,' they cried. Those Palestinian communities were generous but stretched beyond their ability to comfortably sustain the increase in numbers.

The younger people searched further. Omar and Sabah tramped east with close friends, bright memories of the hills of Galilee drawing them on. In the spring, it was as if a giant hand, with broad sweeping strokes, painted them blue, white and red. They stood in picturesque confusion: narcissus—the Rose of Sharon; wild anemone—the Lily of the Field; pink flax; crowfoot; iris; broom; rape and borage. But just as the flowers faded rapidly under the heat of the sun, hope of a home for the fugitives evaporated as quickly.

The day they left the shores of Tiberias, Omar rose early. The lake, covered in a grey shroud of silence, waited patiently for dawn. One remaining solitary star burnt bright. Slowly the faint pink on the distant hills became stronger. Cocks crowed in a chorus, the scream of swifts filled the air. Through the still air of morning, men with camels and donkeys led their beasts to water. Eventually the sun leapt over the hills—a new day had come to Tiberias.

'I would love to stay here,' Omar said to Sabah. But the Palestinian community had conspired against them. Scowls from angry faces had repeated the refrain, 'No room for you here.'

The party of pilgrims travelled south. Two donkeys struggling under the weight of oversized sacks gifted by villagers picked their way along ancient paths. They plunged down into the breathless northern end of the Jordan Valley through parched hills, through *Beit She'an*, encountering further heartache. The valley was like a tropical trench filled with fierce heat. Omar knew Sabah would struggle to survive the summers, so they retreated, travelling north-west.

The Harod River revived their faded spirits—the delicious sound of running water in a thirsty land, luxurious and extravagant. The small, exhausted company pressed on further, towards Jezreel and Nazareth a little further to the north. But again, 'there was no room in the inn.'

So they headed towards Haifa.

On a few occasions, Jewish soldiers checked their papers and possessions for guns and then allowed them to travel on.

~

Omar took a long swig from his waterbag and glanced at Sabah. 'How are you?'

'I'm tired, but I can manage. I hope we can find a place soon. I'm over this.'

'We're around a day's walk from Haifa—I'm sure we'll find something there,' Omar replied. He looked high into the dense branches of the cypress that hid him and his friends from the heat. 'I'm glad we're not in the desert,' he quipped. 'Give me the north any day.'

The sound of a truck caught their attention. It bounced along from the south, a large cloud of dust following its progress. An ancient Bedford decommissioned by the British appeared—a wreck on wheels, carrying major dents in every panel. Obviously, it was a refugee from a war zone. Futile attempts had been made to preserve its rusting body with varying colours of house paint, but clearly, corrosion was winning. Black smoke spewed from the exhaust, indicating an engine rebore was well overdue. The dirty windscreen was cracked in several places.

'How does it keep going?' Omar exclaimed.

The brakes complained loudly as it ground to a stop. Grinning faces of three Palestinians greeted them from open windows.

'Salam,' Omar said.

'Salam,' came the response in unison.

'Where're you going?' the driver asked.

Omar hesitated, then replied, 'We're headed towards Haifa, looking for somewhere to stay.'

Omar explained a little of their exile and how they'd been treated by the Jewish soldiers.

The driver nodded. 'You can stay with us tonight. About twenty minutes walk up the road. I know our people won't mind.' The driver's grin appeared again, revealing missing teeth. 'I can take some of you now if you want?'

'Thank you.' Sabah gasped with relief and glanced at Omar.

Conversation erupted amongst the tired travellers, and they agreed to spend a night at the settlement.

The young Palestinian driver leapt out of the truck and rearranged shovels and gardening equipment. 'Three or four can fit on the back, and I can take one in the front.' The young Arab was slim, energetic and wore khaki shorts. His dirty red and white checked headscarf provided a small measure of relief from the blazing sun.

'He seems nice,' Sabah said.

'Yes, he does. It won't hurt us to spend a night here. Everyone needs a break.' Omar scanned the exhausted remnants from their village. 'You go in the truck, and I'll bring the others on foot.'

Minutes later, bodies loaded, four tired exiles braced for a bone-shaking ride to the shade and respite of a promised oasis. 'Take the first turn off this road on the left and follow it for about 500 metres,' shouted the young Arab driver to Omar and the weary refugees.

The truck rattled off, and Omar and the group quickened their steps along the uneven road, blinking their way through reddish dust. The exit road soon appeared, and with renewed energy, the exiles followed it through low scrub, past a clump of pine trees until they came to impressive cultivated gardens on either side of the road. Young corn plants, cucumbers, and tomatoes covered ground that sloped gently to a group of distant stone houses nestled amongst a small cluster of pines. On the higher slope to the north, a grove of olive trees, citrus, and figs caught their attention. Further down the slope, stone houses nestled amongst a small cluster of pines.

'This is a nice place,' one of the women commented.

Omar and the group spotted the ramshackle truck when they entered the village. A small group of residents welcomed them, pouring coffee and offering small cakes.

Omar approached the excited gathering, and one of the men stepped forward to greet him. 'Salam. You must be Omar? I'm Joseph.'

'Salam. Yes, my wife is Sabah.'

'I've met her. She's resting inside. My wife Miriam is taking good care of her.'

'You're most kind in your welcome,' Omar replied.

'You've been on the road for many days.'

'Yes. Four weeks.'

'Already I heard a little of your story … it makes me sad to hear how you've been treated. Anna, please give coffee to Omar.'

A young woman in a pink hijab appeared with coffee and a plate of small cakes.

'Thank you.' Omar took the small cup and relaxed in a padded chair under a sycamore tree.

The afternoon sun sent the weary exiles and their hosts to the shade of trees on the eastern side of Joseph's home. More village residents arrived with food, and young children stood and stared at the visitors from a distance. The exiles ate hungrily from plates heaped with fresh baked cakes and varieties of fruit.

'How long have you been here?' asked Omar, sipping coffee.

'Our families took over this land fifty years ago. We are blessed to have good soil and water from the stream. God has been good to us.'

Omar spotted a cross hanging on a pendant around a woman's neck. 'Are you Christians?'

'Yes, and you're Muslim; we're brothers. We both come from the same Father, Abraham.'

Omar smiled and selected an orange offered to him by one of the older women. 'The women's dresses are woven with great skill. My wife loves embroidery.'

'It's our tradition here. Ima was a fine dressmaker and taught the women. They're proud of their creations,' Joseph replied. 'Now let me see; what I can arrange?' He beckoned two young men. 'Omar, when you're ready, they will take you and your people to the spare houses. We have two.' Joseph pointed to the stone cottages on the far side of the plantation and lowered his voice. 'We had families leave. They're scared of the soldiers. The soldiers came through and checked our village months ago, but didn't return. Some of us think they still might come back. But … God will protect us.'

Omar shifted uneasily in his seat. 'I believed Allah would protect us. We've lost our homes, but we're still alive. It's Allah's will.' Omar sighed. 'Our land had many trees and crops. It's a large area and the soil was good, like yours.'

'Our area is small, as you can see,' Joseph said. 'Maybe the Jews are only interested in larger farms. I'm not sure, but I wonder if our relationship with Kibbutz Atak may help.' He pointed to a small hill to the north.

Omar gazed at the buildings perched on the hillside. 'I didn't spot them …'

'You can only see the main building, which is the dining hall, and one dormitory,' Joseph said. 'The remainder are built down the other side of the hill. We've always had a good relationship with them. We help them when harvest is on and they help us.'

Omar smiled. 'That's the way it should be.'

As the afternoon sun sank lower in the sky, Omar and the exiles relaxed. Soon the smell of barbequed chicken, roasted potatoes, salads and pita bread summoned the united body of guests and hosts to a meal. Music and laughter soon filled the dry hot air.

'I like these people,' Sabah said to Omar, picking up a chicken leg.

Omar nodded. 'So do I; they're so friendly.'

~

Abdiel and Maya stood on the steps of the dining hall and watched the old Bedford rumble its way into the small Palestinian village below. They could just make out tiny figures leaving the old truck, in which, they, too, had suffered on a few occasions.

'Looks like they have visitors,' Maya observed.

Neither knew these visitors would join the community and become local *Atak Fellaheen*. Neither knew that two of the visitors would become entangled in their lives. Abdiel shifted his gaze to the right and surveyed the western slope descending to the killing-fields of the recent Arab attack. A shudder ran down his spine. He'd never walk through that area again.

Part Three

Chapter Nine

October 1949
Abdiel, Omar, Maya and Sabah

How life can change with a chance meeting. That was true for the Atak community. Significant moments in history often turn on an unexpected encounter, and profound, unforeseen consequences follow. Abdiel's random act of kindness would trigger a chain of events that would bring much joy, but also unspeakable suffering.

Abdiel bumped his way back to the kibbutz, avoiding the worst holes in the dusty road. It was mid-morning, and he felt satisfied with his purchase of a load of potatoes in Haifa. He approached the track that led to the Arab settlement and noticed a young Palestinian and his wife, kneeling by the side of the road. The brakes squealed and the vehicle came to a stop. 'Is everything alright?' Abdiel asked.

'My wife isn't feeling well. We're resting here for a break,' the young Arab replied.

'You're from the settlement here, aren't you?' Abdiel asked.

'Yes. We're searching for two goats that escaped. You haven't seen them?'

'No, I can't say I have.'

The young woman suddenly twisted in agony and gripped her stomach. 'Oh, what's happening?'

The young man's face became a mask of fear. 'My wife is six months pregnant. It's our first child.'

The woman took a deep breath and bent forward gripping her stomach. She exhaled and took another deep breath.

Abdiel weighed up the situation. 'I'm no doctor, but I think we need to get her to a hospital.' He leaned across and opened the door on the passenger's side.

'*Shukran. Shukran,*' the husband said, turning to his wife. 'I'll help you.'

With her husband's help, the young woman rose unsteadily to her feet and climbed onto the front seat of the truck.

'You're most gracious to do this,' the young Palestinian said.

'Your wife's welfare is far more urgent than anything I've planned for today. It'll take us a little less than half an hour to get to Haifa.'

'My name is Omar, and my wife is Sabah.'

'I'm Abdiel; I live up the hill in Kibbutz Atak.'

'Yes, I've seen you in the fields from a distance. You people work long hours.'

Abdiel was only half listening as he reversed the truck and negotiated the potholes along the uneven road back to Haifa. His anxiety rose as he noticed blood on the front of Sabah's robes. She gripped the edge of the well-worn bench seat, and he was conscious of every bump, which resulted in Sabah giving a short gasp.

She remained silent for the entire journey, regulating her breathing to manage her pain. The hospital staff met her at the entry into the emergency department with efficiency and care. Abdiel sat patiently in the waiting area as nurses and doctors in white coats breezed past. A wardsman wheeled a young man with a leg strapped in a splint through the swinging doors into the central section. An old Jewish man's raucous cough broke the silence. Abdiel counted six people in the waiting area, glad his patient had been given priority. He was no doctor, but his sense was that she wasn't in a good way.

Omar came through the swinging doors and walked over to Abdiel. 'They're admitting her and will keep watch. I'll stay with her. You've been most kind. I don't know how to thank you.'

'You've thanked me already. I'll drive back now and let your people know.'

'*Shukran Shukran*, Abdiel; I hope I can return your kindness someday.' He grasped Abdiel's hand gratefully.

Abdiel drove back along the old familiar road to the kibbutz deep in thought. *How crazy this land is. Arab and Jews fight each other. Jews help Arabs; Arabs help Jews. Arabs, they're just like me, we're brothers.*

~

Uncertainty hung heavily in the air. Everyone was on guard, vigilant, watching for an unseen enemy. While the appearance of normality presided over the small country, pockets of violence and terror exploded intermittently. Yet in the midst of strife and uncertainty, genuine acts of support and friendship survived between the 'tribes.'

Five days after the trip to the hospital, as pink sky coloured the west, a familiar face appeared at the dining-hall entrance at Kibbutz Atak. A small group of kibbutzniks preparing the Shabbat meal were glad of the interruption. It was Omar, the husband of Sabah, who Abdiel had taken to hospital earlier in the week. Concern for the mother and the child she carried had impacted the small Jewish community. The women of the kibbutz had made friends with Sabah during the embroidery classes they shared in the settlement every month.

Omar approached with caution, looking uncertain. 'My apologies for interrupting your preparations. We've just returned from hospital. The news isn't good.'

Abdiel appeared at Omar's side. 'Omar, please come in. How is Sabah?'

Both men entered and stood with the concerned kibbutzniks who offered both men a seat.

Omar sighed and glanced away, then returned his gaze to Abdiel. 'We've lost the child,' he said with a sob, his lips quivering.

A stunned silence took hold of the group. Eyes stared in disbelief at the haggard face lined with grief. The women knew the life that Sabah carried was special. A precious life desperately longed for, prayed for. The joy of the announcement of her pregnancy had lit up the community. The women's excited chatter infected the embroidery group with unrestrained advice, and snippets of information had been heaped upon a beaming Sabah. But now that life had ended. How cruel! The gentle little flame had been snuffed out, extinguished. Tears began to stream down the women's faces, their chests heaving under the weight of grief. The sobbing continued in waves.

In a momentary silence, Abdiel said in a frail voice, 'That's so sad. I don't know what to say. I'm so sorry.' He shook his head slowly, hands extended towards the broken Palestinian in a gesture conveying helplessness.

The women embraced each other, desperate to gain support from the shock of the tragic announcement.

'How is Sabah?' one of the women asked.

'She's very weak and, of course, she's devastated.'

The women nodded, red eyed as the words fell from Omar's lips like molten lead.

'The saddest part is that Sabah may never be able to have children. We'll have to wait and see.'

Abdiel moved his chair closer and placed his hand on Omar's shoulder. Tears streamed down Omar's face and splashed onto the floorboards. In the midst of the sea of sadness, something inexplicable was happening in the hearts of those that sat united in grief. An unspoken bond of understanding and empathy drew them together. Here was an Arab from the adjoining community, a husband, a brother, in pain. It seemed unbelievable that Jews were taking the lives of Arabs, and Arabs taking the lives of Jews in acts of violence throughout the country. Yet here, Arab and Jew joined together in grief for a single life, not fully formed, a life snuffed out.

Omar shook his head and wrung his hands. 'Not only have I lost my land, I've also lost a child.'

Abdiel felt the ache in Omar's heart. He grieved over losing his beloved olive and citrus trees. The soil that had supported him and his family for generations had been violently wrenched from his grasp. Abdiel felt helpless, unable to lighten the load of the invisible shroud that hung heavily over Omar. The added grief of their lost child was very real and created a bond deeper than friendship. The bond, forged between Omar and Sabah, and Abdiel and Maya in the crucible of suffering, was only a foretaste of a far greater agony, yet to come.

~

October 1956

The friendship between the Jewish kibbutzniks on the hill and the Arabs on the plain grew as years progressed. Not only did they share the additional demands of harvests but also their religious festivals. *Yom Kippur* brought the Christians and the Muslims to the grounds of the kibbutz. Tables strained under the weight of steaming casseroles, egg dishes, smoked fish, kugels and sweet cakes. *Eid Al-Fitr*, the 'festival of the breaking of the fast' of Ramadan signalled a welcome invasion by the Jews into the open spaces in the settlement where they joined their Muslim and Christian friends in roasted lamb and the extravagance of all that is sweet and rich. Abdiel always headed for his favourite fare, *Ma'amoul,* a shortbread filled with dates and pistachios or walnuts.

Christmas drew the kibbutzniks to the settlement in the cooler days of winter at the invitation of the small Christian community, who created a spectacular tree with lights and tinsel. Chicken, kosher meats, salads, desserts, dates and figs provided a feast that united their communities. Everybody looked forward to the times of celebration, a joining of cultures, a blending of blood—Arab, Jewish and Christian.

Omar's eyes lit up. 'We're truly blessed to have so many celebrations—more than most of my Muslim friends,' he said to Sabah.

The founding of the PLO on the second of June 1956 raised the eyebrows of Israelis. However, the impact of Israel's invasion of Egypt with France and Britain, when President Nasser closed the Suez Canal on 26th July that year, did nothing more than feature headlines in newspapers in Israel. It hardly rated a mention in the communities of Atak.

The painful news for two couples in that multi-faith community was that 'there was no news'—no sign of conception. Maya and Sabah had become like sisters, sharing the pain of childlessness. Maya would wail, 'God! Why are you punishing me? *What* have I done? How have I sinned?'

Sabah's cry resonated with Maya's furtive tears, 'Allah, you've forgotten me ... I've been cursed.'

Their pregnant friends looked on with pity. Maya and Sabah bravely summoned a smile whenever the beginnings of new life were announced in their communities, but inside they cried. Abdiel often blamed himself, wondering if the trauma of Auschwitz and the camps may have reduced his fertility.

As time passed, so the heaviness of barrenness increased. Rabbi Yousef often said to them, 'I pray for you regularly.'

'You'll need to pray a lot harder, Yousef, because it's not working!' Abdiel replied in frustration.

'Remember Sarah was ninety years old and Abraham one hundred when their son Isaac, was born. Be patient with God,' Yousef said in encouragement.

Maya replied, quick as a flash. 'I don't want to be ninety when my child is born.'

'And I don't want to be a hundred, either,' Abdiel added.

~

Just over eight years later, Abdiel received news of a miracle. Maya was pregnant. Maya could hardly contain her joy, torn between wanting to shout it from the hilltops, to hiding it from the world in case something might go wrong. The memory of the agony of her dear friend Sabah, sat just below the surface of her emotions. It took her weeks before she plucked up courage to tell her. How would she react?

Finally, she baked some sweet cakes, stole away after her kitchen-duty had finished in the afternoon and found Sabah gathering in bed-sheets from the clothesline. They sat together under a cypress tree and Maya took her hand.

'I'm pregnant,' she blurted out. 'I can hardly believe it myself but the doctor in Haifa confirmed I'm around fifteen weeks.'

Sabah sat open mouthed, speechless. Then came a smile and a squeeze of Maya's hand. 'Oh, that's amazing news,' she shrieked. Sabah leapt to her feet and hugged Maya. 'I'm so happy for you. I know it'll be hard for me, but I'm so thrilled; I really am.'

The two women forgot their duties, the time of day and the rest of the world and immersed themselves in talk of preparations for the arrival of the miracle baby.

Abdiel found his delight difficult to disguise. In spite of his well-practised skill at hiding his depression, joy escaped unrestrained. It touched all who surrounded him. People found the natural care and protection he provided for Maya remarkable, and it moved people to say, 'He's so gentle and tender.'

The kibbutzniks had experienced a man of the outdoors, a Holocaust survivor, tough, resilient, mild mannered and often depressed. Now they saw softness.

'It's wonderful what a baby can do, isn't it,' Rabbi Yousef said to Abdiel with a smile.

Maya knew only too well what the baby was doing to her. To carry a child through a Middle-Eastern summer was no easy task, but for a woman in her thirties, sometimes too much.

'You carry your baby heavy today,' Sabah observed as she wiped the perspiration from Maya's forehead. 'But you're doing so well.'

The sun punished any who dared to leave the shelter of a building, and Maya rested in the coolest part of the Kibbutz, the lounge area, where two large cypress trees protected the wall from the afternoon sun. Maya freed herself from the heat, nausea and discomfort by focusing on the anticipated joy of holding the precious life she carried in her womb in her arms.

The moment finally came. Abdiel, Sabah and three women from Kibbutz Atak, who were sitting on the edge of their chairs in the waiting room, heard the announcement from Maya's obstetrician, '*Mazzel tov*! A son is born.'

Abdiel sprang to his feet and thanked the doctor, who beckoned him into the delivery room. Maya lay back on the pillows, exhausted but smiling, the beautiful reward of her months of discomfort cradled on her breast. 'We have a boy, Abby.'

Abdiel blinked back tears and in a quavering voice responded, 'How amazing; how wonderful.'

Maya handed the precious new life to his care.

Abdiel tenderly folded his son in his arms. Tears flowed. 'Thanks be to God,' he whispered.

Abdiel and Maya prepared for the traditional *Bris Milah* held on the first Friday night after the birth. On the Thursday night, the night prior to the *Bris*, they followed the custom for children to see the newborn and recite the words of *Shema Yisrael* in his presence. They provided sweets to encourage them to come. The baby was dressed in white clothes and wine brought for the blessings.

Rabbi Yousef led the ceremony in the presence of the kibbutzniks, Omar, Sabah and a small number of their Arab friends.

'*Mazzel tov!* A son is born. A son who will, with God's help, be a source of pride and joy to his family and the entire Jewish people, and his name will be Uri. And God said to Abraham: "You shall keep my covenant, you and your descendants after you, throughout the generations."'

The ceremony continued, and towards the end of the service, a thunderstorm brought a downpour of heavy rain. Yousef, acknowledging the current need of rain for the thirsty land, commented, 'May Uri bring nourishment to a thirsty Israel.'

Celebrations and the meal followed with much singing and laughter.

On the eighth day after the birth, in keeping with Jewish custom, Rabbi Yousef organised a *Mohel*, a God-fearing professional practitioner to perform the circumcision.

~

Two months later, Maya heard footsteps coming up to her door. She placed Uri in his crib and ran to open it.

'It's only me, Maya,' came Sabah's excited voice.

Maya opened the door, to be greeted with overflowing energy, bursting joy and smiles from her dear friend.

'You'll never guess, Maya; I'm pregnant!' Sabah's eyes filled with tears which spilled down her face.

Maya jumped forward and seized Sabah in her arms. 'You're … you're pregnant. How wonderful. How exciting …'

'I'd given up hope,' Sabah said amongst her tears. 'I really didn't think it would happen, but it has.'

They sobbed in each other's arms, cheek to cheek, faces awash with tears of relief. Finally they released, 'Just look at us,' Maya exclaimed. 'What a mess: wet faces, soggy hair. When's the baby due?'

'I'm about twelve weeks. I wanted to be sure everything was certain before I told anyone. It's been so hard to keep it a secret … but now …'

'I can't believe it. Two miracles in one year.'

'Allah has heard my prayers, praise be to Allah.'

The news spread through the community like a bushfire.

The Rabbi quipped, 'Atak might become a holy site for infertile couples—it's in the water.'

~

On a cold night in February after a difficult pregnancy, Sabah woke Omar from a deep sleep. 'We need to go, now!' she said, her voice urgent. 'The contractions are regular and becoming stronger.'

Omar fumbled for the keys to the car and eventually found them exactly where he'd left them. He was not at his best at 2 a.m. The road from the settlement had received many makeovers since his first trip on it, and it now provided a smooth ride to the main road.

At 10 a.m. the following day, the doctor decided to perform a caesarean section. Thirty minutes later, a nurse invited Omar to see his exhausted wife and meet his newborn.

Sabah searched Omar's face and saw his eyes moisten. 'We have a boy,' she said with a smile.

'A boy, thanks be to Allah, and you're well?'

'I'm very tired, but I'm fine. Here, would you like to hold him?'

Omar reached out and cradled his tiny son in his muscular arms; his eyes full of joy and wonder as he held his precious gift, lovingly admiring his reddish face and wet hair.

'He's been a real fighter,' Sabah said with admiration.

'Then we'll call him Ghazi—warrior, conqueror,' Omar announced.

'Ghazi, yes, I like that.'

Omar returned to the waiting room where two women from the settlement sat chatting, holding a small basket of sweet cakes. Then the celebrations commenced. Minutes later, Omar and the women gathered around the newborn. The first practice was to make the *Adhaan* in the ear of the baby, so the first words the baby hears is the name of Allah and the *Kalima*—declaration of faith. The *Tahneek* followed. For this Omar softened a date, placed it on his finger and rubbed Gahzi's palate from left to right. After offering up prayers, he returned to the settlement to be greeted by the overflowing joy of the community.

After the seventh day of Ghazi's arrival, the community celebrated *Aqeeqah*, a form of welcome and thanksgiving to the One who gave the blessings. Omar slaughtered two sheep and shaved Ghazi's head, then the ritual circumcision was performed.

Sabah threw every part of her being into caring for her 'gift from heaven.'

'She's such a wonderful mother,' came the constant chorus from the community as they observed her over the months following the birth.

Abdiel understood that he now took second place in Maya's life, and he admired her gentleness and patience in the way she cared for their beautiful boy. When Uri became responsive to Abdiel's *pops* and *cackles* sounds, he muscled in for a greater share in caring for his son.

As Uri grew and the time for him to go to the children's house drew near, Abdiel became aware of Maya's increasing silence. Kibbutz Atak, like most kibbutzim, functioned on the socialist philosophy that children need the care of the community, and so at six weeks old, the children were separated from their parents. Kibbutz life was the instrument required to create the 'new breed' of young people to survive in Eretz Israel: a cooperative, a religion of labour, a way of life, a blend of necessity and realism. Kibbutzim centred on agriculture and facilitated the emergence of the 'new man.' While Abdiel enjoyed the benefits of this new creation, Maya's maternalism paid the price.

'I don't know how I'm going to manage,' Maya blurted out one evening after her caressing lullaby had settled Uri.

Abdiel tried to comfort her: 'It's hard for me, and much worse for you, but we can still see him in the afternoons.'

'It's not the same.' Maya's eyes filled with tears. 'If he's sick during the night, one of the older children will ring the adult on duty. It's so hard even thinking about it.'

Weeks passed without any mention of the subject. Then one night, again after saying good night to her precious bundle of joy, Maya sat beside Abdiel on their well-worn but comfortable lounge and placed her hand on Abdiel's hand.

'Abby. I want to move from here,' she said softly.

For a moment, Abdiel froze, feeling as if he'd been struck by lightning, then he turned his head to look at his wife.

Maya's eyes fixed on the door, avoiding his gaze, and her lips trembled.

Abdiel breathed deeply and took his time before responding. 'The problem is the children's house, isn't it? You're a good, no, a great mother. Uri is bonded to you so well, but the time has come to let go.'

'I've waited so long for this. God's been so good … and now, I've got to give him away!' Maya's sobs erupted from the part of her being that had ached for years for the movement of life in her womb.

Abdiel cradled his arm around her shoulder and drew her close.

Maya relaxed, resting her wet face on his welcoming shoulder.

He felt stuck, completely helpless. Life in the kibbutz was demanding but satisfying. He was well respected, dependable and had developed considerable skill in managing the crops and the orchard. To leave the support of their friends in the kibbutz and their close relationships with the Christian and Arab communities was unthinkable. The birth of a son had completed his dreams. The freedom, the love he enjoyed in his new home had brought a small measure of healing from the trauma of the past. Where would they go? How would they manage? Where would they find another place like Atak? Abdiel's mind raced like a deer in flight. His breathing quickened, but he remained silent.

'I'm sorry, Abby,' Maya whispered. 'I know you love it here, and I do too, in so many ways, but maybe not every kibbutz has a children's house.'

Abdiel kissed her on the forehead. 'Maybe there are, but I don't know of any. Give me time to think about it. I know you're desperate, but I want to be sure it's right for us.'

'Thank you, Abby. It's good to know you understand.'

'I'll talk with Rabbi Yousef.' This comment, Abdiel believed, was a stroke of genius. It gave him time to think. He loved Maya and wanted the best for her and his son. But buried inside was a belief he would not admit to himself, let alone to Maya: *there's no way I'm going to leave Kibbutz Atak.*

Abdiel never raised Maya's concern about the children's house with Yousef. The issue became an invisible, unspoken wedge between them that infected their marriage. Conversations between Abdiel and Rabbi Yousef were usually about the increasing tension between the Arab States and Israel. It became a familiar conversation of concern and mutual support. On one occasion Yousef said, 'We've tried for seven years to negotiate with our Arab neighbours but without any success. Remember back in October 1960 when Golda Meir challenged Arab leaders to meet with David Ben-Gurion to negotiate a peace settlement? Nasser said Egypt would never recognise a Jewish State, and the PLO has been getting stronger under Arafat. There's been more attacks so far this year than in the previous two years, likely because the Palestinian guerrillas are getting their orders from Egypt.'

'It's always civilians who're attacked,' Abdiel said. ' Syria shelled the Huleh Valley so much last year that children had to sleep in bomb shelters for months, and the United Nations did nothing to stop them. United Nations, pah! United Nothing!'

'They did criticise us for retaliating, though,' Yousef reminded him. 'I'll not forget the words of Nasser two years ago: "We shall not enter Palestine with its soil covered in sand; we shall enter it with its soil saturated in blood."'

'What do you think will happen next?' Abdiel asked.

'It'll come to another war, that's for certain,' the Rabbi replied.

'When?'

'Soon.'

Abdiel felt strangely relieved. More fighting was imminent, but he had the answer he needed. They would stay at Kibbutz Atak. Nowhere was safe in Israel, but at least he knew this place—the land, the people. That had to count for something.

Chapter Ten

October 5 1973
Uri

I brush a speck of dust from my white robes and lay another plate on the table. Everyone is wearing white because we're preparing for *seudah hamafseket,* the last meal before our fast tomorrow, and after the meal, we'll light candles. I'm looking forward to that, but even now I'm still buzzing from the day's excitement of getting ready for *Yom Kippur*. It's the holiest day in the year, and it's happening tomorrow. Rabbi Yousef led special services today, one was for confession where we repented our sins, but I couldn't think of anything much to repent, only silly little things.

'There are a lot of trucks with soldiers going north,' someone says.

I leave setting the table and run outside to the edge of the clearing. I can see a line of army vehicles going towards the Golan Heights.

I return to the hall and ask Papa, 'What's happening?'

'It's just a precaution, Uri,' he says. 'Nothing to worry about. It happens.'

I go back to my work.

Later, a little after we've finished dinner, I see Papa sitting with a group of men around a table. They're talking quietly and seem very serious. I creep closer and listen.

'We felt good jumping the gun and beating the Arabs in the Six Day War but now we're paying the price for it,' Papa says. 'It seems like they're looking for a way to overcome the humiliation of their defeat and to regain the land they lost. Sadat lost a lot of respect amongst Arab nations when he lost. He needs to overcome his shame before he can talk peace.'

'And the Soviet Union is doing its share to stir the pot,' says the Rabbi. 'The way they're pouring arms into the region.' Everyone listens when Yousef talks.

Papa adds, 'The Arab States are taking greater control of their oil resources and that lets them flex their muscles like they've never done before.'

My heart beats faster when I hear the men talk like this. I don't know what it really means.

One of the senior men enters the room and walks up to the group. 'We've just had the phone call,' he says. 'We need to get into uniform. We leave at midnight.'

Papa looks shocked. 'Where are we going?'

'No word. We report to base and we'll get instructions.'

Papa takes time to get to his feet, and I run to his side, my heart racing. 'What's happening? Where are you going?'

'I'm not sure, Uri. The army needs me.' He looks down at me and holds out his hand. 'Come, I'll take you to the children's house.'

I hold his hand tightly as we walk. I don't like the big frown on his face.

'I'll be gone for a little time,' he says when we get to the door, 'but I'll be back soon.'

'Goodbye, Papa. I love you,' I whisper.

I run into the house and jump onto my bunk. Tears flow. I know children whose fathers said that and then never came back.

~

It's been one week since Papa and the men left. Every time the siren sounds we have to run into our safe room. It's a large room with thick concrete walls and no windows. A big water container sits on a shelf in one corner, and food in packets and tins fill the rest of the shelves. When we're there, our teacher leads us in singing songs. Some of the children cry. Every day we hear the boom of the big guns from the Golan. Jets scream overhead. We're not allowed to leave our kibbutz, and we've not heard from Papa. Ima is worried. Will we see him again? Will he get hurt? The days are long and we have extra work to do.

I lie in bed and count the bright stars through the open window. I've never heard so many big explosions from the guns in the north. Suddenly the siren screams and children fall out of beds and run towards the safe room. We've done this many times, but I'm always scared running across the grass from the children's house. It's a big relief to get to the door and run to our place and sit on the floor. The door closes and the singing starts.

~

October 25 1973

Today I'm so happy. This morning we heard that Papa and the men from our kibbutz are alive and will be home soon. We offered prayers of thanks when we found out, and now we're all excited. I can't wait to see him.

Our teacher holds a newspaper up and tells us to be quiet. 'Children, for our news this morning I want to read a little part from this newspaper to help you understand what has just happened.'

The children suddenly become strangely quiet.

She reads: *'The CIA reported a war in the Middle East was unlikely, while the Israelis prepared for battle, convinced it was imminent;* that means very close, very near.'

'What's the CIA?' I ask. 'I've never heard of them.'

'Good question, Uri. You're always asking helpful questions. The CIA stands for the Central Intelligence Agency in America. It advises the American government on what's happening in the world, which helps their leaders make decisions about what they should do. Let me continue:

'At 5 a.m. on October 6, General David Lazar, Chief of Staff recommended a mobilisation of forces for an air strike on Egyptian forces in the Sinai. But Prime Minister Golda Meir refused to authorise any military action. She was concerned a pre-emptive strike would upset the United States who had warned against such action. She believed Israel needed the backing of the US because they couldn't defeat Egypt and Syria and any other Arab nations that might join in.

'On October 6, 1973, Yom Kippur, the holiest day in the Jewish calendar and during the Muslims' holy month of Ramadan, Egypt and Syria launched a surprise attack against Israel from the Golan Heights. Israeli tanks faced an onslaught of 1400 Syrian tanks. Along the Suez Canal, 600,000 Syrian soldiers, backed by 2000 tanks and 550 aircraft, attacked fewer than 500 Israeli defenders with only three tanks. Nine Arab States actively aided the Syrian war effort. Arab oil-producing states imposed an embargo on all oil exports to the United States for

their support for Israel, causing a great shortage of petroleum in the United States.

The Soviets gave their support to the Arab invasion and began an airlift of weapons. US Secretary of State, Henry Kissinger, decided the United States couldn't afford to allow the Soviet Union and its allies to win and organised a massive airlift of military hardware into Israel, which ultimately gave Israel victory in the Sinai. In the Golan Heights, the Soviets responded with direct military involvement, countered by the US placing troops with conventional and nuclear weapons on alert. On October 22nd, the UN Security Council called for all parties to cease fighting. The fighting claimed 2688 Israeli soldiers. Egypt and Syria's dead totalled 7700 and 3,500 respectively. Kissinger's shuttle diplomacy allowed Egypt to retain control of the Suez Canal and create buffer zones between the two forces and surrounding territories.'

A big gasp came from the children when they heard so many Israeli soldiers had died. After a brief silence the teacher continued.

'Syria was more difficult but finally an agreement was made. The fact that the Arabs had succeeded in surprising Israel, inflicting heavy losses in the early part of the war, was a traumatic experience for Israel. Its government reacted to the public's calls for an enquiry by establishing a commission, which concluded that Israeli intelligence had sufficient warning of the attack from a variety of sources, but failed to interpret the information correctly. Although Sadat lost the war, he had restored Arab honour, which helped him to enter into a peace agreement with Israel. Hmm … I think that's enough.'

'So we weren't prepared for this attack, were we?' All heads turned to who asked the question. It came from one of the older boys.

The teacher thought for a moment and then said, 'No, we weren't. There were signs, but we didn't think it would happen on Yom Kippur or Ramadan. That's why so many of our soldiers were killed at first. I think it's taught us a lesson to always be on guard. We have a strong army, and they will make Israel a safe place to live.'

My mind asks why we can't have a place to live like other people. Why do Arab nations want to drive us out of our land? They have a homeland, why can't we? It's so unfair.

I glance out the door hoping to see Papa coming up the road, but there's no sign of him.

Every day we wait, but it's the first day of November before I see Papa again. Ima hugs him and cries most of the day. So do I. My sisters and brother follow him around everywhere. It's like a little holiday. Everyone is so excited that the men are back that we take time out from the gardens and the orchard and have a big feast with chicken and special dishes, and lots of singing and dancing.

Papa doesn't say much about what happened, except that he went into Sinai. I ask him to tell me all about it, but he just says, 'One day, when you're older.'

Why does he have to be so secretive?

~

August 1976

It's been twelve months since I secretly watched the movie *Breakout*. My teachers are pleased with my progress and have given me harder work to do. I love science and maths especially. Whenever I can I go into the room off the hall, which we call the library, and read about the War. Ima and the other women are so full of fun, but Papa is so quiet and keeps mostly to himself. I know Ima is worried. I still want to know about his past, about what has made him like this.

It's late in the afternoon and Papa has gone into Haifa to pick up supplies. Ima is sitting alone on a bench seat under the big tree beside the children's house.

'Ima. You look tired,' I say.

'Yes, Uri, I need a break. It's been a lot of work to make the special food for the 'fifteenth of Av' tonight.'

'I love this festival. It's so mysterious.'

'Yes. Did you know that it's believed that centuries ago, the daughters of Jerusalem came out to dance in the vineyards on the full moon, looking for a husband.'

My eyes widen. 'I didn't know that. So it's not only a spiritual time but also a matchmaking time?'

Ima smiles. 'Yes, Uri, I suppose so.'

'A long time ago you said you'd tell me how you and Papa met after the war and how you got married. Can you tell me now … please?'

Ima looks away to the younger children playing hide and seek among the trees and then at the buildings lower down the slope. She gives a big sigh. 'Well … you're getting older, I suppose …'

'It's my *Bar Mitzvah* next year!'

'Yes. But I don't want you growing up too quickly.'

'What do you mean?'

'There are some parts of our lives that … well, aren't very nice.' Ima looks at me and then stares at the ground. She appears awkward and a little embarrassed.

'You want to protect me from that stuff?'

Ima sighs again and nods her head.

'I've read in the library about what happened in the war. I know you want to shelter me from that bad stuff but it's ... it's important to me. It's part of your story ... our story.'

'Oh, you are growing up, aren't you?' Ima says with a quick smile. She hesitates for a moment and then says, 'Well, it might help you understand Papa a little more.'

My heart leaps. This might give me a clue to what happened with Papa at the Wall.

'I can't be too long. I need to get back to the kitchen.'

'Okay.'

'You know that we grew up in Poland and when the Nazis came, we escaped but our parents were killed ...'

'Yes.'

'Well, Papa went to Auschwitz, and I went to the women's prison at Ravensbrück.'

'How did you find each other?'

'You know Papa came to Haifa on the Exodus and was taken back to Europe, to Austria, and placed in a camp at Poppendorf ...'

'Yes. I read that in the diary.'

Ima nods. 'You're a very inquisitive young man, and I should scold you for that, but I can see how important all this information is to you.' She pauses for a moment and chases a fly from her face. 'Now where was I? Oh yes, I ended up in Poppendorf too. One of the women in my cabin called to me and said she had just found someone who knows me. When I saw Papa, I burst into tears. I'm not sure he recognised me at first. I had lost a lot of weight. The dress I salvaged from the Red Cross looked terrible. My skin was wrinkled and my lips chafed. I looked like an old woman. Papa stood there just looking at me. He was shocked, and I couldn't take my eyes of his face. He'd aged, too. Then he stepped forward and we hugged—for ages. I cried; he cried. It was so emotional. I said, "I can't believe it's you, Abby! I didn't think I'd ever see you again."' Ima bit her lip and blinked away a tear.

'What happened next?' I said impatiently. 'Tell me everything.'

'He wanted to know what happened to me.'

'Please tell me what it was like?'

Ima hesitated for a moment before continuing. 'I went from Poland by train to Ravensbrück. The guards squashed us into cattle trucks like animals … horrible … no sanitation … little food … the air stank … people dying … but I made it. When the doors at last opened, we crawled out into sunlight so bright that it hurt my eyes. Women screamed for water. I saw a beautiful blue lake, sycamore trees and what someone said was the Fürstenberg church spire. The guards ordered us to march. We marched along the lake for about half an hour. People stared at us and turned away. You could see the anger and revulsion on their faces. Others had shame … pure shame in their eyes … they turned and looked the other way. We staggered up a hill, and there was the town of Ravensbrück.

'Near the town you could see the camp sitting in the valley: rows and rows of grey barracks; tall concrete walls with guard towers. In the centre, a stack spewed dark smoke into the sky. We tramped on and stood outside the compound, guards staring down at us from the towers. Massive gates opened and we marched through freezing water, spraying from faucets. It poured over our stinking bodies, removing the filth we'd picked up from the cattle trucks. Exhausted we collapsed on to piles of straw lying on the ground, only to find it was alive with lice.

'The first three days we spent in tents. It poured and the area turned to thick mud. On the fourth day, we went to a building, stripped off, and walked past the leering SS guards into the shower room. We were given a prison dress and a pair of shoes—that's all. Sewn on the back of the prison dress was a large X. On the way out, SS men searched us, touching every part of our bodies. The barracks were terrible—mouldy, with five of us squeezed on to a smelly mattress. Our barracks were full of lice—invisible torture; so hard to sleep.'

'Oh, that must have been terrible. I've never seen lice.'

'They're very tiny and difficult to see. But their bites are awful. Most of the other barracks appeared to be relatively free, but our place was alive with them. I don't know what it was,' Maya continued. 'We're not sure, but we wondered if the lice saved us from being … well, taken by the guards. They came regularly and took women. They did whatever they wanted with them. You could hear the screams … the beatings …'

Ima's voice becomes softer. I take her hand. 'The guards took women to a building for "discipline"—an excuse for the guards to do whatever they wanted … rape … beatings … all kinds of torture … I'll never forget those screams … it froze the blood in my veins.' Ima shifts her gaze to the ground and becomes silent. She shakes her head.

I try to distract her. 'What time did you get up in the morning?' It's probably a silly thing to say, but I needed to say something.

'Roll call came at 4:30 a.m. Then came a stampede for a slice of bread and whatever it was they called coffee. If you got there late, you missed out. We had to wear coloured triangles. The Polish wore red; Soviets, red; criminals, green; us Jews, yellow.'

'What did you do during the day?'

'I worked in the factory and the munitions centre, assembling parts for V2 rockets. Conditions were a little better there than in the camp. I also helped with secret education classes that helped those who were poorly educated. The Nazis knew nothing about it. We spent the time creating simple games, making necklaces and bracelets. I still have a necklace in my room—a small length of fishing line threaded with small, highly polished coloured stones.'

'How could you do that?'

'That's the advantage of working in munitions. It's amazing what you could do when the guards weren't looking,' Ima said with a smile.

'When did you and Papa start liking each other?'

Ima thought for a minute. 'It was in Poppendorf. A day or so after we were reunited, Papa said, "You're the only one I have from the past … and I'm glad … I'm really glad … it's you." He seemed awkward and a little embarrassed. Your papa was the 'boy next door' when we were growing up. He was like a brother to me. We'd grown up together: played in the streets; walked to school; explored the old castle; shared Friday evening meals—Shabbat. We were like family. Then Papa stood looking into my eyes. It was as though he was blind to my straw-like hair or the wrinkles and hardness of my face. He looked into my eyes, and I saw his … longing … an invitation. I felt excited and embarrassed. I'd never felt like this before. He whispered, "I'm not going to let you go, ever again".'

'That's so romantic.'

'It certainly was, and I said I didn't want to let him out of my sight. I knew then that I loved him.'

~

Maya was selective in what she gave to Uri. Like any mother, she wanted to protect him yet realised it was important he knew the truth, well, maybe some of it. She struggled to know what his young mind could manage. The last thing she wanted was to leave a dark imprint that produced nightmares and robbed him of sleep. Her husband's darkness was more than she could manage. She didn't dare tell Abdiel that she'd mentioned anything of their experiences in the camps to Uri. It was an unspoken rule imposed by her traumatised husband who tried to lock the past away, unsuccessfully. She had no idea of the reason for Abdiel's emotion at the Wall. She was as curious as Uri as to what had triggered it. She often replayed the events in the camp in her mind, looking for clues.

Chapter Eleven

November 1947
Abdiel and Maya

One afternoon soon after Abdiel's and Maya's reunion in Poppendorf, as they walked together towards Maya's barracks, Abdiel commented, 'There's Ruth. I really feel so sorry for her—got a terrible fright today.'

'I heard about it,' Maya said. 'She had a dreadful time with the guards at Ravensbrück. She was in a different section from me, but she told me that at the end of the first week in camp, they took her and raped her. She was one of the most attractive women there—long hair, slim figure. She screamed and fought them, but they beat her. Two nights after the first attack, she said she was going to 'run the wire.' I talked with her, and I think that helped, but I wonder now … maybe she would have been better off dying? She went through so much … I said to her at the time that *I wanted to survive*. I wanted to prove something to the Nazis … maybe to the world … I talked to her about how she could survive.'

Abdiel sighed and shook his head.

Maya continued, 'After that, she stopped fighting when they came for her. She became one of the camp prostitutes. Now her pain isn't physical; it's in her mind. She feels guilty that she survived and gave pleasure to those filthy swine. Some of the other women shunned her for getting pleasure and privileges from those bastards, but I said we do whatever it takes to survive. I helped make rockets that killed Allies. I'm just as guilty.' Maya, animated now, moved her free hand with sweeping gestures.

After a short silence, Abdiel became agitated and, appearing distressed, said, 'You're right. We do *whatever* it takes to survive!'

The way he said it brought a frown to Maya's face.

The following day, tension mounted in the camp. The gunshot heard the previous day came from the rifle of one of the German police who raided the camp looking for black market contraband. He'd fired a warning shot over the heads of a group of inmates who'd refused to disperse. The British had recruited German soldiers, including SS officers, to help keep order in post-war Germany, and the reaction of Jewish inmates in the camps was predictable to anyone who would've bothered thinking about it.

Simon, the man from Hungary who'd been transferred from the American camp, was livid. 'The Americans want us to help rebuild the German economy, which the Germans destroyed with their own evil and violence. Now the British expect us to help these bastards! They have sawdust for brains. The Germans confiscate the goods and sell it on the black market themselves!'

Abdiel repeated his mantra, 'There'll be a special place in hell for them.'

'I don't know if there's a hell or if there's a god,' Simon responded in frustration, 'but I want these swine to suffer like we have.'

Everyone in the small group seated around Simon nodded as he said this, but no one spoke. His words were enough. Powerlessness had seeped into their souls. Weakened by persecution, discrimination, humiliation and defeat, they saw the world as unspeakably cruel. Why spend energy mouthing words?

'Sometimes I get tired of being angry,' an older woman finally offered.

'It's the only thing that keeps me alive,' Abdiel said.

'He keeps his feelings padlocked away,' Maya advised the group. Turning to Abdiel, she added, 'I worry about you Abby. I want to see you shout or scream sometimes. You hold everything in.'

'Anger gives me energy,' he replied. 'I use it to survive. One day, I don't know when, I'll show the world we're a people to be respected. I'll fight to see my children live in peace in Israel and walk safely down the streets of Jerusalem. Now … yes, I'm tired. Sometimes I feel like giving up. Then, I remember what *they* did. I look around and see what they're doing now. The anger returns, I fight on.'

Maya looked at Abdiel with mixed feelings. She was proud of Abby—everyone had to find a way to survive—but his body seemed so heavy and his mood, so quiet and brooding. Darkness had robbed him of the energy and vitality she'd seen in him as a boy. He'd lost his youth. She missed his laughter and energy for life. *One day*, she thought, *he'll find it again, and I want to help him.*

The days crept by at a snail's pace towards an icy winter. The daily ration was raised to 2800 calories per day. Stealing and crime were rife. The British continued to treat the inmates as an unwanted, incurable, irritating disease that had invaded the earth, and the response of the survivors confirmed their beliefs.

As one Polish inmate admitted, 'Some of our behaviour may be difficult to understand. After living in the woods for a couple of years—the ghetto—then the camps, our manners, our behaviour, are not the best.'

Finally, after three months, Jewish relief ships delivered tons of machinery into the camp and trade classes commenced in carpentry, welding, electro technology, radio mechanics, bricklaying, boot making and dressmaking. ORT, a Jewish relief agency formed in 1880, was a prime force in providing education and training in the camps. Goods were produced and exchanged, and the black market thrived. Gradually world opinion strengthened the resolve for a better deal for victims of the Holocaust.

Abdiel taught his trade in shoemaking, and Maya channelled her energies into teaching the children. She said to Abdiel at the end of her first week as a teacher, 'These children have forgotten how to smile. They've forgotten how to have fun.'

She sat with her group and helped them draw their stories—drawings of non-existent families, of nightmares, of what they thought their new homeland might look like, *Eretz Israel.* The crude sketches of nightmares were usually grotesque shapes in black and red crayon. Children chose if they wanted to destroy them. Some tore their intimidating figures into tiny pieces. Others bashed their scary images with sticks. The old yellowing newsprint absorbed their horrific dreams and helped release a layer of pain from their dark memories. They avoided any ceremonial burning of their therapeutic art. Every child in the camp had witnessed the never-ending pall of human smoke spewing from the chimneys of the crematoria in their camp. The Nazis had classified children to work in the camps, and they did. Otherwise the gas chamber and the oven became their fate also.

Musical instruments scrounged by Jewish relief organisations helped create an orchestra. The formation of theatres, choirs and various sporting events, with results published in newspapers set up by inmates, brought meaning and purpose into their lives. Stories collected from the survivors were placed into the 'Yizor' and published in Yiddish. Commemorative services were held for victims. Commemorations ranged from traditional Jewish rites to new and different forms. Political parties emerged, religious and secular—Zionist and Socialist.

Abdiel found himself caught between the two. His mind was a mess. His roots were firmly planted in Judaism, but like many survivors, the evils of Nazism had reduced his beliefs to ashes. His constant refrain joined the chorus of the masses, 'Where was God in the Holocaust?' He secretly admired those who maintained the faith.

Yousef, the Rabbi, was one who'd befriended him on the *Exodus* and looked out for him in the camp. Yousef's slight figure could be seen wandering through the camp, hiding a recently acquired, highly prized prayer shawl under his coat. His friendly manner and a pocketful of candy provided by Jewish Relief made him popular with the children.

On one occasion when the two were reflecting on their future and Abdiel's depression had expelled from him all hope of going to Israel, Yousef said, 'Abby, our people have suffered over time. We've been slaves in Egypt. Europe has become a cemetery for our people. The Promised Land is our destination. God has provided it for us.' The Rabbi glanced at Abdiel and waited for a response.

'Who's going to be our Moses this time?' Abdiel growled after a long pause.

'The UN are about to vote on the Resolution … maybe they're our Moses.'

'How will it work? How will Arab and Jew live side by side?'

'They've done so for hundreds of years in Palestine. You must remember that both Arab and Jew come from a common Father—Abraham. We're brothers.'

The Rabbi spoke with confidence and strength. Though his passionate plea instilled a faint ray of hope in Abdiel, Abdiel saw nothing but conflict. The Arabs were resisting mass Jewish immigration. Even his Jewish countrymen, born and bred in Palestine were not welcoming of new arrivals.

'Where are immigrants going to go?' they asked. Life was good for them. They called Holocaust survivors 'soaps'—a horrible term describing the 'end product' of Nazi efficiency of disposing Jews in the extermination camps.

Abdiel respected the Rabbi. This thirty-something man with a jet-black beard and rimless glasses had experienced his own share of pain. Persecution by local townspeople in central Poland where he'd lived had triggered his early distress. The Nazis arrived, broke into the synagogue, and forced him to urinate on the Torah. They laughed and clapped in unison as he danced, at their insistence, on the sacred books. They ordered him to pile all the copies of the Talmud, prayer books, and his library onto the street and set it ablaze. In the camps he tried to keep a low profile as guards usually gave extra 'treatment' to Rabbis.

Here in Poppendorf, survivors were divided: the faithful—those who joined his regular religious gatherings—and those who may have once been part of the faithful but were now cynical, angry, abandoned by God. God was far away, so they blamed Yousef. It was easier that way. Abdiel was caught in the middle.

Abdiel loved many things about Maya, especially her optimism. Her family had been strong in their faith and shared the Shabbat meal on Friday evenings with Abdiel's.

'Abby,' she said, 'you may not like me saying this, but I pray for you, every day. God will help us.'

Abdiel usually remained silent when Maya declared her 'care for his soul,' and immediately changed the subject. 'Where would you like to go in Palestine if we ever get there?' he asked, irritation creeping into his voice.

'I'd be happy to go anywhere as long as I'm with you.'

'I think if we can find a kibbutz in the north that'd be my choice.'

'Let's see what opens up. Maybe around Haifa?'

Abdiel and Maya were drawn towards Zionism. The horrors of the *Shoah* helped them understand that they couldn't continue to exist as an unwelcome minority in Europe. Zionism had energy. Life in Europe for most Jews—the Diaspora—was a dog's life. In Ben Gurion's *Eretz Israel,* the promise of a new type of Jew emerged, strong, muscular, alive. It was more than the talk of political parties that proliferated before the war. Zionism was organised and made sense of the Holocaust.

The survivors in Poppendorf and other holding camps heard about the experiments taking place on a farm near the German town of Eggendorf. In the summer of 1945, a group of Jewish survivors left the liberated Buchenwald concentration camp and established an agricultural-training community they called kibbutz Buchenwald, which helped survivors prepare for eventual immigration to Palestine. The training in agricultural methods flowed into the camps, including Poppendorf. The concept of a farming collective caught Abdiel's attention, and he was soon immersed in learning the skills of cultivation, fertilisation, irrigation and harvesting. Yet part of him wondered if he'd ever make use of them.

On the 29th of November 1947, the U.N. General Assembly adopted the Plan as Resolution 181(II), partitioning Palestine into two separate states. British impotence and indifference had given way to a groundswell of sympathy and guilt by nations who'd remained closed to the unprecedented refugee crisis. The pockets of violent anti-Semitism in Poland and parts of Europe that prevented the return of Holocaust survivors to their homes had made newspaper headlines around the world. There appeared to be no other choice than a divided Palestine. (Note 1)

In Poppendorf, groups of survivors danced the *Hava Nagila* joyfully in the cold afternoon on the doorstep of winter. The orchestras played, choirs sang. Abdiel and Maya embraced and kissed.

'It's just a matter of time,' Maya said, her eyes sparkling. 'Soon we'll be together in the land of our forefathers. I can't wait.'

'I don't know how long it'll take. We need to be patient,' Abdiel cautioned. 'I'll get excited only when I have my feet on Palestinian soil!'

'Yes, but it'll happen. It *will* happen.'

'I hope we can get out of here before winter turns us into ice,' Abdiel added with a half a smile.

'We have each other to keep warm.'

They kissed again. Skin on skin became electric. Two souls had escaped the ghetto, the ovens, and burial in the cemeteries of Europe. They'd survived, as one *Shoah* victim had said, 'living in the holding camps—rubbish heaps of human leftovers, eyes darkened from the sight of the dead.'

Abdiel gently shifted his weight to support Maya. The warmth of the embrace of their tired bodies brought sweet memories of their reunion in September. Then it became a desperate clinging to each other as sole survivors of their families, bonded by treasured memories. Forces beyond their control had fused them together, forged by horror and suffering. Now, their union was one of choice. They released and stood back from each other, reflecting on their commonality and complementarity.

'No longer are you like a big brother,' Maya whispered. He was becoming her lover. Childhood and adolescence had vanished. Now they were adults, and they chose each other.

A freezing morning in February 1948 farewelled two survivors from Poppendorf, bound for Palestine. Abdiel left Europe, but he couldn't leave the memories of Auschwitz burnt into his brain—memories he never dared mention to fellow survivors; memories he hid from his beloved Maya. He'd tried to bury them in Poppendorf, but they'd refused to leave him. So he locked them away deep in his inner dungeon and threw away the key. How would he survive the torment? And how would he manage the anguish of not knowing whether his brother Daniel was dead or alive?

~

(Note 1) The United States State Department proposed a UN trusteeship to give more time but President Truman refused. Partition was adopted only after ruthless arm-twisting by the US government and by 26 pro-Zionist US senators who, in telegrams to a number of UN member states, warned that US goodwill in rebuilding their World War-II devastated economies might depend on a favourable vote for partition.

Chapter Twelve

Maya often reflected on Abdiel's reaction to his nightmares. The early morning conversation she'd had with him after the attack on the kibbutz in 1948, replayed in her mind like a horror movie.

'You're shaking, Abby,' she'd said when she'd awakened from sleep, disturbed by his thrashing around. 'You're sweating. Oh dear, are you okay?'

'I've just had the worst nightmare.'

'Tell me about it … it'll help.'

'No. It won't.' Abdiel's chest heaved as he gasped for air. 'Just let me lie here and rest.'

Maya stretched her arm across his sweaty chest and held his trembling body. After a short silence, she asked, 'Was it the fighting today?'

'Most likely.' Abdiel sighed. 'I'm not cut out to be a soldier.'

'You've seen enough violence in your life … more than most would see in a lifetime.'

'It took me back to Auschwitz … the camps. Faces of lifeless bodies ...' Abdiel sobbed.

'My darling. I'm with you. I'll always be with you, I promise.' After a long silence, she continued, 'We'll face it together.'

Abdiel shifted his body and wrapped his arm around Maya's shoulder, drawing her closer. 'I'm so glad to have you … I don't know what I'd do without you. What time is it?'

'A little after 3 a.m. Try and get some sleep.' Maya continued to hold Abdiel until the rhythm of his breathing slowed. Relieved he'd finally found sleep, thoughts flooded her mind. *How long will these nightmares continue? Some nights he wakes with a start, distressed, but returns to sleep quickly. Other times he tosses and turns for hours. He puts on a front, even smiles, and then collapses. He's lost his joy! He seems confident, but then, so fragile.*

Maya watched his chest rise and fall, his nightshirt wet with the perspiration from the terror of his return to the dark past. She leant over and kissed him lightly on the lips. 'Sleep well my darling,' she whispered. Maybe the answer to his strange behaviour at the Wall lay hidden in Auschwitz.

~

Another incident she remembered in her search for an answer to Abdiel's behaviour came in June 1961, during her struggle to conceive.

'Abby, I've made another appointment with the specialist in Jerusalem,' she'd said.

Abdiel had glanced at Maya, shaken his head, and stared out the window.

'I know you're tired of me going on with it, but there're new procedures being developed all the time. Also, the

Eichmann trial is on in Jerusalem and you might want to go and sit in …'

'I've no desire to listen to that swine,' Abdiel snapped.

Maya looked at Abdiel, shocked by his outburst, then returned to her embroidery, soothing her hurt. The long absence of any sign of a child had taken its toll on their relationship. The pendulum swung between supportive understanding to days of agonising tension when Abdiel snapped at the slightest hint of any disagreement. Maya hid her tears. More than ever, she wanted a child, and she knew that not having a son to carry his name devastated Abdiel. Their lovemaking, once fun and pleasurable, was now work, mechanical and unfulfilling. Maya had secretly turned for support to the women in the kibbutz and to her Arab friends. Sabah became her closest friend and ally. They leant on each other, sharing their childless journey.

Omar and Abdiel went about their work. Whenever they met, their conversation was always about crops, irrigation, pest control, and complaints about the weather. Abdiel, content to suffer in silence, took comfort from the respect he commanded from his kibbutznik colleagues. He diverted the frustration of his childless marriage into his manual work in the outdoors, and his knowledge and expertise in the gardens and orchards, and his dedication and commitment drew compliments from his community.

The capture of war criminal Adolf Eichmann, a major cog in the Holocaust death machine, created an avalanche of pain and anger. Images resurrected by his arrest haunted a generation of survivors. His cruelty was indelibly burnt into their psyche. Jews throughout the world celebrated the capture of this vile monster, found hiding in South America. But his arrest came at a cost—the reignition of the nightmares of thousands of survivors.

With the help of Rabbi Yousef, Abdiel had managed to find a way to soothe the demons that robbed him of sleep. Now, as Eichmann's face appeared on TV screens and across the front page of newspapers, dark, violent memories retraumatised him. While Eichmann's trial resurrected the horror of Auschwitz, it also provided an unexpected twist of fate.

On a warm day in the middle of May, Abdiel and Maya set off in the kibbutz vehicle for Jerusalem after a breakfast of pita bread, eggs and fruit. Maya had arranged accommodation for two nights with their friends in Jerusalem, and Abdiel's mood had changed as the day drew near. A break from the kibbutz was long overdue. They reached the hospital and the rooms of the specialist soon after midday, and Abdiel sat with Maya, who nervously fiddled with her sleeves.

'There's still hope,' the specialist eventually told them.

After the consultation, Abdiel returned to the car and, after negotiating the erratic traffic, parked outside the walls of the Old City, on the edge of the demilitarized zone near the Tower of David. The Jordanian soldiers who controlled the Old City were clearly visible on the ramparts.

'Will we ever see the Western Wall?' Abdiel lamented.

They walked on, stomachs growling—it was well past lunchtime. 'Let's stop here,' Maya said outside a café that had partially emptied.

Within minutes, two plates of *shwarma*—shredded lettuce, olives, cucumber and onions with pita bread—were served. Two small cups of strong coffee followed. Maya glanced around the walls decorated with artefacts and paintings from a local artist. She loved the grey stone walls, the slate floor, the rustic wooden tables.

A British family with two small children sat in the far corner. Two Arab women with white hijabs buried themselves in conversation beside them. A group of well-dressed men in western clothes sat in the opposite corner. Next to his table, two Jewish men sipped coffee and conversed in Yiddish. Multicultural masses continued to stream past the door. Maya knew how much Abdiel loved people watching, and no better place existed to do it than in Jerusalem. She noticed two Rabbis pushing past the door, avoiding eye contact with the masses.

Abdiel nodded to the door. 'Rabbi Yousef is not like them.'

'What do you mean?'

'When Yousef walks down the street, he's happy to meet and greet people.'

'He's a remarkable man,' Maya replied. 'He gives me hope.'

Abdiel finished his meal and leaned back in his chair. After a couple of minutes, he tilted his head towards the two Jewish men and said to Maya, 'They're talking about the Eichmann trial. The man closest to me was in the public gallery today.'

'Abby! You shouldn't be listening to other people's conversations!'

'Why not? You never know what you might learn.' Abdiel grinned, but minutes later, his expression changed, and he turned to take a closer look at the man who'd been present at the trial.

'What's up?' Maya asked.

'This man was in Auschwitz.' Abdiel swung his body around on the chair and faced his fellow survivor, a man a little older than himself. 'Forgive me for interrupting but I couldn't help hearing you talk about Auschwitz,' Abdiel said. 'When were you there?'

The man studied Abdiel's face and didn't answer. Then his eyes lit up and a smile creased his lips, 'Abdiel. It's you!' His companion looked away and fidgeted with his clothing. 'I've often wondered where you got to. How's Daniel?'

'I've not seen Daniel since Auschwitz. I've tried to trace him, but he's disappeared.'

'I saw him in Brussels some time ago.'

'You saw him … he's alive?' Abdiel gasped in disbelief.

'He most certainly was … very alive. He was working on a farm in the country somewhere.'

Abdiel slumped back in his chair, a shocked expression on his face as he stared at the face of his colleague. 'You're … Fishel … yes I remember you.'

'And you might remember Mendel? He was there also.' Fishel nodded to his companion.

'Yes, I remember you, Mendel.'

'I certainly remember *you*.' Mendel spat the words out as though he'd tasted poison, then without another word, he strode to the counter, paid the bill and left the café.

'What was *that* about?' Maya stared at Fishel and her husband sitting stunned in their seats.

'The war does strange things to us,' Fishel said without hesitation.

Abdiel's faced flushed. 'My apologies, this is my wife, Maya.'

'It's nice meeting you, Maya.' Fishel paused, reached into his pocket and handed Abdiel his card. 'I really have to go, but if you're in Jerusalem again, please let me know.'

'Thank you,' Abdiel replied, and without another word, Fishel disappeared through the door.

Maya frowned. 'What was going on with that other man … did you say his name was Mendel?'

Abdiel shifted uneasily in his seat. 'As Fishel said, the war does strange things to us,' he mumbled.

The question mark hung uncomfortably in the air while Abdiel paid the bill and walked out ahead of Maya into the afternoon sun.

They left Jerusalem plagued by questions. Maya sat in silence. The main reason for visiting Jerusalem had been the appointment with her gynaecologist, now pushed to the back of her mind. Mendel's angry response became the focus of her mind—an unwanted distraction. Why would one fellow inmate be so welcoming and the other so offensive? She couldn't make sense of it and felt anxious about raising it with Abdiel, having seen his dismissive reaction at the café. Conversation on the return journey north centred on whatever caught their immediate attention—a car accident, birds in flight, healthy crops, and the pleasure of sealed roads.

Abdiel, stunned to hear his brother was alive and somewhere in Belgium, tortured himself by wondering what he should do. Place an advertisement in a Belgian newspaper? But if Daniel was living in the country, he might never see it. And Fishel's companion, Mendel? Pain rose in Abdiel's chest when he remembered him. He immediately wiped Mendel's face from his mind, and the pain subsided. But he couldn't let go of the conversation about his brother with Fishel.

Two weeks passed before he picked up the phone and rang the number Fishel had given him. *No answer, damn!*

A week later, Abdiel phoned again, and this time Fishel replied.

'Abdiel; yes it's Fishel. Just returned from the U.S.'

'Shalom, Fishel. You travel regularly?'

'Yes. I work for an American company in electronics, and I move around.'

'I wanted to see if you'd thought of any way I could track down my brother. I've had the Red Cross looking since the war, but nothing has come up.'

'It's very frustrating, Abdiel. I know of so many of our people who're searching for family or friends. Our meeting in the restaurant was really a chance in a million.'

'What did Daniel look like?'

'He looked very much the same as when we were in the camp, except much healthier, of course. He'd put on weight, like most of us.'

'What else did he say?' Abdiel asked.

'Nothing much. Most of our conversation was around Auschwitz, and he talked a little about the farm he was on. It seemed as though he moves around, depending on where he can find work.'

'Did he ask about me?'

Fishel paused before replying, 'No, I can't say I remember him asking about you. He had plenty of questions about what I was doing. I guess that's what happens when you're sitting in front of an old friend.'

'Did you leave him your address or contact number?'

'I offered him my card, but he didn't take it. Strange, I thought at the time. Seemed like he wanted to stay ... private.'

That word—private—pierced Abdiel's heart. He sat silent, shocked.

Fishel, sensing Abdiel's reaction, once again said, 'The war does strange things to us.'

'It does,' Abdiel replied. 'It sure does.'

Chapter Thirteen

5th August 1977
Uri

In February this year Rabbi Yousef promised to help me prepare for my bar mitzvah. He said, 'Uri, I'll help you with your studies and how to select your project.'

I'm so excited. Today is my thirteenth birthday, and we're travelling to Haifa to the synagogue for the ceremony. Last week my parents purchased the *fillin*, black leather boxes containing parchments inscribed with the Shema and other biblical verses. They're worn on the forehead and upper arm to remind us that we use our intellect, emotions and actions in the service of God. I've already prepared my speech thanking my parents and those who've helped me, especially the Rabbi. I've chosen as my project *chesed*—kindness—one of the most important Mitzvahs in the Torah. My project is to 'love your fellow man as yourself.' That's going to be a challenge for me.

~

The ceremony is joyful. All our Jewish friends are here and some of our Arab friends too, including Omar, Sabah and their children. Everyone thinks my speech was great. We have platters overflowing with food, singing and dancing. Papa wants to make a speech. The music stops and everyone gathers round.

'Thank you for coming to this very important occasion,' Papa says. 'I've looked forward to this day when my firstborn son, Uri, is welcomed into society and takes up his responsibilities ...' Tears run down Papa's face! 'I'm very proud of Uri ...' People clap and Papa's tears continue to fall. 'I'm so emotional ...' He continues his speech with a broken voice, and at the end he says, '... thank you again, and may God bless you.'

The celebration finishes, and friends shake my hand and kiss me, saying goodbye. My mind is spinning. I've never seen Papa so emotional. Four years ago at the Western Wall, I saw a single tear, but tonight *he cried!* I've seen other men cry, but not Papa—he's so strong. *I wonder what the tears are about?*

A few days later, I've just completed my homework, and I'm walking through the dining hall on my way to report for kitchen duty when Ima arrives, walks over to where Papa is sitting nearby, and hands him a letter.

'I wonder who it's from,' she says.

I stop while Papa reads the letter. His face goes white and his hand shakes.

'What's wrong Abby?' Ima asks.

Papa looks at Ima, but says nothing. He just hands her the letter. She reads a little and gasps.

Turning to me, Papa says, 'Uri, I can't believe this is true.' His eyes fill with moisture. 'It's a letter from my brother, your Uncle Daniel, congratulating you on your Bar Mitzvah.' Silence follows, until Papa says, 'I haven't seen or heard from him since the war. How does he know where we are? How does he know I have a family and how old you are? I don't know what he's doing? Why is he hiding from us?'

I'm shocked. Papa speaks so loudly and strongly about Uncle Daniel. It seems so strange; creepy that he knows about us, but we don't know anything about him. Was there a problem between them that Papa isn't telling us about?

~

On Sunday, the following week, we go to Banias Springs as part of the ongoing celebrations for my Bar Mitzvah. Many of our friends are here. Omar's and Sabah's eldest boy, Ghazi, calls me into the water. He's a little younger, skinny but strong. We're good friends, but sometimes he's a pain. A mess of black hair flops around when he runs, which is most of the time. I'm stronger than he is, but he can run faster.

I change into my swimmers behind a tree near the edge of the stream. Joseph's little dog is barking at birds, and adults are talking and laughing together. My sisters and brother— Sabella, Sachi, and Abraham—and I jump into the shallow water. Ghazi's sister, Aalia, and his brothers, Ibrahim and Khalil, are not far behind. Shrieks of laughter and cries of 'Oh, it's cold,' come from some of the kids splashing around in the clear, cool water.

Banias Springs was my choice for this special day. Hampers are packed with my favourite food and lemonade; the sun is shining; it's such a happy day. We float sticks down the stream and skim smooth rocks on the surface. Music sounds from the men and their instruments.

'I'm taking the children back now,' Sabella announces. She's nine years old and a second mother to Sachi and Abraham.

I don't want to get out yet, even though I'm shivering. Ghazi and most of the other kids have left the water. I love the quiet and peace of being by myself as I float further downstream, near where the soldiers found me.

By the time I walk back upstream, clamber out of the shallow water, and find my towel, my fingers look like white prunes. Where are my shorts? I search around but they're nowhere to be seen. I walk back to the picnic area and hear peals of laughter. *What's going on? What's all the fun about?*

I walk into the open space and can't believe my eyes. Someone has managed to put my shorts on Benny, Joseph's dog. His body is small enough to fit through one leg hole. Benny is enjoying the fun, running around barking as the kids chase. Even my sister Sabella is laughing and pointing at Benny.

'Oh, that's funny,' she giggles.

'Shut up, Sabella!' I scream. I can feel tears swell in my eyes, but I'm not going to cry. I'm going to be angry. 'Who did this?' I shout at the rabble.

'It's only fun,' Aalia, says with a smile. 'Can't you take a joke?'

'Who did it?'

At that moment, the dog lifts its back leg and pees onto a small bush, but the shorts have slipped down and the pee wets my shorts. I'm furious.

'Oh no!' Sabella cries, placing her hand over her mouth.

All the kids look at Ghazi. He's sneaked to the back of the bunch. I sprint towards the group, feeling the blood rush to my head. Ghazi flees, racing along the edge of the stream and scrambles up the slope overlooking Pan's Temple.

I hear Ima's distressed voice say, 'Uri, stop.'

But I don't. I'm embarrassed and humiliated. *I'm not going to let Ghazi get away with this.* All I want to do is hit him as hard as I possibly can.

Ghazi sprints up the broken, rocky slope like a mountain goat, but I'm determined to get him. Sharp rocks cut into my bare feet, softened by the water, but I feel no pain. The only pain is in my heart, and it'll go when I give him a good beating. Calls from my parents and Omar come from a distant place, but we race on. Ghazi gets to the top, and I know I can't reach him. I'm exhausted, so I stop, reach down, and pick up a flat rock, about half the size of my hand. Ghazi sees I've stopped and pauses, breathing heavily. My anger explodes and I throw the rock with all my strength.

I've no special ability at throwing balls or anything, but the rock sails through the air and strikes Ghazi on the side of his head as he tries to duck. It's more good luck than any skill on my part. Ghazi falls to the ground, clutching the side of his wounded skull. He curls up in a ball and cries, his body shaking like a leaf. I climb up to Ghazi and kneel down beside him. Blood flows from the gash, and my rage turns to guilt.

'I'm sorry, Ghazi,' I say, but he doesn't seem to hear. He continues to sob and hold his head.

Papa, Omar and two of our friends clamber up the slope behind me. Papa arrives breathless. 'Uri, what have you done?' he shouts.

'He'll live,' Omar says, examining the wound. 'It's not too deep.'

'You could've knocked his eye out or caused him brain damage,' Papa says in a furious tone.

'I can understand how Uri feels,' Omar says, trying to make peace. 'Ghazi provoked him.'

'There's no reason for violence,' Papa replies.

~

Silence fills the car during the drive back to our kibbutz. Ima washed my shorts in the stream, and they're drying on the back shelf of the car. My feelings are mixed up: guilt at having injured Ghazi; relieved that I didn't injure him badly or kill him; and satisfied that he suffered pain. After all, he had humiliated and embarrassed me on my special day.

It's evening after dinner. Rabbi Yousef arrives and asks me how the day went. I tell him everything and search his eyes for his response. All I see is softness and kindness.

'Your anger is a great challenge,' he says. 'The Mitzvah you've chosen as your project, *chesed* is a very difficult one, Uri. May God give you power to make the project strong.'

Later in the children's hut, I undress with Yousef's words still in my mind. I can't forget them. This day is a spiritual day when I acknowledge to society that I'm accountable for my actions. I chose kindness as my mitzvah, but if I reacted so violently to someone who offended me as Ghazi did, how would I ever manage if a person did something *really* bad? Great shame comes over me; I've a long way to go. Can I ever achieve my mitzvah?

Chapter Fourteen

September 1978

'Abby, I think Aalia has eyes for Uri,' Ima says.

She doesn't know I'm close enough to hear her.

'Oh … she may have a crush on Uri,' Papa says. 'Nothing to get concerned about … well … maybe we should start thinking about a *Shadchen*.'

A *Shadchen?* I don't know what to think about that.

We're finished for the day and preparing a special meal to celebrate the signing of the Peace Accord between our Prime Minister, Menachem Begin, and the Egyptian President, Sadat, in the White House. Jimmy Carter, the US President, is a friend of Israel, and we're happy to know Sadat has finally agreed to peace. I think that deep down, we knew it wouldn't take much for him to change his mind.

I watch Aalia talking with the girls as they spread the white tablecloths over the boards mounted on wooden trestles. I like Aalia; she's sweet, kind and affectionate. She's a good friend and scolded Ghazi about his practical joke when he dressed Joseph's dog in my shorts. But I've no interest in girls.

Rabbi Yousef says I need to concentrate on my studies because I'm a good student. 'Your parents may employ a *Shadchen*,' he says when I ask what he thinks about the idea.

'That will stop you having to even think about a wife. Girls can come later.'

The Rabbi has chosen not to marry, and maybe I will, too. Men and women usually find their partners in Israel without the help of a matchmaker, except for the ultra-orthodox. Yousef said Papa and Ima had friends where they grew up who used a *Shadchen,* and they think it's good for us. The kibbutzniks don't encourage or discourage it.

I carry a bowl of figs from the kitchen. Papa is turning the chickens on the spit. His shoulders are slumped forward while he stares at the chickens sizzling over the fire. I know his mind is somewhere else. Ima says his nightmares are getting worse after he received the letter from Uncle Daniel. Papa can't understand what's going on with his brother. It's all rather crazy.

~

June 1980

My heart is heavy today. Papa is becoming more distant. I called on him after school, but no matter how well I do in my studies, he doesn't seem to notice. I don't know if he's proud of me—he doesn't say a thing! I know Ima is concerned; she says he's depressed. Papa placed an advertisement again in newspapers in Brussels, but he hasn't received any word about his brother. I wish he'd just get over it! Rabbi Yousef is worried too because Papa isn't talking with him as he usually does. I think I've forgiven Ghazi for the practical joke and Rabbi Yousef is pleased with my spiritual progress.

I'm working on a history assignment about the Six Day War in June 1967, while Abraham, my brother, now eight years old and spoilt, is running around with a football even though he hasn't done any of his homework. I get frustrated because he can wrap people around his little finger with his cute smile and funny antics. He's solid with dark brown eyes and light-coloured skin, much lighter than mine. He likes playing with the other kids more than schoolwork and has fights with the boys. I think the parents and teachers need to be tougher on him.

My sister Sabella is eleven years old; she's done her homework already and is mothering the younger kids as usual. Sachi, who's ten, isn't always pleased with Sabella fussing around, but I guess they'll work it out. They're both keen to do well at their schoolwork and do their jobs in the kibbutz.

I turn my attention back to the book before me, looking for extra information for my assignment. My fingers flip through the pages, then stop suddenly, and I stare at the photograph before me, a sudden realisation dawning—it feels as if someone has turned on a light in my mind. The image shows soldiers standing in front of the Western Wall after the battle for Jerusalem at the end of the Six Day War, and they have tears in their eyes. *Tears in their eyes?* Could this be a clue to Papa's emotion there, too? I'd always thought it was because of the camps but maybe somehow, *this* is the trigger. I need to talk with Rabbi Yousef, and I need to think carefully about how I might approach the subject.

I spot him after dinner. 'Hi, Rabbi, have you a time to help me with my history assignment?' I ask.

'Most certainly, Uri. What's the subject?'

'The Six Day War.'

'Ah; what do you want to know?'

'What was it like for you and Papa when Jerusalem was taken and we had access to the Wall again?'

'Unforgettable. Let's take a walk. It's such a nice evening.'

We leave the hall and walk, embraced by the cool evening, across the grass and down the slope towards the orchard.

Rabbi Yousef is always pleased to talk about the past, and I think he has a special interest in me. 'Let me start at the beginning,' he says, 'and I'll tell you how I saw it. It was late May in 1967. I remember it clearly. While the afternoon shadows lengthened, we sat together with Omar and his community.' Yousef nodded towards the valley. 'Jewish and Arab representatives sitting together under the cypress trees near Joseph's home.'

'Yes, I know that tree.'

'The water pipe exchanged hands among the men, and sweet cakes were passed around the group, but the atmosphere was very tense. Joseph spoke with concern, ensuring he made eye contact with each of the nine men present. "We are again anxious about the state of affairs," he said. "Our Arab brothers, although I find it hard to use that term about them sometimes, are making life difficult for everyone in Israel."'

The Rabbi stumbles on an uneven part of the track, and I catch his arm. 'Thanks, Uri,' he says. 'I must be getting old!'

'Older but always wiser,' I quip.

'Now where was I? Oh yes; I said to Joseph that we wanted to assure him of our loyalty and support. One of the senior members of the kibbutz nodded and said, "We know your heart and know you're people we can trust. We've been in this place before and we've stood together." The problem was, Uri, that the PLO had increased terror attacks over the previous twelve months. We understood their instructions were coming from Egypt, and Syria had commenced direct attacks. We all knew we were close to being invaded.' Rabbi Yousef removed his rimless glasses and cleaned them on a handkerchief.

I've no idea why he does that, but I think it might be a habit that gives him time to think.

'Most of us believed war was inevitable,' he continues, 'especially since Nasser had closed the Straits of Tiran, blocking any supplies for Israel and free passage for any nation. It was a blatant act of war. Nasser had already moved around 80,000 troops, over 500 tanks, and nearly 1,000 artillery pieces into the peninsula.'

'That would've been scary.'

'It certainly was. I believed Israel needed to strike first. We're so small and so vulnerable; we can't allow any attacking forces onto Israel's soil. Where would we retreat to?' (Note 1)

'Exactly,' I reply. 'You'd cop it from every side, too.'

'The tension from the build-up brought back memories of the 1948 War. Many who'd been in the camps, like Auschwitz, had terrible nightmares. Those kinds of threats do terrible things to former inmates.'

'Was Papa affected?'

'He certainly was. I spent many hours with him during that time.' The Rabbi completes his polishing exercise and returns his glasses to their rightful place.

'Where was the main threat?'

'As you said, on every side. Syrian troops could attack from the Golan Heights and the Sea of Galilee and, of course, threaten our main water supply. Jordan could come in from the hills on the West Bank—Samaria and Judea. Egypt had troops in the Gaza Strip, only thirty miles from Tel Aviv. We should've attacked earlier than we did.'

'Why didn't we?'

'Many were furious with Levi Eshkol, the Prime Minister at the time. Our people wanted him to respond to Egypt's provocations. "What's he waiting for?" they said.'

'Why was he waiting?'

'He was hoping for US or British intervention. The U.S. Secretary of State, Dean Rusk, announced the United States was not planning a military intervention in the Middle East. He didn't think it's the business of the US to restrain anyone.'

'We were on our own.'

'Exactly,' Rabbi Yousef said. 'Arab oil producers had agreed to boycott any countries that assisted Israel. Nasser warned that the Suez Canal could be blocked. The Arab world felt bound by the death sentence expressed by President Aref of Iraq. "Our goal is clear," he said, "to wipe Israel off the face of the map."' Our walk leads us to the far end of the row of citrus trees, and the Rabbi pauses to glance at the oranges ripening on the trees.

I'd read about the Six Day War, but hearing about it from Rabbi Yousef sends a shiver down my spine. I can imagine Papa and Ima listening to the news reports and talking between themselves of an evening. I can only imagine how scary it must have been.

'Let's head back up the other side of the orchard,' the Rabbi says.

I follow without question.

'I recall reading an article by a journalist Yossi Peled in which he summed up the mood before the Six Day War. We'd seen photographs of the victims of Egyptian gas attacks in Yemen during the early 1960s, and we believed Nasser was intent on a similar annihilation of our people. During the nerve-wracking *Hamtana*, 'the waiting period' of May 23rd to

June 4th, the mood of our people came as near to despair as it'd ever come. It was like a great bandwagon had formed. Jordan's King Hussein came to Cairo and placed his armed forces under Egyptian command. The radios of the Arab world dropped their attacks on one another and concentrated their attention on Israel in a conspiracy of hate.' (Note 2)

Rabbi Yousef's voice drops, and his mood becomes sombre. 'I stood with your Papa and others crowded around the radio in hushed silence. The news came that Israeli planes had taken out the Egyptian air force on the ground; Syrian tanks and installations had been destroyed by our air force. Celebrations broke out everywhere—through the whole countryside. We had a big party here at Atak with singing and dancing.'

'I've seen photos. It must have been such a relief.'

'Yes. Our nation came from a terrible low to a spectacular high.'

'And then Jerusalem was captured,' I added.

'Oh, Uri. That was the *pièce de resistance*.'

'I saw photos of our soldiers weeping at the Wall.'

'It was a very emotional moment. For the first time in 2000 years, we could have access to the Wall. Legally, Jordan was supposed to give us access to it after 1948, but they never did. They used it as a rubbish dump to insult us. Within twenty-four hours of the capture of the Old City of Jerusalem, the Arab dwellings crowding the Western Wall were demolished.'

I hesitated for a moment, and then I asked the question that had motivated me to raise the subject. 'Do you think Papa's tear at the Wall was like the soldiers' tears?'

Rabbi Yousef stopped and looked at me. 'I've wondered if that might have been the case—so emotional to finally have it within his reach. But I really don't know. I suspect there's more to it. The way you've described it to me before ... it sounds as if it was a very profound, a very powerful, experience.'

'Would he have been embarrassed to cry in public?'

'It's common for men to shed tears when they come to the Wall, especially for the first time. He would know that, and I remember him shedding tears at your Bar Mitzvah. But he's not given to showing his emotions readily. No, Uri, I'm certain there's something much bigger that triggered that emotion at the Wall.' The Rabbi's face lost seriousness and a smile creased his lips. 'Hah; you're still a detective on your case.'

'I certainly am, and I'm not going to give up.'

'You're a determined young man, if ever I saw one.'

'I want to help him. Maybe if we know what it is, we can help him.'

Rabbi Yousef's smile turned to a frown. 'Hmm, I wish you well. Whatever it is, I suspect it's something that he's seen that he doesn't want us to imagine or even think about. He's probably protecting us.'

'I wish he wouldn't. He's becoming more distant. I feel so sad.'

'I pray every day for a miracle.'

'Thanks, Rabbi. I feel so much better when I talk with you.'

~

1. Israel stretches 250 miles from Eilat (the Red Sea port in the south) to Metulla (the village on the border with Syria and Lebanon in the north).

2. Conor Cruise O'Brien, *The Siege: The Saga of Israel and Zionism*, New York: Touchstone Books, Simon and Schuster, 1987, p. 413.

Chapter Fifteen

For the Israelis, the Six Day War was won.
For the Palestinians, it had only just begun.

June 1982

The Israeli Defence Force—the IDF—have moved into our region after attacks by the Palestine Liberation Organization— the PLO. The tension has been building for the last number of years, and the last straw was the PLO's attempted assassination of Israel's ambassador to Britain. The IDF attacked Southern Lebanon, and now the PLO is firing rockets into the Galilee with many casualties. The government has restricted travel to keep the roads clear for military use.

My Arab friend Ghazi has a job in Haifa as a trainee motor mechanic, and his sister, Aalia, has commenced nursing in Jerusalem. My plan is to commence medical studies next year in Jerusalem. I want to become a doctor and Rabbi Yousef has encouraged me to apply.

'You'll make a good doctor, Uri,' the Rabbi had said when I told him my intentions.

'Ima is supportive, but I'm unsure of Papa's thoughts,' I confessed.

'I'm sure your Papa approves.'

'I wish *he'd* say that,' I replied with frustration.

'Your Papa is a good man. He works very hard in the orchard and the gardens.'

'Yes, but he buries himself so much in his physical work that he has no energy or time for other people or me,' I lamented.

'Your Papa has been through tough times. You'll meet many patients in your work who're suffering from their trauma. I know it's a challenge, but accepting them is more likely to be helpful than getting angry with them.'

Deep down I know Yousef is right, but when it's your own father ... sometimes I just want to shake him. When I see him now, which isn't often, he's lost in his own world. He's present in body ... lights on, but no one home!

~

December 1982

'Papa, I finished my schooling today, and now I'm preparing for the entry exam for medicine,' I tell him. We've lost contact with each other over recent months. He has no idea what's been going on in my life.

Papa frowns and in a lifeless voice says, 'Medicine is very hard, you know.' He avoids my gaze and looks across the lounge room through the open window at the red sun in the western sky.

'I know, but my teachers have said I should apply for a place at university.'

A long pause follows. 'Your mother and I've been thinking ... you should take a wife.'

I sit motionless, stunned by the change of direction in conversation and into a topic we've never discussed.

Papa continues, his voice gaining more life, 'We've talked with a *Shadchen*, and she's made a selection we think will be a good match.'

I sit speechless, mind in a whirl.

He turns and faces me. 'We want you to meet her soon; we're sure you'll like her.'

Anger rises in me, and I take a deep breath and restrain my instinct to scream. I've worked hard to control my anger, holding high in my mind my Mitzvah, but I want to fire questions: *Why didn't you ask me first? Why haven't you asked how I'm doing in my studies?* I stop myself because if I don't, my angry words will wound him. How can I respond without exploding?

The Rabbi's words about respecting and honouring return to me, and that and my controlled breathing helps me relax. 'This is a surprise … a shock. I'll need time to think about it,' I say. 'I'm sure you want the best for me,' I add, attempting to disguise my insincerity.

'We've always wanted the best for you, Uri,' Papa replies, softening his voice. 'Can we plan a meeting soon?'

'Give me time, please,' I plead.

'Thank you, Uri. Let's play a little pool.'

Play pool! We walk into the games room, and my frustration returns. How can he, just now, invite me to play a game of pool? It's been years since he's offered to do anything with me. It's manipulation—he's just being nice to me to get his own way!

Three weeks later, the *Shadchen* introduces her 'selection' to me.

'This is Miriam, Uri,' she says.

I sit beside Ima and Papa, and Miriam and her parents sit opposite us.

'It's lovely to meet you, Uri.' Miriam's nervous fingers betray her anxiety.

After a quick smile, I avoid her eyes and stare at the *Shadchen*. She's old, with grey hair tucked under a head scarf, dressed in fine … *How would she know what young people … what I want?*

'Miriam comes from a village further south, just north of Tel Aviv,' the *Shadchen* says, smiling and looking at me as she talks. 'She's very intelligent, doing well at school and good at baking. She's made sweet cakes for you.'

Ima pours coffee and Miriam's sweet cakes are passed around. When Miriam speaks to Ima, I risk a quick glance. A colourful headscarf covers her dark wavy hair; she has brown eyes and a large nose, similar to her mother's, and a large mouth reveals well-arranged teeth when she smiles.

I'm not nervous and realise that I'm disconnected from this charade. I'm going through the motions: smiling, nodding, saying 'thank you' and 'how nice.'

After an awkward hour, Miriam and her parents leave. They appear to be pleased with the meeting.

'What do you think, Uri?' Ima asks.

'I remember you saying years ago that if you want to see what a young woman will look like when she's older, you only have to look at her mother. Well, if that's the case … she'll be like the side of a house.'

'Oh, Uri! She'll be fine for you. She comes from a good family, and we believe Miriam will be very compatible with you. Marriage involves the marriage of two families, not just the young people.'

Frustration tightens my throat, and I can't contain myself any longer. 'You never had a matchmaker tell *you* who to marry!' The words leap out of my mouth before I have time to think.

Ima and Papa stand dumbfounded. I see the hurt in their eyes, and Ima and Papa seek refuge through the open door.

Early the next morning, I lie on my bed, blanket in a mess—evidence of a restless sleep. The ceiling becomes my focus. I'm torn. Most youths in Israel are able to choose their partners. How can I honour my parents and make my own choice? The kibbutzniks will be my allies, but I know they won't interfere.

Guilt, a familiar enemy, returns as I replay my outburst of yesterday. I decide I need to talk to them sooner rather than later. I drag myself upright and stand by the window, watching the sun creep above the horizon, announcing a new day. Maybe tonight.

Papa responds to my knock on the door of their tiny room. He greets me with half a smile and avoids eye contact. Ima sits in her chair, an embroidery hoop resting on her lap. She looks up and smiles a sad smile. Papa shuffles his body into his chair, and I take my place on an old wooden, straight-backed chair. The relic is part of the furniture Papa received when he arrived at the kibbutz. I don't know what to say, so I sit motionless.

A long awkward silence follows, then Ima says, 'Uri, we know we've pushed you about finding a wife, but please understand, we only want the best for you. We see mistakes young people make when they look for a wife or a husband. Wisdom comes with age. Parents know what's likely to be a good match ...'

Papa interrupts with an answer he's thought about since our previous conversation, 'No, Uri, we didn't have a matchmaker, but our families knew each other. We knew we were suitable for each other.'

The words run off me like water off a duck's back, and I stare at the blank wall above their bed. The fight within returns: honour and respect for parents versus asserting my independence and individuality. It was easier thinking about it away from them, but now, in their presence ...

Ima fills the silence, 'Your father and I grew up together, separated by war and reunited by a miracle. We survived, our families didn't; we were reunited—God's will.'

I want to respond with as much care as I can. I take a deep breath. 'You were brought together by amazing forces, but you still had the power to *choose* each other.'

'Yes, Uri, that's true. We clung to each other as survivors at first. However, we did choose and chose to love each other. Love grew over time.' I haven't heard Papa speak like this before. Here's a rare glimpse into the man who has hidden himself from me.

His eyes moisten and he wipes away the emerging tears.

'You're our miracle baby, Uri.' Ima's voice is heavy with emotion. 'I'd given up hope of having a child when you came along. In fact, your sisters and brother are all miracles. We're so thankful to God for you all. Your Father never wore a kippah until after you were born. It's his way of saying thank you to God. Your birth revived his faith.' She shakes her head.

Papa sits silent, staring at the old red rug on the floor— another relic inherited on their arrival.

I don't know what to say and fidget with my sleeve.

Ima takes the lead again, her embroidery now relegated to a small table beside her. 'We want you to have what we didn't have. We were robbed of our childhood and youth. We want the best for you.'

Papa switches the conversation as he often does. It feels like a sweetener. 'And that means that if you want to be a doctor, you have our blessing. I always believed you would find a place in the kibbutz—you're intelligent and could make a great contribution here—but if you must, then follow your heart.'

Those words were like soothing ointment on an open wound. I played them over in my mind. No! I wasn't hearing things; the words were real.

Papa's eyes fix on me, searching for a response.

'Thank you, Papa … Ima. Thank you.'

'Let's leave thoughts of marriage until you're ready,' Ima says. 'You have much to fill your mind if you're going to be a doctor.'

Her white flag is a welcome relief. I'm on my feet, and with one step, we're united in a hug. For the first time in my life, a window has opened, and I'm touched by their vulnerability. A mix of fear, grief and appreciation envelops me. I understand their desire to give me what they never had while risking, fearing, they could lose me in the process. It's important to have their blessing. But are they trying to live their lost youth through me?

Chapter Sixteen

1982
Ghazi, Omar and Sabah

Ghazi wiped black grease from his hands and threw the soiled rag into the corner of the cluttered workshop. He glanced at Abdul who was rummaging through his overall pockets searching for his car keys. Abdul and Ghazi were good friends. Abdul—two years older, thickset, jet-black hair, bushy eyebrows—possessed a pair of long legs that carried him swiftly away from danger, of which there's plenty. The early stages of the Lebanon Civil War between Palestinian Forces and the Marionite Christians took the lives of Abdul's parents in 1975, but Abdul's streetwise cunning helped him survive, and he commenced a new life in Palestine. His adoption as an orphan by one of the many Arab villages south of Haifa provided him with new opportunities, profoundly impacting the lives of those who crossed his path. Ghazi liked Abdul and admired his courage, cunning and confidence. The rebel in Abdul, mixed with genial charisma, appealed to Ghazi. He secretly looked up to this 'survivor from Lebanon' and wanted his acceptance and approval.

'Want to come and play Bastra?' Abdul asked.

'Now?'

'Yes. I play once a week with friends.'

'Okay.' Ghazi's eyes lit up. He longed to enter Abdul's world.

Ten minutes later, seated with two other Palestinians around a vinyl table in a small rundown house on the outskirts of Haifa, Ghazi's world changed. He guessed Dharr and Farid were a similar age to him, and they appeared to be the only occupants in the untidy and neglected house. Ghazi felt the eyes of both men on him as he shuffled the deck. He was careful not to appear inquisitive, but rather wait for answers to the questions that filled his mind. He dealt four cards to each player and the game began.

'Always you live in Atak?' came the first question from Dharr.

'I was born in Palestine. My parents moved to Atak when Israeli soldiers took their land.' Ghazi raised his eyes without moving his head and saw Dharr glance at Farid.

'Same as us,' Farid responded without looking up.

Dharr said, 'One day, we get our land back from Israelis.'

Ghazi remained silent. The menace in Dharr's voice sent a chill down his spine. Dharr and Farid gave their attention to the game, which ended in Abdul emerging the winner. A second and third game progressed through clouds of smoke from the water-pipe.

Two hours later, Ghazi left the company of three, fired up his prized possession—an old motorbike he'd restored—and headed back to Atak. He found it satisfying to enter another social circle outside the few who worked in the garage and the familiar faces in the settlement. He was eager and poised to spread his wings.

~

Weeks later, Sabah watched her son return to the village at midnight. 'What's going on with Ghazi?' she asked her husband with concern. 'He's gone into himself in the last month.'

'Maybe a stage he's going through,' Omar replied.

'He's getting home very late. I don't know who these friends are he sees.'

'He's an adult; we can't keep watching him forever.'

Sabah knew her husband was right. 'But there's something about his manner that disturbs me. I can't quite describe it. He seems to avoid us, not look us in the eye,' she said frowning.

'As I said, it's probably a stage he's going through. I don't think we need to worry.' Omar's response was an attempt to reassure himself, but a vain effort to placate his wife.

Over the coming months, Sabah's concern only grew.

~

The small circle of Palestinians who frequented the house of the card-playing quartet nurtured Ghazi's friendship. Ghazi was surprised to learn that every one of the group were displaced, either they, or their parents, had been forced from their homes. This shared background gradually strengthened their friendship and formed an unbreakable allegiance. Into this crucible of discontent, a figure by the name of Ammam found his way. His entry was planned—intentional—designed to achieve a specific purpose. That time was imminent, and when it came, it would bring profound suffering and change.

Part Four

Chapter Seventeen

1983
Uri

My farewell from Atak brought mixed emotions: sadness at leaving the kibbutz, my home for all of my eighteen years; but also excitement at finding a place in Hadassah Medical School in Jerusalem, set on the green slopes of Mt Scopus in West Jerusalem. My heart sang as I explored the campus. I'm privileged to have the opportunity to be a student in a university that's recognised internationally for its standards and research, and I'm prepared to give it my best.

Towards the end of my first week, I'm standing in line at the cafeteria when a familiar voice behind me says, 'Uri.' I turn, and before me stands a beaming Aalia. 'It's so good to see you,' she says.

'Likewise. I haven't seen you for … how long? … over twelve months. You look well. Nursing must agree with you.'

'I'm enjoying it, but it does have its challenges.'

We pay for our food and find a quiet corner amongst the mix of students and medical staff immersed in animated conversations around laminated tables. The absence of soft furnishings contributes to the difficulty of hearing intimate conversations.

'Tell me what it's like working here,' I ask as we settle into our seats.

'I really enjoy the study and the work in the wards. It's something I've always wanted to do, as you know. There're one or two matrons who're tough, but generally life is pleasant, but hectic. I've made some close friendships, but I still miss my family and friends at Atak. I miss you, too. How are you finding your way around?'

I finish swallowing a mouthful of falafel. 'It's rather overwhelming, but I'm managing. I have a short walk from where I'm boarding in West Jerusalem which will keep me fit.'

'I'm fortunate to have accommodation in the nurses' quarters on campus, both good and bad. When I'm not on shift, I meet a couple of friends and we explore Jerusalem. I love the Old City, its history, the markets, the amazing mix of people, and pilgrims from everywhere.'

'Jerusalem is an amazing place. So much history, so much to learn, so much to see,' I respond. We talk about hospital life until I see Aalia looking over my shoulder and biting her lip.

'Don't look now,' she says, 'but behind you are sitting two Jewish girls who give me a hard time. The rest of the staff are accepting of me but these two—they behave in a terrible way—call me names, heckle me.'

'Have you complained?' I ask, frowning.

'I think that'll make it worse. I try to avoid them as much as possible. They're leaving now.'

I intentionally drop my serviette on the floor, turn and glance at two figures exiting through the main door of the cafeteria.

'They go everywhere together,' Aalia added.

'They may be so insecure they can't exist without the other,' I offer with a touch of sarcasm. 'If they get worse, report them. I'm sure there're ways of dealing with them that can be done without implicating you.'

'I'll let you know. I'd better run now. My shift commences in ten minutes. It's been so good to catch up with you. Hope we can meet again soon.'

'I've enjoyed it, too. Yes, maybe we could catch up for lunch again.'

Aalia strides to the door. She pauses and glances over her shoulder. I nod in response to yet another beautiful smile, then she's gone.

I finish my coffee and head to the library, feeling lighter. Aalia has been a friend ever since she was born. Over the years, our families have shared lives, celebrating birthdays and significant events together. She was part of the group that played games in the orchard, swum in the river, and explored the countryside. Now we're no longer children. Strange sensations I've never experienced before stir within. I find myself keen to see her again and soon.

That evening, I phone the kibbutz.

Ima's voice sounds tired. 'I miss you, Uri; we both do. Your father isn't sleeping well. He's disturbed every night by nightmares. It's wearing me down, too.'

'He can get treatment at the hospital,' I say. 'They've specialists here who can help.'

'He knows that but ... oh, I don't know what he thinks. My guess is he doesn't think it'll make any difference. He's becoming obsessed with finding his brother. So far he's been in touch with the British Red Cross, the American Red Cross, US Holocaust Museum's search department, and Yad Vashem Museum's missing persons' group in Jerusalem. Nothing has come to light so far. He's never been quite the same since he received the letter from your Uncle Daniel at your Bar Mitzvah.'

My pathetic response reveals my feeling of helplessness: 'I'll try to talk with him when I get back to Atak.'

~

Abdul finished replacing a muffler on an old jeep and sat on a drum outside the workshop. 'Ghazi,' he called to his friend inside. 'You coming for a few rounds of Bastra later?'

Ghazi's eyes lit up. 'Sure, wouldn't miss it.'

'We've some new players tonight, so we may have two tables.'

Ghazi's friendship with Abdul, Dharr and Farid had strengthened over the months. The theme of their dispossession became central in their conversations: the injustice; the ongoing struggle of feeling 'second class'; the continual suspicion and mistreatment by Jewish authorities.

Later that afternoon in the neglected house on the outskirts of Haifa, the four regular players had just pulled their decrepit wooden chairs around the familiar table when a voice sounded from the back door. Dharr sprang to his feet and walked to the closed door.

'Who is it?'

'Ammam,' came the brief reply to his query.

Dharr opened the door a little, peered into the twilight at the faces of three men, then stood back to allow them to enter. The first was tall and handsome with bushy eyebrows. The other two—shorter and stockier—eyed the men seated around the table.

Abdul rose from his seat and greeted the tall Lebanese, 'Ammam, it's good to see you after all these months.' He introduced the card players to Ammam, but Ammam's accomplices remained nameless and silent. The four friends carried an old sofa into the room and an extra chair from the kitchen to provide seating for the visiting trio.

Ammam moved his gaze from Dharr to Farid and then Ghazi in turn. 'Abdul says you're good men and can be trusted. You share the pain of many of my countrymen in Lebanon who've been abused by Israel and America. Your families have suffered because of Israelis taking Arab land. Do you want to be free? Do you want the land of your fathers back?'

Dharr, Farid and Ghazi stared at each other and remained speechless.

'You've protested about the Jewish occupation; you talk about it often. I'm asking whether you want to *do* something about it rather than just talk.' His voice gathered strength, demanding a response.

The men sat stunned.

The heavy silence suddenly broke. Ghazi spoke, his voice eager, 'What do you mean *do* something?'

'Be part of a group to drive Jews into the sea … wash your hands in their blood. My job is selecting fighters who want to get rid of the Jewish scourge. We'll use everything possible: rockets; suicide-bombers; anything. Allah is with us.'

Ghazi's gaze fixed on Ammam as he spoke, and a strange awakening stirred within. 'I'm in,' he said without further thought.

'What about you two?' Ammam stared at Dharr and Farid.

Dharr nodded without saying a word, and Farid, after thinking for a few moments, replied, 'I've never fired a gun. I'm not sure how I'd go.'

'We've training camps for everything. How to shoot, make bombs, gather information,' Ammam replied. 'There's a place for anyone who wants to rip these infidels to shreds—wipe out Jewish occupation.'

Ghazi's mind was working overtime. 'So you're part of the PLO?'

'Yeah, and we're stronger every day. Yasser Arafat declared he'll never accept the State of Israel. It's brought many groups, Arab brothers, together. Those who fought each other are now united to push Israelis into the sea.' Ammam's powerful presence filled the room; his quiet confidence, poise, and measured words, compelling.

Ghazi sensed an opportunity to break free of the monotony of Atak. Free from his father and mother who frustrated him with boundaries that stifled his thirst for adventure. Here he saw the possibility to be someone. 'Count me in,' he repeated.

Dharr and Farid nodded and declared their allegiance to their newfound cause.

'Good. Don't breathe a word to no one—not even family—otherwise I swear by Allah you'll be punished. You'll receive further instruction later.' Ammam stood and nodded to Ghazi, Farid and Dharr. Turning to Abdul, he said, 'I'll be in touch in the usual way next week.'

Ammam's two accomplices stood and followed their leader to the door, then they disappeared into the night.

'Congratulations. You're part of a new brotherhood,' Abdul said with a grim smile. 'I pray to Allah that you'll have courage of a lion.'

Something about Abdul gave Ghazi confidence. Scars testifying to his courage covered the man's face and body. His history of violence, written on his body, attracted and also repelled Ghazi.

Farid scratched his lightly bearded chin and said, 'I didn't think PLO had much power after Israel's attack on Lebanon last year. They were tossed out of Lebanon. The leaders went to Tunisia, and the others went to Sudan, Yemen, and South Yemen.'

'Yeah, the PLO was split up,' Abdul said, 'but Arafat is smuggling arms into Palestinian camps in Lebanon now, and there's new organisation happening, especially in the south. There's a lot you don't know.'

'Maybe that's where we come in,' Ghazi suggested.

Abdul raised a cautionary hand. 'That may be the idea. But we don't come up with plans. We follow orders.'

Minutes later, the new recruits went their separate ways, excited. A new era had begun.

~

Aalia entered the cafeteria and immediately noticed the 'Velcro Sisters' sitting together. She'd named them appropriately—the way they 'stuck together' was pathetic. No matter if it was in class, the cafeteria, or the toilet, they were joined at the hip. They lived in one of the many illegal settlements in the West Bank, deemed so according to the Oslo Accords.

The Velcro Sisters glared at Aalia as she walked past. 'Go back to the desert, you Arab bitch,' one of them spat.

Aalia paid no attention. She continued walking and sat at a table some distance from the pair. She knew they came from a new Israeli settlement near Ramallah in the West Bank, north of Jerusalem. The area had a history of fighting between Arabs and Jews. She imagined that was why they hated her. But she wasn't going to give them the joy of a response. (Note 1)

The Sisters finished their lunch and chose a path to the door that included Aalia's table. They stopped beside her.

Aalia fixed her eyes on her plate and continued to eat.

'There's no place for you here,' one of them said in a caustic tone that cut Aalia to the bone.

Aalia took a deep breath and glanced up from her plate into the blazing eyes of the pair. She fought the impulse to throw her plate at them or the urge to cry. Steeling herself against showing tears, she said with a fixed stare, 'Where I come from, Jews and Arabs work and live together peacefully. I can't see why we can't do that.'

'Good for you.' The speaker was the taller of the two—green eyes, pencilled eyebrows, silver Star of David earrings hanging from each ear. 'Where we come from, Arab terrorists killed my uncle and nephews. I'll never forgive you for that.' The words flew like darts from her twisted mouth.

'I didn't kill your family—'

'Your fighters did,' she interrupted, 'and you're an Arab.'

Aalia turned her attention back to her plate and continued eating.

The pair stood glaring at her for a moment and then left. 'Bitch,' the shorter sister said as their final word.

Aalia waited until they left the cafeteria, then hurried to the women's toilets, locked herself in a cubicle and burst into tears.

~

Two weeks after my reunion with Aalia, when I'm walking through the orthopaedic section, I catch sight of her tending a patient and pause in the doorway of the four-bed ward. The patient commanding Aalia's attention lies in a bed in the far corner of the ward. The man has suffered a compound fracture of the right leg, fractured ribs, and deep lacerations to both forearms.

Aalia, her back to me, gently raises him up onto his backrest of pillows, rearranging them to the patient's satisfaction. She checks his temperature and pulse, then offers water from a glass by his bed. I'm struck by her patience and care. Her ways are so gentle. Calmness and tenderness flow from her into the broken body and bruised spirit of this accident victim. She touches everything and everyone with beauty, grace and reverence. Angelic. *I love the way she cares.*

She turns, catches sight of me, and smiles.

'How's the patient doing?' I ask in a professional tone.

'He's managing well, doctor,' comes her equally clinical reply.

'That's good to hear,' I respond with half a grin. My heart rate increases. The brief encounter has made my day. I continue walking through the ward, wondering when I can see her again. Should I check the nursing roster to see when she's on next?

I allow one lift to go, hoping she might pass by me, but no such luck. The lift door opens. I enter reluctantly and descend to the car park.

A week later, I'm sitting in the car park feeling frustrated. I've not set eyes on Aalia since I saw her in the orthopaedic ward. I'm certain her shift has finished, and when I see her leave, I plan to join her for the short walk to the nurses' accommodation. I'm aware of the risk of being seen together. Doctor and nurse relationships are frowned on, and a female Arab nurse fraternising with a Jewish doctor would be scandalous, but I have to talk to her again.

There she is! Descending the steps to the car park. I open the door but stop with one leg out of the car. *Should I walk with her?* My heart races as I watch her slim body glide across to the lower exit. In a minute, she'll be out of sight. *Should I risk it?* Two staff members stand in the far corner of the car park. I hesitate and … she's gone. I sink into despair. It would have been risky, but …? I chastise myself for lack of action and vow it won't happen again. The engine springs to life and I drive to my flat, nursing disappointment.

~

At the conclusion of the first semester I decide to visit the kibbutz for a few days. Ima is concerned for Papa and thinks I might be able to persuade him to seek help for his depression. The initial therapy of kibbutz life gave him some relief from his torment. Open air, hands in the soil, reaping the rewards of his toil at harvest, and the camaraderie of colleagues provided temporary respite. Now, his past is imprisoning him.

On the familiar road into Atak, I wave to friends finishing for the day. It's been hot, and I head for the water cooler. Children gather for reading time after outdoor play, and parents walk back from the orchard. I wait. Papa approaches. The lines on his face have deepened; his shoulders now carry an invisible weight, heavier than when I saw him last.

Ima looks exhausted. She spots me and quickens her steps towards me. 'Oh, Uri, it's so wonderful to see you.' Her tears flow with happiness.

'It's good to see you, Ima.'

She holds me in a long hug. Papa arrives and stands beside me, and I give him a hug. His body stiffens.

'How are you, Papa?'

'Managing as best I can.' He provides no effort to match the strength of my embrace.

'Let's sit under the trees and have a drink,' Ima says, and she goes to collect a jug of iced water, and some olives and figs.

'How are your studies going?' Papa enquires as we walk to the bench seats a few metres from the dining hall.

'I think I did well. I'll get my results in a week or so. I'm enjoying the course. It's really what I want to do,' I reply. Ima is delayed, talking to two other women, so I see an opportunity to sound him out. 'How are you going, really?'

'I'm now fifty-three years old and not getting any younger. I like the work in the orchard, but on days like this it's too hot. I'm not sleeping well; the nightmares still wake me and … oh, you don't need to hear all this!'

'Of course I do. It concerns me to know you're missing sleep. I've a duty of care to you, not only as a son but also as a doctor.' I grin.

Papa's face remains blank. 'Yes, you're my son, but you're not a doctor yet.'

'I know enough to know you can be helped. There's a department in the hospital that deals specifically with trauma; they can help you.'

He rubs his chin, thinking, and looks at Ima, who's finishing her conversation with the women. 'I'll think about it. It's a long way to travel.'

'Two hours by car, at the most,' I remind him.

'I'll think about it,' he repeats as Ima sits beside him.

The figs and olives are delicious and the water brings energy back to my weary body.

After dinner I retire to the hall and mix with old friends and catch up on happenings in the region. I hear that Ghazi is doing well in his work at the garage and has moved into accommodation in Haifa. Before I retire, I call in on Ima and Papa. Their simple room, unchanged, provides them with a comfortable space away from the kibbutzniks.

Ima tells me the latest about Sabella, Sachi and Abraham and then asks, 'Have you any more thoughts about Miriam?'

The question throws me. The visit by the *Shadchen*, Miriam, and her parents has not entered my head for months. 'Not really,' I respond truthfully.

'I don't want to trouble you, but we're concerned you have the best wife. Don't leave your decision too late. Miriam and her family are good people,' Ima replies, watching me.

'Thanks for your concern,' I reply. 'I know you have my best interests at heart. I'll try to get some sleep now. I want to help out tomorrow.'

'We could use you in the orchard, if you have time,' Papa says.

'I'd enjoy that. It's good to get my head out of books for a few days.'

~

Ghazi closed up for the day, the rattle of the workshop door the only sound in the almost deserted street. The only sign of life was a familiar figure seated quietly in his weather-beaten vehicle, parked metres from the garage. The door swung open and a voice said, 'Wanna come for a drive?'

Ghazi slid into the front seat and shook hands with Ammam. Ghazi was always pleased to see his mentor, and they met regularly. The engine sprang to life, and the men motored casually through the outskirts of town and into the darkening countryside.

'How's your day been?' Ammam asked in a quiet voice.

'Aw, just the usual. When do we see some action?'

'Be patient. But I like your keenness.' Ammam paused and glanced at Ghazi. 'You're shaping up but still a bit of an unknown. The leadership are concerned about your parents— so tight with the Jews.'

Ghazi moved uncomfortably in his seat. 'I haven't seen them in … months. They don't know what I do. I don't care about them. They don't know about you and the others.'

'That's good; that's how it should be. Our cause is more important than family. I shot my cousin last year because he had a friendship with a Jewish soldier. I couldn't trust him.'

Ghazi's mouth opened and closed without words.

'There's us and there's them,' Ammam said. 'If you're not for us, you're against us.'

Ghazi remained silent.

'You're suddenly quiet?'

Ghazi took a deep breath. 'It's pretty gutsy … doing what you did … your own family … were you close to him?'

'Well, I guess so, but he wanted to be a peacemaker, even when the IDF invaded Lebanon last year—traitor!'

The coldness in Ammam's voice sent a shiver down Ghazi's spine.

'How badly do you want the Jewish pigs out of Palestine?'
he continued.

———'I won't stop until every last Jewish swine is pushed into
the sea,' Ghazi replied with vigour.

A smile emerged on Ammam's face. 'That's what we need
to hear. Your opportunity will come, and take it when it does.
You'll be tested, and I'm sure you'll pass with flying colours.'

Ghazi sat back and relaxed on his seat. It felt good to be
accepted. He liked Ammam and wanted to impress him. 'I'm
very pleased to be part of the brotherhood. You're my new
family. I'm gonna make a difference. I'll do anything you
need.'

Ammam smiled and nodded at his new convert. *He's ready
for his initiation.*

~

1. Ramallah contains significant historic, cultural, and religious sites and has been
a focal point since 1948 for conflict, not only between Palestinians and Jews but
also between Palestinian factions seeking control.

Chapter Eighteen

My return trip to Jerusalem couldn't come quickly enough. While I enjoy the outdoor life at Atak, catching up with my parents, family and friends, my heart lies with Aalia. I've resolved to contact her and become more intentional. No more chance meetings in corridors, cafeterias or car parks. My love for her demands me to be upfront. I believe we can overcome any fallout from our relationship. However, a question tortures me: *Are these feelings infatuation or love? How will I ever know unless I explore them? And what about Miriam?*

Rabbi Yousef says we can learn to love over time. It's not necessary to have the chemistry bubbling to form a love relationship. He told me that, 'The problem about marriage in the West is, the pot on the stove is boiling at first and then as time goes on, it cools. For us, the pot starts cool and gradually, over time, it heats up.' On the drive back, his words ring in my ears and disturb me. But there's an ache within that drives me to her. I long just to see her, to be with her.

Before I go to sleep I picture her in my mind, her beautiful slim body nestled between the sheets, her brown eyes closing gently as she settles for the night. What does she think about before she sleeps? Does she think about me? I'm sure she likes me. Her reaction in the cafeteria—she was delighted to see me—shows that. But I know she'd be anxious about showing her feelings. If anyone found out, like her family, there'd be much talking—much wailing and gnashing of teeth!

Yet if we truly love each other … *I believe love will find a way*. Our parents and friends would be horrified. While our communities in Atak have lived and shared their lives together, there's never been inter-marriage. What would happen in the hospital? I imagine there'll be talk, but it'll blow over. We've Arab and Jewish doctors who work together harmoniously. Arab and Jewish nurses cooperate in their duties—well most of them. But then there's the Velcro Sisters. I can imagine what their response would be. *Love will find a way*. That's now my mantra. I can't wait to see her.

The following day, I enter the cafeteria during lunchtime and search the tables for any sign of Aalia. I'm enjoying the break from books and managed a slow jog around the Old City earlier. Now, after a coffee and a shower, I'm ready to put my plan into action. I position myself in the corner to gain the best view of the gradually filling tables. Aalia walks through the entrance, and my heart leaps. Then I'm devastated—she has someone by her side. My eyes follow her as she and her friend queue for food, then find a spare table in the middle of the room. Patiently I wait, irritated, nibbling away at my *shwarma* and pita bread. My interest is focused more on the table in the centre of the cafeteria than my meal.

By the time I finish eating, Aalia and her friend have also completed their lunch. They stand, and I'm on my feet heading for their table. I arrive as they walk towards the exit. 'Aalia,' I say. 'What a surprise.'

'Uri, you've been eating here, too? This is my friend Mary. Mary, this is Uri. I grew up with Uri at Atak.'

'Nice to meet you, Mary. You're nursing here with Aalia?'

'Yes, we're in the same year. We look after each other,' Mary replies with a laugh.

I'm so glad Aalia acknowledges our connection. Thinking quickly, I say, 'I've been back to Atak for two days, and I'm happy to bring you up to date with the latest, if you have a little time.'

'I'd love to, Uri. I've tomorrow afternoon free.'

'Excellent.'

'Maybe we could meet in the car park at … 2 p.m.?'

'Could we make it four?'

'That's perfect. See you then, Uri.' Aalia smiles and turns to Mary. 'Let's go.'

After they disappear through the doorway, a huge sigh of relief escapes my lips. My spirits soar. That was easy, and so natural. The bonus was to have a witness to us arranging a meeting—just two people who grew up together, catching up on the latest news. Just perfect.

The next morning, before my alarm sounds, I'm showered and breakfasted. It's going to be a long drag through my shift to 4 p.m. Already my heart rate is up.

The day passes slowly, but finally I walk down the steps to the car park, my excitement growing.

Aalia appears, wearing a beautiful pink headscarf. '*Shalom*,' she beams as I open the car door.

'*Shalom*. You look as though you're ready for an outing.'

'Where do you want to take me?' She giggles.

I shrug. 'How about Mt Herzl.'

'Mt Herzl! Where the national cemetery is and the graves of all the prime ministers?'

'Yes, it's a huge area with lots of open space—lawns, trees—and Jerusalem Forest is on the Western side with some interesting tracks; if you're feeling energetic.'

'Why not. I've never been up there, ever, so educate me.' Her energy in jumping into my car with her radiant smile shows she's pleased to be with me.

We chat about Atak and our families as we wind our way up to the Mount on the Western side of Jerusalem. I park and we walk to the edge of the forest on a rough pathway, then gaze across the valley of green at Jerusalem in the afternoon sunlight.

'Aren't we so lucky to live here,' Aalia reflects. 'It's such a beautiful city.'

'We're blessed, and I'm so fortunate to be with you.' The words tumble out before I have a chance to retrieve them.

Aalia stops and faces me. She thinks for a moment, then asks, 'What do you mean?'

'I *really* enjoy being with you.'

Pink floods her cheeks. She looks stunned and avoids my gaze. 'The way you say that, Uri ... it ... it embarrasses me.'

My heart skips a beat. It seems like I've overstepped the mark. Awkwardness grips my tongue, but I manage to stutter, 'Do you ... you ... want to stay here or walk?'

She smiles, but an embarrassed silence falls, until she asks, 'What do you mean? We've always been friends ... good friends.'

My heart is racing. Should I back off or reveal my hand? I take a deep breath, 'I often think about you. When I see you around the hospital ... I ... uh ... it's ... so good.' My face heats as the words tumble awkwardly out of me. I feel foolish.

She glances at me with amusement. 'Are you saying you have ... feelings for me?'

It's now or never. I take another deep breath and force the words out. 'Yes. I think that's what I'm trying to say.'

Aalia gasps and covers her mouth with her hand. 'Oh, Uri ... I had no idea ... oh, that's ... I don't know what to say!'

I regain my composure. 'I can understand you being surprised.'

'Surprised? ... shocked!'

'Okay ... shocked. I know you've always been the-girl-next-door, but why wouldn't I have feelings for a woman who is not only beautiful on the outside, but also on the inside.'

'Oh, Uri,' she gasps, 'you say the loveliest things, but ... what will people think?'

'Frankly, I don't give a damn what people think! It's what *we* think that matters.'

Aalia appears stunned by the force of my response. 'Well ... I think it does matter. Life could become very difficult for us both. I can hear my parents, especially my father, ranting at me. He'd probably disown me ... I like you, Uri. I really do. You're smart, intelligent ... whoever snares you will have a good catch, but ... I don't know what to think. I'm so confused.'

Aalia waves her hands around as though she's at sixes and sevens. My disclosure has thrown her off balance. Secretly I wanted her to say, 'And I have feelings for you, too; I can't believe it; I'm so excited.' To have her throw her arms around me and scream for joy would transport me to the seventh heaven. But to see her shock and reservation and hear her confusion ...? It's painful.

We walk a few paces further without saying a word. It gives me a minute to engage my brain. Yes, I can understand her caution. I need to give her time. She'll come round. What was I thinking to expect her to fall straight into my arms? You idiot! 'I hope my rashness won't affect our relationship. Whatever happens, I want to be your friend. I apologise for ambushing you and causing you embarrassment.'

Aalia smiles and nods. 'I'm certainly taken back, but I love your honesty, and I'm flattered. But I can't see how a romantic relationship would work. But, anyway, we can always be friends, good friends.'

'Good friends we'll be,' I reply with a laugh. My body is now more relaxed, and a strange air hangs over us. Our relationship *has* to change as the result of my declaration. How it will change remains to be seen. Undoubtedly moments of awkwardness will appear, but I need to be patient. A quick glance at Aalia tells me she's reasonably comfortable to continue walking. She's not desperate to head back to the car and return to her flat. We walk on in silence, and I risk further glances.

I drink in her loveliness: olive, unblemished skin, soft yet firm; brown eyes shine and invite me to play; a small, cute nose, perfectly shaped; a genuine smile revealing pure white teeth, and full lips, beautifully formed. Here's the girl who lived next door, who romped with me in the fields around Atak, who swam with me in the rivers and dams around Haifa, and who joined in family celebrations. She was just a kid then, but now, she's a stunningly beautiful woman. My eyes caress her body. She takes my breath away.

'What are you thinking about?' she asks suddenly.

The blood rushes to my face. I search for an answer. Does she know what I'm thinking? 'Oh, I … I was thinking about our days of growing up together and how you're so easy to get along with. I've always enjoyed your company; you're fun to be with.'

'Yes. They were great times, and I'm so grateful for them. I couldn't have had a better childhood.'

We stop under a cypress tree on the dirt track under the canopy of green shielding us from the heat of the sun. I desperately want to kiss her, but I know that would finish things for good. The desire I feel is so strong it shocks me. I need to take charge of myself. Stop it! Turn away.

I look around. The birds in the trees are our only witnesses. The moment passes and voices sound from further along the track. Two young men, sporting back packs, speaking German approach. The rhythmic 'click' of their walking sticks signal their rapid progress.

'*Guten Nachmittag,*' they greet in unison.

After meandering for another five minutes, we retrace our steps back towards the car park and see the two Germans disappearing in the distance. We drive back to Aalia's quarters, sharing casual conversation centred on whatever catches our eyes.

'Thanks, Uri. I did enjoy discovering new territory today,' she laughs. 'Let's catch up soon.'

'I hope you can sleep well tonight,' I say with a smile.

That night I lie in bed with my emotions in a scramble. Guilt, frustration, uncertainty, and relief swirl around in a muddle of … did I overstep the mark? She was shocked but didn't get mad at me. Her initial distress from my confession did cause me guilt, but I think, deep down, she seemed to like my honesty. She likes me, but is there anything more?

~

Ghazi heard footsteps and peered out from under the car where he lay, tightening the plug on the oil sump of a car. He knew who the sandals belonged to and the voice that said, 'Ghazi.'

'Ammam.' Ghazi found his excitement hard to hide whenever Ammam walked into the workshop. Any conversation with Ammam always involved another chapter of the adventure that had taken him captive. He'd finally found his place in life. Now he had a cause, a just cause to which he could devote his passion. Ghazi slid out from under the dirty vehicle, and grinned at Ammam. 'What news have you got for me today?'

Ammam glanced around the workshop, eyeing every corner. 'Only you here?'

'Yeah. Abdul will be in soon.'

'There'll be a shipment coming in next week. You'll receive six car batteries with false tops. Remove the tops and the fuses will be wrapped in plastic inside. I'll sort out a night the following week to show you how to put them together.'

'Want a drink?' Ghazi asked, removing grease from his hands. 'There's a can in the fridge in the corner. I'll have one, too, if you're having one.'

'Sure, thanks.'

Both men sat on an old steel crate filled with used car parts that Abdul deemed too good to throw away. The strong smell of oil and petrol filled the workshop.

'We've picked up another dozen recruits from the area,' Ammam said after taking a long swig from his can.

Headquarters are very pleased with the response, and your efforts have been noted. I like your dedication, your commitment, Ghazi. I think you'll do well.'

Ghazi nodded but kept his smile on the inside. He didn't want Ammam to know how much his words meant to him. 'Any idea when we'll have action?'

'Not yet. We have to get the goods assembled first. Also, I need you to pick up an order from Haifa soon.'

'I'm ready for anything.' Ghazi leaned forward in his chair. He admired this mysterious, tall, Lebanese man with his calm, cool, and collected manner, who blew in and out of the workshop every couple of weeks. Every word, every movement of his body was calculated, measured, and efficient.

'I'll be in touch after next week's delivery,' he said after draining the can. 'Thanks for the drink.' Then he was gone.

~

Abdiel sat in the shade of his favourite tree with Maya by his side in the familiar surrounds of the settlement. Omar and Sabah had invited them down for a birthday celebration for their youngest, Khalil.

'We named him Khalil, meaning 'brave' because we thought he needed it to survive his three older siblings,' Sabah said with a laugh.

Maya passed her freshly baked cakes to Omar, who accepted one gratefully.

'How's Uri going?' he asked, resting back into his armchair.

'Uri is doing well at his studies, but we don't see him very often. Though that's understandable.'

'His future is certainly secure if he succeeds at medicine,' Omar replied.

Maya frowned. 'I wish he'd think more seriously about a future with a wife. He's never got back to us after the meeting with the *Shadchen.*'

'He is a sensible young man,' Omar said. 'He's level-headed and has good common sense; I'm sure you'll find that it'll work out well in the end.'

'I hope so. He can be impulsive at times, as you know,' Maya replied.

Omar turned to Abdiel. 'How are you, Abdiel? You're rather quiet today.'

'Not sleeping well again. My demons usually arrive around 3 a.m. and torment me for the rest of the night.'

Maya looked at Omar with concern. 'I keep telling him he needs to see someone professionally.'

Abdiel shook his head. 'I don't know what anyone can do for me.'

'You'll never know if you never go, will you?' Maya glanced at Omar as her words of frustration bounced off her husband's invisible shield. She desperately wanted Omar to add his voice to her own.

Omar only shook his head and said, 'Maybe time will heal?'

An awkward silence fell over the group.

Abdiel deflected attention away from himself onto the main topic of conversation—the collapse of Israel's four major banks. 'I'm pleased the government has taken over the banks,' he offered tentatively. 'It'll mean they can never manipulate the stock market like they've done in the past.'

Omar nodded. 'Yes, but the price we've paid to achieve it is a significant loss in public assets.'

'I don't know why it took the government so long before they acted,' Abdiel added.

Omar scratched his head. 'Maybe they wanted to ensure the banks fell hard enough, so they had no option than accept a government takeover.'

Sabah offered a second round of coffee, accepted by all. Maya, concerned conversation would head into the current debate about public finances, of which she knew little and had no inclination to explore, asked, 'How's Ghazi finding his work in Haifa?'

'We don't see him very often now,' Sabah replied, 'but he's enjoying his work as a mechanic. Whenever we go to Haifa, we call in for a few minutes and take him some cakes. He's always busy.'

'Is he interested in having a *Shadchen* find him a wife?' Maya asked.

Abdiel shook his head and looked at Omar. Omar gave him a quick glance before returning his gaze to Maya. He knew what his good friend was thinking.

'We've talked to Ghazi,' Sabah replied, 'but he wants to make his own choice. I don't understand young people these days.'

'Maybe he wants it to be a surprise,' Abdiel offered with half a smile.

'I agree,' Maya said. 'They can end up making a mess of their relationships, but you can't tell them anything!'

'Allah will take care of our children,' Omar assured them. 'What we cannot do, Allah will do.'

'I hope you're right,' Sabah said. She didn't accept Omar's simplistic, theological prediction.

Suddenly Omar sat forward in his chair and scratched his head.

'What's the matter?' Sabah asked.

'I just remembered. Yesterday when I visited our supplier in Haifa, the salesman mentioned that Ghazi had called in and purchased two bags of fertilizer. The salesman thought it strange and asked him what it was for, knowing he worked in a garage. Ghazi said he was picking it up for us, here at the farm. I've never asked him to do that. Strange?'

~

My mood is up. Aalia is about to join me for a coffee in a quiet café in the Jewish quarter. A month has passed since our time at Mt Hertzl, and during that time, momentary glances at each other were the only connection I've had with the woman who's stolen my heart. Caution prevented me approaching her for time together. I hoped the natural course of our weekly routine might place us together, but it didn't happen. My frustration grew to the point where I had to arrange a rendezvous.

'Sorry I'm late.' Aalia sat on the chair on the other side of the cloth-covered table.

'No need for apology. It's good to see you again outside the wall of work.'

Aalia's beautiful smile revealed pure white teeth. 'It's been so frantic with study and work. I've missed you.'

'You've missed me? Truly?' I reply, signalling the waiter.

'Of course. I always enjoy your company,' comes the quick response with a laugh.

'Two Arabic coffees and two pieces of coconut cake,' I say to the waiter.

He nods and withdraws.

'You remembered.'

'Remembered what?'

'That I like coconut cake,' Aalia says playfully.

'That's not hard to forget. It's also one of my favourites, too.'

'And how have you been after our last time together?' Aalia's voice drops and becomes more serious.

'So glad you're still my friend!'

Aalia laughs. 'You'll always be my friend—I hope.'

'That's my wish, too. How did you feel?'

Aalia fiddles with her sleeve and glances casually at me. 'It was sort of strange. I felt pleased. It's a huge compliment to have someone like you … ah … interested in someone like me.'

'What do you mean someone like you?'

'Well, I'm just a simple Palestinian country girl—'

'Simple!' I interject with disbelief. 'You're an intelligent, beautiful woman—'

'Oh, there you go again, Uri,' she says, her cheeks blushing. 'Keep your voice down.'

'I speak the truth,' I protest vigorously.

Aalia smiles, then bites her bottom lip and sighs. She avoids my gaze, waiting for the coffee to be delivered by the waiter, now standing beside her. 'Thanks.'

The young, well-mannered Jewish waiter retreats.

'If you were Palestinian, I'd have no hesitation … oh, I don't believe I said that!'

I laugh. 'How can I become a Palestinian?'

Aalia's cheeks colour again, and she says in a more serious tone, 'It's ridiculous, isn't it? This race business. People should be free to choose who they love.'

'I agree,' I say instantly.

'But to be practical, here in Palestine, Israel, it's such an issue. I'm sure my father would disown me. My world would change.'

'In a few cases mixed couples have migrated overseas …'

'Yes, but then you're removed from your family.'

'If the love between the couple is strong—I mean really strong,' I say, 'that could outweigh the negatives that come from family. If parents and family saw the genuineness and the strength of the commitment of their son and daughter over time … I think they'd come around.'

Aalia is quiet and slowly sips her coffee. I wait for a response hoping I've not pushed too hard. 'You might be right, but for us … I don't think it could work … I really don't.'

My heart sinks. And then I remind myself to be patient. *Slow down, Uri. Rome wasn't built in a day.* 'Let's leave it in the lap of God,' I offer with a light-hearted grin. To show my disappointment could have damaged my cause.

'That sounds like a wise move,' she says, nodding in agreement.

~

Ghazi, though now over six feet tall, still wasn't quite as tall as Ammam. With his slim and sinewy-but-strong build, his olive complexion, and his shot of black hair loosely tamed into a wavy style, he'd caught the eye of many young women. Ghazi, however, had skilfully avoided any close relationships with women except for Leah, who worked at a bakery close to the workshop.

Whenever Leah spotted Ghazi approaching the shop, she'd do her best to organise her colleague at the counter so that she could serve him herself. They occasionally met after work and wandered around Haifa Port, looking at boats moored in the harbour. Not only was Ghazi physically attractive to Leah, she was strangely drawn to an enigmatic air that he carried naturally. 'You never tell me what you do apart from work,' she complained.

'Nothing much to tell,' Ghazi replied. 'My life is basically boring.'

Leah knew there was a lot more to learn about this energetic mechanic. Sometimes he went away for a few days, but he never divulged where he went or what he did. He kept his cards close to his chest. She loved the way he moved. His actions were quick and decisive. Once they went to a hill overlooking Haifa. She climbed as far as she could, and Ghazi, wanting to reach the summit, scrambled up the remaining distance like an antelope. She knew Ghazi liked her, but it seemed purely platonic. Leah had waited for six months for a sign of greater interest, but nothing was forthcoming. It made him even more attractive, the perfect gentleman. But there was also something mysterious about him—an edge that made her shiver.

~

Six months have passed since I made my declaration to Aalia on Mt Hertzl. Our meetings have been mostly in the company of medical staff in the canteen and friends who see us as 'childhood friends from the north.' Aalia's eyes usually search me out, and she smiles when I return her gaze. There's something in the meeting of our eyes that excites me. My boldness, I believe, hasn't blunted our friendship. My stoic discipline, I believe will bring rewards.

But today I decide to test the waters.

'I feel alive when I'm with you.'

Aalia glances at me with a soft smile, then moves her gaze to the river. 'I search for you at the hospital every day, and I'm so excited whenever I see you,' she says, renewing eye contact.

'Your eyes are beautiful, clear and mysterious, not like the Jordan.'

Aalia laughs and blushes a little. 'You say the sweetest things.'

We're in paradise, a fertile patch of intense green covered by a canopy of trees beside the ancient river Jordan, well-off the beaten track. This is the time I've ached for. To relax with Aalia in cool shade under a cloudless sky as the sun warms the gentle contours of the countryside. My mind is alert, my heart sings, and poetry escapes my lips. 'Your eyes are like the clear sparkling water of Banias Springs, beautiful and invigorating.'

Aalia's complexion colours pink. 'You're so … romantic.' She appears a little embarrassed and deflects my love offering. 'And that beautiful clear water ends up here, looking like this! Have you ever swum in the river?'

'Yes, after a kayaking trip, but further south, closer to the Dead Sea. It's not as bad as it looks. The brown sediment in this part of the country gives it that colour.'

Aalia stares at the gentle flow. It gives me another uninterrupted opportunity to drink her in: the soft contours of her body as she sits serene on the grass-covered bank; her slightly elongated face; her small rounded nose, perfect; lips soft and slightly full, with the faintest touch of lipstick— anything artificial spoils natural beauty. I long to stroke her smooth olive skin and kiss her rose-coloured lips. *I wonder what they taste like?*

'You're looking at me,' she says suddenly with a grin.

'Guilty as accused. I confess.'

Aalia laughs.

'And why shouldn't I?'

'Oh, Uri, you're a hopeless case.' Aalia adjusts her legs.

'Are you comfortable?'

'My leg has gone to sleep. I'm fine—perfect.'

'I have a rug in the car. I'll get it.'

'Okay.'

I move with restrained energy, not wanting to appear too eager. My thinking as I drove the winding track from the main road to our hideaway by the river was to spread it over the grass as soon as we arrived. But then I wondered what she might think. Playing it safe was my best option.

The colourful rug, a present from my parents, provides a thin layer of comfort. We settle side-by-side, and Aalia takes my breath away by throwing back her head and removing her headscarf, carelessly shaking her long dark hair. It falls lightly beyond her shoulders and glistens in the filtered sunlight.

I gasp. I've never seen her hair before. 'You have beautiful hair.'

The moment is life-changing. Back lit by the sun, I find her angelic form and playful smile breathtakingly beautiful and irresistible. Then comes a moment of panic. She's breaking the rules! This is forbidden in her religion.

'What if someone comes?' I say, my voice heavy with concern.

'That's highly unlikely,' she replies in a matter-of-fact tone. 'If anyone does appear, I'll simply put it back on.'

My heart races. Aalia's bold, if not brazen, abandonment of her religious restrictions excites me.

She says, 'I feel so safe with you.' This intimate disclosure comes without a smile, sincere, softly spoken with an intensity that thrills me. It's an invitation, an offering from the heart. Her eyes match her words—they don't leave my face.

I want to say something, but words won't come. So far, I've taken the lead, suggested the outing, selected this place, provided the rug, and she's responded. Now her eyes are searching, longing for *my* response. Her free-flowing hair, her voice, our bodies facing each other have created an intimate space; we've moved beyond the boundaries of good friends.

My mind races, and my breathing accelerates. Here we are, once childhood friends, but our religions and cultures are worlds apart. She's forbidden territory. Untouchable. *But I love her.* She's the one who brings meaning, purpose and joy into my life. She says she loves being with me. *This is the moment I've longed for ... now, she's waiting for me. Be a man! Step up! What are you waiting for?*

The atmosphere is electric. The anticipation in my chest is so intense I can hardly breathe. The smell of her perfume intoxicates me and my head swirls. Our eyes are locked together in a gentle, cautious embrace. The rapid rise and fall of her breasts move in rhythm with my breathing. It's not enough now just to be together. A powerful unseen force pulls me towards her. No longer am I in charge of my body. My hand creeps forward and meets the softness of her touch. The connection is sensuous, beyond my expectation. My heartbeat races as I move my head, ever so slightly forward. Aalia's breathing is rapid. Her face is centimetres away, eyes still transfixed, searching for me. Her rose-coloured lips, slightly parted are irresistible. Our lips meet, gently.

The touch electrifies my body. The taste is moist and sweet. A moment apart, and then our lips meet again, this time hungrily. Aalia responds to the strength of my passion with equal intensity. Her desire astounds me. It feels like she's released an ocean of hidden passion. The dam wall has broken, and it now threatens to overwhelm me. Aalia's long slender hands grip the sides of my face as the length and intensity of our passion produces an ache and wetness in my groin. Our lips release and we both struggle for breath.

'You're so beautiful,' is all I can manage.

'Oh, Uri,' she says breathless.

Aalia nestles her soft face into the crook of my neck. Her heartbeat pulses through my body with erotic energy. Our bodies, folded together, is the stuff of my dreams. We lie together without speaking, listening to the call of the birds, content to bathe in the beauty of young love.

The heat of our bodies and the growing warmth of the day calls for a reprieve. We both move. Aalia sits upright and arcs her back. The soft curve of her breasts and her upturned face to the heavens delights me.

'I could stay here with you forever,' I say. I take her hand and caress the softness.

She smiles and leans down and kisses me playfully on the cheek.

Our bodies are weary from the constant surge of adrenalin and the prolonged arousal of the chemistry the body labels as love.

'What brought about your change of heart?' It felt safe enough now to ask the question.

'Your courage to be yourself, to challenge the taboos, and as time has gone on, I realised how much I love you.'

'Courage or stupidity,' I respond, smiling as I shrug my shoulders.

'Time will tell, but, as you said, if we're both committed … in the long term, our parents, family and communities will respect us.'

'We can be agents of change, and this land needs change,' I say confidently.

'Exactly … oh look, there's a heron and two moorhens.' Aalia points to the mass of oleander bush. Three birds ignore us as they scratch haphazardly in the undergrowth.

The sun reaches the top of its arc, and we reluctantly fold the rug and turn towards my car.

Aalia says, 'Wait a minute.' She reaches down beside the riverbank, breaks off two long reeds, and plaits the two together with the speed and skill of a weaver, then knots each end. 'This is us,' she says, holding the creation in her extended hands.

A warm glow of satisfaction radiates from my chest as I receive her simple, symbolic gift, her declaration of love. She falls into my arms. 'This is all I've dreamed of,' I whisper as our lips unite.

The release from our lingering embrace triggers the question of what I should do with this precious symbol, marking the milestone in our relationship. Do I take it with me or leave it by the bank?

We wind our way back through the willows and jujube trees to the car, leaving the union of reeds to commence an uncertain and slow-moving journey down the Jordan towards the toxic waters of the Dead Sea.

~

Our return to Mt Hertzl has been planned for some weeks. We've decided to keep our relationship secret for the present so as to work out the best way to introduce it to our parents and friends.

'We'll need to be careful where we see each other, won't we?' Aalia says at the end of our walk.

'Yes, but I think we can manage. We can always visit here, and people will think we're patriotic—visiting the graves of our prime ministers and war heroes. Although, it isn't the most romantic place in Jerusalem!' I say with a smile.

'That's for sure.' She chuckles.

I think for a moment. 'There's a place on the rooftop in the Christian Quarter that's safe, not far from the Jaffa Gate. I imagine only the locals living near it would know about it. If you know the route, you can find your way to the Damascus Gate by rooftop. We could arrange to meet there, much more romantic than here—particularly at night. It's only a short trip for you from the hospital by bus.'

Her face lights up. 'That sounds so exciting. When can we meet?'

'I can show you the place now, if you like.'

'Okay.'

'We can drive to the Jaffa Gate, and I'll drop you off and park. If you go through the Gate, you'll find a café, fifty metres on your right. Take a seat there, order a coffee and when I walk past, follow me.'

Twenty minutes later, I pull up beside the Jaffa Gate. Six young soldiers with guns stand in two groups either side of the ancient entrance, observing the colourful flow of human traffic. I watch Aalia join the multi-cultural mass. *This is a good place to meet.*

After parking the car, I stroll through that same imposing gap in the wall and walk the gauntlet of tiny shop fronts, shopkeepers selling jewellery, clothing, food and coffee. The constant babble of voices rises above the narrow street. A middle-aged, bearded man with a wooden trolley pushes a bag of flour down the well-worn cobblestones. The smell of spices and fresh coffee mingles with tobacco smoke. I approach the café where Aalia sits, sipping coffee. She's spots me, and I turn to my left and inspect postcards on a stand outside a gift shop. Aalia pays the café owner, and I continue, with slow steps, down the gentle slope of the street. I glance behind to see if she's following, then make a right turn into the Jewish Quarter, taking time to feign interest in the displays of small shops. I resist the invitations of eager salesmen.

Minutes later after negotiating a twisting laneway, I see stone steps ascending from street level. The first five steps take me to a platform and a second set of ten lead me behind a stone building wrapped in darkness and up to the flat roof. I climb to the top and wait.

Within a minute, Aalia's beaming smile greets me from the top of the stairs. She looks around over a maze of rooftops, dotted with clotheslines. 'I thought you said it would be romantic.' She giggled.

I laugh. 'Wait till you see it at night.' I point to a space near a pile of cartons and add, 'That's the way to the Damascus Gate.'

'We can have fun exploring it at night,' she replies, drawing closer.

'I can't wait,' I say, my heart racing.

~

Late that afternoon in the grey time, the colour of a dove's wing, when there are no shadows, I sit on the balcony of my small room and ponder life. The day is over and night has not yet unfolded her wings, a strange in-between time, when earth seems to listen for wisdom from the sky. Stillness soothes; all sounds an invasion.

Without warning, disturbing questions invade my bliss. My relationship with Aalia is no longer a dream. The fantasy that's lived safely in my mind is now a reality. The raw starkness of it suddenly shakes me. Am I foolish in pursuing what is forbidden? How can I seriously think about following my heart? Is it infatuation? Will my hunger for her last? What would a broken romance do to Aalia? Is it worth the risk? Doubts attack my feelings, but I'm prepared for a fight.

The rising moon silvering the trees breaks the impasse. I picture her sitting beside me, gazing into her large sensitive eyes. Eyes are the windows of the soul, and whenever I look at her, her eyes are bright with a deep inward happiness. Aalia radiates happiness and life. We live in an uncertain land in difficult times. Everyone dies, but not everyone lives. Life is for the taking; now.

Grateful for the wisdom from above, I rest easy in the growing love for the woman who has stolen my heart.

Chapter Nineteen

1984

Every opportunity to observe Aalia in the wards is a gift. My spirits soar when I see her graceful figure breezing along the corridors. Our eyes meet, but there's no sign of recognition. To reveal the power of the emotion binding our hearts together would be premature and could detonate catastrophe. During the winter we choose to meet in a variety of cafés, off main thoroughfares. We feel safer in Old Jerusalem, hidden amongst the masses of tourists, pilgrims and rabbis—always in a hurry. We are careful not to set a pattern that invites questions or comments from proprietors or regular customers. Our contact is frustratingly irregular, at the mercy of the demands of my studies and Aalia's shifts.

I sit opposite her in a rather new café in the Armenian Quarter. Aalia admires my ability to find suitable cafés and locate tables in darkened corners.

'You're so clever, Uri,' she says as we settle into our seats. 'You've done it again!'

I laugh and feel the electric touch of her soft foot brush my lower leg. We've been careful in maintaining the 'no-touch' rule, except for a variety of under-the-table, leg and foot intimacies. The playful stroke of her stockinged leg raises my heart rate. Sitting with her is delicious. Her beautiful presence breathes life into my body. Daily I crave her, and now, to have her all to myself is intoxicating. I lose myself in the swell of emotions.

Two small cups of coffee arrive. The aroma instantly draws us to taste the fresh brew, and with the addition of the sticky baklavas, I'm transported to paradise. We're in our own little world, content, happy and talking about nothing in particular. All that matters is that we're together.

'Now the worst of the cold nights are over, we can venture onto the roof top,' Aalia says with longing in her eyes.

'Do you remember how to get there?' I ask.

She smiled. 'It's burnt into my memory. How could I ever forget?'

I laugh. 'Well, maybe next time we'll try for a rooftop rendezvous.'

Her smile broadens and I marvel at the whiteness of her teeth and the soft curve of her chin. She notices my gaze, blushes, bites her lip and looks down at her coffee. 'Do you think anyone knows?' she asks, taking another sip of coffee.

'About us?'

'Yes. Is there anyone you know who's made any comment?'

'Nobody has said anything,' I reply with a playful shrug.

'May that continue.'

We chat about family and the hospital until Aalia checks her watch. 'I must be off. I need to be back in thirty minutes for my shift.'

I always dread saying goodbye. I gaze into her eyes and drink deeply, filling myself with her in our final moments. Our feet touch under the table and her cheeks blush a little.

'Goodbye, my dear,' she whispers as she slips her feet back into her shoes.

'*Shalom,* my love,' I respond, holding her in my gaze as she walks across the slate floor into the narrow street that leads back to the Jaffa Gate.

~

Ghazi and Abdul had finished their day's work when the sound of approaching footsteps caught their attention.

Ammam appeared at the doorway. '*Salam.*'

'*Salam,* Ammam.'

'Goods arrived?'

'Yes, last week,' Ghazi replied. He'd taken over the role of being the spokesman for the pair.

Abdul didn't appear to mind and took a back seat, pleased at Ghazi's energy and enthusiasm. 'I'll make coffee,' he volunteered, walking towards a small stove in the corner of the workshop.

'We need the door lowered,' Ammam said.

The chains rattled, and the metal door descended, separating the outside world from the trio. The untidy workshop provided a perfect environment for hiding any illegal goods. Old vehicle parts lay around the perimeter of the walls; drums and tyres filled the corners, and an array of tools hung from a greasy pegboard. Ghazi removed rags from the 'batteries' stashed in a corner and placed them on a large solid workbench.

'We're planning a strike soon,' Ammam said, taking a coffee cup from Abdul's outstretched hand. 'Would you be interested?' He glanced at Ghazi.

A knock at the side door, hidden from the road, brought Ammam to his feet. 'That's likely to be Farid and Dharr.'

Abdul left his coffee duties and opened the door slowly. Farid and Dharr entered and the tension suddenly increased.

'Take a seat,' Ammam said coolly.

Farid and Dharr looked around for something suitable and chose two empty drums resting in the corner.

'I was just saying that we're planning a strike soon. The fuses are here.' He gestured at the batteries on the bench. 'Is everyone ready?' Ammam stared at Farid, waiting for a response.

The aroma of coffee couldn't overpower the smell of oil and petrol that hung in the garage. Ghazi was used to it but wondered if it was the cause of Farid's sudden coughing.

'I don't … I don't … think I'm ready … just … ah, just … yet,' he stammered.

'Just as I thought!' Ammam's voice, hard as steel, hit Farid like a sledgehammer. 'If you're not ready now, you'll never be ready. You've no more courage than a woman!' Ammam's smile that had greeted Ghazi minutes ago turned to a vicious ugly scowl. 'I heard you wanted to back out. Your honour is no greater than a pig's! You make me sick.'

Farid whimpered.

'Shut up.' Ammam's voice burned like acid. 'You stink like a camel's fart. You howl like a sick goat. You don't deserve to live here … or anywhere.' Ammam reached into his pocket and slammed a revolver onto the bench.

The air was electric. A single spark could blow the place apart. Ghazi's eyes became like saucers. Nobody moved except Farid. He shook uncontrollably in the shrieking silence.

Ammam's gaze remained fixed on his weapon.

Ghazi broke the silence, speaking with confidence, 'I'm ready for whatever you want.'

The tension eased and Ammam turned his attention onto Ghazi. 'You've the courage of a lion,' he said, his voice measured and controlled.

'Where will it be?' Ghazi asked, feeling proud of his offering and Ammam's approval.

'It'll be either Jaffa or somewhere on the West Bank.'

Ghazi's face lit up. This was his big chance to show everyone what he could do—to prove himself. He felt strong, especially seeing Farid still quivering, avoiding the eyes of others by staring at the greasy floor.

Ammam pocketed the revolver. 'I'll be in touch soon, Ghazi.' He turned to Farid. 'Get out of here. I only want to see you again if you're ready to join your brothers for the fight.'

~

The night is young as I climb up the steps to the rooftop for our rendezvous. Aalia is twenty metres behind me. A large moon lifts itself above the glow of the city, threatened by a bank of heavy cloud. So far we've been successful in maintaining secrecy about our meetings in the cafés in the Old City. It's a strange tension of daring and dread. I sometimes wonder if Aalia was Jewish would I have the same intensity of passion. *Is it simply the attraction of forbidden fruit?* My answer is always, no! Her inner beauty matches her outer beauty. Her presence in the hospital amongst the pain and suffering is a soothing balm. Her smile and words of comfort bring a healing light, overcoming the darkness of patients' despair. I see the glances of males in the wards and know they, too, find her attractive. I'm so fortunate to have her, but the infrequency of our meetings is painfully frustrating. Tonight we can venture to our secret place. Two weeks ago at our first attempt to meet on the rooftop, a violent October thunderstorm prevented us from even leaving the hospital.

I reach the rooftop and look eastward, towards the Mount of Olives. The soft orange lights of the Old City create a perfect setting for our risky liaison. How I've longed for her touch, her gentle caress, the music of her laughter, her playfulness. My heart beats faster as I wait in the shadows. There she is!

'Uri.'

My heart leaps. My angel steps out of the darkness and glides towards me, arms outstretched. Her eyes sparkle and reflect the subdued glow of the city lights. I can't wait to hold her.

She comes up beside me and glances around the open space—an unnecessary distraction; there's nobody here but us. I chastise myself; she needs to feel safe. For a moment, she hesitates. I take her hand. It's soft. How does she manage it with the demands of her work? There's no resistance as I explore the shape of the palm and the length of her slender fingers. Her eyes follow the gentle movements of my hands until she looks into my eyes. I gaze into her soft brown eyes. They search my face, and my chest swells with excitement. These are the eyes I see in my dreams. No words are necessary. I see deep longing—desire—a hunger that brings to life feelings I've never experienced before. Breathless and transfixed, we meet in silence.

Urgency builds, and then I have to say it. 'I love your eyes; I love your lips.' The words tumble out, and I'm breathing heavily. I feel so boyish—a force I can barely control seizes my body.

'After all this time, we're alone,' she whispers and grips my hand tighter as I pull her closer.

We face each other; my body becomes electric. Any hesitation has gone. No embarrassment, no shyness, no biting of her bottom lip. The world around us fades—nothing else matters. Her eyes invite me into her. Her lips, slightly parted, are full and inviting.

'Oh, Uri.' Our lips touch, gently, ever so gently. My chest quivers, and a wave of sheer ecstasy floods my body. Her eyes close, and I'm transported to heaven. I'm alive. My groin throbs with excitement as our lips meet hungrily. Breathless, we rest for a moment. 'You've the most beautiful, delicious lips, my love.'

Aalia smiles, nestles into my shoulder and presses her body even closer. The smell of her hair and the scent of her body are intoxicating. The softness of her breasts on my chest and the rhythm of her heart make me feel that I'm one with her in a special, sacred space. Our bodies, our minds, our spirits, united. Our breathing synchronises as our lips meet in a long, lingering kiss. One of her hands holds me firm around my lower back and the other grips the back of my head as her lips devour me.

Suddenly a loud crash shatters our world. The sound of a truck engine rises between the stone walls of the old buildings beside our 'love space.' It's the garbage truck. I picture the workers feverishly running beside the vehicle, throwing boxes and plastic bags of refuse to the men balanced on top of the truck. The powerful odour of rotting vegetables and food waste hits our senses.

'Very romantic,' I say with a grin.

Aalia laughs and squeezes me tighter. 'I don't care where I am. As long as it's with you, that's all I need.' She unlocks my arms and spins around and leans back into my chest, wrapping my arms around her stomach. She shivers and draws my arms even tighter around her body.

'Are you cold?'

'Just a little, but you'll keep me warm, won't you?'

'Try and stop me,' I reply, nibbling her ear.

The silver moon emerges from behind a curtain of grey cloud. A sword of light cuts through the darkness.

A long period of silence follows as we gaze into the night sky. No words are necessary, for we are both content to bathe in the sheer ecstasy of being together, hidden from the eyes of the world. I move my hands slowly up and down her slender arms, enjoying her response as she thrusts her soft cheek into the crook of my neck.

Half an hour passes, and the moment I dread approaches.

'I'll need to go if I'm not going to break my curfew,' she whispers.

She turns and we embrace again for a long kiss.

'I'll let you know when I can see you again,' she says with a touch of sadness. 'I think of you every day and just before I go to bed. Goodbye my love.'

I wait until I no longer hear her footsteps before I make my descent. The cold air on my chest brings a shiver now Aalia's warmth has gone. Sadness grips my heart as I pick my way along the deserted street. The shutters are down, vendors gone to their homes. Frustration overshadows the joy of our meeting like a storm cloud covering the sun. I can't continue like this. I'll break apart if I can't see her more often. It's exciting arranging our clandestine meetings, but it's also draining. I imagine what a spy must feel like, being on guard twenty-four hours a day, seven days a week, month after month, year after year—exhausting!

The question is how long can I maintain this?

As long as necessary.

~

A month later, I sit opposite Professor David Androski in his cramped office. Two filing cabinets stand beside an open window that overlooks the car park and Jerusalem in the distance. Behind him, four bookcases bear the weight of volumes of medical knowledge distilled from years of study which has helped him gain high recognition in Jewish and Arab communities within Israel and medical academics worldwide. A human skeleton hangs from a support in the opposite corner to the window, and an array of crafted body parts rest on a shelf above the skull.

The professor leans back in his large black-vinyl chair and looks over his rimless glasses. I imagine he's in his late sixties, but he appears much older. Overgrown tuffs of white hair surround a bald patch that's usually covered with a kippah. Age and worry have wrinkled his olive skin. Large puffy bags hang from under his eyes, the result of the rigorous hours he maintains in his care of students and lecturing load. He sits with his hands clasped together, thumbs rotating in opposite directions.

I feel relaxed and comfortable with the old professor. He reminds me a little of Rabbi Yousef—his gentleness, firmness, acceptance of people, and his interest in pursuing peace between Arabs and Jews. Aalia wondered if he'd had a quiet word to the Velcro Sisters who'd been giving her such a hard time. She hasn't made a complaint, but she thought someone on staff might have noticed their abusive behaviour and reported it. Their insults have stopped all of a sudden, but their silent, piercing, hateful looks still find their mark. Aalia is resigned to living with their hatred, and has little to do with them.

'You called for me, Professor?'

'Yes, Uri, I wanted to see how you're finding medicine. You're now in your fifth semester.'

'I enjoy it immensely. I don't have any regrets whatsoever,' I reply.

'That's good to hear. I know students sometimes manage the first year, which can be quite a shock compared to the demands of their schooling, but run out of steam midyear in their second.'

'It's demanding, but I try to keep up to date. I attempt to give my studies priority.'

'What are your hopes for the future? Do you have any special interest yet?' He reaches across his desk and selects a pen from a container of pencils and paraphernalia.

'I rather like neurology.'

'Very demanding, Uri, but you've got the brains and determination to be an excellent neurologist. It's an important area, too, given the brain injuries that are prevalent in Israel and the trauma of survivors of the *Shoah*.'

'Thank you for your confidence in me.'

'There's one matter I want to raise with you, Uri. You may say that it's none of my business, but I believe I've your best interests at heart.'

I catch my breath and wait while he looks out the window and then fixes his gaze on me. What's coming that I might consider 'none of his business'?

'I've noticed the way you look at Aalia when we're doing patient rounds. I'm not sure if she's aware of it, but in my experience, women usually are. Are you interested in Aalia?'

I maintain eye contact and struggle to give an answer. My heart's in my mouth, and I fumble for words. After what seems an eternity, I stutter, 'She's ... ah ... an attractive woman.'

'She is indeed, and an excellent nurse, highly regarded. But as you're fully aware she's an Arab, and while the hospital is open to training Arabs and Jews, or students from any race or religion, you'll find life difficult if you were to pursue Aalia. If the relationship was to get serious, to the point of marriage, it could have serious consequences for your career. Also socially. As you well know, Arab and Jew coexist in Jerusalem and many parts of Israel peacefully, but culturally, intermarriage is forbidden. What's been your experience in the north?'

My mind races. If I become defensive, he'll know there's a relationship. I tell myself to relax. 'In Atak where I grew up, we were fortunate to have, just as you said, peaceful coexistence. Our community was a mixture of Jews, Arabs, and Christians; we were very close—almost family.'

'You're fortunate to have had that upbringing. But do you understand that for a Jew to keep company with an Arab, or to marry, would bring unrest within the families, the community, and the workplace?'

'Yes, I do.'

'Of course you do, Uri. I'm probably overreacting, but I like you, and as I said, you've got great potential. It's men like you we need to help build society. Hassadah Medical Centre will be proud to have you as a doctor when you complete your training. I don't want anything to get in the way of your career. I hope you don't mind me raising the issue?'

'Not at all, sir. I appreciate your concern for me and my career.'

'That's good. I better let you get back to whatever you have on your plate today.'

'Finishing an assignment that's due tomorrow.'

'Thanks for chatting with me, Uri.'

'Thank you for your interest in me, Professor. *Shalom.*'

'*Shalom.*'

I walk into the corridor in a state of confusion. I feel undone. Does he know more than he's letting on about my relationship with Aalia? Has he seen us in one of our café liaisons? Is he being a gentleman in giving me a little 'nudge?' Or is that 'I like looking at her' all he knows? My feet are heavy as I walk to the library and throw the half-written assignment onto a small wooden table. How the hell am I going to concentrate on this? I won't tell Aalia about this—well, not yet.

Chapter Twenty

June 1984

Mid-afternoon in a small café north of Jerusalem, Peter Wiseman opened his briefcase and extracted his cryptic notes. The brief trip from Ramallah, a little further north, had been long and hot. An accident between an army vehicle and a truck had severely disrupted traffic in both directions. Tempers had flared; violent words had been exchanged, and time had dragged on.

A glass of cold water quenched his thirst while he waited for coffee. Three months in Israel had been a steep learning curve. Ever since his graduation from college, a thirst for everything Middle-Eastern had overtaken him. Completion of his studies in journalism and political science, combined with an uncanny ability to relate to people of any race or culture had landed him a position with a major US newspaper, but he found his immersion in this 'dumping ground' of Jewish humanity overwhelming. Close relationships with Jewish friends in the USA had brought him to the Holy Land overflowing with sympathy for the exiles from Europe—a people without a land. Since planting his feet on its soil, the pain of dispossessed Arabs in their communities also disturbed his peace, especially the rage in Ramallah. He felt caught in the middle.

'Your coffee, sir.' The young Jewish waiter placed a cup of strong Arabic coffee on the small table beside his notes.

'*Shukran*.' Peter glanced around the dimly lit café. A small counter containing large glass jars of homemade biscuits and small cakes stood in front of a doorway that bore the sign 'staff only.' Through this door a small plate of salad emerged in the hands of an attractive Jewish woman. The plate was delivered to a neighbouring table where a tired young mother sat nursing a baby while her toddler explored the small cracks in the timber floor. Three businessmen in the corner buried themselves in deep conversation. The eldest of the three, a man of large proportions with a grey-black beard puffed on a cigarette. Two older women dressed in white dresses without headscarves—tourists—laughed as they inspected a camera. At a larger table in the far corner, a group of Jewish students played cards and sipped on fruit juice. The toddler waddled a few steps towards Peter and embraced his left leg. Two large blue eyes gazed up at him.

'She likes men,' the woman said with a smile.

The baby, wrapped in blue, remained asleep, cradled in his mother's arms. Peter was tempted to develop conversation, but chose to remain silent after an intense week, immersed in the depths of Arab anguish in Ramallah. Glad to be out of the sea of human suffering, enjoying a brief respite, he responded with a smile. The toddler staggered back to his mother and looked back at him with a frown. *Such beautiful children, soft, innocent,* he thought. The mother was attractive, too, wearing a blue dress covering her ankles and a colourful headscarf. Peter surmised she was orthodox and a woman of reasonable substance, given the quality of her clothing. He had an eye for attractive females.

Over the years, he pursued an interest in women, but never allowed it to overtake him. His work demanded long hours living out of a suitcase. Readiness to fly to any corner of the globe at a minute's notice, together with his journalistic skills, placed him high on the ladder of respect with his employer. Peter loved his work more than he loved a permanent relationship with a woman. His tall athletic build, blue eyes, and rugged features ensured he was never short of female company.

He glanced down at his empty cup and plate and felt energized. Caffeine and cake had revived his spirits. He pushed back his chair and walked towards the men's toilet in the corner, opposite the entrance to the café, leaving his notes on the table.

A young Palestinian man wearing a blue shirt and faded-blue jeans entered from the street. He casually removed his backpack and placed it carefully under a chair, then inspected the menu board. The waiter took the young man's order, and when the waiter returned to his work area, the young man stood up and calmly walked to the door.

The mother busied herself with her bag as she prepared to leave. She glanced up, saw the young man hurrying across the roadway, and ran to the doorway. 'You've forgotten your backpack,' she called.

The young Palestinian broke into a run.

The mother turned to the backpack and froze with terror. 'No!' she screamed.

The horror of her insight hung in the air; her piercing scream a split-second warning of what was to follow. It was her last word. The violent explosion obliterated the agonising sound that burst from her lungs: a blinding flash; shattering glass; splintering wood; flying body parts; smoke; dust and blood.

Peter was reaching for the door handle when the blast shattered the building. Its force propelled part of a wooden chair across the café, splintering the door and shattering his shoulder. He fell and lay writhing in excruciating pain on floorboards covered with dust and debris, fighting for air in the acrid fumes of gelignite and against the smoke and dust filling his lungs. Blood oozed from a deep wound in his aching head, but the ominous crackle of burning wood registered through the pain. He had to move. He crawled across the café floor, coughing through the haze of smoke, but collapsed, exhausted, and lay among dismembered bodies, shattered tables, and splintered chairs, his gaze transfixed on blood-spattered walls.

The fire coming from the kitchen area behind the counter intensified, and Peter's need for survival overcame his agony. He dragged his throbbing body over shattered glass, leaving a trail of blood on a vile carpet of debris. Groans came from a corner. The fire gathered strength, and he set his eyes to the brightness that once was a doorway. He had to make it to the opening. Human figures appeared—or were they angels? Peter lost consciousness.

~

Aalia adjusted the drip, allowing life-giving plasma to flow into Peter Wiseman's broken body. 'He's the best of the four who've survived,' she commented to a colleague. The curtained area with the usual clinical smells of an emergency ward contained the registrar, two trainee doctors, Aalia, and a junior nurse.

The registrar appeared concerned. 'His blood pressure hasn't stabilized. I'm worried about his blood loss. We need to do a transfusion.' He directed his instructions to Aalia.

She moved with clinical efficiency to the blood bank and quickly selected an A-positive bag. Minutes later, life flowed freely through the cannula into Peter's left wrist.

'He's got a reasonable chance of pulling through,' the registrar observed, 'but we need to keep him sedated.'

The following day, Peter emerged from the clinically induced fog that had helped him manage the violent shock that had almost robbed him of life. Aalia was back on day shift and checked his blood pressure and pulse.

'You've a gentle touch,' he whispered through dry lips.

Aalia smiled and lifted a glass of water with a bent straw to his lips. 'Take a sip.'

Peter took a long draw. The water was cool and luxurious.

'You're lucky to be alive,' she said, returning the glass to the bedside cabinet. 'Someone was watching over you.'

Peter made it clear to friends and his readers that he had no faith in a God. His journalistic career had exposed him to the darkest evil humanity could inflict on itself. This latest event in the café confirmed what he already believed; *No God would allow the innocent to suffer.* He had no strength to protest and lay silent as Aalia wrote notes on his records and slid the folder back into its holder at the foot of his bed.

'We'll take you down for an X-ray later to find out the damage to your shoulder.'

'Thank you for your care. You're an angel,' he whispered.

'Rest now and I'll be back later,' Aalia replied with her trademark smile.

~

Two weeks after the café explosion, Omar sat staring out the open window over the blossoming citrus trees, while Sabah stood in the middle of the living room wringing her hands, 'I know something's wrong.'

He stiffened at the anxiety in his wife's voice, but remained motionless, facing the window.

'I can feel it, Omar. A mother can sense these things.' She remained still, waiting for a response.

He shifted his weight in the chair but continued to stare into the green void. He had no answer to Ghazi's disappearance, but after a long silence, said, 'I don't believe what Abdul said.' He moved his gaze to the empty coffee cup sitting beside him. 'When I spoke to him at the garage, he seemed rather evasive.'

'No. Ghazi wouldn't just up and leave his job and go to another part of the country without telling us.' Sabah shook her head.

'But who knows?' Omar half turned towards his wife. 'He's become more distant and secretive in recent months. Who knows what's going on inside his head?' Frustration crept into Omar's voice.

Sabah moved to stand beside Omar. She leaned forward and wrapped her arms around his shoulders. 'Do you think he's in some sort of trouble?' Her frightened voice resonated with the dread that lay deep within, and her hot tears spilled on to Omar's cheeks.

He clasped her hand. 'I pray to Allah every night for him.'

~

Maya held out an envelope. 'There's a letter for you.'

Abdiel could hear the excitement in her voice. He took it and tore open the envelope. 'It's from Fishel … my friend in Brussels!'

'I know. I saw his name on the back,' Maya confessed with a smile. 'What does he say?'

Abdiel studied the writing and remained silent until he finished reading. 'He saw Daniel in Brussels again, at a train station … can you believe this?'

Dear Abdiel,

I thought you would be interested to know that I saw Daniel yesterday at Brussels Central railway station. We had five minutes to talk before my train was due. He seemed to be in good health and said he is working on a farm in the countryside. He would not tell me where or give me an address. When I said I spoke to you earlier and you wanted to contact him, he reacted rather strangely. He mumbled something about wanting to stay where he was … needed privacy, acted rather weird. I know this must be frustrating for you. He appeared nervous talking about you, though it was only a couple of sentences. He then talked about some incidents in Auschwitz for a few minutes before we parted. He broke off into speaking German for a few sentences, which I didn't understand. It was a strange meeting. I gave him my phone number and address on a card, but he made no promise to write or call. I guess I'll have to wait and see what happens.

If you are ever in Brussels please let me know. We can provide you with a bed for as long as you want to stay. I

Abdiel's face darkened and his eyes moistened as he placed the single page letter onto a pile of papers on his desk.

Maya gave him a worried look but remained silent. She knew he needed time to work through the pain of the latest news.

Abdiel slumped into his favourite chair, leaned forward and buried his head in his rough hands. 'He doesn't want to know me! What have I done?' His words were slow and his voice heavy. 'What do I do? What do I do?'

'Abby, it's hard feeling so helpless. But I'm not sure it's just *you*. By the sound of it it's about *everyone*. He doesn't want to see anybody.'

Abdiel lifted his head from his hands. 'I can't be sure about that.'

'Auschwitz, war, affects people in different ways.' Maya's skill in providing understanding and empathy tempered with reason had helped steady her husband over the years, but Abdiel avoided her gaze.

Whenever he looked into her eyes in a moment of despair, he saw her concern and desire to help. But the thing he feared most was her ability to see into the darkness he kept hidden deep inside.

Maya placed her hands gently on his shoulder and kissed the top of his head. She knew that tonight the demons would return with vengeance.

~

I hurry through the Jaffa Gate, past the familiar group of armed police, appearing disinterested in the rhythm of human flow through the ancient archway. Yet any sound or sight of the unusual will trigger them to full attention, guns at the ready. Separation from Aalia for over a month is killing me. Occasional fleeting glances across crowded corridors were the only moments of connection in our crazy lives. Those brief encounters created a greater longing, adding to the pain.

The sun has sunk behind the Tower of David by the time I emerge onto the rooftop of our secret space, and dusk paints the stone buildings with a soft brush. I drink in the cool air of the evening. Squeals of children playing in a distant lane merge with the harmony of human traffic murmuring from the street below. I hear Aalia's footsteps on the stone staircase and my heart begins to race.

Her eyes light up when she sees me, and she throws herself into my arms, her lips searching for mine. She pulls my head forward, kisses my lips hungrily, and presses her slim body against me. I respond, holding her tight, breathing in the intoxicating fragrance of her perfume. Our lips meet again. She pulls back and gazes deep into my eyes, then leaps up and wraps her legs around my waist. I grip her buttocks. Her kisses become longer and deeper. Her firm breasts press tight against my chest, and my body aches for her. We lose ourselves in each other. Quivering, breathless, we pause. I've never felt more alive, electrified by a powerful primal urge to know her deeply.

'I love you more than you'll ever know,' she whispers.

'You're the most beautiful woman in the world. I want to kiss every part of your body.'

The smile in her eyes brightens. 'My body longs for you, Uri.' Her eyes speak louder than words. Their longing, their intensity, arouses me in a way I've never experienced before.

'I love you, too, and I want to be with you forever,' I whisper.

She continues to embrace my neck but unwraps her legs from my waist, and we stand, content in each other's arms, her head nestled into the nape of my neck. My shirt, moist with perspiration from our passion, clings to my back. 'I don't care what people think. We shouldn't keep our love secret any longer,' I whisper. I'm surprised how easily the words flow. 'I'm tired of how we have to hide our feelings. The secrecy is driving me insane.'

Wrinkles crease her forehead. She moves her arm around my waist. 'What about your career? What will our families say? How will our friends react?'

'I'm at the point of not caring what family or people think. If they love and respect us, they'll want the best for us. When they see how strong our love is, they'll understand. As far as my career goes, I ... we can go to the United States to finish my studies. Last week I saw an application for a scholarship at MedStar Georgetown University Hospital in Washington.'

Aalia remains silent, frowning. 'I've never thought about that option—leaving the country.'

My straightforward comments have taken her off guard.

'Would we get married before we left?' she asks.

'I haven't got the scholarship yet, but Professor Androski reckons I've a good chance of getting it.'

She gasps in surprise. 'You've already talked to him?'

'Yes, I've raised the matter of completing my degree in the US with a view to moving into neurology. As for getting married; why wouldn't we get married before we left?'

'My mind is racing at a million miles an hour.' She releases her arms from my neck and frees herself from my embrace. 'I can't think straight when I'm all wrapped up with you like that.' We release each other and stand apart, facing each other. Then she flings her arms around me and laughs. 'Oh, this is so wonderful, so exciting and so … scary. How about we take time to think about what happens next?'

My heart returns to its normal rhythm. My mind is clearer now. Aalia is right. 'I'll talk to Rabbi Yousef as soon as I can and see what he says. We can trust him.'

'That's an excellent idea. I know he'll be surprised.' She giggles.

I smile and look at the sky. It's now dark and stars sparkle in the heavens. 'Look there's a shooting star.' I point to the southern sky. A blazing stream divides the darkness.

'Oh.' Aalia looks over my shoulder startled.

'What is it?'

'I feel like someone's watching us,' she whispers. Her eyes narrow and she scans the perimeter of the rooftop of our favourite hideaway.

I follow her gaze until we spot two doves perched on the iron railing, metres away, watching us. We both laugh. 'I wonder how long they've been here?' I say.

'I love doves. They're a beautiful bird, so peaceful,' Aalia whispers.

'Lovebirds watching lovebirds,' I reply with a laugh. 'Could this be a sign from above?'

The odour of spicy chicken from a local café indicates the breeze has changed direction. All of a sudden I realise I've not eaten any food for hours. 'I'm hungry. Let's eat.'

'Yes, let's go and celebrate.' Aalia seizes my hand.

Two doves watch two lovers leave their secret place. And a shadowy figure on a rooftop, fifty metres from their love nest, lowers Soviet-made night binoculars, then follows them at a distance, clinging to the shadows.

~

Early November 1984

Professor Androski has called three doctors and me for a conference in his office. He stands beside his desk, fiddling with a pencil while we find a seat in his crowded office.

'What I'm about to tell you must remain secret, top secret,' he says, gaining our full attention. 'The IDF and the CIA are working together to airlift out of Sudan around 8,000 Ethiopian Jews who are under persecution. Hospitals throughout Israel have been asked to provide staff for an initial assessment of the health of these new arrivals. You have been selected as part of the medical team to perform that assessment.'

We glanced at each other, somewhat stunned by this invitation from out of nowhere. 'How long will we be required?' I ask.

The professor takes a sip from a glass of water before replying, 'We're working on a two-week commitment, and then we'll replace you with new staff.'

Silence. Each of us is deep in thought, the pages of our diaries turning over in our heads.

'I know this will be a sacrifice for you. Plans will need to be postponed, but you'll be part of history. Nobody can force you to go. You do have a choice.'

The idea of being part of history is not driving me to accept the invitation, rather the thought of a community who've been persecuted and abused for years. How could I not help? My response comes with little thought. 'Count me in.' The image of Papa sitting behind barbed wire in Poppendorf flashes before me.

The others follow my lead, their faces reflecting their concern, moved by what they imagine the physical and emotional state of the refugees would be like.

'Thank you for your willingness. I'll get back to you tomorrow with details about when you'll be transported to the holding camps. Please, please remember, this is highly confidential. Not a word to anyone.' (Note 1)

Emotions fight each other in my head. I dread telling Aalia that I'll be away from her. Yet the opportunity the professor is giving me is exciting and will be good for my career. I'll talk to Yousef when I return.

~

1. Operation Moses brought approximately 7,800 Ethiopian Jews who had fled the deteriorating political and economic situation in their country to Sudan. They were transported by aircraft from Khartoum to Tel Aviv from 21/11/84 to 5/1/85.

Chapter Twenty-One

January 1985

It ended up being four weeks immersed in the suffering of the Sudanese survivors. A time I would not swap for anything. Their expressions of gratitude were overwhelming.

Now, I sit with my good friend and mentor, Rabbi Yousef, watching his eyes widen as I tell him of my relationship with Aalia. Yousef is one of the most accepting people I know. There's nothing I can ever remember that's thrown him. He's sat with many of the kibbutzniks who've crossed the line in different ways and never appeared shocked. Rabbi Yousef always looked past their transgressions into the eyes of the transgressor and loved them. Powerful. That embrace of his eyes usually brought confession, and then restitution when needed. Everybody loves Yousef in our community, Jew and Arab alike. Yousef and I meet from time to time when he visits Jerusalem. He's involved in teaching students the Torah, but always makes time for a coffee when I'm free.

With a straight face, Yousef says, 'When I said we are to love our neighbour, I didn't really mean this!' The sting of disapproval softened with a touch of humour makes it easier to hear. An awkward silence follows. Yousef's eyes search mine. Intensity creeps into his voice, 'Uri, you've allowed your heart to rule your head.'

His words thump my chest. They're not violent, but an iron fist inside a velvet glove.

I motion with my hands, feeling defensive. 'I've not come to this decision overnight. Aalia and I have kept our secret forever!'

Yousef lets out a long sigh and returns his gaze to the empty coffee cup sitting on the table in front of him. 'You'll make your life difficult, not only for you, but also for your family and Aalia's family. Our communities will be shaken.'

'We know it'll have an effect on our families, our friends, our work, but we're prepared to take the risk. Our families have lived side by side for decades—'

Yousef interrupts. 'Co-existing harmoniously is one thing, but marriage is another!' I hear the exasperation in his voice. 'And who'll perform a ceremony for a Jew and a Muslim?'

I avoid his gaze and look across the almost deserted café. 'Well … er … we wondered if you would be involved. We could find an Imam … combine elements of both traditions, or maybe have two ceremonies.'

The pain on Yousef's face is clear. His eyes lose contact with me and stare at the centre of the small round table that separates us. I stop talking and wait. Finally Yousef raises his head and renews eye contact. The pleading in his gaze intensifies, and disappointment grips my chest. I look away and allow myself to feel the sadness. I was longing for some small hint of hope—at least something like, 'that's a brave move, challenging the taboos.' Maybe I've misjudged Yousef, always accepting of differences, encouraging Jewish and Palestinian communities to accept and work together.

Yousef senses my pain and manages a faint smile. 'Uri, I love you like a son, and don't want you to be destroyed by a bad decision. Are you able to postpone your decision for a little longer?'

His invitation is gentle, but disappointment is overtaking me. I've lost energy and hold back tears. 'Yes, we'll wait,' I mutter in a strained voice, lowering my gaze to focus on the pearl buttons that secure his white shirt.

'I know how you must be feeling. You come to me, overflowing with love for Aalia, seeking my blessing. But I need to be true to what I believe. I need to be honest with you, Uri.' Yousef is torn. He loves me and doesn't want to hurt me but … 'How about we meet again soon?' he offers.

'Sure. Let me know when you're in Jerusalem again.' I embrace him without the usual familiar warmth and seek refuge in the balminess of the fading afternoon sun.

~

It's three o'clock the following afternoon when I spot Aalia, waiting in the shade at the edge of the car park. Her blue hijab catches my eye. A minute later, she's beside me in the car, looking radiant as we accelerate towards Mt Herzl. During the short drive to the parking area beside the National Cemetery, I direct the conversation to her work, and she willingly complies. But as soon as the car door closes, the inevitable question bursts from her lips, 'What did Yousef say?'

We stride towards the path leading down to Ein Karim. I want to ease my way into the subject but have no choice but to jump in the deep end. 'He was shocked and, to put it bluntly, tried to talk me out of continuing the relationship.'

Aalia's reaction wasn't as severe as I thought it might've been. Maybe she sensed his response by my reserve on the phone when we made this date. After taking a deep breath, she says, 'That's sad, disappointing. I really thought he'd be more understanding.'

'Has he ever been in love?' I ask rhetorically. 'I can't remember him ever having a relationship with a woman.'

'He's always given himself to study and teaching. I don't think any woman could survive being married to him.'

'He pointed out all the difficulties we'd face being married—socially, culturally—how it would divide our families.' Sadness and disappointment slow my words.

'I don't care what he thinks.'

The strength of her defiance surprises me.

'Love conquers everything,' she continues. 'Our love is strong enough to overcome any divisions and prejudices of our people.'

I nod. 'You know, I believe that, too.' We're alone on the track where we met the two German hikers. I take her hand, which she welcomes with a gentle squeeze. 'We're not the only ones. I read in the paper recently of a couple in Jaffa who tied the knot. They had a photo on the steps going down to the water from Kaufmann Street.'

'I believe our families and friends, those who love us, will come around. It may take them a little time, but I think Yousef will, too, in time.' Aalia smiles.

'Time. I get so frustrated with keeping everything so secret.' The words fly from my mouth.

'I know, my darling,' Aalia says in a comforting tone. 'I'm tired of holding it in, too. Should we try to arrange a celebrant before we make it public?'

'I believe when our families accept our decision, we'll find someone to officiate. It may take a little while … but we can always get married in the USA.'

Aalia looks at me in disbelief. 'What about our family? What about our friends? That would be awful!'

'If our families never give us their blessing, I don't want them to be present! They wouldn't want to come.' I can't believe what I'm saying. The pain in my chest grows stronger. How could I even think about my parents not being present for my wedding?

We stop walking and remain motionless on the track, reflecting the stuckness we both feel. My arms reach out and draw Aalia towards me, embracing her. She welcomes the warmth of my body and the comfort of my arms. We hold each other for what seems like an eternity, locked in our own world. The road ahead appears too hard, too uncertain, the demands too much. But I choose to enjoy the moment. I love holding her. Her breath caresses my neck and she draws me closer.

'We have each other, and that's all that matters,' she whispers.

~

Ghazi finished his breakfast of meat, boiled egg, and fruit. His first major mission had met with enthusiastic approval from the leaders of the Palestinian Islamic Jihad to which he had become attached—more radical and exciting than the PLO. Ghazi felt alive, strong, and powerful. The devastation he caused in the Israeli café had put the Jews on notice. Arab youth on the West Bank where he now hid were stirred into action. For too long the Muslim Brotherhood had been preoccupied building schools and clinics, which was necessary, but action was now needed against the occupying Jews. The occupation had to cease. The *Qur'an* commanded the expulsion of the invaders. Every day Ghazi talked with other young Palestinians who were ready to fight. They were unarmed, but they were tough and angry.

The Muslim Brotherhood tried to quench the fire in the belly of these angry young men, but the momentum was building. Ghazi repeated the words daily, like a mantra to the frustrated youths he met on the streets, 'We will not stop until the Jews are driven into the sea.'

They were prepared to form groups, set tyres alight, throw rocks at the Israeli soldiers, damage equipment, and undertake any action to pressure the Israelis to leave. Eventually they would have guns. The promise of money for weapons was mesmerising, but Arab nations needed to see the commitment of the fighters. Ghazi wanted to show them.

~

'Uri!'

I swing around and trace the source of the whispered call. Aalia stands smiling at me from the medicine room. It's early evening and she's preparing medications for her patients before they sleep. I look around. Nobody in sight. Only the night-shift are active in the wards. I slip into the room lined with shelves of boxes and bottles, and Aalia closes the door quietly behind me.

She throws her arms around my neck and kisses my lips firmly. I'm surprised by her sudden passion and respond with equal hunger. We've not seen each other for days, and desire overtakes me as I envelop her softness.

'Oh, darling, I've missed you so much,' she gasps.

'There's not a moment goes by when I'm not thinking of you,' I whisper in her ear.

Her hands caress my neck. 'Let me get rid of this stupid stethoscope!' She places the obligatory instrument on a swivel chair and kisses me again. Our lips and bodies are one again.

Suddenly the door opens. Two quizzical eyes peer from a startled face. 'Oh! I'm sorry to interrupt … I … I didn't know anyone was in here.' The face flushes and the door closes.

I stand in shock, holding Aalia, who's rigid, staring at me with opened mouth, frozen to the spot. We stare at each other speechless until Aalia says, 'Do you know who that was?'

'Can't say I do.'

'That's one of the Velcro Sisters. They're the pair who give me grief. This is going to get around the place faster than an outbreak of typhoid.' Horror fills her eyes. 'What're we going to do?'

My mind goes into overdrive. A thousand thoughts race through my head. What will the staff say? Could the hospital kick me out for unprofessional conduct?

Tears stream down Aalia's face. 'I shouldn't … I shouldn't … have pulled you in here,' she stutters guiltily.

'You're not to blame. I didn't say *no* did I?' I let out a long sigh and draw her close. 'Maybe this is for the best; I mean, having it come out. We're thinking about getting married … maybe this will push it along. Mind you, I would've liked to have been in control of who we told and when, but maybe we can still manage that. When can we go back to Atak?'

'I'm free the day after tomorrow,' Aalia replies, wiping away tears. Her rapid heartbeat against my chest tells me her anxiety level is high.

'I'll take the day off, and we'll go to Atak and tell our parents. I don't want them to hear from any other source,' I say gently, as I stroke the curve of her back. 'Let's see what happens. I'm not going to say anything yet.' I reach for my stethoscope.

'I'm scared, Uri. What are people going to say?'

'I believe our love is strong enough to sustain us. We have each other. We're not alone. If we stay focused on our work and ignore any bad comments, just let them drop to the ground, we'll get through. I know we can.' I say it with an air of confidence but suspect I'm trying to convince myself as much as I'm trying to reassure her. It appears to work. She looks up at me with sad eyes and half a smile, and places a quick kiss on my lips. 'We'd better go,' I suggest, releasing my embrace.

'I'm so glad I've got you, Uri. You're so strong. I love you.'

'I love you too, my darling, and we'll find a way through this; I know we will.'

Aalia's beautiful smile returns, and I open the door. The corridor is quiet, but we step back into an uncertain world. What will the future hold? Those minutes in the medicine room may change our lives forever.

The following afternoon, I'm wondering if I'm being paranoid. Am I imagining the quick glances of staff as I pass them in the corridor? I know my sensitivity has skyrocketed. When I enter the crowded lunchroom, conversations appear to cease as I pass by tables. I must stop it. I'll drive myself mad if I keep this up!

I've been granted a day's leave tomorrow without giving any specific details. I wrote 'personal issues' on the form, and my superior didn't question it—maybe he guessed?

It's a long afternoon, waiting for respite from what feels like a thousand eyes piercing my soul. I try to practice what I preached to Aalia—focusing on the patient or the task at hand.

I'm a dismal failure and wonder how my dear Aalia is managing. I hurry from the building at the end of my shift, convinced that 'Little Miss Velcro' has infected the entire staff of Hadassah Hospital.

~

The first hour of our two-hour journey has gone quickly, buoyed by the confidence we've gained from rehearsing our planned conversation with our parents. As the green hills of Amikam appear, however, my anxiety starts to rise. The final kilometres seem never-ending. We follow the road northeast before it swings west again and heads towards the sea. Conversation ceases when we take the exit and wind our way to Atak.

'Looks like they've done the road up,' I comment, trying to appear relaxed.

Aalia nods and fiddles with her hands. We've agreed to visit my parents first. They have no knowledge we're coming, and they'll be surprised to see us. We drive past the potato fields and the citrus orchard, and drop to a lower gear for the final two-hundred metres climb to the cabins and the community centre. The joyous sounds of children singing flow from the schoolroom.

I glance at Aalia as we climb the wooden steps to the deck leading to the community hall. 'Well, here goes.' My voice is more confident than my mind.

'Allah is with us,' Aalia replies with half a smile.

Ima is preparing chicken in the kitchen when she spots me. Her face lights up. She wipes her hands on her white apron and runs toward me. 'What a lovely surprise. It's so good to see you, Uri … and you, Aalia.'

'I wanted to surprise you,' I say, embracing the fullness of Ima with both arms.

'Would you like some coffee and sweet cakes?'

'You know I would.' I laugh.

She slips from my arms, turns toward the kitchen, and looks over her shoulder. 'Your father is in the garage. Why don't you call him?'

Minutes later I enter the large shed where patient men with limited mechanical experience attempt to do the impossible with ageing machinery.

At the sound of my footsteps, Papa looks up from under the hood of a truck. 'Uri! Wait till I clean my hands. What a surprise.' He appears to be in reasonable spirits; that's a relief.

Papa removes the grease from his wrinkled hands with the help of hand degreaser and an old rag. The surprising warmth of his embrace shows his sincerity. I wonder what it'll be like when I leave later?

Ima sets the coffee and sweet cakes at the far end of the table in the community hall, and we seat ourselves around the table that has absorbed conversations from my youth. The workers are busy with their tasks, providing us with welcomed privacy.

'Papa, we're visiting today because we want to let you know about a matter that's very important to us.'

Papa frowns at Ima, then returns his gaze to me.

'This news may surprise you, but please ... please understand it comes after much thought.' My chest is heaving and my heart racing. Papa and Ima fix their eyes on me, and I sit rigid. 'I ... we ... I mean ... Aalia and I have been friends for many years as you know, but our friendship has changed in recent times and we realise … we … we've fallen in love.' I want to continue but my voice has gone.

Papa and Ima remain motionless, just staring in disbelief.

Aalia looks down at her coffee, unable to manage their stunned expression any longer. A long, deafening silence freezes conversation.

Finally I break the agonising awkwardness. 'I know you weren't expecting this. I didn't know any other way of telling you …'

'Did you know anything about this?' Papa turns to Ima, his tone severe. He studies her face, searching for any hint of conspiracy.

She returns his stare and waves her hands. 'I know nothing of it. We both know they've been friends, like brother and sister since they were children.'

'That's true.' Papa clenches his fists in frustration. 'Brother and sister, you are, almost … brother and sister.'

'We were surprised, too, when we discovered we loved each other.' Aalia manages a gentle smile.

Papa has moved past the shock, and frustration overtakes him. 'Do you know what this will mean for your career?' he wheezes, fixing his eyes on me. 'This will cause huge problems wherever you go. And you'll not find a Rabbi to marry you … not in Israel.'

I decide not to mention the 'M' word and remove any thoughts about having the ceremony in America. *This would be enough for today.*

'We love you both; we really do,' Ima says. 'But you know this is such a shock. It'll be difficult for both our families here, and our communities. I don't know what they'll say.' Tears flow down her face and her pleading voice stabs my heart.

I take a deep breath. 'I know what they'll say. There shouldn't be inter-marriage between Arab and Jew. We can be friends and live together in community harmoniously as we have done in Atak and Jerusalem, but marriage is forbidden. We want to challenge that rule. The world is changing; our country is changing, and we need to challenge some of these so-called prohibited restrictions we've invented.'

'Invented! Uri, have you forgotten the Torah?' Anger creeps into Papa's voice. 'The law about marrying a Gentile is not a human invention; it's from God!' His fist slams the table, rattling cups with coffee still untouched. Papa sits back on his chair, believing that he's made his point and there's nothing more to discuss.

I'm not going to engage him in theological argument. My anger rises, and I try to breathe slowly. Hypocrite! How can he play the Torah card when he's so hot and cold about his faith? Aalia has lowered her eyes and is staring blankly at the table, avoiding engaging with Papa or Ima.

I choose my words carefully. 'I love you both, and I include Aalia, also. *We* would never do anything to intentionally hurt you. I can tell you our love for each other is real. We believe it's strong enough to overcome the challenges ahead. You and the kibbutz have taken good care of me since childhood, and I love and thank you for that. Now I'm a man, and you must trust me to make my own decisions. Aalia and I are responsible for our decisions.' Strength increases as my words flow, frustration empowering my resolve.

I continue, 'Yes, there're traditions which we keep that are helpful for our culture. There're, well … traditions … laws, which were helpful in the past, but in this new age, they need to be revised. If two peoples, Jew and Arab can live together harmoniously, as we have done, surely they can marry. If we're to develop a secure future here in Israel, we need to rethink some of these old prohibitions. There needs to be more flexibility.'

Papa has gone to a dark place somewhere inside him. His face is a mask of despair. To continue pressing my case will not advance our cause. Ima's hands fidget as she glances at Papa. Lingering will only continue the discomfort. 'Maybe it's best if we leave; it'll give you time to think,' I say.

Papa remains motionless, his eyes now defocussed in a trance-like state.

'Won't you stay for lunch?' asks Ima with a weak smile.

'Thanks but we need to call on Aalia's parents, too.' My words shake her and her tears well up. I feel for her. What have I done? Sadness takes hold of me. I know Ima thinks she could lose me. If Papa cuts me off, she'll have to also distance herself from me, and that will tear her apart. I need to move, now before I'm plunged into grief. I stand and take a deep breath. 'Thanks for the coffee and cakes, Ima. I'll be in touch soon. I'm sorry we have to keep moving.'

Ima embraces me with a desperate hug and repeats her emotional embrace with Aalia. 'No matter what happens, know we love you,' she says, tears returning to her red eyes.

Papa is still in a trance. Awkwardness stands between us. He's standing but not moving towards me. I'm determined to embrace him as we've sometimes done, so I step a pace forward and slowly take hold of his body. It's lifeless; arms hang loosely by his side. 'I love you, Papa. I'll be in touch soon.'

His mouth doesn't move, and a nod of his head is his only response as we move to the door of the community hall.

Chapter Twenty-Two

Omar gasps when I confess my love for Aalia to him and Sabah. Blood drains from his face and he sits in stunned silence for over a minute before he utters, 'You're crazy!'

I'm not sure who he's speaking to—Aalia or myself, or both of us. He's looking at Aalia, but I'm sure I'm included.

Tears spill from Sabah's eyes, and she runs from the room.

'You know it's forbidden for a Muslim woman to marry outside her religion. I cannot permit this, Uri. How will your parents react?' Omar's head shakes vigorously, and he throws his hands in the air in despair.

'They were surprised …'

'Surprised? They would've been shocked!' Omar springs from his chair and paces the floor, wringing his hands. 'Uri, I implore you, do not pursue Aalia. It will lead to disaster. Can you imagine what the community will say when they find out? This is unthinkable.'

I swallow hard and keep breathing deeply. Omar and Sabah are like family. It distresses me to see the fear in his eyes, his writhing hands, and his sandals pounding to and fro across the floor. He stops when I speak again.

'I know you're distressed, and it hurts me to see you like this. It wasn't our intention to hurt anyone, especially you. We couldn't help falling in love. I know our religions have their traditions, but times are changing, the world is changing—'

'Some things are not to be changed!' Omar slams his fist into an open hand.

My sense is to let the dust settle. Omar and Sabah need time to recover from the shock. To press the conversation further would be like pushing against a brick wall.

Aalia's hands had fidgeted nervously during our brief encounter. Now she stands, and for a moment, I think she's going to give her father a hug, but she just shrugs her shoulders and says gently, 'I love you father, but I love Uri, too.'

An awkward silence follows until Sabah returns and seats herself at the table. 'Let's finish lunch, and we can talk about this another time,' she says, staring at Omar.

Omar remains silent while Sabah steers conversation to local happenings within the community. The tension hanging heavily in the room reduces our appetites, and soon we leave a tearful Sabah and an angry Omar, who froze when Aalia attempted a hug.

Heaviness slows our return journey to Jerusalem. Aalia blinks away tears as she reflects on our morning of trauma. 'Do you think father will renounce me as his daughter?' she asks, her voice quivering.

'If he made a decision now, maybe yes. But given time and your mother's soothing, I believe he'll accept us.'

Sadness fills Aalia's eyes. 'It'll be horrible, waiting. I don't know how I'll manage?'

'We have each other, and any of our friends who are true friends will support us.' I try to sound confident. 'I need to talk to Rabbi Yousef again. He's had some time now to think about our situation.'

'Can I be with you when you talk to him?'

'Certainly, my love.'

By the time we finally reach the outskirts of the new city, I feel like I'm running on empty. The events of the week were enough to drain me, but the trauma of today has removed any remnants of energy.

~

Professor David Androski sits observing me in his office. Nothing appears to have changed. The familiar mountain of files scattered at one end of his huge desk; the friendly skeleton near the window, his faithful silent companion.

'Looks like I was right, Uri,' he says, looking over his rimless glasses. 'I can't say I'm surprised.'

Energy drains from my body as he leads into a conversation I knew had to take place. 'Yes, Professor, we've been seeing each other for some time. We told our parents yesterday.'

'I can only imagine how they reacted.'

'Yes, it was a shock, but I hope they'll mellow over time.'

The professor shifts his gaze to his two thumbs, circling each other on his lap, and frowns. 'I hope for your sake they do. Are you planning marriage?'

'Yes, we are. It's something we'll talk about soon, but we're taking one step at a time,' I reply, recovering my confidence.

'My concern is what happens in the hospital. Of course you're free to do whatever you wish in your own time, but your relationship will ... already is, having an impact on staff. There're some who will happily work with you; some will shun you. We've not had a precedent of this kind in the hospital. If it becomes disruptive, you may need to go to another facility.

As you're aware, the climate is volatile with what's going on in Gaza and the West Bank.'

'I understand the heightened sensitivity at present, and if I have to go—well, I'll go. I'd like to think that we have intelligent, well-educated people here who'll respect our decision. I'm hoping our example will count for something.'

The professor smiled. 'You're either crazy or courageous to think you can be a change-agent on such an explosive issue!' Sympathy touched his smile more than humour.

'I have to be honest with you, Uri. There's a member on the hospital board who'll want you out of the place. I know what he'll say when he finds out. I'll argue as best I can and try to persuade other members to be tolerant.' He moves his arms onto the armrests of his chair. 'One thing in your favour is your excellent academic record and your strong work ethic. The board would not want to lose someone of your calibre. I guess we'll have to see what happens.'

He fiddles with a pencil, continually rotating the pointed end in slow motion, for what seems an eternity. I sense it mirrors his mind. What is he thinking?

'I want to be honest with you, Uri,' he continues eventually. 'I care for you, and I know I need to respect your choice, but it's important for me to say that I've real concerns about your future if you pursue your relationship with Aalia. It'll bring limitations to your professional development in Israel. I'm sure you're aware of how life will become increasingly difficult for you. Not just with both your families, but socially. If you married Aalia, your children will also face the ire and hostility of both communities.'

Now I fiddle. The sudden turn in the direction of the conversation surprises me. 'Yes, I know it's a huge decision. We're not taking it lightly.'

The professor fixes his eyes more intently on me. 'I want to assure you, Uri, that I have your best interests at heart. I don't want to sound like a father; rather I'd like you to see me as your mentor. You have a good mind; you're an excellent student who has the potential to go a long way in medicine.' He pauses. 'I wonder what's driving your pursuit of Aalia? Yes, she's an attractive woman with beautiful manner, but the cost? Love is a decision. If we allow our body chemistry to override our brain, it can bring dire consequences.' He shakes his head. 'I don't understand you. What drives you so ferociously to cross the cultural and religious lines?'

'With respect, to be frank, I don't see the lines as sharply as you do. I grew up with her and her family. I've lived in a community where there's respect and acceptance of cultural and religious differences. In fact we often join together to share in each other's festivals.'

'I understand that and applaud your communities for what's been achieved there, but in Jerusalem, as you know, it's different, and you're becoming a public figure. Your profile will be raised as your career develops.'

I remain silent. I'm saddened by the professor's attitude and persistence. His genuineness and care are evident, but he just doesn't understand.

He clears his throat and says, 'May I speak even more plainly?'

'Most certainly.' I brace myself for whatever's coming, my anxiety rising.

'I could be wrong, and forgive me if I am. I'm no psychiatrist, but I've a hunch there's a battle going on inside you. I don't know who it's with, and you may not know either.'

His words hit me like a sledgehammer. 'I'm not sure what to say.'

'Who are you angry at?'

My first response is to slam the door shut on his words. How could he make that accusation? But his gentle, firm tone and pleading eyes neutralise my flash of anger. 'I'm not aware of being angry with anyone … I get annoyed with my father from time to time … well … for most of my childhood, he's been distant. But on the other hand, I want to care for him. He needs help.'

'And he refuses help?'

'Yes; it's so frustrating!'

'And he doesn't like your relationship with Aalia?'

'No, he's not at all happy. Ima, I think, is more accepting. They arranged a *Shadchen* some time ago, but I didn't want a bar of it.'

'Could it be that your decision in pursuing Aalia is also a statement? A statement of defiance to your father?'

I'm lost for words. My mind is blank. After a deep breath I stutter, 'I'm … I'm not sure … I've never thought of it that way.'

'We all have our blind-spots, and as I said, I could be wrong, but it's worth thinking about.'

'Thank you,' I say weakly. 'I respect you and appreciate your concern for me.'

'You're one of my top students, and I like you. I want the best for you and want to be sure that you know what you're doing. Are you okay to finish now?'

'Yes, I'm fine,' I reply without conviction. 'You've given me something to think about.'

'I'm happy to chat any time, so don't hold back,' he says, signalling the end of our conversation.

'Thanks for your honesty and support. I'll do my best to continue to serve the hospital. I'm grateful to be in such a rich environment and for the support of mentors like yourself.' Bruised, but not broken, I take my leave.

The day unfolds better than I expected. No outbursts of vitriol, no hints of savage silence amongst colleagues. Maybe they don't know? I leave the hospital in the late afternoon at the end of my shift, thinking I'd mistakenly feared the worst.

My phone rings as I open the door to my accommodation.

It's Aalia. She struggles to speak through great heaving sobs. 'Uri … I need … I need to talk.'

'I'll come now,' I reply, turning back to the open door.

I find Aalia standing on the footpath, arms folded, eager for my arrival. I stop, and she bundles herself onto the front seat. 'Drive, Uri, drive.'

I accelerate up the hill and look for a place to talk. Dark bags have formed under her red eyes, telling me she's been distressed for some time. An unsealed side road appears on the eastern slopes of the hill, and minutes later we sit, facing each other.

'I've had a terrible day,' she sobs. 'It feels like a thousand eyes are watching me. The Velcro Sisters were vile.'

'It sounds as though you've had a day in hell.'

'It's been horrible, and I don't know if I can go back.'

The distress on her face pains me. I feel it in my stomach.

'They said—those vile bitches—"Get out of the hospital. You're ruining his career. You have no right to seduce him. You're nothing … nothing … nothing but a whore!"' Aalia crumples, shaking violently. Her sobs erupt from a depth I've never witnessed before, with anyone.

I lean forward and hold her. Five minutes pass, and she continues to weep, despite my efforts to soothe her. How can there be any tears left? I feel so helpless. What can I do? What can I say? Guilt creeps into my mind. My day has been better than I ever expected. Why should they take it out on her? This is so unfair.

Aalia takes a deep breath and raises her head. Salty tears saturate her face. The sides of her hijab are soaked, as is the left shoulder of my shirt. She turns her head and looks through the dirty windscreen towards Jerusalem, now backlit by the setting sun.

'Isn't it beautiful,' she whispers. 'Just look at those golden rays beaming down.'

Again, I don't know what to say. She needs a breather.

'It's a beautiful city, so much joy, but it also hides so much pain.' Aalia wipes her tears. 'What am I going to do? I'm not sure I can go on if they keep this up.'

My stomach tightens as I think about what might happen if she reports the abuse to her superior. If this filters through to the board and to whoever this character is, it's fuel for removing me from the staff.

The sound of a door closing grabs my attention. I turn and look through the rear window to find an army jeep parked three metres behind and three young soldiers walking towards us.

The older of the three, a sergeant, beckons me to lower the window. 'Excuse me, sir, your identification please.'

While I fumble for my wallet, he peers inside and sees Aalia, staring wide-eyed at him. I imagine the question forming in his head: What is this Jewish man doing with this red-eyed Arab woman on an unsealed side-road hidden from the main road by the trees?

The sergeant studies my identity card. His two sidekicks stand behind him, rifles at the ready. He returns my card, then glances at Aalia. 'The same for you, please.' After returning her identity card, he rests his hand on the roof of the car, and appearing more relaxed, asks, 'What are you doing here?'

'We needed somewhere to talk privately,' I answer, staring into his dark eyes.

He maintains eye contact. 'Sorry for disturbing you, but we're keeping a close eye on the area.'

'I understand, sergeant. You need to do your job, and we're grateful for your diligence.'

He smiles. 'Take care. *Shalom.*' The three return to their vehicle.

Aalia is more settled now, in spite of the unwelcomed intrusion. 'You're so wonderful. I feel safe with you,' she says with a smile. 'I love it when you hold me. I really needed that.'

Her hand is soft in my grasp. 'I don't know what to do,' I say. 'Do you think reporting them will make a difference?'

'I wish I could just let their venom run off my back,' she replies with a sigh.

I'm angry at these bitches. 'Can you put on some invisible body armour? Can you see them as shallow, pathetic, miserable, human beings who can only find joy in life by abusing other people? *They* have a real problem.'

'I'm going to try selective deafness. I know I'm giving them what they want if they see me upset. I'm not going to give in to them!' The determination in her voice convinces me she's chosen to switch sadness into strength. But will she be able to do it?

'Allah will help me,' she adds.

She offers her lips and I respond with passion. They are salty but so sweet. 'I love you so much,' I whisper.

'I love you, Uri, and I'll love you forever. Nothing will ever separate us, nothing,' she says, stroking my hair.

~

A week later Rabbi Yousef eyes me with interest as he peers over his rimless glasses. 'It's a cold day. The temperature is hovering around ten degrees,' he says, rubbing his hands together. 'How are you?'

'I'm managing—only just. Aalia's the one I'm concerned about. She's had a rough start after the word got out in the hospital, but she's weathering it as best she can. Most of the staff appear to accept her, knowing we're an item. At least, they're not openly offensive. Two Jewish nurses are the offending flies in the ointment.'

'How about the hospital hierarchy?'

'So far, so good. The old professor is sympathetic ... well, in a kind of a way. I guess it's a matter of wait and see. How are things at home?'

Yousef glances away and studies two old Jewish men playing chess in the corner of the café. He's thinking carefully before he answers. 'I'm saddened to tell you this, Uri, but all is not well at Atak. After you left, your father and Ima went to see Aalia's folk. Omar blamed you for pursuing his daughter without his knowledge or consent. Your Papa jumped to your defence and said it wasn't a matter of one "chasing" another. Words were exchanged … they were still in shock. They needed time to settle down. Their brains weren't functioning.'

'Oh no …' I sighed. 'How's Ima?'

'She cries a lot. So does Sabah. Your folks have kept their distance from them ever since. Your Papa is struggling—blaming himself …'

'Blaming himself?'

'He believes he's failed as a father. Your Ima and Papa are struggling with each other.'

Stunned, I sit in silence. Our parents after decades of harmony are now divided! My father will retreat into himself and become even more depressed!

'I pray for you and your family every day, Uri. It's been a shock for them. They're traumatised, and I pray as time goes on they'll be more accepting.' Yousef's voice softens as he sees the distress on my face.

I knew consequences would result from the discovery of my relationship with Aalia, but now, as it's happening, it's so distressing to know my parents are suffering and there's conflict between them, and Aalia's folks.

Yousef turns to greet a Westerner who has entered the café, '*Shalom* Peter, good to see you.'

'*Shalom*, Yousef.'

Yousef says to me, 'I met Peter at the university some months ago. He was in Hadassah Hospital with horrible injuries after a terrible explosion near Ramallah. This is my good friend Uri, who is a doctor at the hospital.'

I offer my hand, to which Peter responds with a welcoming handshake. He frowns and is about to say something and then stops. It's an awkward moment. I break the tension. 'I saw you in emergency, Peter, when you were first admitted after that terrible attack.'

He nods. 'Yes, I remember you. The staff were amazing, especially a nurse by the name of Aalia. She was so caring, so attentive.'

'We have an excellent team. It's a privilege to be part of the place,' I reply with little enthusiasm, hoping he'll move on, knowing my time with Yousef is limited.

'I don't want to interrupt your conversation, but good to meet you, doctor. Hope to see you soon, Yousef. *Kol Tuv.*'

'Very good, Peter,' Yousef says. '*Kol Tuv.*'

Peter heads for a corner table, and Yousef returns his gaze to my face. 'Interesting man, Peter—an American journalist.'

I decide not to comment on Peter Wiseman. My mind is wrestling with what he was going to say before he stopped himself? Does he know about Aalia and me? I decide not to distract myself but focus on my conversation with Yousef. I fidget with a napkin and say, 'I feel so sad to hear of the fallout with our parents.'

'Predictable, wasn't it?'

'Yes, but now, when it's happened, it's very hard to bear.' I sigh.

'I'll keep in touch with them, Uri.'

'I wish Papa would get some help with his depression. I'm concerned that one day he might decide to end it all. I hope this stuff won't push him over the edge.'

'You're right to be concerned. I've tried to encourage him many times to get help. But … you can lead a horse to water …' Yousef shrugs, opens his hands and looks at me helplessly. 'I'll keep my eye on your Papa, but he's so stubborn!'

'I'm so grateful for your care of him and Ima, and myself. I appreciate you listening to me. I know you can't tell me what to do, but you understand me.'

I head back to the hospital and find emergency wall to wall with bloodied bodies. The fighting on the West Bank has blown out again, and I walk into a sea of suffering. When will this carnage cease? The afternoon explodes with more victims, bodies burnt from Molotov cocktails, bruised and broken from truncheons.

When the evening arrives, I retreat to the cafeteria, exhausted. I'm so tired I've lost my appetite but force down a sandwich, and with a welcome coffee, temporarily revive my failing spirits. The clock on the cafeteria wall reminds me of my duties, but I need more time before I face the masses again.

Suddenly a nurse is at my side. She is shocked and breathless. 'Doctor, you need to come to emergency.'

Frustration rises. Why can't I have a few minutes to myself? I'm not superman! 'I'll be there in a few minutes,' I snap in annoyance.

'Please doctor. It's not good news for you. You need to come now,' she persists.

Not good news for me? What does she mean? Her distress is obvious. She blinks back tears, pleading with her eyes. I hesitate, trying to make sense of it. My body feels like lead, my mind is racing.

'Doctor, it's … it's … Aalia,' she gasps. Tears flow as she walks towards the door. She stops and turns her head, imploring me to follow.

A tight knot forms in my stomach. I'm on my feet, but my legs won't respond. What's happened?

The nurse waits as my mind urges my feet into action. 'Come … come,' she repeats through tears.

My heart races and my mind's a blur as I hurry in her footsteps to the all-too-familiar space, overflowing with human misery. My guide leads me to a bay with closed curtains. I enter. Four of my colleagues are bending over a motionless body. Life is flowing into the body from a drip. I can't see the face. There's blood, too much blood! The bloodied face, half hidden by the oxygen mask is difficult to identify. A blood-soaked bandage covers the head. Eyes are closed. Is this Aalia? I can't tell.

'She's been hit by a car, Uri. She's in a bad way,' says Ben, one of my good friends and an excellent doctor. 'We'll take care of her. She needs to go into an induced coma. So sorry, Uri.'

I stare in disbelief. Her name is written above her head, but it can't be her! Not my darling, my beautiful Aalia. They must have it wrong. The monitor shows an irregular heart beat and low blood pressure.

The blood transfusion is complete, and the nurse removes the tube from the cannula. I catch sight of the hand, and a ring. A sapphire ring! I gasp as I see the near-lifeless hand unveiled by the sheet, bearing testimony that this body is my beloved. My heart sinks. I want to touch her, hold her, but the team surrounds her. It's not appropriate! How many times in the past have I turned distressed families away from touching their loved ones when medical procedures must take priority? I want to stay, but I need to go.

Chapter Twenty-Three

My office is my refuge. Head buried in my hands, all I can do is pray. I only pray when I'm in a crisis, and that leaves me feeling guilty. 'God,' I mumble, 'I want to do a deal. Save Aalia and I'll do anything you want. Anything!'

Half an hour has passed since I retreated from the horror of those first moments. I must go back. Cold water from the tap in the bathroom injects a small measure of life into my exhausted body. The mirror reveals fatigue in my bloodshot eyes.

Staff have made space for her in intensive care. Zena, who heads the IC team nods at me when I arrive, and I move to Aalia's side and gaze at my beloved. Her hand is soft, as white as a sheet. I caress it with gentle strokes. Her blood pressure is still low, and the oxygen flow has been increased. Blood smears remain on her face; bandages cover her arms and legs. *Fight on my darling, fight on.* The rest of the world is now a million miles away. I'm deaf to the cries from the distant cubicles in emergency. My Aalia is my only concern. *I'm fighting with you my darling. Don't give up. You can make it.*

The staff have done all they can. It's now up to Aalia. I stand beside her as long as I can, but exhaustion overtakes me. I lean forward and whisper, 'I love you,' and kiss her gently on the forehead. I back away from my sweetheart, allowing my eyes to take in her brave struggle for life until I am outside the partition.

'Uri, she's a fighter,' Zena says in a soothing and empathic voice. 'But her liver, kidneys, spleen, and stomach have been badly crushed. It's not looking good. I'm so sorry.' Zena is perfect for IC: calm, coolheaded, professional.

I don't want to know any more detail. All I want is for my darling to live. 'Thank you, Zena. I know you, and everyone, are doing their best.'

I wander, dazed, past the hospital busyness and hide in my office. I collapse into my chair, wondering if this is simply a terrible nightmare. It doesn't seem real. My body is numb. I want to cry, but no tears come. I stare at the spines of medical textbooks on a shelf beside my desk, and they become a blur. My head is heavy and I fall forward onto my desk.

When I wake, I've no idea how long I've dozed. My head aches, my neck aches, my body aches. I retrace my steps to emergency. The area is quieter.

'No change, Uri.' Zena's words are a comfort but no comfort. *At least she's no worse.* I stand beside her slender body watching the rise and fall of her chest, the hypnotic hiss of the oxygen the only sound as my darling continues her battle. I let go of Aalia's hand, and my mind switches to the accident. I'm shocked to think that I've no knowledge of where or what the circumstances were.

'I believe she was hit in Derech Shechem St—runs down to the Damascus Gate. Looks like a hit and run,' Zena says.

'A hit and run!' I spit the words out, my anger flaring. Fortunately exhaustion robs me of the luxury of maintaining the rage in this sacred space where life hangs by a thread. And this is no place to show it.

'The family have been informed and they intend to come down from the north tonight,' Zena adds.

I creep out of emergency to taste the night air. It's 2.30 a.m. and a cloudless winter's night allows cold to grip the city. A slight breeze sends a shudder down my spine; I wrap my jacket tighter. The sudden burst of icy air encourages movement, and five minutes later, I'm standing at the top of the car park, the lights of Jerusalem flickering like specks of gold in the distance. It's obscene: people are in their beds, sleeping while my precious love fights for life. Life is so unfair. I'm now half-frozen and my breath is visible in large clouds of ghostly white. I turn my gaze to the starry heavens and lose myself in their expanse.

'If you are watching, God, hear me. Hear my prayer. Don't let my Aalia die.'

The brief, frozen respite from my bedside vigil calls for coffee. The welcome caffeine warms my core and I glance at a newspaper, which I soon discard—it's too hard to focus. I need to return to Aalia.

Emergency is strangely quiet, given the volume of patients in the area. Zena's eyes are filled with sorrow. She shakes her head and sighs. Aalia's face is pasty white; her heartbeat weak. I stand beside her and touch her forehead—cool. Tears well up as I take her limp hand and caress it gently. *She's losing the fight.* Minutes tick by while I tenderly hold her hand.

An agonising hour passes. Zena has broken the rules and brought me a small stool. My head, heavy with fatigue, rests on the white sheets beside the almost lifeless body of my darling. Her hand is now cold. How long will she last? The minutes tick on. I lift my head from the sheet, face wet with tears. Her face has turned from white to grey. My hands tremble. Surely there's something I can do.

'Fight on, my darling,' I whisper. 'Don't give up. I'm here. You can do it. Stay with me.' I massage her hand gently, frantic to fight the ever increasing cold with my warmth. Long cold fingers of desperation grip my stomach. It's no use. I angle my body over her and hold her face with shaking hands. 'Take my heat, my energy, my strength; you can do it.'

Minutes pass. The coolness of her body chills my chest. I stare at the heart monitor, waiting, dreading … then … the line goes flat. My body refuses to move. I kiss her tenderly on the forehead, my tears covering her face. 'I'll always love you … always.' My eyes search her face, now deep grey, without life. Death cannot hide her beauty. I strain to absorb every detail of the face of the woman that was my reason to live. The shape of her eyebrows, the contour of her small nose, her lips—those lips, so sweet.

I remember the first time we kissed: the touch, the taste, sheer excitement, and joy as our bodies embraced. I hear her laughter as we run through the trees beside the Jordan and swim in the cool clear water of Banias Springs. Images of walking on Mt Scopus, listening to her chat about her day, flash before my eyes; sipping wine on my balcony as the sun sets over Jerusalem; passionate embraces on our rooftop hideaway; dreams of marriage, of going to America.

I sit stunned, broken, overwhelmed with grief. Angelic Zena sweeps past me and turns off the oxygen and the monitor. I feel her hand on my shoulder, then she leaves me in silence to say a final farewell to my beautiful Aalia.

Later—I don't know how much time has passed—a hand touches my shoulder.

A young nurse says, 'Doctor, Aalia's family is here. I didn't know whether to disturb you or not.'

I look up and see I'm in my office. I don't remember walking here, but obviously I did. Blinking at the messenger in white, I say, 'Thank you, nurse.'

Omar and Sabah sit in the private room set aside for visitors. They're seated together on a lounge. Aalia's younger brothers, Ibrahim and Khalil, occupy two plastic chairs beside them. Omar's brother, Ishmael, and Sabah's sister, Sophia, are preparing cups of coffee from an urn sitting on a table by the window.

How will they receive me? My heart is heavy as I step forward.

Omar stands and extends his hand. He's shaking. Ever since childhood, a warm embrace signified the depth of our relationship, but now both his unsteady hands envelop mine in an act of genuine warmth. 'I can't believe it, Uri? My darling daughter ...' Tears fill his eyes.

Sabah pulls my hand towards her, gripping it with both hands. She releases her grip and throws her arms around my shoulders. 'My Aalia, my dear Aalia,' she wails.

I hold her while she sobs uncontrollably, her tears saturating my shirt. When the tears subside I kiss her hands tenderly.

Her question comes, mingled with grief. 'Why? Why?'

I learn of Omar's car accident; it happened an hour earlier as they drove from Atak after hearing of Aalia's accident. Fortunately, no one was injured, but the car hit a post and required emergency repairs before they could resume their journey.

Dawn breaks. Omar makes a phone call to the Imam in Haifa who'll conduct the ceremony. Heaviness hangs over the room as each individual commences their journey of grief.

~

I stop twice on the drive to Atak to release tears. Two of Aalia's friends from the hospital wanted to drive me, but I prefer to be alone—alone in my grief. I know I shouldn't be driving, due to my exhaustion, but I make it.

The burial tradition flows with great emotion through the afternoon: the washing and braiding of the hair; the ceremonial washing of the body; the inexpensive white sheet wrapping the body and tied with ropes; the prayers at the mosque. Members of the Atak community are present for the burial: Christian, Jew and Arab—both men and women. Usually only men attend a burial, but this community is all embracing. Now forty days of mourning have begun.

As I leave the cemetery and farewell the broken figures of Omar and Sabah, I catch a glimpse of a figure peering from behind a distant tree.

Back at kibbutz, Ima fusses around me, and Papa does his best to be buoyant. No signs of the strain of our last departure remain. It's as though nothing has happened. Ima is full of warmth, and Papa even manages a hug.

'I'm so sad to hear about this dreadful accident,' he says. 'It feels like I've lost a daughter …' His face flushes, his expression awkward, and he changes the subject. 'I hope they find the person responsible.'

I clench my fist and feel the blood rush to my face. 'I'd like to get my hands on whoever it is.'

We have a light meal together before I move to my bed in the bunkhouse. It feels like I've not slept for a week.

The next morning, I mope around the kibbutz. Ima makes a meal for Omar and Sabah and walks down the road with Papa to deliver it. The kibbutzniks are in full swing, repairing machinery, pruning, and painting. Yesterday my tears burst without warning. Today I'm numb. I felt awkward amongst the community yesterday during the proceedings. People didn't know what to say to me. Conversation flowed around Aalia. 'We'll miss her smile. We'll never have anyone like Aalia again; she's one of a kind.' My heart is glad hearing the respect in which Aalia is held.

Papa and Ima return by a track easier to negotiate ascending than descending. It reduces the distance a little. Papa's face is ashen and Ima is sobbing into a handkerchief. At first I assume it's ongoing grief about Aalia, but I've a hunch it's something more.

Papa draws close to me and places a trembling hand on my shoulder. My anxiety rises. This is not what my father does. What could've happened? Ima looks with fearful eyes over the handkerchief that covers her mouth.

'Uri. I have terrible, terrible news.' Papa pauses and shakes his head, as in disbelief. 'It wasn't an accident!' he gasps.

I freeze and stare into his eyes. 'What are you saying … Aalia's accident isn't an accident?' I cry in horror.

'The police rang Omar this morning. They have a witness who saw a silver car hit Aalia as she crossed the road. But then'—Papa shakes his head again, not wanting to say the words—'the car … the car … reversed back … over her body.'

My heart leaps into my mouth, and I steady myself. 'She was murdered! This was intentional! Someone killed her!'

Papa fixes his eyes on me.

His announcement stabs me in my chest. 'Who would do such a thing?' I bellow in pain.

Papa and Ima stand in silence. A confusion of horror, helplessness, understanding, and grief, is written on their faces.

I must sit down. I glance around. The first refuge I see is my car, parked thirty metres away in the car park. I stagger like a drunk towards it.

'Uri.'

Papa is calling, but I don't want to hear him. I need to be alone. Their footsteps follow behind me. I quicken my pace. The car door opens, the key is in the ignition, and the engine springs to life.

'Uri, don't drive; please don't drive!' Ima's pleading voice fades behind me as the car moves out of the car park and down the hill.

I drive with no care as to whether I live or die.

~

The hill overlooking Pan's Temple at Banias Springs appears steeper than in childhood days. The last rays of the sun enrich the red rocky face of the cliff. The sun sinks behind the trees, flinging the last light onto the adjacent hill. I stagger on, climbing higher.

The hill holds the light of the vanished sun for a long time. In spite of the cold wind from the northeast, perspiration drips from my forehead. My ears are deaf to the bubbling stream that brings life to a dry and thirsty land. Silence is deep. A robotic trance has seized my mind. I've no idea how I've got here. I see my car parked below, but I don't remember the trip—it's time forgotten. A burning rage inside is the only strength that propels me to the top of my favourite hill.

This is the place where I chased Ghazi and hit him in the head with a stone. I was angry then, but now it's blind rage, murderous rage. I collapse, hitting the hard-baked earth on the stony edge that drops twenty vertical metres to the oldest Canaanite site in Israel.

If I ever find the bastard that murdered my Aalia, I'll tear him apart!

I couldn't conceive of a woman committing such a horrendous deed—it *had* to be a male, but who? My tortured mind searches names and faces. No one stands out.

Unannounced, the rage returns, and I lurch upright. A large rock at my feet becomes a missile. My body strains under the weight as I lift it above my spinning head. The scream that erupts from the deepest part of my being is enough to wake the dead. The rock, powered by fury, smashes the edge and crashes down the cliff face, exploding into fragments below. The force of exertion throws my unsteady body off balance and I lurch forward, losing my footing. My chest slams onto broken rocks, and I slide forward, almost plunging over the edge to where the object of my wrath exploded. Head and shoulders extend beyond the edge, I look down. All I need to do is push a little further and I can end it. How can I live without my Aalia? I can't go on.

Sobs commence and convulsions shake my exhausted body. I draw my arms up and grip the edge. It would be so easy to finish it here, in my favourite place. I lie vulnerable, staring into the darkening void and let the tears spill into the wind.

Eventually my sobbing subsides, and I wriggle back from the edge. The top of the hill still holds the light of the vanished sun. My hands are bloodied, skin broken by rough rock, jacket and trousers dusty. What will I do? I lie and stare into the deep silence.

Unhurried, I stagger down the slope and kneel beside the freezing spring water. My bleeding hands sting as I plunge them into the steadily flowing stream. The icy water provides a mixture of pain and pleasure in my mouth. What will I do?

The path beside the stream beckons, and I follow the gentle flow of water. Through lush grass and swaying trees I tread, lured by the sight and soothing sounds of the stream.

'He leads me beside still water ... Though I walk through the valley of the shadow of death ...' Where did that come from? The words of Psalm 23. I'd memorised that Psalm in childhood, a Psalm of David.

Dusk descends while I retrace my steps to the desolation of Pan's temple. I remove a blanket from my car and caress it. The red fabric holds precious memories of picnics and playfulness—a sacred symbol of our romance. I handle it gently. A stale packet of biscuits, an apple, and a banana are the only food I can find. Now, to find the cave of my childhood.

It doesn't take long. Memories flood back. Here's the small opening leading to a space the size of a small room. Two startled birds fly past my head as my eyes adjust to the darkness. I gather dry sticks and a few dead branches. Minutes later a smoky fire crackles inside the entrance with the smoke finding its way into the night. Ghostly shapes appear on the walls and move in rhythm with the flames. The wind drops, and I consume the dry biscuits and the apple. When the cold of the night enfolds me, I consider retreating to my car, but here is the place of memories—beautiful images of childhood. The walls of this cave witnessed our childhood games, stories of adventure, and hopes for the future. I bathe in the warm glow of reflections that hold me secure.

Night's icy hand shakes me from sleep. Lying cold in a green wash of starlight, I stare at the faint embers of fire. My mind seizes the stark images of the previous afternoon, and they return to haunt me. The respite of a few hours sleep and the frigid air have sharpened my mind. Cocooned in my blanket, I roll onto my side and feel the bruising on my chest from the collapse on the cliff edge. That terrifying image, staring down at the uneven rocks below, longing for death brings bitter tears.

What was I thinking? My breathing quickens, shocked, as I realise how close I came to losing my life. I can see Papa, standing beside my grave with Ima. 'Why? Why?' I hear him say. I can only imagine how Papa and my family would suffer if I threw away my life.

Then I think of Papa fighting for life in Auschwitz, surviving the horrors, and here am I, tortured by grief and tempted to finish it all. He must have been tempted to throw himself onto the wire, like many in the camps, but he didn't. He fought on, struggling to create a better future.

The insight gives me strength. Strangely, a memory awakens. I see myself waiting at the Western Wall as an eight-and-a-half-year-old, the swifts darting into cracks. Beside me Papa stands, suffering in silence. I study his face and see a single tear drop from his eye. 'Why are you crying, Papa?'

Silence.

'Why won't you go to the Wall and pray?'

His chest heaved as he turned away.

What secret is he hiding? Whatever it is, it's powerful. He carries the darkness with him, locked inside. Yet he chose not to die, and neither will I. He needs my help, and I won't go to my grave until I find out.

Chapter Twenty-Four

I wake suddenly. Someone is tapping on the window.

'Uri, Uri.'

The cold of pre-dawn has driven me from the secure place of childhood memories to the relative warmth of my car. I stare through the frosted window and recognise Abe, my youngest brother.

'Uri, are you all right?' he asks.

I resent his intrusion. This is my space, my place. I push the door open and spot a thermos of coffee in his hand with a basket of food. Hunger wins.

Abe's face is serious. 'We were so worried about you. Papa and Ima are beside themselves.'

Then I notice Yitzhak, a senior member of the kibbutz and a good friend of Papa. He offers a sad smile and says, 'Uri, you've been through so much. If you need to stay here for a longer time, then do it. Your family is ready to welcome you whenever you're ready. I'm just glad you're safe.'

A sigh of relief escapes my lips and I relax. It's helpful not to be coerced into doing what others think is right for me. '*Toda raba.* You're kind to come out here to look for me.'

Abe smiles. 'Papa rang the hospital last night and was worried when he heard you weren't there. I had a hunch you might come here. I know how much you love this place.'

Abe is now a strapping five feet ten. He's headed to being the tallest in the family. People comment about his height and sandy coloured hair. 'Are you sure he's your son?' friends used to joke with Papa and Ima.

'It's the revival of a distant family gene,' Ima would reply with a smile.

I'm glad to take a cup and the sweet cakes and head for the stream layered with a thin wisp of mist.

The early pink fingers of dawn disappear as we sit on a rock beside the life-giving waters of Banias Springs. This beautiful place that gives life to a thirsty Israel also gives me life. Soon the terror of the dark night of the soul will cease its torment, but the imprint will remain, forever etched on my spirit.

I stay until late morning, then wind my way back to Atak.

~

Abe and Yitzhak left hours earlier. In spite of the filth on my clothes, I feel as if I'd had a shower, an inner cleansing. The well of tears is reduced but not emptied. Previously I was fearful I wouldn't stop crying. Grief hung like a claustrophobic cloud, but somehow I found the strength to manage. An army jeep passes me, heading north. I wonder what may have happened if a patrol had discovered me. Lucklily the place had been deserted—not unusual for this time of year.

Ima is the first to greet me as I enter the kibbutz community hall. Casting aside her apron, she flings her arms around me and sobs, 'You're here, Uri. I love you.'

I give in to her embrace and pat her back. Papa appears and Ima releases me into his best attempt at a hug. He's filled with emotion and without words, he grips me. His quivering body says it all.

A shower and a change of clothes that have remained in a corner of my parent's wardrobe become a priority. Soon I'm seated at the far end of the hall, away from the kitchen. A few friends pass by and offer their condolences. Most of the kibbutzniks are busy with their tasks.

Ima produces chicken and vegetables with flat bread, and I refill my tank, emptied from the enforced fasting of the previous day. Papa pours another glass of homemade lemonade. Ima glances at him but he doesn't return her gaze. He's breathing heavily.

'Uri,' he says. 'There's news we received from the police last night that will shock you …'

I wait and feel my chest tighten. What news could be worse than what I've already received?

'The police believe they've identified the person responsible for Aalia's death.' Papa stares at the floor, avoiding eye contact.

'Who is it?' I demand.

Papa takes a deep breath. 'They believe it was Ghazi.' The words fall like vomit from his mouth, his revulsion clear.

I glance at Ima. She's sitting helpless in her chair, tears flowing down her cheeks. 'Uri, it's terrible, so terrible. I can't believe anyone, let alone Ghazi, would do such a horrible thing.'

The words bring a chaos of thoughts that physically shake me. I take hold of the table to steady myself. 'Ghazi!' I gasp in disbelief.

'The police believe he's been working with a terror group for some time,' Papa continues.

'Why would a brother kill his own sister? His own flesh and blood?' I explode.

Papa and Ima sit motionless and stare at me. Thoughts fly in confusion through my mind as I try to make sense of this craziness. Did he know about Aalia and me? If he did, is his hatred for me so strong he'd kill his sister? Or was he trying to preserve his family's honour?

I spit words as icy as cold steel. 'I'm going to find him and kill him.'

Papa and Ima remain silent, avoiding my gaze.

After a long silence, Papa leans forward on his chair and raises his head. 'The police have picked him up, Uri.'

Part of me feels relief; at least they have him! The other part, rage and frustration. I want to find him and tear him apart. Any benefits of my deep soul searching from last night have been swept away.

Workers enter the hall for lunch. Even though they fill up the far tables, giving us space, I decide to leave.

'I need to walk.'

Ima's face becomes a mask of panic.

'No, I'm not going to drive. I just need some time alone,' I say as firmly and respectfully as I can. 'I'll be back for dinner, at the latest.' Without waiting for a response I hurry to the door, brushing past the workers hungry for their midday meal.

I hasten around the back of the hall and take the path that winds its way along the top of the hill towards the north. Rage boils inside me. I want to scream. As soon as I'm clear of the perimeter, I break into a run. I've not run for years, and soon I'm perspiring, my heart thumping. I push on through the trees along the track that leads to another kibbutz, five kilometres north. My legs are screaming, but there's a strange masochistic feeling of pleasure from the pain. My body signals 'stop' but my anger propels me on. The endorphins kick in, and now the high, which I know is temporary, lightens my legs.

At last, exhausted, I collapse on a grassy patch overlooking the boundary of the adjoining kibbutz. It's been good to run. It's taken the top layer off my anger. As I lie here breathless, chest heaving, horrible images hijack my mind; my lovely Aalia, crushed by the wheels of a car. Sobs erupt. I lie prostrate on the ground, pleading, 'Why? Why?'

~

Ghazi lay on the floor of the van. Two hours earlier Shin Bet agents had burst into his hideout on the West Bank and seized him and two other members of the group. His mind was a mess of thoughts. How did they know about his secret location? Had he been betrayed?

His hands were numb, the result of handcuffs clamping his wrists firmly behind his back. The blindfold ensured he had no idea of where he was or where he was going, and his head banged against the metal floor of the van as it bumped along an uneven road. Eventually the van stopped and its door opened. Soldiers dragged him to his feet, and he staggered up some stairs and into a foul-smelling room. He could hear people and shouting in Hebrew.

A soldier removed his blindfold and handcuffs. He blinked and stared wide-eyed at the small room, empty except for a wooden table and a brown filing cabinet.

Will this be the time for interrogation? Will I be beaten? Tortured?

He waited barely five minutes before the door opened and two soldiers ushered him down a narrow corridor, past a man in a white coat, whom he presumed was a doctor.

The guards pushed him into another room and handcuffed him again. A dark green hood was pulled over his head. It smelt of vomit, putrid, like it had never been washed. Ghazi tried to hold his breath, and then gasped as the filthy odour flooded his mouth. He panicked, fearing he'd suffocate if the bag wasn't removed. Hands searched him, removing his wallet, papers, belt, and bootlaces. A hand grabbed him by the hood and dragged him down another corridor, moving left and right, left and right, and through a doorway. Cold air told him he was outside. Strong arms bundled him into a vehicle, which accelerated and sped through what he presumed were the streets of West Jerusalem.

Finally the vehicle stopped. He was dragged by the hood upstairs, down a long corridor, and then he was pushed into a cell. The hood was removed and handcuffs unlocked. He glanced around. An Israeli officer in uniform sat behind a desk. A soldier pushed Ghazi onto a seat, handcuffed him to the right arm of the chair, and shackled his feet to its front legs.

The Israeli's eyes fixed on Ghazi. 'What's your name?' he asked in a soft voice.

'My name is Ghazi.' Ghazi stared back, trying to sound strong, but his shaking knees betrayed him.

The interrogator held eye contact. 'Do you know why you're here?'

'I have no idea.' Ghazi took a deep breath and stared back at the soldier.

'We have evidence that you were the driver of the vehicle that killed your sister Aalia.'

Ghazi's gaze flickered. 'You're wrong. I know nothing about her death.'

'Aalia is your sister, isn't she?'

'I do have a sister called Aalia. I've not seen her for months.'

'Ghazi, we also have evidence to link you with the bombing of the café in Ramallah in August.'

'Don't know what you're talking about.' Ghazi's knees continued to shake. He shifted his weight on the chair.

'Ghazi, you're in big trouble. I want to help you, but I need you to tell me the truth. Do you have anything to tell me?'

'I don't know what to tell you,' Ghazi replied shaking his head. 'What will happen to me? How long will I be here?'

'As long as it takes,' the officer replied in a stern voice. 'It depends on whether you're willing to cooperate. We have plenty of time. Think about it, Ghazi.'

The soft-spoken interrogator nodded to the guard. The foul-smelling hood was pulled back over his head. He was released from the chair and his hands secured with handcuffs, then a soldier dragged him to his feet and bundled him down a darkened corridor towards an empty cell.

~

The guard leads me down the musty corridor to the waiting area. My request to visit Ghazi has finally been approved. Shin Bet has allowed contact with him, hoping he might shed light on his motive. A month has passed since his arrest and confession to Aalia's death and the café explosion in Ramallah. I'm the only one, other than his lawyer, permitted to visit. The well-fortified prison on the outskirts of Jerusalem holds a number of 'notable terrorists' awaiting sentencing. My motive is to hear what caused him to take the life of his sister, my beautiful love.

I sit and wait. My heart rate has increased, my palms sweaty. What am I anxious about? How will he react? Will he spit in my face? Will he break down and cry when he's confronted by someone he once regarded as a brother? My thoughts cease as a door opens on the other side of the transparent barricade, and a thin figure of a man is led handcuffed into the room. I step forward and sit on an antiquated chair opposite the now seated figure. I stare. Nothing is familiar: a scruffy beard, a mass of unkempt hair, pasty skin, and dark, sunken eyes betray a soul lost in time. My heart sinks as I stare deep into the depths of his emptiness. It is Ghazi—dishevelled, disoriented.

'Ghazi,' I gasp.

He doesn't respond.

'Ghazi,' I repeat louder.

His vacant eyes flicker, and his face changes to a ghostly white. Terror fills his eyes, and his chest heaves.

He's recognised me! 'Ghazi. Why did you do it? WHY?'

His head drops forward, and he fixes his gaze on the floor.

'Why did you murder your own sister? Why did you kill Aalia?' Anger fires my words like arrows. I want to hurt him, badly.

Ghazi doesn't lift his head.

I can't take my eyes off him. For weeks my tortured mind agonised to make sense of his evil act of terror. Every night, uncontrolled thoughts, ignited by rage, formed questions demanding answers and shaping statements I need to utter. My breathing is heavy. 'Look at me,' I demand. 'Why won't you look at me?'

His head doesn't move. A mass of unwashed, untidy hair is all I see.

An eerie silence fills the room. I wait, but there's no response. 'When I first heard you were the one responsible, I wanted to kill you. Now … I don't want you dead. I want you to know you have destroyed the lives of your family, and mine … and all for what? What have you achieved? You've thrown petrol on the fire. We were like brothers, once. But you've gone a different path … violence. Spend a week in emergency with me and see what your violence achieves.'

I don't know if my words are finding a place to settle and germinate, or if they fall on rocky ground and fail to grow; I've said what I need to say. I'm surprised my voice is calmer. The sight of this pathetic shell of humanity has almost extinguished my anger. Part of me feels sad for this wretched soul, who has lost his way. There's still no movement from the mess of black hair.

'If you ever have anything to say to me, Ghazi, I'm ready to listen.'

It's difficult to discern, but I see a few slow movements of his head. Was that a nod? I wait a little longer.

Silence, an empty silence. I glance up at the guard standing behind Ghazi, convey my thanks with a nod and leave without speaking, still none the wiser to Ghazi's murderous motives.

~

A small group of the Arab community surrounded Omar and Sabah. The truck, fully laden, groaned under the weight of their worldly possessions.

Sabah, torn between rage and grief, pleaded with her husband for weeks not to leave Atak. 'I know it's hard for you to live here now, but it'll be harder going to Ramallah!' she begged. 'We don't want another grief. We've lost our land, a child, and now our friends, our community.'

Omar's response was always the same. 'I've lost face and I'm full of shame. I cannot look my people in the eye here. I cannot meet with Abdiel and Maya. Ghazi has disgraced our family.'

'Our friends here understand, Omar,' she protested. 'You're going to a dangerous place. It's safer here. Are you punishing yourself for what Ghazi did?'

Omar couldn't answer. Since Aalia's death he had slid into a deep depression, a man devoured by a kind of smouldering inner fire. Most days he moped around the small settlement, attempting to do his share of work, but he achieved little. Nobody worried. They saw a man devastated by an act of terror that had shaken not only Omar, but also the entire community.

Tears mingled with embraces brought an end to the farewell ritual. Omar released himself from Joshua's embrace, turned and walked to the truck, and lifted an object from the front seat. 'Please give this to Abdiel and Maya. It's our gift.'

Everyone knew what it was. A pottery jug painted with a small cluster of grapes—the most precious possession Omar and Sabah owned. Nobody knew its age, but it had been in Omar's family for generations. Every family in their community had tasted grape juice poured from this sacred vessel. A gasp came from the witnesses.

'I cannot bear to say farewell to them. Please give it to them with our love.'

Joshua nodded.

Omar, tears streaming down his face, turned back to the truck. The engine roared and they were gone.

~

'Abby, there's a letter for you. It's from overseas,' Maya said, returning from the kitchen. She'd found the envelope in their pigeon-hole near the front door of the hall.

In recent times, the pit of despair had drawn Abdiel deep into its chamber of darkness. He'd grown more distressed and withdrawn from those who wanted to support him. The news of Uri's relationship with Aalia had shaken him to the core. To learn of her violent death at the hands of her brother; the devastating impact on Omar and Sabah, and the accumulated anguish was too much to bear. Abdiel's grief at losing one he regarded as a loved daughter and another, Ghazi, who'd been like a son to him was overwhelming.

The distance he felt between him and Uri, his eldest son, compounded his grief. Ever since Uri announced his love for Aalia, it felt as if he'd lost him. He'd complain, 'Life is so complicated. How much can a man bear?'

Maya sat with him and attempted to soothe his distress with words of support. 'You've been through so much, my love. You're not alone. I'm with you and will never leave you.'

But Abdiel felt alone. Distanced from his friends and his children, grieving a lost brother, battling the demons of the past, life was a never-ending story of suffering.

Abdiel's eyes opened wide as he took the crumpled envelope from Maya's hand.

'It looks as though it's had a rough passage,' Maya commented as Abdiel removed the contents.

'A photograph; it's Daniel!' Abdiel exclaimed in disbelief. He examined the photo like a detective seeking forensic evidence, studying it without comment. At last, he said, 'He looks much older. I can see a tractor in the distance—taken on a farm by the look of it.'

'Now see this,' Maya said, examining the post mark on the envelope, 'it's dated just over twelve months ago!'

'Maybe it got lost along the way,' Abdiel replied. 'There's nothing written on the back; no letter!' he added. 'What am I supposed to think?'

'Well, at least you know he's alive, that's something.'

'This is *so* crazy. It feels like he's playing with my mind.'

Silence.

Then Abdiel's voice rose in frustration. 'What am I supposed to do with this?'

Maya looked at him in despair and sank into her chair. 'Abby, I know it's hard for you, but maybe all Daniel wants you to know is that he's alive. Is it possible, for whatever reason, he's not ready to tell you the rest of his story?'

Silence.

'I love you, Abby, and there're times when you're with me, but not present—you're far away. I don't know where you go; I have my hunches, but I don't know what's going on for you. You shut me out. You shut your friends out. Sometimes I don't understand you, and you don't understand Daniel.'

Abdiel took a deep breath.

Maya could see her honesty had struck a chord.

Abdiel nodded and looked at Maya with softened eyes. 'You're right, Maya. You always are. When Daniel is ready, he'll return from the war.'

Part Five

Chapter Twenty-Five

1986

A clandestine meeting took place in Hebron, just south of Bethlehem. Seven men sat in secret planning. It would become an historic day. Sheikh Yassin sat in his wheelchair. Muhammad Jamal al-Natsheh from Hebron and Jamal Mansour from Nablus were present. The highly esteemed Sheikh Hassan Yousef and Mahmud Muslih from Ramallah took their seats. Jamil Hamami had made his way from Jerusalem and Ayman Taha had travelled from Gaza. At the end of their sinister meeting, the men took a solemn oath. Hamas was born. [Note 1]

~

December 1987

The radio announces escalating violence in Ramallah on the West Bank. Arab youths are burning tyres and throwing bottles and rocks at Israeli soldiers.

'That's just what we need! We'll have casualties from one end of the hospital to the other,' I growl.

An Israeli plastics salesman named Shlomo Sakal is stabbed to death. Then word comes through that four people have been killed in a traffic accident in Jabalia refugee camp in Gaza. The truth of the incident gets twisted, and word spreads that Israelis had killed them in revenge for Sakal's death.

'Fuel the fire,' is the cry from Hamas' leadership.

A seventeen-year-old throws a Molotov cocktail, and an Israeli soldier shoots him dead. The incident sends crowds of protestors flocking into the streets in Gaza and the West Bank. A new kind of war begins: the First Intifada.

~

June 1989

We drive south for a day, escaping the hypnotic power of Jerusalem. I love the Old City. To walk its streets is to walk through history. Beneath the feet of priests and pilgrims, tourists and traders, rest the bones of the past scattered in every direction. The sacredness of standing at the Western Wall is to know that beneath lies thirty-nine layers of history. The colour of Jerusalem is the colour of a lion skin: tawny yellow, dark browns, and pale golds. The walls are the armour and shield of Jerusalem in troubled times. You are inside the Old City, embraced and sheltered from the world, or outside looking in, as it shields itself from the modern world. Wonderful and terrible things have happened behind her walls.

The glorious sight of the sun greets us rising behind the savage hills of Moab, lighting the still waters of the Dead Sea and shining over the grotesque spectral hills of the Jordan Valley. The brown hills rise like a barrier streaked with violet shadows, contrasting with the emerging blueness of the sea. Beyond lies the dead city of Petra, silent in the red sands of Jordan.

I tap the car's indicator and turn right toward the golden glow of Masada. Masada, without walls and perched high on a pinnacle, stands in bold contrast to Jerusalem. Its lofty elevation guarantees its security, but its brown soil, too, is covered with Jewish blood. Here the earth aches from the sun, and the sky is a lid above it.

'Just look at it, Yousef! I'm always in awe of this place and its story.'

'Likewise,' Yousef replies. 'I can understand why Abe wanted to have his Bar Mitzvah here.'

Today Yousef and I are meeting my brother Abe and a small group of his army mates for his birthday lunch in the restaurant. Yousef spots two camels.

'They look their usual arrogance,' I say.

Yousef smiles. 'Here's a little piece of local trivia. The Arabs say that anyone with a protruding lower lip portrays superiority. They believe that God has one hundred names, but man knows only ninety-nine. The camel knows the hundredth and that's why his expression is always arrogant.'

I laugh.

Masada is located on the top of an isolated rocky cliff at the western end of the Judean Desert, set in a sea of glaring sand that can weary the eye. As you stand on the eastern side, the sheer drop is about 450 metres to the plain that borders the Dead Sea. The western edge stands about 100 metres above the natural landscape.

A short walk from the car park to the cable car fills us with the baked scent of the earth. We pause and watch the effortless ascent of tourists in the cable car to the tabletop garrison, set against a china blue sky.

We enter the restaurant and follow the noise to a corner where Abe and his mates are already seated. Abe and the group arrived earlier to climb the Snake Path to the top.

'A bit of a macho thing,' Yousef had said.

Abe takes my hand, 'Thanks for coming, Uri.' He introduces us to his six mates who appear relaxed to have a Rabbi as part of the gathering.

After we've eaten, the evidence of the meal lies in the remains scattered on plates.

Abe rises to his feet. 'Thank you for joining me for this celebration.'

'We felt sorry for you, didn't want you to be here alone,' quipped one of his mates.

Laughter.

'You know the importance of this place for me, us, and all Israelis,' Abe says. 'Let me remind you of the story.'

Abe's comrades fix their gaze on the clean-cut model soldier, carving a distinguished place in his regiment. Of course every soldier knows the story. It doesn't need to be told. It's the very heart and soul of the New Israel. But in telling it, you declare yourself at one with the passion of the people. Masada has become a striking memorial. The story of Masada has become a mantra.

Abe's solid, erect stance, searching blue eyes, and unblemished olive skin give power to his measured speech. Unspoken respect is written on the faces of his friends. 'Herod the Great built Masada for himself somewhere between 31 and 37 BCE. Around seventy-five years after his death, in 66 CE, at the beginning of the revolt of the Jews against the Romans, a group of Jewish rebels seized the Roman garrison here. When the Romans destroyed Jerusalem in seventy CE, Zealots and their families joined the ranks of the rebels. For three years, the Zealots and rebels attacked passing Romans and retreated to the fortress. Finally Rome vowed to put an end to their harassment. In seventy-three CE governor Flavius Silva arrived at Masada with the Tenth Legion and thousands of Jewish slaves. He established a camp and built a wall around the base of the mountain.'

A waiter appears to clear the plates but senses this isn't the right moment. A quiet reverence has settled over our gathering. 'The stuff of Masada is our DNA,' one soldier had commented earlier.

'The wall was just the start,' Abe continues. 'Over the following eighteen months, Jewish slaves driven by Roman whips constructed a rampart on the western side, moving thousands and thousands of tons of earth. As you know, you can still see it. The rebels and Zealots knew their time would soon be up, so the Zealots' leader, Elazar ben Yair, decided that every man should slay his family. [Note 2]

Two surviving women told of the final hours to Josephus. Almost 1000 men women and children, led by Ben Yair, burnt down the fortress and killed each other. The Zealots cast lots to choose ten men to kill the remainder. After the slaughter, they chose one man among their group to kill the survivors. The last Jew committed suicide.'

Poignant silence follows, a statement of respect to the fallen and a recognition of the impact of the violence that marks this place as special for Jewish people. [Note 3]

'Brothers, we will return here soon to graduate. Masada is the essence of the New Man of Eretz Israel. This is where we connect with our national history—the passionate survival of our people. It's here we'll take our vow as thousands of soldiers have in the past. Masada shall not fall again.'

The soldiers rise as one, clink glasses, and repeat the refrain, 'Masada shall not fall again.'

Abe is at his best telling stories and doesn't need an event like a birthday party for the tales to flow. I'm proud of him. He's articulate, fluent, and humorous. The lunch is a great celebration during which he shares recollections from his youth and exaggerated tales of his early days in the military.

The mid-afternoon heat beats down upon us without mercy as we head north. Yousef remarks, 'You can understand, with the poor soil conditions, the harsh climate, rugged terrain, little fresh water, and a small population, why the Negev has largely been ignored.'

'I could never live here. Give me the north, Atak, any day,' I reply. 'Even better; give me Banias Springs.'

'Interesting,' Yousef reflects. 'Your favourite place is Banias—green, plentiful, peaceful. Your brother Abe chooses Masada—desert, dry, harsh, and bloody.'

'We're so different, aren't we?'

'Strange how it happens in families. Sometimes I'm concerned about Abe,' Yousef continues. 'He's disciplined, determined, and strong minded, but rigid.'

'I guess that makes him popular amongst men. They like that in him; you know where you stand.'

'He's black and white, doesn't have your flexibility, your empathy.'

'But I'm older. I'm sure he'll mature,' I reassure Yousef.

'I hope so, Uri. Life will be difficult for him and others if he doesn't. Anyway, how are *you* managing?'

'I have my moments. Every so often I break down, but it's not every day, as it was at first.'

'You give yourself permission to feel. That's good and healthy,' Yousef responds.

'I still have times when I want to rage!' I confess.

'You're human. It's only ... how long ... just over three years since Aalia was taken from us. If in three years time you're still angry I'd be concerned. To hang on to anger forever, is to commit yourself to a life-sentence. You went to see Ghazi, didn't you?'

'Yes. I wanted some answers, but I'm none the wiser. He just sat and stared at the floor. No sign that he heard anything I said. The lights were on, but nobody home! He was pathetic. A small part of me actually felt sorry for him.'

'He's been radicalised,' Yousef says.

'You'd think after the strong relationship he and his family had with our community that he'd be harder to influence,' I reply.

'He'll have not forgotten his family being forced off their land, and when that's joined by the undercurrent of hate from his Palestinian countrymen, it's a force that's hard to stop. For a brother to kill his sister ... that shows real hatred.'

'Do you think it was some kind of "honour killing"?'

Yousef nods. 'That's my theory. Then you add to the equation his ambition to rise in the ranks of PIJ, his stage in life as a young man when everything is black and white, the formula becomes explosive.'

Sadness swells my chest, and I allow myself a distraction, glancing at the rugged, chalky-coloured cliffs of Qumran.

Yousef notices my interest. 'Amazing discovery, wasn't it? That Palestinian shepherd boy had no idea what he stumbled on in that cave.'

I knew from my early religious education that the unearthing of the Dead Sea scrolls in 1947 was one of the most important discoveries, ever, in Israel. Those ancient records scribed by a religious desert community, the Essenes, confirmed the authenticity of the Old Testament.

I choose to change the direction of our conversation. 'How do you think Papa is managing?'

Yousef strokes his greying beard and returns his eyes to the road. 'He seems to have picked up a little after receiving the photo of Daniel. It only occurred to me last week that the photo may have been sent by somebody else. Your Papa assumed it was from Daniel. It could have been sent by anyone. Strange business.'

I point to a brown hawk hanging in the hot air. Conversation returns to a theme Yousef and I have spoken about forever. 'I'd give 10,000 shekels to know what Papa has locked inside him. Do you know that he's never been to the Western Wall since the day he took me, when I was eight and a half years old? I was so excited. He said he'd been looking forward to it for so long—dreamed about it when he was in Auschwitz and the camps. Yet when he finally has the opportunity, he just stands there. I can still see that tear and his chest heaving.'

'Whatever it is,' Yousef says, 'It's powerful. I don't think he's told anyone—certainly not your Ima, or me. We may never know. He may take his secret to the grave.'

'He's locked himself in Auschwitz and is rarely in the present. It's sad that I, or any of our family, have had very little of Papa over the years.'

Yousef doesn't answer.

My pronouncement about Papa brings unease. Is the pot calling the kettle black? I need to let go of the anger and trauma of losing my beloved Aalia if I'm to embrace the future. But then, I remind myself, grief must find its own way.

~

It's mid-afternoon and I've managed to secure a few minutes break from the incessant flow of wounded humanity. Fractured bones, stabbings, missing limbs, burns, a never-ending stream of suffering sweeps through the door of Hadassah Hospital.

'Doctor, a call for you. It sounds urgent. It's your father.'

Papa! That's strange. He never calls me at the hospital. I hurry to my office and lift the receiver. 'Papa, how are you?'

'I've had enough, Uri.' The heaviness and lack of energy in his voice disturbs me.

'You've had enough?'

'I can't go on … I'm tired … exhausted.'

My heart rate increases, and I move uneasily on the padded seat.

'It's too much for me. I want to end it.'

My mind explodes, tempting me to panic. I need to slow down. *Remember your training.* 'When you say you want to end it, what do you mean?'

'I want to kill myself.'

I pause, stunned. 'Have you ever had these thoughts before?'

'Many times,' comes the cold reply.

'Have you thought about how you might do it?'

'The most painless—a tube from the exhaust pipe into the car.'

Calm yourself, Uri; stay calm. 'This is a hard question to ask but have you ever tried to kill yourself?'

'No, but I know I'm closer to doing it now than I've ever been before.'

'Have you ever told anyone about taking your life?'

'No. No one.'

'Have you set a date, a time?'

'Not yet.'

I give myself time to think.

'Will you promise me one thing? Will you phone me before you do it?'

A long silence. 'I'll phone you only on the condition that you don't try to talk me out of it.'

My heart sinks. How can I agree to that? But there's nothing else I can do! 'Okay, it's a deal.'

'Thank you for listening. I never wanted to interrupt you at the hospital.'

'Please call whenever you need to,' I reply, my heart pounding.

Then he's gone.

A nurse appears at the door. 'Doctor …'

I shake my head and wave her away.

She retreats obediently.

I couldn't believe the conversation I've just had. What the hell do I do now? Do I call Ima? No, that will be too much for her. Should I call one of his friends at the kibbutz? If Papa finds out, he'll be angry and feel betrayed. He may never phone me if he becomes desperate. The knot in my stomach tightens. If he phones again, what do I do? I've promised not to talk him out of suicide. How can I allow myself to do that? Maybe just listening to him, letting him talk will be enough to stop him. Yet, if his suffering is so great, who am I to stand in his way? Maybe I need to respect his decision. He's suffered for a lifetime. I can't blame him for wanting to opt out.

~

Two weeks later on 2nd August 1990, Uri tries his gas mask on.

Saddam Hussein sent the Iraqi army into Kuwait, the invasion fuelled by a long-standing border grievance and Kuwait's policy on oil production. The rumour was that Iraq's ultimate goal was to dominate the Gulf Region, unite the Arabs, and overcome Israel. Palestinians are going crazy, and security is tight throughout the country.

'Soon the occupation will be over,' is the Palestinian catch-cry. 'Our brothers are coming to our rescue.'

The Israel Defence Force distributes gas masks to every citizen. The Palestinians receive one per household. Old sheets are taped onto windows. All eyes are on TV news. Palestinians cheer with each warning of an incoming missile, while Uri and the staff at Hadassah Hospital brace themselves for a tidal wave of wounded.

~

Abdiel and the kibbutzniks couldn't believe their eyes as they studied the TV. Forty scud missiles hit Tel Aviv, lighting up the sky.

'It's amazing only two Israelis were killed in that attack,' Abdiel said.

The Palestinians thought Israel was lying, but it was true. Later the IDF found out that Iraqis had fiddled with the missiles to make them go further, but sacrificed power and accuracy. The UN forces were too great for Saddam Hussein and forced him back to Baghdad, leaving the Palestinians angry and bitterly disappointed. 'Why is the war finished?' they asked. 'Israel is not finished,' they cried. 'Nothing has changed.'

In November 1990, President Bush ordered a significant increase in US forces in Saudi Arabia, and twenty-eight countries responded to the call. On 15 January 1991 'Operation Desert Storm' forced Iraq to withdraw its troops and Kuwait was liberated. President Bush said it was time to put an end to the Arab-Israeli conflict.

~

A nurse approaches me while I'm taking a break in the cafeteria and says, 'Doctor, we need you in Emergency.'

I drain my coffee cup and follow the nurse. Unrest has broken out on the West Bank again today, and Bethlehem hospital are sending the critical cases over to us at Hadassah.

Minutes later I gaze into the fierce eyes of a rock-throwing Palestinian youth. Israeli soldiers at the checkpoint retaliated with force, and he's lost a significant amount of blood. His head injury doesn't look too promising, either.

'What's your name?' I ask.

Silence. Eyes full of fire glare at me.

'Can you feel my hand on your feet?'

Again, no words, only eyes blazing with hatred.

'Can you move your legs?'

Silence continues. Jaw set. Rage remains.

Anger seizes my throat. 'Speak. Help me. Do you want to die?'

His hatred is palpable. I stare into his eyes, and they become the eyes of Ghazi. I see the soft, broken body of my beloved Aalia. Here in emergency, in this same space, I sat with her as she lost her bitter battle against violence. I watched her die from the toxic hatred of a terrorist. I fight the chaos of emotions with a confused mind. The conflict within me has a history and my body remembers. My chronicle of vitriol flashes before me: the rock that felled Ghazi; the murderous rage against Ghazi when I learnt he'd murdered Aalia; the frightening violence that came close to finishing my life on the cliff at Pan's Temple.

Breathe, Uri, breathe. Remember your mitzvah: Chesed. Kindness. Chesed. Kindness.

The firm voice of a senior nurse breaks the madness. 'Send him back to the West Bank,' she says in disgust.

The young Palestinian closes his eyes and loses consciousness. The event triggers a medical response. The sight of the deep puncture to his head and the bloodied wound from bullets in his leg, overtake my compulsion to exact revenge.

'No, we won't,' I reply, my head still spinning. 'We'll treat him here and do whatever we can to help.'

Two hours of difficult and delicate surgery save his life. Later in the afternoon, I'm about to head to the cafeteria when I receive word that the youth's father is in the waiting room. He's spent a brief time with his son in intensive care. I introduce myself to the middle-aged Arab. He shakes my hand warmly and produces a sad smile. Through tears he expresses his deep gratitude. It's genuine—why wouldn't it be? We saved his son's life. Then, comes the unexpected:

The Palestinian father grips my hand with both hands and looks into my eyes. His appreciation is powerful. 'What you did today, doctor, not only save my son's life, but you gave him new eyes.'

'I don't understand.'

'To my son, an Israeli is a soldier with a gun. He has never been to Jerusalem. He has never been out of the West Bank. All he knows about an Israeli is camouflage clothing and a gun. My family do not hate Israel. We teach our children not to hate. My son became infected with violence by his group. He's not a bad boy; he's been misled. When he was brought to you today, he thought he was going to die. He told me he was so scared he couldn't speak.'

My heart leaps into my mouth. I'm speechless. The meeting with his son in emergency replays at lightning speed again and again. It becomes a nightmare. How could I have been so mistaken? The light dawns: his eyes were not filled with anger or hatred. *They were full of fear.* Fear of being in the hands of an Israeli doctor? Fear he was going to die? How could I have missed it?

A gasp escapes my lips as the realisation takes hold. How could I have made such a terrible error? Guilt grips my tongue and I stutter, 'I've … I've… great respect … great respect … for … for your son. Thank you for your words of thanks.'

'Thank you again, doctor. You've given my son a different understanding of an Israeli. He will never forget it. I pray it will change his life.'

I bid goodbye and head to my office, shaking. I need to be alone—to hide. The turmoil swirls inside my head. The sudden eruption of a murderous impulse shocks me.

The knowledge that rage and grief still lie hidden in my darkness brings shame. Will I ever get over losing my Aalia? My Mizvah of 'kindness' is an impossible dream.

~

1. Mosab Hassan Yousef, *Son of Hamas,* Carol Stream, IL: Tyndale Momentum, 2010, p. 19.

2. Elazar's final speech was a masterful oration: 'Since we long ago resolved never to be servants to the Romans, nor to any other than to God Himself, who alone is the true and just Lord of mankind, the time is now come that obliges us to make that resolution true in practice ...We were the very first that revolted, and we are the last to fight against them; and I cannot but esteem it as a favour that God has granted us, that it is still in our power to die bravely, and in a state of freedom.' *Jewish Virtual Library.*

3. *Jewish Virtual Library.*

Chapter Twenty-Six

1991

It's been an eventful year. From 30th October – 1st November 1991, George Bush Snr led the peace initiative with Secretary of State, James Baker, in a three-day conference in Madrid. Israel refused to recognise the PLO so the Palestinian representatives were included in the Jordanian delegation. Extremist groups like Hamas and Islamic Jihad denounced the process as a 'sell-out' of Palestine. The process agonised like a woman in labour, struggling to give birth to new life.

Then the UN voted to condemn Israel for its treatment of Palestinians; Soviet forces stormed Vilnius as Lithuanians created the 'Singing Revolution' to protest their freedom; Iraq repeatedly fired Scud missiles into Israel; the Gulf War finished with Saddam Hussein's troops setting fire to Kuwait's oil fields; Latvians barricaded the streets of Riga to symbolically prevent the entry of Russian tanks; US Department of Justice announced Exxon would pay one-billion dollars to clean up the Exxon Valdez oil spill in Alaska; George Carey was enthroned as Archbishop of Canterbury; and "Terminator 2" and "Silence of the Lambs" was released.

While the kaleidoscope of world events pass me by, the pain of my loss is shrinking. The raw, gaping wound has shrunk to a small hole of manageable size. It's been six years since the light of my life was taken from me. The initial numbness soon moved to rage and then to overwhelming loss. The staff at the hospital were concerned and pleaded with me to take time off. After a week of drifting in and out of sleep in a bunk bed in Atak, I resumed duties at Hadassah. While the hills around Haifa and the care of the community gave me temporary respite, I came to the realisation that Atak was no longer my home. My parents and friends were well intentioned, but I needed space. Strangely enough, I could hide in the multitudes that swarmed the streets of Jerusalem. While memories triggered by sights and sounds brought sadness, strangely some comfort came from the familiar. After finishing my shift, I often walked aimlessly around the crowded streets. I'd pass by the steps leading up to our rooftop hideaway, sense her presence, and blink back tears. At first the wards were full of her. I saw her leaning over patients, tenderly reassuring them with love. Her care was never dispensed cold and clinical, but flowed with understanding, respect, and love.

Guilt was my torturer. The months following her death I blamed myself for creating the scene that led to her passing. I'd crossed the line of social and religious conventions. If I'd listened to Yousef and my parents and taken note of the gathering storm around me, it wouldn't have happened. I drove myself crazy with thoughts of 'if only.' My mind became a confused mess of messages and I fought to maintain sanity. Often I believed I heard her voice at night speaking to me. Once in the Old City I hurried twenty metres through the crowds, convinced a young woman was Aalia, until I saw her face. Then came the self-recriminations—*don't be so stupid.*

Somehow I managed my work; I don't really know how. It became a helpful distraction. At first a wall of silence surrounded me at Hadassah. Many colleagues appeared awkward and unsure of what to say. While the bittersweet absence of words became a protection from me facing my pain, it also left me feeling alone. Loneliness was a cruel companion that accompanied me for too long. I felt torn, withdrawing from the world whenever I could, yet desperately needing the human touch of those that understood me. Yousef was my rock; dear Yousef.

Friends have become more understanding and supportive of my varying moods while I've negotiated my journey of grief. Well-meaning friends are encouraging me to seek marriage now that I'm slowly letting go of the past. I still have a way to go, but I'm more prepared to consider the future. Ima, in particular is keen for me to find a wife. She told me she's made discreet enquiries and knows that Miriam, the choice of the *Shadchen* lives in an apartment in New Jerusalem. Her story is one of sadness, too. She married a Captain in the IDF, killed by a Scud missile twelve months after their wedding. I don't know what to think. How would Miriam feel after the way I rejected her?

Shabbat commences at sundown, in exactly one hour. I've agreed to go to the Wall to pray with Yousef and then to a mutual friend's place for the meal. The ritual and rhythm of going to the Wall on Shabbat has aroused orthodoxy in my life. I'm rediscovering my faith. Jewish men in black suits and white shirts, the tassels of their prayer shawls sway beneath the edge of their coats as they hurry through the Jaffa Gate. I spot Yousef, his slim energetic figure arrives with a smile, his rimless glasses perched precariously on the end of his large nose.

'Apologies, Uri; I've been delayed.'

'I don't mind people-watching for a while. It's a change from watching people in a hospital ward,' I reply. 'Do you want to have coffee?'

'I'm happy to walk on, if you are.' Yousef reaches into his pocket and produces sweets for two Arab children. '*As-salām 'alaykum*. Hello.'

'*As-salām 'alaykum*.' They giggle, then respond in unison with, '*Shukran,*' before running off.

Yousef chuckles. 'They always seem to find me whenever I walk this way.'

We join the human flow down King David Street.

Yousef appears in good spirits. 'How's your father?'

'Still lurching through life with a limp,' I say with a sigh. 'Nothing ever changes.'

The multitude multiplies in late afternoon. Not only Jewish men and women in black and white swell the narrow street but also Armenians, Orthodox, Catholics, and Protestants all head to the Wall to join the celebrations. I spot visiting European Rabbis, with perfectly formed ringlets dancing on their cheeks, striding to the sacred site they've no doubt dreamed of visiting for decades. Local Rabbis power past, wearing expensive black hats of all shapes and sizes, avoiding eye contact with the masses.

'I love Shabbat,' says Yousef after observing the crowds, people from all faiths, every culture, all walks of life, celebrating together.

'It's special,' I reply, then excuse myself to a middle-aged American tourist who stops in his tracks without warning to peer into a spice shop.

Since Aalia's death, I've taken some comfort in my faith. Even though I couldn't make sense of her death, I believe God is still there. In the Torah God says, 'It is mine to avenge; I will repay. In due time their foot will slip; their day of disaster is near and their doom rushes upon them.'

Revenge was not something I had to take responsibility for. If I did, I knew it could become a life sentence. What amount of revenge would satisfy me? These matters I talked over with Yousef, and he affirmed my thoughts. I understand but lament Papa's continuing, agonising refrain, 'Where was God in Auschwitz?' He holds on to the horror, or does the horror hold him? As I think of Papa and what he must have endured, the edges of my pain soften—no longer hard and sharp, but soft and smoother, manageable.

We descend the steps to the courtyard at the Wall and join the masses. Men hand-washing at the fountain; davening; singing and dancing; clapping and swaying to the rhythm of the singers. Once my ceremonial washing is complete, I head for the Wall and find a space. I never come to this place without the image of Papa, standing at a distance, full of emotion, fighting a tear.

'God, help my Papa,' I pray.

~

The other great joy for me at Shabbat is the meal with friends. It's become quite a ritual. I've brought a bottle of wine as a gift for my hosts, Joshua and Esther. We sing the *Shalom Aleichem* hymn, welcoming the angels, who visit every home at the start of Shabbat, and request their blessing. Then follows the song of *Eishet Chayil*, a tribute to the Jewish woman, written by King Solomon, extolling her for the wisdom and hard work she's invested in her home, making it safe and nurturing. We stand as Joshua recites the *Kiddush*, holding a cup of wine, and everyone takes a few sips, then we move to the sink for the ritual hand-washing. Joshua recites the blessing over the bread and then distributes *challah*, first dipping each piece in salt. After *challah* comes fish, salads, followed by soup, and then a meat or chicken course. And then, of course, dessert!

Conversation travels in any direction: humorous anecdotes; amazing achievements; short stories; tall stories, and deep and meaningful topics about grappling with the mysteries of life. Tonight it appears it's headed for the deep-and-meaningful department. Peter, the son of our generous host, is talking about a young woman he's found attractive and is dating.

'I *love* her,' he says.

'You *think* you love her,' his father says.

'I would call it infatuation,' Joseph says.

Yousef interjects: 'I call it fish love.' Whenever Yousef throws a stone into the pond, it catches everybody's attention.

Sarah and Jonathon, Peter's younger siblings, stop eating, and their brown eyes fix on their favourite Rabbi.

Wrinkles crease Peter's forehead. 'Fish love?'

The Rabbi smiles and points to Peter's plate. 'Why are you eating that fish?'

Peter glances at the fish and returns his gaze to Yousef. 'Because I love fish.'

Yousef nodds. 'You love fish! A fisherman caught it, took it out of the water, killed it, and boiled it. Now you eat it. Don't tell me you love the fish, you love yourself.'

Peter rests his knife and fork on his plate and waits for the next part.

'Because the fish tastes good,' Yousef continues, 'you approve of someone taking it out of the water, killing it, and now you're happy to eat it. So much of love is fish love. And so a young man and woman fall in love. What does that mean? It means that *he* saw in this woman someone who he felt could provide him with all his emotional and physical needs. *She* felt that in this man is someone she feels she can be with. Each one is looking out for their own needs. It's not love for the other. The other person becomes a vehicle for one's gratification. Too much of what is called love is 'fish love.' Real love is not one I'm going to get, but one that I'm going to give.'

The light goes on in Peter's eyes.

'It was Rabbi Dessler who said that people make a serious mistake if they think you give to those whom you love. The real truth is, you love those to whom you give. "True love" is a love of giving, not a love of receiving. End of lesson,' Yousef quips with a short laugh.

I stare at the remains of the fish on my own plate. Yousef's illustration hits me between the eyes. For months I've been struggling with thoughts of Miriam. A matchmaker selected her for me. How am I supposed to feel? My chair suddenly becomes uncomfortable.

Yousef says, 'Can you spare me one more comment?'

I see the wheels turning in Peter's head; he smiles and nods as he picks up his knife and fork.

'The West has a different way of approaching marriage. They insist that what they call love—infatuation, passion—has to be hot. Two people marry, and as time goes on, the pot on the stove loses heat and grows cold. We are different. We start with the pot, cold on the stove, and as time progresses, it becomes hot.' Yousef's words find a place in my heart like seeds in soil.

'Ah, more wisdom from the Rabbi,' Joshua says, handing Yousef a piece of fish.

'I've never been brave enough to allow anyone to find me a wife,' Yousef says.

I've never explored that topic with Yousef. He always said he was content to be single, that his calling as a Rabbi consumed his waking hours. I often wonder if he feels lonely. He's such a wise, amazing man. I love him.

The Shabbat meal, sprinkled with Yousef's wisdom, brings a shift in my thoughts about Miriam and marriage. Yousef's exposition of love challenges me. Maybe I need to learn to love. Maybe the pot doesn't have to be boiling at the start. What was the boiling about? My obsession with Aalia? Was it simply blind infatuation? Why was I attracted to her?

The professor's words came back to haunt me—*love is a decision*. Was part of my pursuit of Aalia driven by an unconscious need to convey to my father that 'I'll do what I bloody well like and nobody is going to stop me!'? Was I frantically trying to fill an emotional vacuum? Was it infatuation? Was I hooked on dopamine? Was it love or was it unconscious rage or both that I allowed to dominate me?

Increasingly I began to question the wisdom of my relationship with Aalia. I battled the feelings of guilt, knowing I'd initiated the relationship. I was the pursuer. *Love is a decision*. If I'd been wiser … she may still be alive.

Plenty of attractive Jewish women are available. But starting with cold water on the stove seems like a mountain too high. Yet many marriages in the East are strong. The divorce rate is much less than in the West. The pendulum swings in my head. My thoughts churn like a washing machine. What about Miriam? She's not unattractive and takes good care of herself. But how can I stop comparing her with my Aalia? And she was married; how can she not compare me with her husband? What skeletons lie in her closet that may emerge if we marry? Can I love her with the love that Yousef talks about? My mind is in a whirl as I drive back to the hospital—my stomach content, but my head, troubled. The following day, I shelve thoughts of marriage.

~

June 1991

I survived another four weeks in a temporary camp on the outskirts of Tel Aviv, immersed in a sea of bruised, but not broken humanity. Hadassah hospital invited me to provide treatment for another wave of Ethiopian Jews—men, women, and children who survived appalling conditions and persecution. When they landed, they just stared at me and the other staff in disbelief that they were safe. Operation Solomon drained me. [Note 1] Daily I saw the fear and uncertainty in the eyes of my Jewish brothers, arriving with only the clothes they wore, aged beyond their years due to decades of inadequate food, health care, and shelter. I found myself staring into the eyes of Papa, Ima, and their kind when they arrived in Eretz Israel. They, too, had survived persecution and the threat of extermination. They endured the hopelessness of being trapped in European camps with every nation's door slammed shut in 1947. Again, as I experienced in Operation Moses, when I answered the professor's call for help, I saw and felt the reality of their past.

However, the dilemma dug deeper because I worked beside Palestinian colleagues, whose frustration and pain increased with every planeload of Jewish refugees. 'Where are they going to be settled?' they asked.

Creating and expanding Jewish settlements is the only answer, which rubs salt into the already open wound for the Palestinians. I understand their pain and their claim. There is no easy answer.

Over the months following my work for Operation Solomon, my interest in a relationship grew.

Is it chance or a divine appointment that I spot Miriam sitting beside a child in the children's ward when I commence my morning rounds today? I think it's her. I check the hospital records at the nurse's station; I'm correct. Her son, Ari, has been admitted with a high fever and is being monitored. Ari is not my patient, but I decide to make an informal enquiry as to how he is feeling.

Miriam recognises me instantly and smiles.

'*Shalom*.' I say. 'I thought I recognised you. I was just passing and interested to know how Ari is feeling this morning.'

'His temperature is almost back to normal and the antibiotics appear to be working.'

'I'm glad to hear it. How old is he?'

'Four last month.' She turns her gaze to the face peering above the white sheet, a small soft brown bear nestled beside his head.

'*Shalom*, Ari. I'm glad you're starting to feel better.'

Ari manages a weak smile and then a cry from a child in the opposite bed catches his attention.

'Thank you for stopping by, Uri,' Miriam says. 'The staff are very helpful.'

'Do you have other children?'

'No. Ari is my one and only,' she replies with sadness in her voice.

Something inexplicable is happening. Miriam falls silent but continues to gently hold me with her gaze. A faint, sad smile creases her lips. For a moment I want to excuse myself to continue my rounds, but something compels me to stay. Miriam glances at the floor for a brief moment and then returns her gaze to me, this time with a confident smile.

Something inside me resonates—it's like someone has plucked the single string of a harp; it stirs me, soothes me. I take a deep breath and smile. 'It's good to see you, and I hope Ari is out of here soon.'

'I'm sure he will be. Thank you, Uri.'

My body feels lighter as I reluctantly leave Miriam. My breathing rate has increased. What was that about? Any encounter could've been awkward and embarrassing, given our circumstances. But there was none of that. I'm genuinely surprised. It was the way she looked at me, relaxed, so peaceful, yet with a touch of sadness in her eyes. Was that longing in her eyes? An invitation? My mind is now in a spin.

~

Two months have passed since my 'chance meeting' with Miriam. Yousef and I have been to the Wall, and we now hurry through the Jaffa Gate towards Ben Yehuda Street where we've been invited for the Shabbat meal in a beautiful home in the new city. Benjamin, a successful businessman, a friend of Yousef, is our host.

Soon we're immersed in a gathering of at least thirty people. Two large round tables have been prepared for the meal. Benjamin's taste in artefacts and art are displayed around the perimeter of the huge room—one that has welcomed diplomats and high-ranking politicians from around the world.

An expensive red carpet with an intricate pattern covers the floor where guests chat animatedly.

Suddenly, I catch my breath. Across the crowded floor I see a woman talking with our hostess. It looks like Miriam; it is Miriam! My eyes refuse to leave her. She's wearing a dark blue, long, loose-fitting dress, elegant but not ostentatious, in keeping with Shabbat. She's enjoying the conversation, smiling and gesturing with her hands.

Yousef, standing beside me, observes my interest. I glance at him, and he smiles back, but says nothing. I pause … *Wait a minute. Is this a setup? Is this Yousef's work? Has he taken over from the Shadchen?* For a moment, suspicion robs me of any joy I have at being present in this amazing gathering. Then, almost instantly, I consider that it's meant to be. Who cares if it's the work of matchmaking friends or the work of the Divine?

The seating for the meal places me opposite Miriam on one of the two tables, but the distance between us isn't conducive to developing conversation, so I talk to those nearby. The delicious Shabbat meal finishes with a torte filled with seasonal fruit, and when our bellies are full and taste buds satiated, we rise and slowly gravitate towards each other.

'*Shalom,* Uri,' she says, her eyes reflecting the relaxed smile on her lips. 'A beautiful meal.'

'*Shalom*, Miriam; most definitely. They are generous people.'

Guests spill out over the large balcony and down the stone stairs into a garden dotted with a variety of mature bushes and palms.

'Care for a quiet walk?' I gesture towards the open door.

'Thank you. I'd love to.'

We walk to the door and descend into the garden. Small groups are chatting, enjoying the night air. 'How is Ari?'

'He's well now, thanks. He bounced back quickly once the antibiotics took over.'

'It's amazing how quickly kids can recover.'

'I'm surprised you remember his name.' Miriam laughed.

'Maybe it's a gift I have,' I respond with a smile.

The warmth of the orange glow from the Old City, with the Tower of David keeping watch, contrasts with the growing chill of the night air under a clear sky. 'Are you warm enough?' I ask.

'The coolness is so refreshing after such a hot day.'

A half-moon smiles, its soft glow backlighting the scarf that covers Miriam's black hair. My eyes scan her face, in shadow but illuminated by fairy lights scattered through overhanging trees. Wrinkles now have formed on a forehead that once was smooth. Maybe it's the early signs of ageing or the evidence of the deep grief she endured through the death of her husband. Her eyes are soft and appealing, with a touch of sadness.

'How long have you lived in Jerusalem?' I ask.

'Ari and I moved into an apartment six months ago. I was successful in applying for a teaching position in a primary school. We both love Jerusalem, so different from Tel Aviv.'

'So you did your teacher training in Tel Aviv?'

'Yes, and that was where I met my husband. He was an officer in the air force.' She turned and looked towards the Old City and sighed. 'It was too hard after his death to stay there. I've tried for two years but there are too many memories: the beach; the cafés; the shops. Friends said I was making a mistake leaving. They said, "We're here to support you." But I have a brother and a sister who live here, and they've helped me settle in. It's been a good move; a fresh start; a new beginning. And how is your career going at the hospital?'

'I love it. It exhausts me, but I'm learning to take better care of myself, now. I'm exploring postgraduate studies in America at the moment. Not sure I'm really convinced I should go yet. My father is unwell, and I try to support him as much as I can.'

A moment of awkward silence hangs in the air. My mind is curious about how she felt about me walking away from a proposed marriage, but my heart says, 'Don't go there; don't embarrass her.'

In her next breath, she plunges into the issue that's causing me to walk on eggshells. 'I really admired you for following your heart after I met you. You are such a strong person to stand up for what you believed was right for you. I must confess, I liked you; I was *very* impressed, so I was disappointed, as were my parents.' She fiddled with her sleeve and smiled. 'But I instantly knew *you* had to choose, and I respect you for that.'

I nodded, looked away for a moment, and then asked, 'How did you meet your husband?'

Miriam smiled and then laughed. 'You may not believe this, but your decision gave me the courage to say to my parents that my husband was not going to come from the matchmaking of a *Shadchen*. Of course they were shocked. They blamed you for influencing me.' She laughed again. 'Living in Tel Aviv is like having one foot in the West. No doubt I was influenced by many of my friends who were secular.'

I smile and say, 'We're as bad as each other.'

Miriam nods vigorously and smiles. It's obvious she's enjoying our conversation. Another silence follows, but this time it's a relaxed, restful silence.

'I read about your terrible sadness in the papers, Uri. I can't imagine what that was like for you.' It was the way she said it that brought a sob to my voice—so understanding and empathic.

Pause. Breathe deeply, I tell myself. I'm shocked that a pocket of raw emotion still exists. 'I'm mostly through it. Every so often the past emerges.'

Miriam senses my grief. 'We're all different, aren't we? The way we deal with grief; it takes time …'

I nod. 'I now believe the wound never completely heals, it just shrinks to a manageable size.'

'You're right. I've spent hours weeping until I had no more tears to cry. I've done what I know I need to do to let go of the past and be ready to face whatever the future holds.'

I nod and realise how much I'm enjoying the growing connection. 'It's been so good to see you again.'

Miriam smiles. 'I've enjoyed it immensely.'

'Have you ever been to celebrate the end of Shabbat in Ben Yehuda?'

'No, I haven't.'

'The place is packed with folk all singing and dancing. It goes on for hours.'

'Oh, I'd love to, sometime.'

'What about tomorrow night?'

'Yes,' she says, her eyes sparkling.

'It's a deal. Let's meet at nine at the Jaffa Gate.'

~

Yousef strokes his beard, a complex blend of shades of grey.

'I don't know what to think,' I say, tapping my fingers on his small wooden table.

His small flat in the Bukharim Quarter, a short walk northeast from the Old City, is one of my favourite places. Spacious mansions with large courtyards similar to those in European cities front its wide streets. Homes are designed with neo-gothic windows, tiled roofs, arches, and Italian marble. Jewish motifs decorate the facades.

I sigh. 'No … I don't know what to think.' The words fall lazily from my mouth. The two meetings with Miriam swirl in my mind in a daze.

'Take your time,' Yousef says.

'It's over six years since I lost Aalia. Most of the time I feel fine.'

'What do you think of Miriam?'

'She's an intelligent woman, a good mother, attractive—though not as striking as Aalia. We have many things in common …'

'I'm careful about saying this,' Yousef says, cutting a slice of teacake, 'but the *Shadchen* selected her for you. Does that count for anything?'

I find myself nodding and smiling, and then, 'Hah! I don't know what I'm laughing about.'

Yousef finishes a mouthful and says, 'You've shifted a little in your thinking?'

'I suppose so … I … well yes! Your oration on 'fish love' still plays on my mind. I hear your voice in my head. My brain was overdosing on oxytocin—the chemical released when people 'fall in love.' My brain went on a vacation! The more I've thought about it, the more I wonder if I was using Aalia to heal a wound. Was I desperate for love to fill the vacuum of not having a close relationship with my parents … well certainly with Papa?'

'You were certainly vulnerable, Uri. I struggled to watch you thrashing around. Your brain was disengaged.'

'Aalia became someone for *my* gratification … it's hard to say that, but it's true.'

'Life is about learning, and you're prepared to think and reflect,' Yousef says seriously.

'The question I'm now asking myself is, can I love Miriam, really love her … give to her rather than wanting from her?'

Yousef smiled. 'When two people who believe that commit themselves to a relationship, it's powerful and it lasts. Love is a decision.'

~

December 1993

My relationship with Miriam grew to the point where I commenced the process of marrying her. I sourced a ring and followed our traditional practice for a wedding. Yousef reminded me, subtly, on a few occasions, quoting from Genesis with half a smile, 'It is not good for man to be alone.'

Yousef officiated on that Sunday under the *chuppah* in Kibbutz Atak, with family and friends clapping, singing, dancing, and celebrating with genuine warmth and love.

As I look back on that cool day in December, I'm grateful to have a wife who is so committed to me. There's not the passion I had with Aalia, but rather a gentle blending of our lives. We are slowly discovering each other as we share limited time out from our professions. Our lovemaking is growing in intensity. It's a surprise to us both that Miriam is pregnant already. We haven't really established our relationship and yet we're going to have a child!

One of the memories, amongst the many of our relaxed wedding, was the sight of Papa's tears. Streams of joy flowed unhindered, reminiscent of my Bar Mitzvah, and a stark contrast to the unforgettable day at the Wall when he didn't give himself permission to cry.

~

1. A total of 14,324 Ethiopian Jews were transported in Operation Solomon on May 24th 1991. More than 36,000 Ethiopian Jews live in Israel. Despite poverty and economic hardships, they are an integral part of Israeli life, with a number achieving significant roles in society. *Source: Israel Association of European Jews.*

Chapter Twenty-Seven

1987

Two years had passed since Omar and Sabah's exit from Atak. At first Maya had agonised over her friend's sudden departure, a wound that kept her awake at night, but now the shock of Sabah and Omar's sudden abandonment of their close-knit community had passed, leaving just a deep grief which hung heavily over Maya. She'd finally tracked down Sabah through mutual friends, and correspondence flowed between the two.

Sabah's grief had refused to leave her, but her rage towards Ghazi had eased. She still found it unthinkable that her son could murder his own sister. She blamed his so-called 'friends'—terrorists. *He's been radicalised, tricked by terrorists into an act of evil*, she wrote. *It was not the behaviour of my Ghazi.*

She told Maya how desperate she was to visit him and that Omar had removed his son from his mind. For Omar, Ghazi no longer existed. He'd made no pronouncement from his mouth, but actions speak louder than words. Sabah had suffered in silence through the imaginings of what was happening to her son in prison. Omar didn't allow her to mention his name—nobody did. As far as Omar was concerned, Ghazi was dead.

Maya decided to support Sabah in what she knew would be a disturbing experience for her long-time friend. Something had to be done, and Abdiel gave Maya his blessing to support their long-time friend. Secretly the two women plotted to visit the prison, carefully hiding their plan from Omar.

In early April, Maya and Sabah received permission to visit Ghazi. Maya drove from Atak and stayed with Abdiel and Maya's friends Leah and Issur in the confusion that invades the Old City at Easter. Someone referred to it as, 'The strange agglomeration of ignorance, cynicism, simple piety, sophistication, and scholarship where observance replaces faith.'

On the day of the prison visit, Sabah left her home in the beautiful, ancient Palestinian town of Ramallah, ten kilometres north of Jerusalem, early in the morning. She left plenty of time to negotiate the infamous Rachael Checkpoint or Checkpoint 300. Sometimes it could take two hours to be processed. Baruch Goldstein, a Jewish doctor, was the one responsible. In an act of terror, he'd massacred twenty-nine Palestinians at the Cave of the Partiarchs in nearby Hebron, and Jewish authorities feared Palestinian revenge on the Jewish settlement of Gilo, so they built the checkpoint, which made life difficult for everyone.

When she finally met Maya in Jerusalem, Sabah held her friend and sobbed for half an hour. Then they drove south, through insufferable heat, beyond the inaccessible mountains of Moab, where black goats grazed beside the road under the watchful eye of their Bedouin masters.

The descent towards the Dead Sea, calm and still like blue glass, progressed to sand-coloured mountains and khaki-coloured chasms. The drive plunged them into even fiercer heat, in the land of fire, the lowest place on earth. Dead rocks, piled high, look as if they'd been twisted in the agony of some prehistoric convulsion. Rocks stained with obscene yellow slime dot the parched wilderness of dirty white and grey. No shells decorate the shore of the Dead Sea, and no weeds or water plants. Instead of water, the vast hole in the earth catches and holds a cauldron of chemicals—mixtures of sulphurous and nitrous matter.

'We're going into hell,' Sabah muttered.

'Looks like it, feels like it, and smells like it,' Maya replied.

After an hour's travel, they arrived at the outside gates of the secure prison guarded by thirsty shrubs. Both stared in horror as they approached the stronghold. The place held all the elements of a nightmare: the surrounding land, drained of colour, appeared sinister and dead; khaki rocks flung back the sun like the sides of a furnace; the heat, unbearable; air hot and still. Their eyes avoided the blinding glare of distant sand hills.

The boom gate rose after a guard examined their papers. The two women parked the car, then rushed through the heat to the shade of the building. Inside, the women surrendered their belongings to a locker—nothing could be taken into the prison. Then another guard ushered them through three heavy, locked doors and told them to wait in a small room in which a few plastic chairs faced a glass screen mounted on a narrow counter. A green metal door was the only entry into the partitioned area. A single chair positioned at the counter, in line with a number of small holes in the glass, enabled the prisoner to speak to visitors.

Sabah fidgeted with her dress while the minutes ticked by. Finally the green door opened, and a figure entered the room. Ghazi stood motionless, handcuffed. Behind him a guard closed the door and stood at the back of the partitioned area. Sabah sprang to her feet, pulled a chair up to the glass and sat down.

Ghazi stood motionless, staring at his mother, and then looked away.

'Ghazi. You have no idea how much I've wanted to see you.' Tears formed as Sabah's eyes searched Ghazi's body. His gaunt, bearded face and emaciated figure shocked her. In a faltering voice she said, 'Ghazi, I want to tell you, you are still my son. I care for you.'

Ghazi's eyes returned to his mother, then focused on the floor.

'Please talk to me Ghazi,' she pleaded.

Without looking at Sabah, he stepped forward and lowered himself onto the chair on his side of the partition.

'Thank you, Ghazi. You're my son … I care for you. … I'm so glad to see you.'

Ghazi's posture softened as if his mother's words caressed him.

'I miss you, so much. I wanted to … to bake some of your favourite sweet-cakes but … we're not allowed to bring anything into the prison … tell me, how are you?'

Ghazi shook for a second and then came a sob. His eyes remained glued to the floor. His lips quivered, 'I thought … I thought what I was doing was right … but now … it's … it's just a …' He didn't finish the sentence.

'You thought you were doing right. You fell under the spell of those who love violence.' Sabah's voice was soft, empathic. She chose her words carefully. 'What you did was wrong, but that doesn't mean I don't love you.'

Still slumped forward, Ghazi lifted his head and peered through misty tears at Sabah. 'I didn't ... I didn't want to hurt ... you, or Father.'

Sabah nodded. 'Your anger was so great; you couldn't think straight.'

'I was so tired of what the Jews are doing to us: taking our land; pushing us around; controlling our lives.' His haggard body moved to a more upright position. 'I wanted it to be ... different.' He rested his hands on the counter and lowered his eyes. 'I thought one day you might come.' His voice softened, and for the first time came a hint of a smile. 'How's Father?'

Sabah frowned. 'Your father is hurting, badly. I believe, in time, he'll forgive you, as I have.'

Ghazi gazed into his mother's eyes. 'I'm so sorry ... so sorry ... I caused you and Father so much pain.'

'Time's up!' The guard stepped forward and waited for Ghazi to stand.

'I love you, Ghazi, and I always will.'

Ghazi's eyes smiled as he whispered, 'Thank you.'

Chapter Twenty-Eight

Tara moved her body to a more comfortable position on her metal-framed bed in her home on the West Bank. It had been in the family for generations. The fancy wrought-iron work of the bed head gave it a 'touch of class' in Tara's thinking. Mica, her husband of four years, had left home earlier for another day's work carving beautiful figures from local olive wood in a small workshop on the outskirts of Bethlehem.

Tara loved the dry climate of Bethlehem, perched on a ridge in the Judean hills, ten kilometres south of Jerusalem. From her window she could see the rolling green hills, scattered with grey rocks. For her they were sacred hills, once occupied by the shepherds who heard the angels sing, announcing the birth of Jesus. She loved the sacred history of her town, but felt saddened by the ongoing conflict.

Tara missed the chatter of the women who surrounded her in the workshop. Seated on low pieces of wood, she worked daily with a skill acquired from her mother, embroidery. Other women created rosaries from the stones of Dora palms. Men sat cross-legged, carving crosses from olive wood and common date palms.

Today, she 'carried her baby heavy.' That's what her mother would say. Her mother died prematurely a year ago from cancer, and her father met an untimely death when an

Israeli shell exploded near his car three years earlier. Today she wondered how she would survive the next ten weeks.

Tara's obstetrician, a Palestinian with Israeli citizenship, worked two days at the local hospital in Bethlehem and the remainder of his time at Hadassah Hospital. He kept a watchful eye on his patient, who struggled with her first pregnancy. Tara loved children and everything was in place for her baby. Mica had created a beautiful mobile with a moon, stars, and a variety of other shapes, all carved from olive wood. His masterpiece, hand-painted in bright colours by Tara, hung above the crib and attracted the adulation of every visitor to their simple home.

A cramp suddenly seized her abdomen. *What's this? Baby's not due for another ten weeks.* Then another, far stronger, forced a cry from her mouth. *Are these contractions? Breathe … breathe.* Another, then another … They kept coming. Tara reached for the phone beside her bed and rang her friend Ruth, a midwife, who lived five minutes away.

'I'm on my way, Tara,' came her immediate response to her friend's gasping cry for help.

Minutes later Ruth sat beside her friend, wiping Tara's forehead with a damp cloth. 'They seem like contractions, but they don't have any rhythm,' she observed.

'They've stopped.' Tara threw her head back onto the pillow with relief. 'What do you think I should do? I don't want to go to the hospital and find out it's a false alarm.'

Ruth carefully examined Tara's swollen abdomen. 'The baby hasn't turned, so it's not ready yet.' Scarcely had the words left her mouth when Tara let out a cry, and fluid soaked the mattress. Ruth looked at the mess, shocked. 'Your waters have broken!' she cried.

Ruth picked up the phone and called the doctor. 'No, she's not dilated yet. Yes … no … very well … thank you.'

'What did he say?' Tara gasped as another pain gripped her.

'He's called an ambulance and has recommended you to go to Hadassah where they have better facilities. This baby is going to be tricky. The doctor's at the hospital now and will be ready for you. My dear, you'll be there in ten minutes. All will be well.'

Tara gave a faint smile. '*Shukran.*'

'That's what friends are for.'

Minutes later two young paramedics stretchered Tara through the open doors of the ambulance and, with siren screaming, headed for the security crossing.

Ruth sat beside Tara, securely strapped to the thin vinyl-covered mattress covered with a white sheet. 'It won't take long,' Ruth said, gripping Tara's hand.

Three cars stood between the ambulance and the boom gate. The soldiers permitted them to proceed, then the boom gate lowered and remained in place as the ambulance approached. The young Palestinian driver turned off the lights and siren, and two Israeli soldiers stepped forward, guns hanging from their shoulders. The driver produced the papers, and the taller of the soldiers, a good-looking young man with a solid build and light-olive skin, examined them.

The other guard, a little older, fumbled with the back doors. 'Where are you off to?' he asked.

'Hadassah Emergency,' came the hasty reply from the driver.

The taller guard handed the papers back to the driver. 'Need to check the wagon.'

The driver leapt out of the wagon and followed the guard around the back of the vehicle. The older guard had opened the doors, exposing the patient and her friend to the blaze of the morning sun.

'This is an emergency …' the driver pleaded, moving his hands in anxious circles.

The taller guard waved his hand to cut off his protestations.

The driver stared at the two guards, desperation in his eyes. 'This patient's situation is urgent.'

Tara let out a scream and gripped the sides of the stretcher. Her white knuckles evidenced the intensity of her pain.

'That won't get you any sympathy,' the tall guard growled. 'We need to search for explosives.'

'Explosives!' The paramedics looked at each other in disbelief.

The driver bit his tongue and thrust his fidgeting hands into his pockets. He wanted to shake sense into these arrogant Israelis, but he knew he had to remain calm. Any frustration or protest was likely to delay the process longer.

On a previous occasion at Allenby Crossing into Jordan, an Israeli found a chess-set in one of the bags of a family. He and his security companion spent an hour playing a game and then went to lunch. It took over three hours for that family to cross the border that day.

Both guards opened cavities, boxes, removed the fire extinguisher from its mounting, and spent ten minutes examining under the wagon. They covered every centimetre of the vehicle.

Tara's groans and cries fell on deaf ears. Even the blood seeping onto the mattress cover in clear view didn't bring a word or hint of understanding or sympathy. While Tara twisted in pain, Ruth held a cold compress to her friend's forehead with her right hand and covered the tears that flowed down her face with the other. The paramedics, stood in silence, arms folded, avoiding eye contact with the guards.

At last, the Israeli soldiers closed the doors. 'All clear.'

The boom gate rose. The ambulance roared to life and raced towards Hadassah Hospital, lights flashing, siren screaming. Twenty wasted minutes at the checkpoint—only to satisfy the arrogance of two Israeli guards! Would they be too late?

Dr Assan paced the floor outside the delivery room, poised, ready for his emergency patient.

'They're here doctor!' came a cry from the corridor.

A wardsman and the two paramedics steered the trolley on which Tara lay. Ruth followed behind.

~

Dr Hamal Assan sat in a corner of the staff cafeteria and stared at his coffee. He had no desire to eat. The unnecessary death of a baby is one of the most distressing events a doctor can experience. He wanted to weep, but tears wouldn't come. *This isn't the place to weep anyway,* he reassured himself. *At least I saved the mother.*

Two hours had passed since the tragedy. An investigation would follow; reports to submit; forms to fill in; interviews. *Could I have done anything differently? No!* Mica, the shattered husband, sat silent beside his distressed wife in intensive care. Hamal knew he had to talk with him soon, but not yet.

Down the hall, Mica sat motionless, blank-eyed, stunned, amongst the soft furnishings and pastel colours of the visitors' waiting room—a contrast to the clinical white and stainless steel of intensive care.

Hamal steeled himself for the conversation and walked up to the grief-stricken man. 'I'm so sorry your baby couldn't be saved,' he said, but his compassionate words didn't appear to register on the face of the distraught father.

'I need to know what happened, Doctor,' Mica said weakly.

'Yes, of course. The placenta separated from the womb, causing a catastrophic haemorrhage. It can happen abruptly with a little bit of bleeding and preterm labour. I suspect the placenta then completely tore away in the ambulance. This caused the contractions to change suddenly and bring on the severe pain, and then, heavy bleeding. The paramedics were wise not to palpate her abdomen to feel the position of her baby; that would have accentuated her pain even more. They put in a cannula and gave lots of intravenous fluid to attempt to resuscitate and put on oxygen via a mask. They didn't give drugs to stop pain as that may have dropped your wife's blood pressure further, which could have affected the baby.'

Mica nodded; his eyes filled with tears.

'Your wife was transferred from the ambulance straight to theatre for an emergency caesarean section to remove the baby,' Hamal continued. 'Sadly the baby died on the way here. Fortunately, however, we were able to control the bleeding after the placenta was delivered.' (Note 1)

'Thanks, Doctor,' Micah replied after a short silence. 'You've done all you could.'

'It was really touch and go with your wife; she lost a lot of blood, but fortunately the transfusion has been effective. We'll continue to monitor her in intensive care.'

Mica's rough, woodworking hands gripped Hamal's hand, then he left the room, nursing his grief.

~

I walk into the cafeteria and notice Hamal sitting alone in the corner, his face drawn.

'Uri!' He waves me over.

'How are you?' I ask, drawing up a chair.

'I'm absolutely stuffed, to put it mildly.'

'I heard about the drama you had earlier,' I say, seating myself opposite his hunched body.

'What's criminal is that it was entirely preventable.' The frustration is clear in his voice. 'The ambulance was held up at the checkpoint for twenty minutes while they searched for bloody explosives!'

I'd heard the news earlier, and it'd made my blood boil. Delays at any checkpoint were common. It depended on the individual guard and his or her attitude; some were pleasant, some obnoxious. The latter kind seemed to derive some sense of sadistic joy from flaunting their power and making life difficult for Palestinians. As an Israeli, I carry great shame for the way my countrymen carry on at the borders, but usually ambulances are given the green light.

'It's pure bastardisation,' I say in disgust. 'Criminal!'

Hamal frowns, looks at me, and then glances away. 'I don't really want to tell you this, Uri.'

'Tell me what?'

Hamal fixes his gaze on me but hesitates.

'Tell me, Hamal; what is it?'

He sighs. 'I've already started my investigations, and I learnt half-an-hour ago that one of the two guards who stopped the ambulance was your brother, Abraham.'

Hamal's words felt like a fist slamming into my stomach. 'Abe!'

'I have it from a reliable source. Apparently, he's gaining quite a reputation.'

My body stiffens. 'How could he do this?' I gasp. 'My own brother!' I sit stunned in disbelief, breathing heavily. After a short silence, I say, 'I'm going to challenge him about this.'

I decide not to contact Abe right now, though. If I saw him in the flesh now, I could strangle him. The shock of hearing it from Hamal recedes, but my anger rages. *How could he do that? He wasn't raised that way. What will Papa and Ima say if they find out?* I decide to confront him as soon as possible—face to face.

Two days after the death of the baby, Abe arrives at our rented apartment in West Jerusalem for dinner. Abe has never visited us here before, so I invited him. Miriam's quiet, no fuss, manner makes her the perfect hostess. Her dark-brown eyes dance when she laughs; her long black hair frames a face of kindness; she is well-loved by my family and respected by her friends, and the dishes displayed before us are a testament to her wonderful culinary skills.

She greets Abe with a kiss and says, 'Something to drink, Abe?'

'I'll have some of your lemonade, please,' he responds.

The meal proceeds with small talk about mutual friends, concerns about how Papa and Ima are managing, and the state of the economy. Afterwards Miriam packs the dishes away and remains in the kitchen as planned.

I watch Abe's face as I approach the main topic of our meeting. 'Any dramas at the checkpoint recently?' I ask, hoping he might volunteer the incident.

'Nothing out of the usual,' comes the casual reply.

I decide to go straight to the point. 'An ambulance was delayed on its way to Hadassah Hospital.' No sign of a visible reaction. His breathing rate remains the same. 'The mother was lucky to survive, but the baby died. That could be called an act of terror!'

His gaze does not leave me. 'That's unfortunate, but these things happen.'

My body stiffens at his dismissive response, and my tension rises as I unleash the next question. 'Rumour has it you were on duty at the time.'

His manner and voice remain unchanged. 'Yes, I was. My colleague and I searched the wagon.'

'Searching for *what*?' I ask, frustration creeping into my voice.

'Explosives, of course. It's happened before.'

My anger rises. 'It took *twenty minutes* to search!'

Without hesitation, he responds in a calm voice, 'It's part of our job. You can never be too careful.'

'Come on, Abe … an ambulance!' I struggle to maintain my calm; anger grips my body. 'A woman almost lost her life … a baby died! That could be called an act of terror!'

He shrugs. 'If you have a problem with it, talk to my superiors,' he replies unmoved. 'I work under orders.'

Following this path will lead nowhere. The laissez-faire approach by many guards at the borders is a nightmare. Morality is a low priority. His superiors would dismiss the incident as simply being 'what happens.'

'You weren't raised this way. What would Papa say?'

For the first time in our conversation, his face changes. He glares at me. 'What would Papa say? What would Papa say! He hasn't said much since I was born!'

The force of his anger shocks me. I look away to gather my thoughts. The penetrating intensity of his gaze is intimidating. I understand what he's saying. Papa's retreat into solitary confinement over the years has left its mark. I know what it's done to me, and for the first time, I understand the impact on Abe.

We sit in silence for a minute, and I decide in desperation to take one last shot. I soften my voice. 'What would Yousef say?'

'I don't care what Yousef thinks! I no longer believe in the faith of my father, not that I saw much evidence of it. There's no God. You can believe in fairy tales if you want to, but for me? No!'

His hardened tone disturbs me. It's reactive, defensive, not coming from reason, but more from silent, solidified anger.

He continues, 'You can be Moses if you want to and try to lead our people to freedom. But I believe in guns … guns without Moses. You can do it your way, Uri, but I vote for guns.'

Abe's words sting me. I give myself time to think and take a deep breath. 'Yes, we need guns and all the weapons of war to provide a safe place for our people. We need a well-trained army to defend our borders. But we *don't* need a cynical, disrespectful, cold-blooded arrogance that de-humanises our Palestinian brothers. My fear is that this cancer will finally destroy us. We're losing our soul—being destroyed from within. Forget about the external threats from Arab nations. This disease, if allowed to continue, will bring us down. It can't go on indefinitely. This is a moral crisis that's within our power to manage. It's how we respond to anger and violence that will make a difference. We can't control others, but we can control the way *we* respond.' I'm surprised by the intensity in my voice.

Abe listens without comment. But I know he's allowing my passion to safely pass him by.

'Abe,' I continue, in a quieter tone, 'I know mothers who weep when their sons and daughters enter national service. Many young men and women are able to maintain their humanity. Some do not. They lose their soul to the cancer, seduced by the power of hate.'

Abe sits in silence, eyes glazed over.

I know I can't reach him. I wonder what needs to happen to him, in order for him to ever regain his humanity.

~

1. If the placenta had not been delivered the doctor would attempt an emergency hysterectomy during which she could have a cardiac arrest from loss of blood and not be recoverable.

Part Six

Chapter Twenty-Nine

July 2002

It's early days in the beginning of a new century. Much has happened in the last eight years. Miriam has provided me with a healthy son, Baruch, meaning 'blessed.' We also have a six-year-old daughter, Shifra, 'beauty and grace.' Very little has changed in my parents' lives. Age has wearied Papa, adding an additional struggle to his demonic fight. Ima is his rock, and her devotion to him should be rewarded with a medal. My two sisters, Sabella and Sachi have reluctantly entered their thirties. Sabella is now married and has two energetic children, whilst Sachi has joined the ranks of the feminists and writes for newspapers or any media institution that will publish her rantings. Abe is married with two children. I don't see much of him now. Militant Zionism has captured his heart and mind, and we find it difficult to speak the same language.

Tensions are running high again in Israel. My hopes were raised when Israeli and Palestinian leaders agreed to cease hostilities at The Oslo Peace Accord in 1993, [Note 1] just after my marriage, and Israel signed a peace treaty with Jordan in 1994. In that year the Nobel Peace Prize was awarded to our Prime Minister, Yitzhak Rabin, Shimon Peres, and Yasser Arafat. Just when peace seemed possible, a fanatical right-wing Israeli assassinated Yitzak Rabin, which threw the country into chaos and shattered peace initiatives. Another incident also caused shockwaves in 1996. Israelis opened a tunnel next to the Temple Mount in Jerusalem, and the clash claimed seventy Israeli and Palestinian lives. Heartrending.

The so-called Al-Aqsa or Second Intifada was a tragic turning point that filled our hospitals and exhausted my energy. Ehud Barak promised to vigorously pursue the peace process, and he defeated Netanyahu's government. President Clinton called Arafat and Barak to peace talks at Camp David, but they failed. Clinton supported Israeli's interpretation of the event that the Palestinians had refused generous concessions offered by Israel. The Palestinians said that 'some concessions were offered' but not enough for a viable Palestinian state with Jerusalem as its capital. The failure of the talks precipitated the leader of the right-wing Likud Party, Ariel Sharon's, visit to the Dome of the Rock, *al-Harim al Sharif*, a holy site for Muslims in Jerusalem, on 28th September 2000. The Palestinians viewed this as an extreme act of provocation and took to the streets in violent protest. A series of suicide bombings followed, killing many Israelis. Hadassah hospital again filled with casualties, making long days and nights for me.

President Clinton's initiative at Taba in Sinai was another attempt to bring peace and raised our hopes, but Ariel Sharon wasn't willing to negotiate until the Palestinians ended their violence. The Arab League Proposals in March 2002 were met with rejection. Israel wasn't willing to return the land acquired through the 1967 War because it would leave us vulnerable to further hostilities. So frustrating! Will anything ever change? (Note 2)

Now it's eight o'clock in the morning, and already the sun threatens to outdo its mid-summer performance of yesterday. The clatter of machinery has commenced along the West Bank; the erratic jarring sounds create an ominous message in a mysterious kind of Morse Code that tells people to keep out. The wall separating Palestinian land from Israel continues to divide land and opinions. I'm saddened to see such a thing happening. Ariel Sharon says it's the best solution to halt the suicide bombers. Over the last twelve months, a procession of shattered bodies has entered our facility. Palestinians killed totalled 862 and around 25,000 injured. Israelis, 239 killed and around 800 injured.

Peter Wiseman is back in Jerusalem. His frequent visits and genuine interest in our ongoing struggles have won him my friendship. I first met Peter as a patient after his terrible injuries. He seemed to have had a special connection with Aalia, who nursed him through the worst of his recovery. No doubt he had a crush on her, which sometimes happens between patient and nurse. The erection of the Security Wall has created international interest, and Peter, now a freelance journalist, is keen to tap into local opinion for a major article.

A brisk walk from my car leads me to the Old City via the New Gate. Every time I enter one of the old gates, I fall under the influence of a strange power—that of a city destroyed and resurrected. I walk where my forefathers suffered the destructive power of the Babylonians, Assyrians, and Romans. Here, blood flowed from the swords of the Crusaders and conquests of the Arabs. The spark of three great faiths create an electric atmosphere, but it's muddled with spiritual barriers and frontiers: the Temple Mount—Islam's holy place; the Western Wall—the Jews most sacred site; and the Church of the Holy Sepulchre—hallowed ground for Christian pilgrims. Each has their divergent beliefs. Each count the days differently.

I descend narrow Bab El Jadid Street in the Christian Quarter and head towards the café where Peter suggested we meet. Two orthodox Jews pass by in deep conversation; corkscrew curls dangle from their temples, tapping against their cheeks. Peter has befriended a young Palestinian named Jabir who is keen to meet me. He's a social worker helping Arab youth in East Jerusalem. Jabir is a passionate, outspoken activist who has led protest groups against the construction of the Security Wall. This will be an interesting discussion, I'm sure.

Life is coming to the stalls and cafés by the time I reach the boundary between the Christian and Armenian Quarters and spot the old café owned by an Armenian family. I enter, greeted by the rich smell of coffee. Peter sits in the corner with a young Palestinian man, Jabir, I presume.

'*Salam. Salam.*' I shake Jabir's extended hand as Peter makes introductions. Once seated, I glance at the young Palestinian's face; he has olive skin, a beard, and piercing brown eyes, and he appears self-assured and serious. My body registers a strange, uncomfortable feeling. Is it his intensity that disturbs me? Why does he want to meet me? Does he have a hidden agenda? My discomfort is more than my physical contact with the hard wooden chair. We order coffee.

'I've heard of you and your work at the hospital,' Jabir says. 'And also through Ghazi.'

The words almost knock me off my chair. I freeze. What kind of relationship does he have with Ghazi? Anger rises. I breathe deeply to manage control.

'I tried to help Ghazi,' Jabir says after a short silence. 'But he wouldn't be helped. What he did was wrong, very wrong. I'm sorry for you.'

My head is reeling. Where is this conversation going to go? I thought it would be political, but it's personal—painfully personal.

Jabir's voice softens. 'I always like to be upfront. I don't like hiding anything from anyone. I see you're upset when I mention his name. Sorry to cause more pain.'

Jabir's compassion and directness commands my respect. Yet the sudden and unexpected reference to the most traumatic event in my life by a total stranger, and a Palestinian, leaves me shaking and vulnerable. How long is it going to take to rid myself of the agony and the anger from which I thought I'd escaped?

'Are you all right, Uri?' Peter enquires.

'I think so,' I lie. 'It took me back to a dark place.'

'I'm sorry you had such a bad experience,' Jabir says, his expression serious. 'We all have a past with pain. My pain came when my family's land was taken for a Jewish settlement. Israeli soldiers forced us from our homes in the middle of the night. Then I lived in a refugee camp for two years. If I visit family in the West Bank, I suffer a bad attitude from many of your soldiers at checkpoints. Now we have a wall! Jews pretend to show respect to us. But when you replace street names with Hebrew, and Arabic name underneath, you don't check to see if spelling is correct. Many times it's not. We are not respected!'

His voice is now firm but pleading—pleading for understanding and respect. I know I need to listen in spite of the pain from the knife that now turns inside me. I summon up my professional persona developed from facing a multitude of patients caught up in the emotion of their dramas. *Leave your pain alone and listen to him.*

'I'm very sad when I hear you've had your home and land taken from you, and that you've been harshly treated by many of the checkpoint soldiers.'

'Checkpoints? Incubators of hatred!'

'I apologise for the way some of my countrymen have treated you. Also, I didn't want the Wall to go up, but our government, in its wisdom believes it will stop suicide bombers.'

'Nothing will stop bombers if they really want to come,' Jabir says, eyes blazing. 'Nothing!'

Peter Wiseman returns his coffee cup to its saucer and says to Jabir, 'Do you believe Israel has put up the Wall for security?'

'We call it the Separation Wall—it takes good parts of Arab land. It's a land grab.'

I remain silent. Many times I've heard that phrase.

Peter looks at each of us in turn. 'Historically, who do you say has title to the land?'

'That's the big question,' Jabir says with a frown.

Peter asks me, 'How far do you go back? King David?'

Jabir jumps in, 'How about Abraham?'

'So we move to a religious view?' Peter says.

'We've no choice,' I respond. 'For both Muslim and Jew, religion and politics are intertwined. You can't touch one without touching the other. Abraham is the first Jew, and in Genesis, we read God's promise of 'the land of Canaan' going to Abraham, Isaac, and his descendants.[Note 3] Religious Jews believe the promise to Abraham guarantees Israel's 'divine right' to the land, as do many secular or atheistic Jews who still value the Jewish Bible as an important historical and cultural writing.'

'However,' Jabir interjects. 'The Koran records Abraham as being a Muslim, and Ishmael is the chosen son, not Isaac. Also, the Koran says Jerusalem and the Temple Mount is a holy place for us because it's the place Mohammed visited before he ascended to heaven and talked to God.' [Note 4 & Appendix A]

'Jerusalem is also holy to us,' I say. 'The rock on the Temple Mount is where we believe Abraham was prepared to offer up Isaac, and Solomon's Temple was in the Temple Mount area. Some Rabbis won't walk in that area because it's so holy. They don't want to step on the ground where the Ark of the Covenant made by Moses may have rested.'

'I understand there are conflicting views between your religions,' Peter says in a conciliatory tone. 'One thing in common to both traditions is the predicted conflict between Ishmael, father of the Arabs, and his half-brother Isaac, father of the Jews. Do I have that correct?' [Note 5]

'Yes, that's correct,' I reply.

Jabir tries to switch the direction of the conversation. 'The root of the problem for Palestinians isn't religious, not Islam, but Palestinians who've been forced from their land.' He leans forward in his chair and fixes his gaze on me. 'We both know the land goes back to the days of Abraham. We share the same father—Abraham. You, from his son Isaac; me, from Ishmael. We cultivated land then, and we try to farm it today, but now the Separation Wall steals our land. Your settlements rob us of pastures and freedom.' Jabir waits for my response.

'I acknowledge our common roots,' I reply. 'Our religions do play a part, and our religions do differ. Who is right? Do we believe the Torah or the Koran?'

Peter strokes the stubble on his chin. 'Just to complicate the question further, you have many Christians who say that the Jewish Bible gives the Jews, God's chosen people, divine right to the land. However, they argue that the Jewish Bible is not the end of the story. They believe the fullness of God's revelation came in Jesus Christ, revealing God not only to the Jews but also to the whole world—every nation. They say the original covenant with Abraham still stands, but now it has little to do with the land. ^(Appendix B)

I frown. 'I'm not sure what you mean?'

Peter flicks through his notebook. 'According to a lecturer in a seminary in the US, and I quote Leviticus 25:23, in the Torah, God says the *land belongs to him:* 'The land is mine and you are but aliens and tenants.' The Jews were to see it as a *gift*, given for a particular period of time, not something they owned by *right*. The gift is a means to a greater end, not an end in itself. There's much in both the Old and New Testaments that says the land is not given to Abraham and his descendants for all time. The coming of the kingdom of God through the Messiah, Jesus, has transformed and reinterpreted all the promises and prophecies of the Old Testament. The Messiah dealt with the root causes of evil and injustice. He lived and died and was raised from the dead in the *land* and has opened the kingdom of God to all peoples, making all who follow him into "one new humanity."'' (Note 6)

I shake my head. 'That's not something I believe. The Christian church should stay out of it. It has a lot to answer for in allowing anti-Semitism to flourish, and allowing nationalism and ideas derived from the Enlightenment to create an environment for Nazism to flourish. The church needs to confess to this darkness which has contributed to the conflict.' (Note 7)

My frustration continues. 'The issue for me is that for centuries, Jewish people haven't had even the smallest strip of land to call home. People have persecuted us for over 2000 years. After surviving Auschwitz, my father was forcibly returned to a German concentration camp—Poppendorf—because no country was willing to open its doors to him or millions of Jewish refugees. Some tried to return to their homes in Poland and elsewhere in Europe, but many were persecuted again, and most found their homes were already occupied.'

Jabir moves uneasily in his chair, and I'm concerned he's reacting to the strength of my voice. He hasn't touched his coffee. I wonder how much he knows about Jewish issues after the war. I know Palestinian schools don't teach Jewish history or anything about the Holocaust.

I finish my coffee and soften my tone. 'I believe God has given us the land, but we need to share it. The tension for me is knowing that the Torah teaches Jews are required to care for any non-Jew, including our Palestinian brothers. The Torah says, "You are to treat the resident alien the same way you treat the native born among you—love them like yourself, since you were foreigners in the land of Egypt." (Note 8) But how can Jews love the "alien," the stranger, when many are intent on wiping us off the land?'

Jabir shakes his head. 'It's our land!'

'From a religious point of view, there's an impasse,' Peter says.

'It's no better from a political perspective,' I respond. 'As we all know, colonial powers for centuries have seen fit to occupy and administer territory under their control—Greeks, Romans, Ottomans, Spain, England, and France. It's the way civilisation has unfolded. England was given the mandate for Palestine, and it became too hard, so they finally passed it to the UN. Globally the UN is supposed to be the recognised mediator if two countries can't come to an agreement. In 1947 Israel was willing to accept the terms of the UN proposal, a two-state solution, but Arabs wanted the lot. The threat to wipe us out, which resulted in the War of 1948, was our desperate effort to stand our ground. The ongoing attacks and threats by the PLO, and now Hamas and Hezbollah, necessitate a "watchfulness" of the Middle East, especially Gaza and the West Bank.' [Note 9]

Jabir spreads his hands in a helpless gesture. 'Palestinian Arabs lacked leadership in 1947. We were not a nation—a majority in Palestine, yes, but too many factions fighting for control. Better if Palestinians had accepted the two-state deal then,' he confessed in a voice tinged with regret.

'Wisdom always comes in hindsight, doesn't it?' Peter offers.

'Jabir, there *are* some changes,' I say. 'Gaza is virtually under the control of the Palestinian Authority, and has persuaded Israel to leave Gaza, and there are indications that complete withdrawal will happen soon. [Note 10] However, Ariel

Sharon isn't prepared to allow munitions or military equipment into Gaza. It's the same with the West Bank. Arab communities can go about their daily lives but—'

'Only on Israel's terms,' Jabir interrupts.

Wiseman sees the frustration rising between Jabir and myself. 'Maybe what's needed is for a strong country to force a settlement. Take it out of the hands of both.'

I hear a pleading tone in my response, 'That's already happened with Britain's efforts and the UN in 1947. What's needed is for our Arab brothers and my Jewish countrymen to look into themselves and their religion and find a way forward. We are *both* victims; the persecutions over the centuries and the recent horror of the Holocaust still cast a giant shadow over my people. The uprooting of Arabs from their territory has been traumatic for them. I grew up with an Arab family whose land was seized in 1947 and were left to wander the countryside until they settled at Atak. I know their story. Their pain is great and has impacted their children, especially Ghazi, as you may know, Jabir. It's shattered their family and caused terrible pain.' I pause, take a deep breath and slow my speech. 'Part of the way forward is for Arab and Israelis to hear each other's stories, to remember that we're brothers, and hear each other's pain.' Emotion creeps into my voice.

Wiseman finishes his coffee, glances at me and asks, 'Did your father ever tell you much about what happened in Auschwitz?'

'No, hardly anything at all, but I can see how it's affected him. I know from my professional life and observing my father that there are usually two extremes: the few who obsessively retell their stories, and those who lock it away. My father is the latter. Survivors struggle with trauma. They have indelible images of death and unspeakable violence burnt into their memories. Also they suffer survivor guilt—*why am I still alive when others have perished?*—and from the intense feelings of powerlessness that they experienced in the concentration camps. There's also concern about survivors' own lack of feeling; they learned emotional deadness in the camps in order to survive. It's as though they internally administer an anaesthetic so they don't feel. Emotional numbness is a defence-mechanism to avoid overwhelming memories, thoughts, and emotions, and it causes the victim to withdraw from human contact. My father moved in and out of his numbness and has emotionally disconnected himself significantly from others, including his family, including me.'

Silence holds sway until Jabir speaks. His voice has the tone of reverence. 'I did a work placement in an aged-care home for Holocaust survivors. There were many rules for us, like not carrying keys; the sound of jangling keys trigger terrible memories.'

I'm surprised and moved by Jabir's sudden revelation. *He's worked in a Jewish aged care facility!*

Peter glances at his watch and then each of us in turn and asks, 'Is peace possible?'

'I hope so,' I reply.

'Peace between conflicted peoples including the Irish has happened,' Peter says. 'Many thought that war would never end.'

'Our conflict is far more complex,' I reply. 'I genuinely believe the vast majority of Israelis and Palestinian Arabs want to live together in peace, as they have often done in the past, and still do.'

'I recognise the problem,' Jabir says. 'Every time peace is close, Hezbollah or Hamas fire rockets onto Jewish settlements.'

'Or maniac Jewish right-wingers assassinate a Prime Minister like Yitzhak Rabin,' I add. 'To compound the confusion within the Jewish world, the religious ultra-orthodox are against the New State of Israel; they oppose Zionism. They believe God alone will establish the state of Israel without any help from guns and soldiers. It will be a pure act of God.'

Jabir nods. 'You don't have agreement among your people, and it's the same for us. Actually, we are worse! We're a crazy people: me against my brother; me and my brother against our father; my family against my cousins and clan; the clan against the tribe, and the tribe against the world; and all of us against the Infidel.' He gives a sarcastic laugh and gestures with his hands.

Peter leans back in his chair, fiddles with his empty cup, and says, 'Even putting the contradictory views between Jewish religious groups aside, I understand Jewish voices aren't unanimous within parliament. Strong conflicting voices, left and right factions argue continuously; it seems there's no one clear voice able to propose a path for peace that suits all Israelis.'

Jabir nods. 'Yes, it's not good for either side. The majority of my fellow countrymen want to live in peace; it's extremists, terrorists, who want to rid the land of Jews. And you must not forget interference by the USA.'

'And also Russia and Iran,' I add. 'Much that goes on behind the scenes by world powers around oil and strategic power adds to our problems.'

'It's so complex,' Peter says. 'Typically we always look to take one side against the other. Declare one is right and the other wrong as though the issue is either black or white. It makes us feel more comfortable. But it's lazy thinking. As an outsider with some understanding of the issues, I describe the scene as a sophisticated dance between Israelis and Palestinians. For observers looking on, that's all they see. But there're others on the dance floor, too, who influence how the two main dancers move. The dance has been going on for so long now that the choreography is instinctive. If one moves, the other responds automatically. The choreography has now become so strong and ingrained, it now drives the dancers …'

'And it's a dirty dance,' I add. 'We always have to consider the bigger picture to understand what's going on. I remember a colleague, a psychiatrist, who had a patient, a young lad around nine years old; the boy presented with behavioural problems that erupted regularly before the evening meal. None of the interventions tried by the psychiatrist made any difference to the boy's behaviour. That changed when my colleague decided to see all the family members together, rather than just the boy or his parents. During the session, my colleague asked the question, "Can you tell me why you're so naughty in the afternoon." His little brother, who was sitting in the corner of the room playing with a toy, said without looking up, "That's easy. My brother plays up when my father comes home from work so he hits him and doesn't hit Ima." Everyone saw the nine-year old as "the problem" but you have to see the family system, the big picture to really see what's really going on.'

Peter pushes his empty cup to one side and clasps his hands together on the table. It seems like a deliberate act, hinting something of significance is coming from his corner. He says, softening his voice, 'Jabir, please don't be upset when I ask this question, but I need to. Many Jewish people believe the fighting over borders and settlements is a smokescreen. Arab nations have been accused of not supporting and caring for Palestinian Arabs. It's been said that Arab nations hate the Jews and their mission is to exterminate them. They use the conflict over the land, border issues, the Separation Wall as a front for their hidden agenda.'

Jabir's eyes flared. 'That's an evil conspiracy theory,' he snaps.

Peter's question has moved us on to what I believe is the real issue, the elephant in the room. Should I speak my truth and upset Jabir further or remain silent and allow Jabir to feel secure in the knowledge that he's embraced by his Palestinian heritage? I decide to speak.

'Jabir,' I commence in a cautious tone. 'Please hear me out. I don't know … you may not believe this, but every outbreak, including the 1948 War, the Six Day War in 1967, and the Yom Kippur War of 1973 were initiated by Arab nations.'

'The intifadas have been aimed at removing Israelis,' Peter says.

Jabir remains silent and looks towards the door. *Is he going to leave?* He returns his gaze to my face. My words need to be chosen with care. This conversation has the dynamics of a sparring match, and I don't want to knock Jabir out of the ring. 'You may not know the threat by Egyptian President Nasser, who led the Arab nations against Israel in the 1967 War, but it's burnt into the brain of every Israeli: *We shall not enter Palestine with its soil covered in sand; we shall enter it with its soil saturated in blood.* Jabir, can you imagine what that does to us Jews? We are a people who've been traumatised for generations. We live in a tiny strip of land surrounded on every side by hostile nations. Israelis live on the edge, knowing an attack could come at any time. Security is never guaranteed. The families of suicide-bombers are rewarded with huge pensions.'

I measure my words without intensity and emotion. 'I don't agree with the Jewish settlements that are increasing on the West Bank, but many of my countrymen fear Israel has to maintain a presence there. They would not want to surrender complete control of the West Bank to Palestinians, fearing it would slip into the hands of Arab nations who could attack Israel on its doorstep.'

Jabir is silent. His eyes search the floor aimlessly for an unknown object. 'You are victims; we are victims,' he says. 'We were forced from my land and home. My uncle had his home near the Western Wall taken by Israelis after the 1967 War. He never had any apology or any payment. We live with the threat of soldiers raiding, controls, checkpoints, limited water and power … we are victims too …'

The way Jabir speaks touches me. His desperate words grip me. His eyes, filled with sadness, plead for understanding. 'Yes, Jabir, I understand. Many times I've treated the wounds of your people caused by Israeli soldiers and heard their stories. I've tears inside. You're right. You are victims; we are victims. We've been forced from our homes in Europe and Arab lands where we lived for centuries. We now live under the constant threat of attack by rockets and armies that surround us.'

Jabir moves his elbows on the table surface and rests his bearded jaw and cups his hands. 'We are both human.'

Peter Wiseman crosses his legs, moves his chair back from the table and says, 'It's not a safe place for either of you. There's one question that still sits with me, Jabir. Isn't it true that the aim of Islam is to create a single worldwide caliphate?'

'Yes,' Jabir replies quickly. 'That's the will of Allah. Every Muslim prays for that day when Islam will rule the world under Sharia law. I don't understand many things in life. I know, Uri, you want me to open my mind, my soul, but the Koran tells me to accept everything in life as fate and submit; it's Allah's will.'

'Of course that means that not only the West Bank will be under the control of Arab Muslims but every country,' Peter says.

'Yes. Whether it takes 100 years or 1000 years, it'll happen because it's Allah's will,' Jabir says. 'I don't believe, like extreme Muslims, that it has to be done violently. When people see the wisdom and beauty of Islam they will convert.'

I choose not to respond to Jabir, and Peter remains deep in thought. While Jabir is a devout Muslim, he's human. He and his countrymen have suffered, caught up in the turmoil of powerful forces out of their control.

Peter shakes his head and looks through the door, intent on recalling something from his past. 'In an article I wrote some time ago, I summed up the situation this way: If home is a 'safe space,' then both Israelis and Palestinians are homeless. The place they occupy is not a safe place; it's living on the edge with violence without and violence within the borders they claim as their own.'

I glance at Jabir and say, 'I believe the vast majority of Palestinians and Israelis want peaceful co-existence. It's only a small percentage on either side who prefer violence to dialogue.' Jabir nods.

The three of us sit in silence and study the surface of the ancient wooden table that may have been a relic from Noah's Ark. Energy has evaporated. A long silence, almost sacred, evidences a mutual respect created from the common crucible of suffering. Confusion, helplessness, insight, enlightenment, understanding, acceptance, and maybe transformation.

Jabir's voice finally breaks the silence. 'I didn't come here just to talk politics. Really, I came today to tell you something I haven't told anyone, not even my wife or family.'

The uneasiness from my first sight of Jabir returns; my body tenses. My intuition was right. What's he going to say?

'You must promise me never to tell anyone. It would cost me my life.' Jabir fixes his eyes on me, lips quivering, hands fidgeting. Any sign of his self-confidence has vanished. 'I was the one who tipped off the IDF about what Ghazi did to Aalia, about him killing her.'

I gasp. Blood rushes to my head. I'm speechless.
Silence.
I want to say something, but words won't come. I glance around to check if listening ears are within reach and realise that the café is almost empty.

Jabir stares at the table, avoiding eye contact. He says, 'I've been torn apart since that horrible day. What should I do? Betray my countrymen, my brothers? Should I stop Ghazi's violence? That day was a turning point. I chose … I decided violence is not a solution. Ghazi would do more terrible things. I contacted your army. I now feel guilty, but I know it was the right thing to do. It's a heavy secret to carry. I had to tell someone; I chose you.' His voice is calm and deliberate.

Our eyes meet, searching for the other's response. I blink back tears at the depths of his courage and strength. Here's a young man who has risked his life and sacrificed his peace to speak the truth and save Arab and Jewish blood. My voice only allows me to whisper falteringly, 'I … will never … never … forget you, Jabir. Your profound act … of courage means more to me … more than you'll ever know.'

~

1. The following year as a result of the Oslo 2 Accord, the West Bank was divided into three zones. Ramallah was classified as Zone A, which prohibited entry of Jewish citizens.

2. In March 2002, Arab League members met in Beirut and unanimously agreed on a comprehensive peace initiative to end the conflict between Israel and the Palestinians. The initiative, which ended years of Arab rejectionism and which many regard as one of the most important contributions to the peace process, was supported by the Palestinian Authority. It called for the complete withdrawal of Israel from territory occupied in 1967, 'a just solution' for Palestinian refugees, and the creation of an 'independent and sovereign Palestinian state' with East Jerusalem as its capital. In return Arabs states would agree to a permanent peace with Israel. Israel rejected the initiative out of hand, ostensibly because of concern that a 'just solution' of the refugee problem would include a right of return to homes from which the refugees were displaced in 1948 or 1967. In reality it had no intention of giving up large swathes of occupied territory. Much of which was still in the process of being colonized through settlements.' Colin Chapman, *Whose Promised Land?* Oxford, UK: Lion, 2015, p. 41.

3. Genesis 15:1 – 21.

4. J. Kristen Urban, 'Isaac and Ishmael: Opportunities for Peace within Religious Narrative,' *Journal of Religion, Conflict and Peace,* Vol 2. Issue 2 (Spring 2009).

5. Genesis 25:19 – 23.

6. Ephesians 2:15.

7. Andrew White provides results of his research and theological reflections in his self-published booklet, *Older Younger Brother: The tragic treatment of the Jews by the Christians.* 2014

8. Leviticus19:34.

9. Five Refusals by Arabs of a two-state solution:

    i.   In 1936 the British Mandate of Palestine Peel Commission investigated the outbreak of violence by the Arabs in 1936 and concluded a two-state solution was the answer. The British offer was heavily in favour of the Arabs, offering eighty percent to only twenty percent for the Jews of the disputed territory. Despite this imbalance, the Jews accepted the offer and the Arabs rejected it fearing Jewish dominance because of increasing Jewish immigration.

    ii.   In 1947 Britain asked the UN to find a new solution to the ongoing strife. The UN recommended a two-state solution, dividing the land (Nov. 1947). The Palestinian Arabs totally rejected it, partly because it was imposed without consultation, and partly because the division of the land seemed unfair and to the advantage of the Jews. It was also deemed to be in contravention of the UN charter, which enshrined 'principles of equality and self determination of peoples'.

    iii.   As a result of the 1948 war, the territory seized by the Jews became an occupied territory under the control of Jordan. In 1967 during the Seven Day War, Egypt and four Arab nations combined to wipe out the Jewish state. East Jerusalem and the Gaza strip fell into Israel's hands. Half of the Jews wanted to return the West Bank to Jordan and Gaza to Egypt in exchange for peace. The remainder wanted to give it to the region's Arabs, hoping they would build their own state there. A few months later the Arab League met and issued its three 'No's: No peace with Israel; no recognition of Israel; no negotiations with Israel. The Palestinians would contest that Ariel Sharon and Ehud Olmer's policies had produced a new paradigm in which Israel was the rejectionist party. The three No's of Khartoum had been replaced by the three No's of Jerusalem: no negotiations with Syria; no acceptance of the Arab initiative, and no peace talks with the Palestinians.

iv.   Prime Minister Ehud Barak in 2000 met with PLO leader Yasser Arafat and offered to the Arabs a Palestinian State of all of Gaza, ninety-four per cent of the West Bank, and East Jerusalem as its capital. Arafat refused. Bill Clinton said, 'Arafat was here fourteen days and said no to everything.' However, the PLO were holding to the position they established since 1988. They called for a two-state solution in which Israel would keep the 78 percent of the Palestine mandate that Britain had controlled since 1948, and the Palestinian state would be formed on the remaining 22 percent that Israel had occupied since the 1967 War (The West Bank, the Gaza Strip and East Jerusalem). Israel would withdraw completely from those lands, return to the pre-1967 borders and a resolution regarding the Palestinian refugees, who were forced to flee their homes in 1948 would be negotiated between the two sides. Then in exchange, the Palestinians would agree to recognise Israel. (PLO Declaration, 12/7/88; PLO Negotiations Department).

v.   In 2008 Prime Minister Olmert extended the previous deal of his predecessor, offering additional land. The President of the Palestinian National Authority, Mahmoud Abbas refused the offer. Between 2000 and 2008, Israel has left Gaza, giving control to the Palestinians, who responded by turning it into a terrorist base firing hundreds of rockets into Israel, and Israel has enforced an embargo on military equipment entering the territory. Abbas said he rejected the deal because he was not given the chance to study the map that spelled out Olmert's offer. 'He said to me, "Here's a map. See it?" That's all. I respected his decision not to give me the map,' Abbas said, 'But how can we sign something that hasn't been given us, that hasn't been discussed?'

10. Israel withdrew unilaterally from Gaza strip in 2005, uprooting thousands of Israeli settlers from their homes. Prime Minister Ariel Sharon said the controversial withdrawal from Gaza was to increase security of residents of Israel, relieve pressure on the Israeli Defence Forces (IDF), and reduce friction between Israelis and Palestinians. Hamas, the Islamic Resistance Movement, claims that the withdrawal is the result of violent Palestinian resistance to Israeli occupation. Right-wing Israelis on reflection see this was a mistake due to the ongoing aggression by Hamas. Source: Jefferson Morley, *Washington Post*, 10th August 2005.

Chapter Thirty

Abdiel sat uncomfortably in a fabric-covered chair. The simply furnished room, surrounded by cool blue walls and bookcases that bore the weight of a legacy of psychological theory and research, provided a safe place for the nervous kibbutznik. This was Abdiel's third visit to the round-faced, middle-aged therapist with a gentle smile, made possible by the financial support of a Jewish welfare agency.

Uri's careful selection had finally convinced a reluctant Abdiel, and the experienced professional had connected well with yet another victim of Hitler's 'final solution.'

Abdiel fiddled nervously. The first time he'd climbed the carpeted stairs to meet his demon-slayer, it'd felt like ascending the gallows, his feet as heavy as lead. His shaking hand had turned the door handle, and the young receptionist had invited him to be seated. What would happen? He'd wondered. How could he survive unlocking the door where he knew his tormentors hid?

'It's good to see you, Abdiel,' the therapist said. 'How are you today?'

'I'm here—not sure what to say.'

'You're here, and it takes courage to walk into this room.'

'I haven't had much sleep since my last visit.'

'Do you have enough energy to talk about it?'

'Where do I start?'

'Tell me about your nightmares.'

'Will it help?'

'I believe it will. 'The darkness' doesn't want to be exposed to the light. The demons want you to keep their evil hidden. Don't hide the truth.'

'I'm scared it'll make me worse.'

'I understand your fear. Your nightmares have grown strong over time—stolen your sleep. They've taken over your life.'

Abdiel gasped, open-mouthed. 'Yes, they have.'

'The nightmares aren't *you*. You weren't born with them. They crept up on you—attacked you. They've taken pleasure in tormenting and chasing you. Do you want to fight back?'

Abdiel shook his head. His breaths became uneven. 'Don't know how to.'

'That's where I come in. I'm your coach.'

Silence.

A huge sigh. 'Okay.'

'What do you see?'

Abdiel's face creased in pain; just remembering his dreams felt as though an invisible, red-hot knife was plunging into his side. 'Hideous faces, distorted, twisted, evil sunken eyes, razor teeth, terrifying mocking smiles, all creeping out of darkness towards me.'

'What do you feel?'

'Terrified. Helpless. I want to run but … I can't.' Abdiel's eyes searched for the door and then returned to the face of his watchful therapist.

'Open your mouth; don't hold your breath; breathe.'

Abdiel panted like a wounded animal, his face twitching.

'You're doing well. Okay to go on?'

Abdiel's chin dropped to his heaving chest. 'I can't.'

'Take your time. There's no rush.'

Minutes passed while Abdiel stared at the floor, longing for a hole to appear to swallow him up. Slowly his hands moved with an uneven rhythm, as though he were juggling invisible hot coals. Fiery, rasping breaths filled the room. He flung the burning coals away and gripped the sides of his chair with white knuckles.

'Tell me … what's happening?'

'I smell burning flesh … stench of evil black smoke … I'm suffocating.' Abdiel's chest heaved violently, lungs screaming for air.

'Slow your breathing … breathe slowly … that's it … long slow breaths.'

Minutes passed. Hot sweat dripped from the survivor's chin. 'I don't think I can go on!'

'What might happen if you do?'

'I don't know … I'm scared …'

'Just rest and breathe … deep breaths.'

Another minute passed. 'My gut's burning. I want to be sick.' Abdiel lurched forward.

The therapist thrust a rubbish bin lined with plastic into Abdiel's lap where his shaking arms and legs created an insecure resting place for the container.

Abdiel dry-retched into the bin and then sat upright, staring, wide-eyed into the container, gasping for breath. 'I want to run … but I can't.' The hairs on his arms froze rigid, a sign of his inner terror.

'Do you hear anything?'

'My name … my name. They're screaming my name … screams echo … I hear children. They're terrified, howling inconsolably for their mother … stop!' Abdiel's convulsing body folded in the chair. The bin fell to the floor, and he slammed his trembling hands over his ears, head swaying violently.

'Slow your breath; breathe.'

'The hideous faces are back; they're laughing, leering, staring, sneering. I want to run, hide,' Abdiel gasped, lifting his feet.

'Keep your feet on the floor … press down hard … harder. Feel the strength in your legs … yes, that's great … now stamp your feet … harder … harder!'

Abdiel's feet gradually and deliberately built rhythm, stomping on the carpeted floor. His body unwound slowly, and he sat upright in the chair while his feet continued to march to the beat of his breathing. Jaw set, determination gripped his face.

'Excellent … you're doing well … fight back.'

Feet continued to pound. Sweat soaked Abdiel's shirt.

'What do you want to say to the faces?'

Silence. Abdiel took a deep breath … 'Stop!' It came as a whisper and fell limply from his lips.

'Use your voice. Open your eyes … they haven't heard you.'

Abdiel, eyes now open but unfocused, leant forward and shouted, 'Stop! Stop you bastards.'

'That's better, Abdiel. Louder. Use your anger. *You're* in charge … tell them!'

'STOP you filthy swine. Go to hell!'

'Louder … use your anger; use your voice.'

'GO TO HELL … GO TO HELL … GO TO HELL.'
The scream is primal.

Abdiel, breathing heavily, rose unsteadily to his feet, fists clenched; he swayed precariously, then, in slow motion, crumpled to the floor like a floppy rag doll. The therapist lowered his body to the carpet and sat beside the exhausted warrior.

A reverent silence followed, only interrupted by Abdiel's rhythmic breathing. The therapist watched the dramatic rise and fall of his patient's chest until gradually the Auschwitz survivor breathed with little effort.

'What are you feeling?'

'I feel relaxed … kind of warm.'

A long silence, then Abdiel lifted his head and with half a smile declared, 'I think I've won round one.'

~

Two torturous weeks have passed since Jabir's disclosure. His willingness to fill the missing gaps in my story unleashed a legion of demons I thought I'd successfully locked away in my dungeon. The open wounds in Aalia's broken body scream, 'Revenge!' Gazhi's face haunts me, a mask of indifference, eyes vacant, empty, like a house deserted by its owner. I scream, 'Why?' but the mask of indifferent arrogance remains unchanged.

Miriam wipes the sweat from my forehead. 'Darling, you're having nightmares again.'

My best efforts to resist calling Jabir fade. The 'why' is a hot needle that pierces my brain; a knife that penetrates my heart. I arrange a meeting, and we agree to meet in the inner courtyard of the American Colony Hotel—a gracious structure fashioned by a famous Ottoman for his four wives, and a 'neutral space' in a sea of tension.

I wander into the cool relief the limestone-walled courtyard provides from the midmorning sun. Jabir is waiting in a corner of the paved courtyard surrounded by palms and potted petunias. The gentle bubbling of a water fountain is the only sound that fills this hidden oasis from the uncertain world beyond its walls.

'*Salam*, Uri. Good to see you.'

'*Salam*. Likewise. Thank you for meeting me again.'

Jabir grasps my hand with both hands and falls back into his white cane chair. 'George will be with us shortly. He's a young man you need to meet.' He smiles, beckons to the waiter, and orders coffees.

I'm impatient for Jabir to shed light on the question that mercilessly echoes in my head. Why, why would Ghazi, a childhood friend, whose family were more than friends with my family, murder his sister, my beautiful Aalia?

Jabir's eyes search my face. 'This may be hard for you,' he says, frowning. 'I don't know everything in Ghazi's brain. I'll try to tell you what I know and what I think is there.' He takes a deep breath. 'He's not a big talker—usually quiet—but anger grew in his eyes over time.'

'*Salam*, Jabir.' The softly spoken greeting comes from a young man smartly dressed in the hotel staff uniform.

'George. *Salam*, my friend.'

George and Jabir embrace, then Jabir motions towards me. 'George, this is Uri.'

George extends his hand. 'I've heard a lot about you.'

'I'm grateful for you taking time to see me,' I reply, returning to my seat around the circular cane table.

'I always make time for people who want to hear my story, especially Jewish.' A genuine smile reveals pure-white teeth contrasting with his deep olive skin and well-trimmed black beard. His waiter's uniform of white shirt and black trousers are immaculate. 'I've a fifteen-minute break, but maybe we talk again if we need to.'

'You're generous, George. You are from Beit Jala?'

'Yes, I leave each morning from my parents' house. I rise at four-thirty. You don't always know how long it will take to go through checkpoints. Sometimes one hour, sometimes two. My permit to travel from Beit Jala to work here is my lifeline. My parents are poor, and I help support them.'

'What's it like living there?' I ask as three coffees are delivered from the steady hand of a young waitress, who smiles shyly at George.

'It's like living in an open-air prison. We can't move anywhere without a permit; in the West Bank there are over 100 permits! Water and electricity are rationed and often stop without warning. Some UN visitors say it's worse than South African Apartheid, but I wouldn't know about that. Living on the West Bank ... it's uncertain ... like living on the edge.'

'Very unpredictable,' Jabir adds.

George continues, 'Things change quickly. Permits can be taken away without warning. If you upset the soldiers for any reason, they take your permit.' He glances at his watch and sips his coffee. 'My uncle has a fruit stall, and his neighbours upstairs are Jewish. My uncle and other neighbours who sell stuff have put wire netting across the street above their goods because the Jews throw all kinds of rubbish down: food scraps, rotting fruit, old clothes, dirty nappies; it's terrible.'

I move uncomfortably on my seat and shake my head. 'I apologise for the bad behaviour of my countrymen. It's inexcusable.'

George nods. 'You're not like the soldiers and settlers. The settlers everywhere on the West Bank are strong. They tell the soldiers who protect them what to do. It's hard to watch settlers take our land. If we fight back, we're beaten, and our permits are taken away; we're helpless.' Jabir studies my face, seeking signs of a reaction.

I study the corner of the white tablecloth covering the circular white table.

'The Israeli policy of encirclement, isolation, and containment has worked very well for Israel for many years,' Jabir says. 'It's theft by stealth.'

I sigh and return my gaze to George. His face is tense; eyes strangely soft despite the violence he describes.

'I come from a Syrian Orthodox family,' he continues. 'My parents told us, "Don't throw stones at soldiers. Don't go with protest groups." When soldiers drove past our school and fired guns, some students started throwing rocks. Then soldiers fired tear gas. Sometimes I ran home with my brother. What good does it do to fight back? Nothing! My parents say, "We don't believe in an eye for an eye. We are Christian. We are to love our enemy." Very hard to do.'

I nod sympathetically. 'What's been your most difficult time with the soldiers?'

George checks his watch and finishes his coffee. 'Let me tell you this quickly, and then I must go. There are many times when soldiers abused me for no reason. But when I was going to university, three times a week I passed through a main checkpoint called Al Container Checkpoint in the Palestinian region north-east of Jerusalem city, where there are no Jewish settlements. The guards were usually tough, and we couldn't go by car—only taxis.

'On one occasion last year when I was finishing my degree, it was particularly stressful. I had my classmates next to me. It was our midterm exam, and I needed to pass because I'd taken a loan to pay for my study. If I didn't pass the exam, I'd lose the semester and would have to pay again and take another loan from the bank, which I couldn't afford. The loans are only short term—only one or two years. I don't have much money, and my parents are dependent on my salary. It has to cover my house and their house, so for me it's a huge issue if I don't succeed.

'The guard stopped the taxi—a seven-seater van—pointed to me, and demanded that I get out of the van. So I did. Then he asked for my ID. I handed it to him, and he said, 'Who is this beautiful lady next to you?'

'"It's my classmate," I replied.

'"Okay, but she is beautiful. Is she your girlfriend?"

'"No, she's my classmate."

'"Do you have sex together?"

'"Excuse me, no, she is my classmate." I continued repeating, "She's my classmate."

'He could see I wasn't happy talking to him. So he said, "Come to the front of the van." I followed him, and said, "Read the registration plate of the car."

'"Why do you want me to read it when you can read it yourself."

'"Start."

'"No. I will not read it. You can read it," I said, but my classmates in the van were becoming anxious. They asked me to read it, saying they wanted to go. So I started reading the numbers. Then the soldier dropped his pen on the ground and ordered me to pick it up. I refused. He insisted. I refused again, so he swung his M16 off his shoulder and pointed at me ready to shoot.'

'"Now pick it up," he said again.

'I'd suffered bad behaviour from Israelis before, and it'd made me angry, but this time I was really angry and stubborn. I said, "Do whatever you want but I will not pick it up."

'One of my classmates in the van started to open the door to come and help me, but the soldier shouted at him to get back into the car. Then he told me to get back in, but he collected all the IDs from everyone in the van and told the driver to park to one side. It was noon by then, and my exam was at two. He held us all there at the checkpoint from noon until 3.30 p.m., and I couldn't study because I was so stressed about missing my exam. He finally released us, but when I arrived at the university for my exam, the teacher didn't want me to enter, even though I told him I'd been held up at the checkpoint. I couldn't believe it!

'The teacher said, "But your other classmates came through that checkpoint and they arrived on time."

'"Yes but *our* taxi; we had problems," I protested.

'"You had problems for all *that* time?" he replied, not believing me.

'Finally he let me in but told me I only had one hour. So my classmates did the exam from 2 p.m. to 5 p.m., and I took it from 4 to 5. I was highly stressed and wrote like crazy, and I passed the exam. My mark wasn't high, but I succeeded and didn't have to take out another loan.'

'George,' I say, 'My blood boils when I hear this. I'm curious to know how you can speak without hatred.'

George smiles as he rises slowly from the table. 'I've forgiven the soldiers, but that's another story.'

I stand and grip the outstretched hand of this amazing young man, but I want to hug him. 'George, thank you. You've given me so much.'

A brief smile flashes from his lips, 'A privilege to meet you, Uri. *Salam.*'

Jabir high-fives his good friend, and we both watch him disappear into the palatial stone building.

'Some story,' I say.

'You've heard just a little.'

The sun has climbed higher in the sky and filtered rays form a pattern on Jabir's face. 'Let me adjust the umbrella,' I offer, moving the large canopy.

'Ghazi is on the other end of the spectrum,' Jabir says. 'He's the opposite to George. Ghazi was targeted by PIJ. Ghazi was angry—easy to influence. His friends, collaborators, were all injured by soldiers. They were and are still brainwashed by extreme Islam—very violent. They believe in extreme Sharia law, in stoning women with bad morals. Also Ghazi needed to be somebody—a big shot. To prove himself with the PIJ, he needed to do extreme violence and show no fear. All these things created the perfect storm for Ghazi.'

'But to kill your own sister!' The words fire from my mouth like bullets. My anger meets Jabir's understanding gaze and is returned as empathy.

'Uri. When a young man lives in a hotbed of hatred, fed with twisted, violent Islam and wants to be a big name, he does anything. He feels trapped, has no hope, nothing to live for, and … Ghazi hated you; he was jealous of you. I suspect he killed her so you couldn't have her.' Jabir's voice is little more than a whisper, his face turns to one side, avoiding my gaze. 'I didn't know he was planning to kill Aalia.' He sighed. 'I still feel guilty; I should have—'

'You didn't know his plans. He's just one of so many angry young men,' I say in support of his guilt, but a familiar pain grips my stomach. I catch my breath. *Ghazi hated me?* 'I never knew he hated me like that. I'm shocked. I never saw him after I commenced my medical studies.'

Silence stills our tongues. A sparrow bravely hops beneath my table, searching for crumbs.

'Jabir, I've lived in a bubble, and you've burst it. It's painful, but I'm grateful.'

~

My Beloved Aalia,

This letter is to say goodbye. I'm not sure if I've ever really said it, or if I did maybe I didn't mean it. The pain in my side is killing me. It has been worse since I've talked with a Palestinian named Jabir. You know I've always loved you and always will, and I'll never forget you, but I'm prepared to release you. I'll let you go and ask for forgiveness if loving you the way I did caused you harm. It has, my darling. I have to be honest; I know it has, and I beg your forgiveness.
I have forgiven Ghazi and pray for him.

Goodbye my love,

Your lover, Uri

I kiss the fragment of paper, roll it into a small scroll, and slide it into the crack between two blocks of stone in the Western Wall. A mass of black and white surrounds me, davening worshippers caught up in their own world, worshipping their Creator. In my private space, I press my hands against the ancient, sacred stone and feel its warmth. Tears spill onto the plaza at my feet. *Father in heaven, hear my prayer.*

Chapter Thirty-One

Ghazi lay motionless in his cell, perspiration dripping from his face. The heat of the summer sun in the Negev needs to be experienced to be believed.

The life-sentence imposed by the court didn't shock him. The absence of any word from Ammam or any of the group, however, left him feeling betrayed—shattered. Even in prison, a secret grapevine operated to convey and receive messages from the 'outside.' But nothing came, just a stony silence. Ghazi's anger grew as the summer heat increased. They were supposed to be his family—a brotherhood. Where were they?

Ghazi's tortured mind still searched for the informer he imagined tipped-off the Israeli security forces. He felt proud that he'd resisted the constant onslaught by the interrogators— he'd protected his brothers. Were they too scared to even send a message—just a 'well done' would do. But nothing … nothing but silence.

Ghazi had never recovered from the rock that Uri had hurled at him. Even though he appeared friendly towards Uri, anger mingled with jealousy towards the 'pin-up boy' of the Atak community had grown over the years. His constant feeble cry to his parents had been, 'Why should he get a better education than me, just because he's a Jew?'

Omar and Sabah had tried to soothe their troubled son when he complained: 'I'm just a grease-monkey; he's studying to be a doctor.'

The growing jealousy towards Uri and rage from the theft of his family's land became fertile soil for the sinister seeds of hatred to germinate. The call to unite against 'the invader' had resonated within this troubled young man, desperately in search for meaning and purpose in life. Ammam's rhetoric of 'us and them,' his call to cease friendship and ties with the 'occupiers,' and his call to arms had excited Ghazi. The brotherhood had given him the hope of becoming someone.

Ghazi became a sponge for Ammam's vitriol. Like a puppet on a string, he'd willingly danced a deadly dance to Ammam's seductive rhythm. Ammam's caution to Ghazi that his parents were friends with Jews had disturbed him, so he'd distanced himself from them. 'I've found a new family,' he'd regularly boasted to Ammam.

Ghazi hadn't believed his eyes when he'd seen Uri walking through the Jaffa Gate with his sister following a little way behind. He'd grown suspicious, followed them up the stairs up to the rooftops and watched from a distance. Every touch, every embrace, every kiss he saw tore him apart. How could his sister betray his family and the Palestinians?

When Ammam had heard Ghazi's report, he'd simply looked at Ghazi with steely eyes and said, 'What are you going to do?' giving him the biggest challenge in Ghazi's life.

Here was the possibility to show the brotherhood what he was made of. A murderous passion that embraced the belief that even family could become the enemy crowned Ammam's mystique and leadership. Ghazi, accordingly, no longer saw

Aalia as his sister. His anger escalated into a blind, evil, vindictive rage.

Now, however, the act of violence had lost its meaning. Nothing had changed in Israel—Palestine. Had he been used? The appearance of his mother and Maya had undone him. Shame melted the remnants of hatred. Now, he couldn't care whether he lived or died.

~

The rollercoaster ride continues. Nothing seems to have changed. It's so frustrating! Whenever there's the possibility of peace, someone sabotages it. Tensions grew in the remainder of the decade with only a brief promise of peace. On 13th September 1993, the White House lawn hosted an historic event, which sent my heart soaring. Bill Clinton presided at a meeting under the so-called 'Oslo Accord', where our Prime Minister, Yitzak Rabin and Yasser Arafat met. For the first time, Israel recognised the PLO as a representative of the Palestinian people, and Arafat recognized Israel's right to exist, committing the PLO to a peaceful resolution of the conflict. Strong opposition came from the Palestinians about the proposed process, and many Jews also opposed it. However, there was genuine hope.

Then, in February 1994, Baruch Goldstein murdered twenty-nine Muslim worshippers and injured 125 others in the main mosque at the Cave of the Patriarchs in Hebron – a terrible act of terror. Immediately Checkpoint 300 or Rachel Checkpoint was built to prevent angry Palestinian reprisals on the nearby Jewish settlement of Gilo. Nevertheless, the possibility of peace continued until the 4th November 1995 when in Kings Square, Tel Aviv, at the end of a rally in support of the Oslo Accords, a representative of the right-wing

Likud Party assassinated Yitzak Rabin. Likud had opposed handing back territories gained in the Six Day War: the Golan Heights to Syria; Gaza Strip to Egypt, and the West Bank to Jordan. Hope was dashed once again!

In 2006, members of the military wing of Hamas attacked a border crossing in Gaza killing two soldiers and capturing Corporal Gilad Shalit, triggering an international call for his release. On 12th July, the Iranian-sponsored terrorist group Hezbollah attacked Israel from the north, killing eight soldiers and capturing two others. The attack began a month-long military conflict in which Hezbollah launched 3,970 missiles at Israeli cities killing 162 Israelis. It became known as the Second Lebanon War. During that time Abe was promoted to captain and led his soldiers into key positions in the Golan, fearing an attack from Syria.

Hamas won by a landslide in the Palestinian legislative elections. The US, Europe, and Israel cut off aid to Palestinians, declaring Hamas a terrorist organization plotting the destruction of Israel. Violence and rivalry erupted between Fatah and Hamas in the Gaza Strip. How can we ever see the beginning of a peace process while these factions fight each other?

I had mixed feelings in 2007 when Israel transferred $100 million in tax revenue into the Palestinian Authority's account to cover humanitarian needs, bolster their president, Mahmoud Abbas, and keep money out of the hands of Hamas. The Battle for Gaza began, and Hamas took Gaza from the Palestinian Authority. The resulting Annapolis Peace Conference called for a two-state solution.

In 2008, Hamas and the Palestinian Islamic Jihad that Ghazi belonged to along with other militant organizations in

Gaza sent a barrage of rockets into the Israeli city of Ashkelon. The Qassam and Grad rockets had been smuggled into Gaza in pieces from Iran. Once they were launched, hundreds of thousands of Israelis in southern Israel had as little as fifteen seconds to find a bunker. I can't imagine how anyone can live life, fifteen seconds away from a concrete cave? This led to the Gaza War.

On 17th June 2008, my brother Abe was part of the IDF assault force that killed seven terrorists on the border of Gaza. Hamas had dug a tunnel under the security fence and planned to abduct Israeli soldiers. Our government responded with heavy shelling and rocket fire.

It's hard for anyone living outside of Israel to know what it's like when rockets can appear at any time, day or night. It's like living on the edge of a precipice.

From 27th December 2008 to 18th January 2009, Operation Cast Lead or The Gaza War lasted twenty-two days. Israel's plan was to stop haphazard Palestinian rocket fire into Israel and weapons smuggling into the Gaza strip. IDF attacked police stations, military targets, including weapon stockpiles and suspected rocket-firing pads, as well as political and administrative institutions, striking in the densely populated cities of Gaza, Khan Yunis, and Rafah.

In response, Palestinians fired rockets to what they characterised as 'massacres,' not discriminating between civilian and military targets, illegal under international law. The photos I saw of children killed by their rockets brought waves of sadness. Hamas' strategy to launch their rockets from sites beside schools filled me with anger.

~

June 2009

Today is a warm summer day in Jerusalem. Old women sit in the shade of white walls, offering vine leaves. The murmurs of a thousand feet on ancient streets mingle with noisy bartering between tourists and shopkeepers. Obama's peace efforts fill the air like a welcome fragrance. Papa and Ima have moved to an apartment in the new city of Jerusalem. Papa's declining health called for closer proximity to medical services and a place where I could keep a closer eye on him. I believe my interventions with medications and advice from my psychiatric colleagues have kept him alive. The attacks of his dreaded demons have not waned, but the anaesthetic provided by the drugs has not only dulled their barbs, but also the joy and gladness that surround him from family and faithful friends. Fire and smoke are instant triggers for him, and great care is taken to avoid them.

I've resigned myself now to not fully knowing Papa or his secrets. It appears he's locked them deep in his dungeon and thrown away the key. I wonder, too, that even if he ever wanted to find the key, the drugs that keep him alive may also prevent him finding the location. When Yousef speaks of him, his voice is sad. 'A lost soul.'

No further surprise cards, letters or photos from Daniel have arrived. I wonder at the impact of these bizarre communications on Papa's disturbed mind. Would he be better off not knowing Daniel was alive, than be tortured by the double message of 'I'm alive' but 'I'm not going to tell you where or anything about me?' That's just plain crazy-making! What was going on in Daniel's brain?

Abe's elevation through the IDF has brought a degree of pride, but his departure from his faith has resulted in pain, even for Papa's nominal allegiance to his religion.

Yousef's observation, shared recently, is disturbing—he's never shared it with Papa, fortunately. 'Uri,' he said, 'there are two kinds of human hearts: one made of clay, the other, wax. As time progresses and the flame of our accumulated disappointments, failed expectations, and injustices rise, the clay hardens in the face of the flame, while wax becomes soft and malleable. Abe is the clay; you are the wax.'

Yousef stunned me. His words are so true. My mind is clear and hand steady as I perform my duties at Hadassah. Yet tears have increased as my years lengthened, especially when I see the plight of needless suffering of both my Jewish and Arab brothers. Abe marches on. A leader, hard, unbending, strong, cool-headed, clever. Israel is proud of him.

~

Uri and the world have no idea that four agents are on their way to a European location following a tip-off. Few are aware of their secret mission. Mossad is described by some as the 'world's most efficient killing-machine.' Deep intelligence, sophisticated forensics, and highly trained agents have killed enemies of Israel who have been 'inaccessible' due to their hidden locations in Arab countries. Mossad are like the official hangman or the doctor on Death Row who injects the lethal dose into the prisoner. The State of Israel endorses Mossad's actions. When they kill, they are not breaking the law, simply fulfilling a sentence sanctioned by the Prime Minister on behalf of Israel. Sometimes, when questions about identity arise, interrogation is necessary, and a 'capture' is required. Often foreign governments have cooperated with Israel in returning war criminals and terrorists to Israel. However, if there's the risk of losing a suspect because of red tape, Mossad will 'fly under the radar,' capture the accused, and smuggle them out. This was Mossad's decision for this case.

Chapter Thirty-Two

July 2009

John Solomon crossed the interviewing room and eased himself into the wooden chair. His smooth manner showed the body of a well-trained athlete. His colleagues nicknamed him 'The Lion' for his stealth and persistence in pursuing his prey. Solomon spends any leisure time away from the demands of his job pounding the sands of the desert, south of Jerusalem. A pistol accompanies him on any activity, whether pleasure or professional. Blue eyes and fair skin demonstrate the British influence in his lineage mixed with Hungarian.

He scanned the pathetic figure seated uncomfortably in front of him: wrinkles, possibly the result of excessive smoking, creased his cheeks and forehead; brown eyes stared from dark cavities, the result of little sleep; skin, pasty—probably the evidence of poor diet; head—bald, except for wisps of grey-white hair, which hung untidily over his ears; height—close to six feet; age—maybe eighty years, give or take. Grey trousers and a blue crumpled long-sleeved shirt hung loosely from his thin body. He sat hunched, avoiding Solomon's gaze.

'What's your name?' Solomon asked.

The fugitive remained still and silent.

Solomon glanced at Ben Friedman, who was recording the session on video, and then returned his gaze to Leib Banii, his close colleague and friend. The powerful pair entered army school together in their teens and moved to Mossad ten years ago. Both are highly intelligent, astute operators, who work brilliantly as a team. Solomon addressed the fugitive again. 'We believe you're Franz Gebhardt, a Nazi officer of Auschwitz.'

The hunched figure remained motionless and stared at the polished floor.

'We have here'—Solomon pointed to a polished table in the corner of the well-lit room—'the uniform of a German captain.' Solomon waited for a response. 'It was found in your room.'

Silence.

'Our agents found these magazines and newspaper cuttings featuring Franz Gebhardt and his abuse of Jewish prisoners in Auschwitz,' Solomon said, holding the yellowing pages in front of the silent figure. 'They were also found in your room.'

Silence.

Friedman checked the computer and video to ensure they were still active. 'I'm going to make a coffee,' he said. 'Anyone interested?'

Banii rose from his chair but shook his head. Solomon nodded. It was a deliberate move to inject a shift in the prisoner, to break the tension hanging in the room.

A small table separated the prisoner and the two interviewing agents. A larger table in the corner contained the newspaper cuttings, personal papers, and the Nazi uniform. Friedman usually sat with his computer behind the prisoner. A flat omnidirectional microphone was fixed to the ceiling in the middle of the room. Its black cable crossed the roof and ran down the wall into the computer. A video camera fitted with a fisheye lens recorded every movement. The walls were intentionally bare and the room empty of unnecessary furniture. The interviewee had little to distract him.

'Franz, may I call you Franz?' Solomon continued. Again he received no reply or indication that he'd even heard. 'Our agents found a birth certificate in the name of Franz Gebhardt. We have records from your youth, awards, and letters to you from family and friends …'

The fugitive remained hunched and rigid. His breathing rate hadn't changed since he'd entered the room. Solomon was unsure if this hapless figure was present in his body or a million miles away.

'You're accused of the murder and abuse of Jewish prisoners in Auschwitz. Do you hear what I'm saying?' Solomon said in a firm voice, his gaze fixed on the silent figure.

The smell of coffee announced Friedman's return with two steaming mugs in hand. He passed one to Solomon.

'Black with one sugar.'

'Thanks.'

The Mossad agents sat silent.

Without warning, the fugitive sprang to his feet, stood at attention and shouted, *'Mein Name ist Franz Gebhardt. Ich bin ein treuer Offizier des Dritten Reichs. Ich habe meinem Führer gut für die Ehre des Vaterlands gedient.'* (My name is Franz Gebhardt. I am a loyal officer of the Third Reich. I have served my Führer well for the glory of the Fatherland.)

Solomon, Banii and Friedman sat in stunned silence.

'You admit you are Franz Gebhardt, officer at Auschwitz?' Solomon asked.

'Mein Name ist Franz Gebhardt. Ich bin ein treuer Offizier des Dritten Reichs. Ich habe meinem Führer gut für die Ehre des Vaterlands gedient,' came the immediate response.

The prisoner remained standing, and Solomon gave no instruction for him to sit. Movement sometimes is more likely to elicit a response than passive sitting. Solomon picked up the newspaper cuttings and studied the photos. The newspapers were old, and the images inferior to the pictures in Mossad's database.

'Can we take a break outside for a minute, John?' Banii asked.

Both men stepped into the corridor, two floors below street level in the well-fortified headquarters of the Israeli Secret Service.

Banii's eyes searched his colleague's face. 'What do you make of him?'

Solomon leant on the wall and stared back into the room through the one-way mirror. The prisoner remained rigid and motionless. 'On the face of it I'd say he's our man. We've personal papers, letters, and a Nazi uniform … but we don't have any medical or dental records.'

Banii nodded. 'Exactly; the only distinguishing physical mark is the scarring on his left arm, no birthmark. His German is good; he speaks like a German officer, authoritative.' Solomon let out a long sigh.

'We'll get some of the Auschwitz inmates to provide identification. I received a call from one yesterday; Abdiel Goldhirsch is interested to identify him. We'll start with him.'

'I'll call him now,' Banii offered. He was one of the witnesses who gave a written statement at the Eichmann's trial, wasn't he?'

'Yeah. He didn't want to take the stand in court. Can't say I blame him—so stressful,' Solomon replied.

~

The following day three men stood in front of the one-way mirror. Inside the interviewing room sat the prisoner, hunched in his familiar stance, staring at the wooden floor.

Ben Friedman, seated with his computer, monitored the signal from the camera.

'I tossed all night,' Abdiel said, staring at the prisoner.

'We're grateful to you for coming in,' Solomon said. 'I know it's hard—'

'I want to do it,' Abdiel interrupted. 'Since I heard the news and saw his face on TV, I've not stopped thinking about him.'

Banii and Solomon watched the reaction of the ageing ex-inmate, his eyes riveted on the prisoner. Some witnesses, when they first see their tormentors, break down and sob. Others, filled with rage, require restraint. Abdiel simply stared at the downturned face of the fugitive, examining every detail. *There's no show of emotion. There's more thinking happening here than feeling,* Solomon observed. *This man is unsure. He can't make up his mind.*

'Can I go into the room?' Abdiel asked.

'Sure you can, but do you really want to?' Solomon replied, frowning.

Abdiel nodded.

Solomon led the way, followed by Abdiel, and then Banii.

The prisoner remained seated, almost lifeless in the wooden chair, his eyes fixed to a spot on the floor, his blue, crumpled shirt and baggy trousers recycled from the previous day. Abdiel stood motionless, two metres in front of the human statue. His eyes searched the details of the face he'd seen on TV, days previously.

One minute passed … two minutes … before a firm order came from Banii, 'Tell us your name.'

All eyes focused on the silent fugitive. Without warning, the hunched statue sprang to life. Standing erect he shouted, *'Mein Name ist Franz Gebhardt. Ich bin ein treuer Offizier des Dritten Reichs. Ich habe meinem Führer gut für die Ehre des Vaterlands gedient.'* Again, the words shot from his mouth like bullets from a machine-gun. *'Mein Name ist Franz Gebhardt. Ich bin ein treuer Offizier des Dritten Reichs. Ich habe meinem Führer gut für die Ehre des Vaterlands gedient.'*

Abdiel gasped, 'My God, my God.' Shaking violently, he staggered towards the table for support.

Banii sprang from his seat and grabbed Abdiel's arm. 'Take my chair,' he insisted, lowering the distressed witness into his seat.

Abdiel continued to convulse. He doubled up, his two wrinkled hands covering his distorted face. The terrible sound of Abdiel fighting for breath gripped the room.

Friedman moved from behind the computer. 'It looks like a panic attack. Do we have any paper bags?'

Banii hastily exited and headed for the lunchroom.

'Abdiel, take long, slow breaths,' Solomon said. 'Slow your breathing … slow your breathing.' He knelt, trying to make eye contact, but Abdiel's hands remained firm on his wet face. 'That's good Abdiel … long, slow, deep breaths … great. You're doing well.'

Banii appeared at the doorway. 'This plastic bag is all I could find.'

'I think he's okay now,' Solomon replied, relieved.

Abdiel gradually straightened in the wooden chair and wiped tears from his eyes. Leib handed him a tissue, which Abdiel took. Both interviewers were in no hurry to continue until Abdiel was ready.

'Are you okay, Abdiel?' Solomon asked. 'If this is too distressing you can leave it. I've stood beside many men in similar situations. You're brave to even consider doing it.'

The response from Abdiel was not what any of the three Mossad agents expected. It was as though Abdiel threw a hand grenade into the room and blew them away. 'He's my brother,' he whispered.

'He's WHAT?' Solomon exclaimed, wide-eyed.

'This man is Daniel Goldhirsch, my brother. I've not seen him since Auschwitz.'

The three agents stared at each other in disbelief. *Has he gone mad?*

Two minutes passed in silence.

The pathetic prisoner continued to stand erect in the centre of the room. Abdiel's drama had taken centre stage, the prisoner, momentarily forgotten.

Abdiel, now composed, rose to his feet and stood directly in front of the fugitive. 'Daniel. It's your brother Abdiel. Remember me … your brother Abdiel? Remember the games we played at home? Flying the kite on windy days; playing hide-and-seek in the cemetery; firing stones with our slingshots? …'

The prisoner didn't move. His eyes were fixed on images a thousand miles away but not on the scenes Abdiel desperately hoped he might recall.

Banii glanced at Abdiel. 'Are you sure he's your brother?'

'I know what you're thinking. It's been sixty-four years since I've seen him. And he's changed and changed dramatically. You think I'm crazy, don't you? I saw him on TV the other night when security escorted him to the car at the airport. Something in the way he moved caught my attention. Yes, his face has aged beyond his years, but as I look into his eyes, I *know* it's Daniel.'

Banii glanced at Solomon and then stretched his back. Solomon was deep in thought, breathing heavily, pondering the next move.

Suddenly, Abdiel fixed his eyes on the prisoner and commanded, '983472; report for duty.'

The prisoner's head turned and faced Abdiel. His fixed gaze returned from the distant place in which he'd been—the first sign of a response or a connection any of the men had witnessed during the interrogation process. 'You were 983472 in Auschwitz, but you're not in Auschwitz, Daniel. You're not a number. You're my brother … Daniel. I am Abdiel … Abdiel.'

All eyes fixed on the prisoner. A long pause ensued. What would be his response?

The prisoner's head moved, his eyes returned him to the distant place, then a familiar outburst shattered the silence. *'Mein Name ist Franz Gebhardt. Ich bin ein treuer Offizier des Dritten Reichs. Ich habe meinem Führer gut für die Ehre des Vaterlands gedient.'*

Abdiel sighed deeply, and his head fell forward.

Solomon turned to his close colleague. 'Where do we go from here, Leib?'

Before he could answer, Abdiel said, 'My brother has three distinct moles on his right shoulder. They almost form an equilateral triangle.'

'Remove your shirt,' Solomon asked the prisoner, who still stood motionless.

The fugitive didn't flinch.

Solomon stepped forward, undid the buttons, and slid the blue shirt from his back. 'Well I be damned,' Solomon gasped. 'Look at this!'

Banii stepped forward and examined the prisoner's right shoulder. 'Just as you said,' he exclaimed.

'I used to tease him when he was lying on the floor on hot nights. I'd sneak up and join the three dots with a pen,' Abdiel said. 'Also, he's removed his number. It was tattooed on his left arm. See the scar?'

'Looks like it's been burnt off ... maybe acid or a flame?' Banii examined the mutilation.

After a long silence, two stunned agents looked at each other, and Solomon said, 'We need Greenberg.'

~

Joshua Greenberg rested his weary body in the comfortable chair in John Solomon's office. He'd sat on that chair on many occasions. As a consulting psychiatrist to Mossad. Greenberg was well respected for his research and experience with Holocaust victims. His day usually started at 6 a.m. with his rounds at the psychiatric hospital. Now he faced the challenge of making sense of the case the two agents had presented to him. Greenberg's sharp eyes peered over his rimless spectacles. Of average build, his body bore the evidence of more than a healthy diet. A well-tailored grey suit covered his slightly rotund figure.

'Thanks for coming in, Josh,' Solomon said. 'What do you make of him?'

Greenberg had a habit of stroking his right knee under stress. Solomon believed it was a way his friend soothed himself under pressure. Now the palm of Greenberg's hand moved in a circular motion over his right kneecap. 'What I saw on the video is one of the worst cases of a delusional disorder I've encountered.'

Abdiel sat in silence, still stunned by the events of yesterday. The team were keen to have Abdiel present for the psychiatrist's opinion.

Solomon glanced at Abdiel but spoke to Greenberg, 'Would a photograph of the family in the early days of his childhood or youth help?'

Abdiel shook his head. 'There's nothing left from our past. The Nazis told us to take one suitcase when they forced us from our home in Poland. We were stripped of everything when we entered Auschwitz … everything, including every hair on our body.'

'I don't think photographs would help anyway,' Greenberg said.

'You saw that moment of recognition when his Auschwitz number was mentioned, and that's a more recent part of his life. No prisoner forgets his number. As you know, numbers were always used in the camps, never names. If we can't reach him through his number, I don't think we can reach him at all.'

'Abdiel, are you absolutely certain he's your brother?' Banii asked, frowning.

'Absolutely. Even though his face has changed significantly, the basic structure is there. His voice … of course, we spoke German, and I could hear the same tone in his ranting yesterday. The three moles ... I've no doubt at all,' Abdiel replied, his voice weighed with sadness. 'Is there any treatment that might help him?' He fixed his eyes on Greenberg. 'Is there anything that can help him now?'

Greenberg shook his head. 'Sadly no ... his delusion is so ingrained, so fixed. If we'd reached him earlier in life, it may have been possible, but now ... unfortunately he's too old; he's too far gone ... sorry, Abdiel.'

'What about the card I received from him around Uri's Bar Mitzvah?'

'Back then he was most likely in the early stages of swinging in and out of his delusion. Often it starts as 'Dissociative Identity Disorder' or DID. Many people who suffer severe trauma end up with DID. It's common among POWs.'

Abdiel frowned. 'What happens in DID?'

'We respond to trauma in different ways. Some, like Daniel, manage by assuming the identity of someone else. I suspect in Daniel's case, he took on the identity of Gebhardt. In Daniel's eyes, Gebhardt was strong and powerful. It was easier for Daniel to 'become' the abuser, than feel his own pain. I've seen many cases in my professional practice where an adult woman who's been severely abused by a parent in childhood or adolescence, reverts to early childhood behaviour. I remember one case of a woman in her late thirties. Whenever she was in distress, she'd drop her head to one side, change her voice to that of a little girl, turn her toes in, like some young children do, and look cute. She was really saying to those who were causing her distress, "Don't hurt me; be kind to me; I'm just a cute little girl."'

Banii shook his head. 'That behaviour would drive people mad.'

'True.' Greenberg removed his glasses and polished them with a clean handkerchief. 'I needed to train the admin staff at the hospital to be aware of these cases. They'd say a child was on the phone going on about some bizarre story. I knew it was one of my patients. Sometimes trauma victims move into MPD, Multiple Personality Disorder; they take on a variety of personas.'

'Do any overcome the problem?' Abdiel asked.

'As I said, if we can provide intervention early, there's a chance of recovery, but it's never guaranteed,' Greenberg replied, glasses now perched securely on his nose. 'Getting back to Daniel, though; I suspect his early response was DID and without treatment, as time went on, the pendulum swung across and became slower to return, until it became fixed. Daniel found it easier to be Gebhardt and then eventually became completely delusional.'

'I understand.' Abdiel nodded. 'Gebhardt was unpredictable in the camp. You never knew what was going to happen. He might smile when he walked past, which none of the other guards ever did, and he could be kind, helping a prisoner to his feet. But it was all fake. He could also walk past and, without warning, lay into you with his cane. He got a thrill from keeping everyone guessing. He loved the power of being unpredictable. He singled out Daniel—not sure why— and pushed him beyond his limits. One day he brought him fresh bread and sardines. Then that night he forced him to stand in the freezing snow for an hour. The chilblains he got on his feet were terrible. Gebhardt was a sick bastard. He only felt good when he was abusing us.'

'It makes sense, Abdiel, perfect sense to me,' Greenberg said. 'Did you see him after Auschwitz?'

'Never. I searched for him when the Red Cross trucks drove into the camp on the last day, but couldn't find him. I've no idea where he went or what he did. The only communication, if you could call it that, was the card, around the time of Uri's Bar Mitzvah in 1978 and also a photo.'

'If he suffered from DID, as I suspect, he probably sent it when he was "Daniel."' Greenberg stroked his knee. 'What did the card say?'

'Congratulations, Uri on your Bar Mitzvah.'

'So the card was not to you but to Uri,' Greenberg remarked.

Abdiel shifted a little on his chair. 'The envelope was addressed to me, but the card was for Uri. Everyone in the family was overcome … it's hard to explain … so powerful. It was an emotional time … blew us away … like a voice from the dead … he's alive … but then the question, *where on earth are you*? The postmark was Brussels, so I placed notices in the newspapers there for him to contact me …'

'But he knew where you were?' Solomon said in a quizzical tone.

Greenberg observed Abdiel: his sad eyes, now glazed; head tilted forward; hands trembling slightly.

'Yes, he knew where I was … so even in his saner moments, he chose not to make contact,' Abdiel acknowledged, head bowed. 'That hurts, and it's been my torture for sixty-four years.' Tears spilled down his face.

'Was there a falling out between you and Daniel?' Greenberg asked.

'No. We were close growing up. In the camp I didn't see much of him. We were in different work parties and different huts. I looked out for him regularly…'

Greenberg sat stroking his chin, evaluating, trying to make sense of what he was hearing. *Is there something more to this than Abdiel's willing to disclose?* The more Greenberg sat with the emotion in the room, and the more he observed Abdiel, the more he sensed that there was a missing piece of the jigsaw puzzle. He had no idea what it was. Solomon's sympathetic words interrupted the long silence. 'Abdiel, the war … Auschwitz … it does strange things to us … I guess one good thing is that you've found your brother.'

Abdiel, in slow motion glanced at the faces of each agent in turn. His words came out heavy with deep sadness, 'I've found his body, but I've not found my brother.'

Chapter Thirty-Three

I enter Papa's room. His eyes are closed. He looks comfortable after what I imagine was a small breakfast. The monitor shows his heart rate at 75 bpm, blood pressure 140/95, oxygen level 98—acceptable. The drip provides him with the necessary level of medication to manage his constant pain. The bristles on his chin catch the morning light, streaming in through the open window. I turn to exit, and his eyes open.

'Uri. It's you!' he whispers.

'Yes, Papa, it's me. I popped in to check up on you. How're you feeling this morning?'

He responds with a faint smile. 'It's just like any other morning. I'm comfortable; I've suffered worse than this in my life. I'd like to have a chat with you when you have a little time. I know how busy you are …'

'Papa. I'll always make time to talk. I can drop by when I finish this afternoon if you like.'

'That's fine by me. I'm not going anywhere.'

I find my way to the nurse's station and wonder what the subject of 'the chat' will be. It's been two weeks since he entered the palliative care ward. The liver cancer remained hidden for too long and has taken a deadly grip on his ageing body. The yellow pasty condition of his skin announces that his days are numbered—maybe two or three weeks at the most.

I return later in the day, close to four o'clock. He's sitting upright in bed with a collection of pillows supporting his frail, eighty-year-old body. His face remains unshaven. The addition of two new greeting cards on the shelf is the only change since my morning visit. His eyes light up, and I sense he's pleased to see me. 'How are you, Papa?'

'No change. The staff are very good. I suppose they need to be since you're a doctor.'

'They're a dedicated team and would give you first-class care whether I was on staff or not,' I reply. 'Would you like me to give you a shave?'

'No thanks. I need to talk to you about something.' He draws his knees up under the sheets as he speaks. His mood changes and becomes more serious.

I wait, wondering what he's going to say.

He takes two deep breaths and shifts his gaze to the bottom of the bed. His breathing becomes laboured, and the hand protruding from beneath the sheets starts to shake.

'Uri, I have to tell you …' He stops and takes another breath.

Whatever it is, it's significant. 'It's alright, Papa. Take your time. It seems like this is *very* important.'

'It certainly is … I've not told anyone about it. But I need to tell you.' His anxiety is obvious in his strained voice. 'I never wanted to talk about life in the camp, but in the last two months, since your Uncle Daniel was found, I need to. Seeing him has taken me back to that place I've always wanted to forget. I can see it as though it was yesterday. I don't want to take it to my grave alone.'

I nod.

'Do you know what it means to open a door to a forbidden room?'

'Frightening I imagine.'

'I have nightmares about Auschwitz, as you know. They continue to rob me of sleep. I see the past so vividly … Maybe I need to start at the beginning … the days we spent in the filthy railway trucks used by cattle without toilet facilities on the way to the camp. We lay on urine-soaked straw. An old man died next to me on the first day, and I lay beside him for the entire journey because the carriage was so overcrowded. Each day the guards handed out water, bearing the faint smell of vegetables. It was supposed to be soup. If you lost your cup you died.' Papa pauses and takes another deep breath.

I'm anxious; aware he's becoming stressed. Yet I know it's important for him to tell his story.

'After the train stopped, the guards screamed at us to get out. We formed a line and marched towards an officer. The flick of his finger sent us to the left or the right. Someone whispered to me, "The right side means work; the left is for the sick and those incapable of work. They get sent to a special camp."'

'How did you feel as you walked up to the guard?'

'I was nervous, but tried not to show it. I carried my suitcase in my right hand and made an effort to walk upright. The SS man looked me over, appeared to hesitate, then put both hands on my shoulders. I tried hard to look strong. He turned my shoulders very slowly until I faced right. I moved over to that side. Of course I knew later what that special camp was—the gas chambers.'

'How old were you then?'

'Thirteen. I was tall for my age and strong. I suspect that saved me. I saw other boys my age going left. A sign across the camp gate read, *Arbeit Macht Frei.* Work gives freedom.'

'You survived the first selection.' I lean forward on my chair to catch his voice, quieter now due to emotion.

'Yes, I survived round one. We were made to run from the station past electrically charged barbed wire, through the camp to the cleansing station—real bath showers. Next we were herded into another room to be shaved. Not only our heads; not a hair was left on our entire bodies. While we were waiting for the showers, our nakedness was brought home to us. We had nothing now except our bare bodies. Everything we owned had gone. Even the hair we possessed. As the days went on, nearly everyone contemplated suicide. It came from the hopelessness of the situation, the constant danger of death looming over us, and the deaths of colleagues, daily. I made myself a firm promise on my first evening in camp that I wouldn't "run the wire." This was the most popular form of suicide. I wanted to survive. I learnt I was a *Häftling*—a prisoner initiated into this misery by an official armed with a sort of pointed tool with a very short needle ... you had to show your number to get bread, soup, or anything.' Papa paused and adjusted his body weight.

'Do you want to lie down?'

'No, thanks. I prefer to sit upright. I can think better that way.'

His story captivates me. On rare occasions I've overheard him giving snippets to Ima, but I've never heard his story like this before. I remind myself not to ask too many questions. His need to share the pain of his story is what this time is about.

'At first I couldn't bear to see my fellow prisoners being abused. One of the most ridiculous exercises was the forced march up and down in the mud mixed with sewerage beside the sleeping quarters. The SS guards took great delight in striking the prisoners with the butt of their rifles. Usually the unfortunate man ended up face first in the bog. But then I passed into the second stage of camp life. I didn't look away. My feelings became blunted. The abuse of others became the norm.'

'It was a way of looking after yourself. It helped you survive. Numbing yourself so you don't feel kept you alive.'

'Yes, but we felt like the living dead. Beatings occurred on the slightest provocation, sometimes for no reason at all. I remember one occasion. Bread was rationed out at our worksite, and we had to line up for it. The man behind me stood a little off to one side and that lack of alignment displeased the guard. I didn't know what was going on behind me or what was in the mind of the SS guard. Suddenly I received three sharp blows on my head. I then spotted the guard at my side using his stick. It wasn't the physical pain that hurt the most; it was the mental agony of the injustice, the unreasonableness of it all.'

A young nurse in her mid-twenties enters and Papa stops. 'Excuse me, doctor,' she says. 'I need to take his blood pressure.'

Her activity gives him a breather and time for me to gather my thoughts. I'd heard from patients and read stories of many Holocaust victims, but when you hear them for the first time from your father … I'm overwhelmed.

'It's a little high at the moment, Abdiel. You may need to rest,' says the nurse.

'Thank you, sister,' Papa mumbles as the nurse leaves the room.

'Do you need a break?'

'Not at all. I've started this, and I need to finish it. It's been a long time … too long.'

I nod as he takes a sip of water.

'There were some brief moments of respite. One of the "privileged prisoners," a Copa, took a liking to me. Sometimes he whispered to the prisoner ladling the soup to dip the ladle to the bottom where the peas were. That was always a luxury and possibly saved my life. Because of the high degree of undernourishment we suffered, the primitive desire for food drove our conversations. One fellow would ask another working next to him in the ditch what his favourite dishes were. Then came the exchange of recipes and the "menu of the day." The gourmet fantasy was interrupted when the warning came down the trench, "Guard coming."'

'What were your rations?' I needed to say something just to respond to him.

'The daily ration was watery soup and a small piece of bread. The so-called extra allowance was three-quarters of an ounce of margarine or a slice of poor-quality sausage or a little piece of cheese. Maybe also a bit of synthetic honey or a spoonful of watery jam. It varied from day to day. In calories, this diet was completely inadequate, especially because we were doing heavy manual work and constantly exposed to the cold. Inadequate clothing made us vulnerable to sickness. Nobody can understand the soul-destroying mental conflict which a famished man experiences.'

'I can only imagine what that would be like.' His words pile up on me. I'm amazed at his memory for detail. I see the pictures he's painting and feel a growing tightness in my stomach.

'I remember regularly, tenderly, touching a piece of stale bread in my coat pocket with frozen fingers, then breaking off a crumb and putting it in my mouth. Finally with a last bit of willpower, I'd put it back again, having promised myself earlier in the day, to hold out till afternoon.'

I change my position and nod, conveying understanding.

'The worst part of camp life was the three shrill blows of a whistle in the darkness of early morning, and we began the struggle with our wet shoes. We could scarcely force our sore and swollen feet into them.' Tiredness creeps into his voice. 'The usual chorus of moans and groans accompanied the snapping of wires we used to replace shoelaces.'

'I don't know how you survived … It's so hard to hear your story, but I want to know.' The lump in my stomach feels uncomfortable.

'You need to know, Uri … Thanks for hearing me. There's more to come. The worst is yet to come.'

What could be worse than this? I wonder.

'One of the luxuries was the shower where we stood frozen, but had the opportunity to remove any parasites clinging to us through the dribble of water from the shower heads. If vermin remained, it ended in a restless night's sleep. The time that terrified us all was the selections. A guard entered the hut and chose a number of men, depending on the quota. The guard first called for volunteers. Those who wanted to end their life stepped forward. If the quota wasn't filled, he made the selection. The prisoners then marched out to face the gas chambers.

'The majority of prisoners suffered from depression and a loss of any sense of self. We were little more than animals. We'd all once been, or fancied ourselves to be, somebody. Now we were treated like we were nothing.' Papa looks toward the cabinet and reaches for a glass of water. After a few sips, I return it to its resting place.

'The SS drove us like a herd of sheep backwards and forwards with shouts and kicks and blows. And we'd think of only two things, how to evade the bad dogs and how to get a little food. Just like sheep crowded timidly in the centre of a herd, each of us tried to get into the middle of our formations. That gave us a better chance of avoiding the blows of the guards marching on the sides, front, and rear. The central position had the added advantage of affording protection against the bitter winds, too. It was an attempt to save our own skin. We tried to merge into the crowd, and this was done automatically in the formations. You didn't draw attention to yourself. To shave regularly, even though it was with a piece of broken glass, was necessary to maintain your health. It cut and left scrape marks, colouring your cheeks. I always stood and walked as smartly as I could.'

An overwhelming sadness grips me. 'You've suffered so much ...'

'... and thank you for listening, Uri. I've so many memories ... I can't ... I can't forget them. The tune the band played when we marched out on road-duty and when we returned still freezes the blood in my veins. The stealing that went on just to stay alive—you never put your beret, knife or spoon down, always gripped them between your knees if you washed your hands. We slept, two to a plank, on top of a hessian bag filled with a little straw, one blanket between two, head to toe. Everyone had sores on their feet that wept at night. The stench was terrible. We had to cut our fingernails by chewing them. Toenails were ground away by our ill-fitting shoes. The rules, and there were hundreds, you learnt by blows to the head or body. Nobody told you what they were … if you didn't know German you soon knew what the words meant …' Papa pauses to catch his breath.

'When I first arrived at the camp and was desperate for water, having had nothing to drink for days, I scooped up some snow off a ledge to eat. A guard stepped forward and hit me with a shovel. *"Warum?"* I asked. *"Hier ist kein warum"* came the sharp reply. There's no "why" here. In camp everything was forbidden because the camp had been created for that very purpose. You learnt skills, like listening to how full the bucket was at night when someone peed into it. If you were the last to use it and it was filled to the top, the rule was, you had to empty it. The rules also stated you had to change into your striped clothes to carry it through the courtyard to the latrines. In the winter, the only advantage was that it provided a little warmth beside your leg as you walked. The downside was that inevitably you stumbled on the uneven ground and the contents sloshed into your shoes. Our shoes were instruments of torture—ill-fitting and laced with wire, stolen, or found in the compound. *"Dicke Füsse"* –swollen feet—was the great fear amongst us. Once diagnosed everyone knew there was no cure and that meant the gas chamber. The stages in camp life were firstly shock and then you moved to apathy. It became a state of negative happiness, freedom from suffering.'

Papa remains quiet, but tremors in his body show a growing agitation. A minute passes, and then he turns his face toward me. In a quavering voice he says, 'This is the part that I don't want to tell you, but I must. It makes me feel so disgusting. I've not told a soul, not even your mother. I've lived with it ever since the camp. It still terrifies me … what I did. You may want to disown me as a father. I wouldn't blame you if you did!' He shakes his head violently.

'Papa, I don't need to know. I can see how distressed you are.' He's shaking, his breathing is laboured, and his heart rate elevates to 125. I look deep into his haunting, pleading, desperate eyes. My body tenses, mind racing, wondering what he could have done to make him feel this way.

'I need to tell you. I don't want to die without you knowing. You must know the truth … I'm not the person you think I am.' His hands grip each other, knuckles white.

'What do you mean, Papa?'

'In the spring of 1942, gas chambers at Birkenau were constructed out of two peasant huts, known as the bunkers. On the outside they looked clean and pretty with a coat of whitewash. Fruit trees surrounded them. The roofs were thatched, but the cottages had no windows. The doors were solid and could be screwed shut. As inmates approached the cottages set in the woods, they saw a sign saying "to disinfection."'

Papa moves his head so he stares at the ceiling. No longer does he want to look at me. His chest rises and falls in a distressing rhythm. 'My job was to welcome the deportees and show them to the large room in a wooden hut where they undressed. I tried to keep them calm and reassure them all was well. Then I'd lead them, pathetic in their nakedness, into the cottage. Their eyes stared at me, searching for answers, for truth I couldn't give. I smiled and tried to hide the pain of my deception.'

Papa holds his breath but is beaten by the sob that explodes from his gut. 'Agh!' He takes a moment to recover and then continues. 'Once they were in the room, a command was given, and the SS would come out of their room, check the prisoners, lock the doors and switch the lights off from outside. At first, you'd hear screams, then murmuring. A member of the SS would climb onto the roof, put on a gas mask, lift the chimney cover off, and open one of the boxes. He'd tip the contents, Zyklon B, into the chimney. On contact with air, it produces a gas. Then came their screams and a rush for the doors. The cries we heard were horrific—terrifying.' Papa sobs and his hands writhe, wrestling each other on his stomach.

I place my hand on his shoulder. 'That must have been horrendous to hear.'

Papa pauses to catch his breath. 'After a few minutes … complete silence. Through the keyhole we could see that no one was moving. Half an hour later, we turned on the aeration system, opened the doors, and the heat dissipated. While we loaded the bodies onto a trolley, the next batch was already undressing in the big room … we pulled the gold teeth from the corpses and cut their hair … then'—his sobbing intensifies—'we … I … loaded the bodies into the ovens. I was a … a … *Sonderkommando*.'

I stroke his shoulder as his chest heaves and the sobbing continues.

'We could fit three … bodies at a time … depending on their size. When the cremation was in full swing, we collected the fat from the floor with buckets and threw it back onto the fire to speed up the process … it went on day and night … seven days a week … the stench of burning bodies … you could smell it through the camp … everywhere … at night you could see the sky glowing red. Towards the end … in 1944 when the Hungarian Jews arrived, it was terrible … the extra number meant we burnt the bodies in open ditches … the heat made the bodies gesticulate … arms and legs waving around … sometimes they sat up … their faces horribly distorted … ahh …'

His sobbing now is so extreme he can't continue. His heart rate has climbed dangerously high, and he's struggling for breath.

'I can understand why you've had nightmares,' I say. 'Rest now.'

I've read and heard about the horrors of the extermination camps … but to hear it from your own father … I'm shaking, too … my whole body. The sickening feeling in my stomach is growing, and I wonder if I'm going to vomit. Papa's chest returns to normal breathing, and I wipe salty tears from his dark eyes. His pillow is damp with the pain he's carried for all these years.

Silence soothes the room from the horror and terror it has just witnessed. The silence is sacred. Here's a man who has bared his soul, freed his darkest imprisoned secret, a confession. I'm the priest, hearing, absolving, suffering, weeping, enabling the healing.

'We'd clean the ditches … collect the ashes … scatter them on a cement block and pulverise the bones with wooden rollers. A truck carried the remains to the little lake in the camp.' A long pause passes. 'Uri, will you ever forgive me?'

I'm shocked and take a deep breath, 'Forgiveness! You had no choice,' I say indignantly.

His swollen eyes search my face. His sinewy, withering hand grips mine. 'I did have a choice. That's one thing they could not take away from us.' His response came slowly, choosing his words carefully. 'They took away our clothes, our belongings, our hair, our name ... but they could never take away our choice ... how we responded. Some of the prisoners refused and were shot. Some 'ran the wire' ... I thought about it, too ... no, I chose to live, but it meant deceiving my countrymen, reassuring them when they were undressing that everything was going to be fine ... then, watching them die ... burning their bodies ... many inmates refused to look me in the eye. I was despised, hated.'

The sobbing returns to rack his exhausted body. Tears fall and mark the front of my shirt. 'I think the worst part was the burning ... the smell ... we vomited ... often. If you didn't keep up with the pace or ... couldn't stomach it ... you were shot. I can still see their faces ... twisting ... burning ... I chose to do it.' His eyes are fixed on the fluorescent light secured to the ceiling, but he's back in the horrors of that little wood in the grounds of Auschwitz - Birkenau. (Note 1)

'Papa, yes, you chose to live. It took courage for those who chose to die, and it was quick. Their suffering was short. But for you, it took courage to choose to live ... maybe more courage. It was easier for them ... they escaped the ongoing torture. You chose life, and you chose to face your torment every day. You've paid the price of your bravery ever since. I respect you ... I've no idea what I'd do in that situation ... no idea whatsoever.'

A momentary silence.

It gives me time to think, and then I reflect, 'No matter what work you did, you were helping the enemy. Building roads, constructing barracks, making ammunition, anything; it all supported their war effort.'

Papa glances at me and then stares at the ceiling.

'If you'd chosen to die, I'd have never existed,' I say with a hint of cheekiness. 'Papa, do you remember when I went to the Wall with you when I was eight? You wanted to go and pray. You were upset, but you didn't want to show it.'

'How could I ever forget it?' He takes a minute to arrange his thoughts. 'Most of us who were forced into this terrible deception couldn't work beyond a couple of hours before vomiting from the stench of burning bodies. If we couldn't continue, we were immediately executed. Somehow I survived. I developed a strange friendship with some of the guards, who also were press-ganged into this evil. One of the German officers attached himself to me. I don't know why - something about my personality or resilience? I don't know. When the end of the war was close, this officer asked me, if I ever made it to the Wailing Wall to pray … he said "please say a prayer for me."

'I couldn't believe it! Me? Pray for an enemy who had contributed to the murder of six million of my countrymen? Pray for the executioner of innocent Jewish men, women, and children? Then I realised that he, too, was trapped, like me. Doing whatever he needed to do to survive —a vile, sickening bond that strangely united us. When you and I went to the Wall that day, it all came back. I could see his face, understand his dilemma; we were both powerless, bound together in evil.'

Papa allows the tears to flow freely. No more fighting the emotion. Gentle drops fall, bringing relief, light, and life. The door to a dark cellar, locked for decades, opens.

After the tears, a faint smile crosses his thin lips. He turns his head towards me. Two lifeless eyes peer at me. His body is now still as he lies exhausted, breathing normally. 'Uri. There's something else.' He pauses and his breathing increases again.

What more could there be?

'Do you remember Yeheil Dinur?' Papa whispers.

'Yeheil Dinur … I remember the name.'

'Yeheil was in Auschwitz, too. He survived and lives in Israel. He was one of the witnesses called to testify against Eichmann.'

'Ah, yes.'

'Do you remember, Uri, when the time came in court to identify Eichmann, Yeheil lifted his head and looked straight into the eyes of Adolph Eichmann, who he'd not seen in eighteen years. Suddenly, Yehiel started sobbing uncontrollably. He fainted and fell on the floor of the courtroom. Afterwards he was interviewed and quizzed about his reaction. News reporters asked, "Was it hatred or fear? Was it the horror of your memories of Auschwitz?" Do you remember what he said?'

'Not exactly.'

Papa gripped my arm, his voice strong, and said, 'Dinur shook his head. He said, "None of it. I was afraid for myself. I saw I had the capability to do that. This was not some godlike authority in uniform who sentenced us to Auschwitz. Eichmann was an ordinary man, and suddenly I realized I was just like him." Dinur was saying, *I looked into his eyes, and I saw myself.* Uri, as I look back at Eichmann and others who committed atrocities against us, I know that I'm capable of that horror, also. I, too, can look at Eichmann and see myself.' [Note 2] His voice is strained and crackles with emotion, but no tears flow. The well is dry, and his ghostly eyes stare in disbelief at the ceiling. 'I'm no better than any of them,' he says with a long sigh.

I allow silence to help me gather my thoughts.

'You're a brave man, Papa, to face your own darkness. Often the things we most hate in others are the very things we deny that exist in ourselves.'

We sit for what seem ages, as he grips my hand. The enormity of his revelation overwhelms me. I want to cry, scream, at the cruelty, injustice, he's suffered. The pain he's endured all these years; the distress it's caused Ima, our family, me!

Finally he speaks. 'Thank you, Uri, for listening to me, for hearing me.'

'I'm grateful to you for telling me, trusting me. I know how important it was to let go of that weight. I love you, respect you so much …' I pause for a long time before asking, 'Do you want me to tell anyone else about these things? Family? Friends?'

'Whatever you believe is best. If you think it's helpful to others, that's okay.' His body starts to shake again.

'Are you cold?'

'No, I'm not cold, but I can't stop shaking. What's happening to me?'

'I don't know. Try and keep breathing normally. Allow your body to relax. Don't fight the shaking … allow it to happen.'

His frail body quivers, out of control. He gasps for breath. Five minutes pass, and slowly the shaking stops. His distress has passed, and his breathing becomes regular. I allow him to rest, eyes closed. Several minutes later, I remove my hand from his shoulder where it offered support during the mysterious shaking.

'My body is tingling all over now,' he says. 'I feel warm.'

'Is it a good feeling?'

'Yes, it's … wonderful … relaxing.'

'I suspect it's your body letting go, letting go of the pain you've carried over all these years. You've given your body permission now to relax, and it's responding.'

The last rays of the sun shine through the open window into calmness—the evidence of deep and profound healing. A figure appears at the door with dinner on a tray. I shake my head and the figure retreats. Papa sleeps, exhausted. 'Sleep well, Papa. May pleasant dreams drive your nightmares away. You can now rest in peace—die in peace.'

I'll never forget his memories. How could I? I wish to God I could. His revelation highlights the tension that exists between Jews looking at the world through the lens of the Holocaust, and not letting the world forget the Holocaust. [Note 3]

~

1. Between January 1942 and March 1943, 175,000 Jews were gassed to death in Auschwitz - Birkenau, of whom 105,000 were killed from January to March 1943.

2. 'Wherever there is humankind, there is Auschwitz, because it was not Satan that made Auschwitz, but you and I. Just as Satan did not create the nuclear mushroom, but you and I. Man!' Yeheil Dinur (Shivitti).

3. Descriptions of the camps are drawn from *Man's Search for Meaning* and *What is a Man?* documentaries and my visit to Auschwitz – Birkenau.

Chapter Thirty-Four

April 2013

'The swifts are back again,' Baruch observes, nodding in the direction of the Wall.

'Yes, it's that time of year,' I reply. We stand in the public space before the Western Wall, my heart smiling. Groups of people sing and dance in circles, celebrating Shabbat.

Baruch is now almost twenty, a fine-looking young man with an intellect far superior to mine. His appetite for food only surpasses his voracious consumption of information about life and computers. Shifra is fifteen, proud of the changes taking place in her slim body. She, too, is a bright student, dreaming of a medical career. We come regularly to the Wall, especially on Shabbat. My faith has held me during the shaky rollercoaster ride of recent years. Papa died peacefully two weeks ago after releasing himself from the remnants of his darkness. No longer do my eyes search the place where my letter to Aalia was posted—a prayer to the Almighty.

'Nothing really changes, does it?' Baruch says.

'What do you mean?'

'The cycle of life goes on; the swifts are back, just like they were last year and the year before that, just like they've been doing for hundreds of years. We have the same problems, here in Jerusalem, in Israel, and Jews … just like hundreds …. thousands of years. It's a never-ending story.'

'Some things have changed,' Miriam says. 'Women can now go to the Wall to read and pray on Shabbat!'

'Oh yeah,' Baruch replies with a smile. 'I think … what I mean is … will it ever be different in Israel. Will we ever have peace?'

'That's why we come to the Wall—to pray for the peace of Jerusalem,' I say, placing my hand on his shoulder.

'We're going down to pray now.' Miriam takes Shifra's hand and walks with pride towards the women's section.

Baruch and I complete the ceremonial washing. I observe the light in his eyes. He's a young man with so much promise. We walk together towards the sacred space where much joy flows from hearts privileged to pray, sing, and dance in our holiest site in the world. Figures clothed in black and white, Torahs in hands, move in an emotional sea of praise and thanksgiving.

The emotion of the moment takes hold of me, or is it a remaining pocket of grief from Papa's passing that's snuck up on me? I allow the tears to flow.

Baruch switches his gaze to my face. 'You're crying, Papa.'

Instantly I'm transported back to childhood, standing with Papa here as a child. 'They're tears of joy mixed with the sadness of the passing of your *Zaydeh*,' I say.

Baruch looks at the limestone Wall and sighs. I know he's not come to terms with the death of his grandfather. Baruch's relationship with the man he called *Zaydeh* was tenuous. Papa's dark moods and depression often distanced him from his grandchildren. Ima, in sheer desperation, poured her soul into them, hoping to make up for the void they felt with Papa.

After his 'confessional,' however, he came alive. He reached out from his hospital bed, tears in his eyes, with quivering arms to hold his grandchildren, who couldn't understand this mysterious change. They didn't know that man. Reluctantly they obeyed his call for an embrace with stiff bodies and confused minds. I stood in the background and watched, with a heavy heart, this awkward human spectacle repeat itself many times in his final days—a lifetime of relationships lost to the *Shoah*. My children robbed of the love and affection of their grandfather—another consequence of Hitler's evil.

Baruch asks, 'Did you come to the Wall with *Zaydeh*?'

I wasn't prepared for that question. A sigh escapes my lips. 'I only came to the Wall once with *Zaydeh*. He'd returned from the war—Auschwitz—some years earlier. He told me on many occasions that he wanted to pray at the Wall. But when we stood where we're standing now, he didn't move. I could see he was full of emotion, and he fought hard to hold it in. But a single tear trickled down his face.'

Baruch frowns. 'What caused that tear?'

I gather my thoughts.

'That tear represented the tears of every Jew and all mankind in every age and in every civilization as a consequence of evil. That tear was the pain of persecution, of powerlessness, the agony of impotence, the unspeakable anguish of choices that are not choices, and the terror when men confront their own darkness.'

Baruch looks at me, puzzled, hoping for clarity, but decides to remain silent. A minute later, he asks, 'He had a difficult life, didn't he?'

I nod.

'Did he find peace?'

'Yes, he did. He found peace.' I'm unprepared for the tears that run down my cheeks. I stand, weeping, and Baruch places his arm around my shoulder. The grief of lost years hits me—a Papa we loved but hardly knew. The pain and torment he suffered, yet relief, knowing he died in peace.

A heavy sigh escapes my lips. Baruch removes his arm from me, and I rest my hand on his shoulder. 'Baruch, I want to give you what he gave me. It may be the best wisdom I've ever received: we need to face our own darkness.'

'What do you mean?' Baruch frowns.

'It's taking the courage to look at things in yourself that you feel ashamed to show other people, things that are part of us, but we think people will judge us for. We sometimes criticize and point the finger at other people who do the same things we did, the things we're ashamed to talk about.'

'That's being a hypocrite, isn't it?' Baruch asks, his eyes searching my face.

'Yes, you could say that. It took me many years to understand and accept that I could hate someone so intensely. It made me feel terrible, so I hid it away inside me—in a dark place. I now know I need to look into the eyes of our enemies and see *their* darkness, understand their pain, hear their story, and know they're human too. And remember that we are all from Abraham and see the image of God in the other.'

Baruch is mature for his years. He nods, and I know that some level of understanding has reached his mind. It'll take time and courage to face his own darkness before it reaches his heart. Instinctively I want to shelter him, protect him from the pain and suffering that inevitably will come. I know I can't shield him, yet I'm aware that I'm avoiding telling him any details of his *Zaydeh's* story. Is it to spare him discomfort? I make a resolution to sit with him when the time is right and provide a fuller picture of Papa's pain. I must trust him to the future. I must be a father who loves his son enough to set him free, and then be ready with the ointment and bandages for when he falls.

We leave the sacred space as night darkens the sky. Miriam and Shifra farewell their women friends, and we walk together towards the Dung Gate. An adolescent Jewish girl in a blue headscarf, a familiar face at the Wall, glances at Baruch. Their eyes meet, bringing a smile to their lips. I realise this is not the first time they've met at a distance. I smile to myself—yes, some things never change.

~

'Israel is an echo of Auschwitz. While meals are more plentiful and health care exists, its borders continue to be defined by barbed wire. Its inhabitants, watched, goaded, threatened, by those outside and inside the fence, intent on their extinction.' Author unknown

*'Truth and forgiveness are the only solution for the Middle East. The challenge, especially between Israelis and Palestinians, is not to **find** the solution. The challenge is to be the first courageous enough to **embrace** it.' Mosab Hassan Yousef*

A Note from the Author

If you enjoyed this book, please leave a review at your point of purchase. I would be very grateful, not only because I love to hear your opinion but also because your review will help other readers decide if they would like to read the book.

If you want some background and resources for further information on events mentioned in this book, please read on for the Appendices.

You might also be interested to read my other book, *Out of Latvia: The Son of a Latvian Immigrant Searches for his Roots*. It's the true story of two men, a generation apart, one growing up in the shadow of the other.

Acknowledgments

Writing a novel is not a solitary activity and I want to thank those who were part of my team. I am grateful for my six readers who gave helpful feedback on the first manuscript: JK, WL, NH, RMc and my wife Chris. A big thank-you to Chris who has encouraged and supported me through the process, and together with John and Kim, proofread the formatted manuscript. I need to acknowledge the patience, encouragement and skills of my editor and publisher, Tahlia, who has helped to steer the course to completion. My thanks to Rose of Velvet Wings Media for her creative design for the cover.

The suggestion of the title by Rob Mc was a great improvement on my early attempt.

My sincere thanks to the Israelis and Palestinians who have entrusted me with their stories and given me permission to be their voice.

Appendix A

Ishmael and Isaac

The ongoing conflict within Israel and Palestine between the Israeli State and Palestinian Arabs is often pictured as mirroring a sibling rivalry that's been part of biblical history for centuries. The story of Ishmael and Isaac is recorded in Genesis 17 and 21: 1- 21. Ishmael is the son of Abraham by Hagar, the handmaid of Sarah, his wife. Sarah had realised in her advanced years that she was infertile and gave her handmaid to Abraham to produce a child. This was an ancient custom to ensure the continuation of the male line.

When Hagar conceived through Abraham, however, Sarah expelled her from the home with Abraham's reluctant consent. An angel of God met Hagar and her son Ishmael on the way to Egypt and told her to return to Sarah and serve her. God promised to multiply her descendants through her son, but he would be a 'wild ass' amongst men. However, the blessing for the Jewish people would come through Abraham's seed with the miraculous birth of Isaac from Sarah.

The Genesis account in the Hebrew Bible is portrayed in the words of Rabbi Jeffrey Salkin as the story of a dysfunctional family. It is the terminal pattern of the book of Genesis: damaged, shattered relationships between siblings and within families. It is a battle of the 'Cain complex'—the battle between siblings, each one battling for the exclusive love of God. The great Rabbi Moshe ben Naham comments that 'when our ancestress Sarah persecuted Hagar, she committed a sin. Abraham, by not preventing her, became an accomplice to that sin. That is why God heard the lament and the tears of Hagar and gave her a wild son whose descendants would torment in every way the descendants of Abraham and Sarah. The sufferings of the Jewish people derive from those which Sarah inflicted upon Hagar.'

However, what constitutes an expulsion within Jewish tradition—evoking a concern for the trauma visited upon Hagar and Ishmael—actually marks the beginnings of the Islamic tradition and is accepted as the action of an unfathomable and all-knowing God/Allah.

From the Muslim standpoint, Abraham was not the world's first Jew; rather, he was a good Muslim according to the history of pre-Islamic Arabs. Mecca was founded as a settlement by Abraham, his concubine wife Hagar and their son Ishmael. It was Abraham and his son who built a simple structure the *Kaba* (the cube) as a centre for the worship of God. Other traditions trace the family of Mecca as the primordial and most sacred of holy sites to Adam the father of humanity but credited Abraham and his family with establishing a permanent settlement there.

Source: J. Kristen Urban, "Isaac and Ishmael: Opportunities for Peace within Religious Narrative," *Journal of Religion, Conflict and Peace*, Vol 2, Issue 2 Spring 2009.

Appendix B
Three Rs

Andrew White in his booklet entitled *Older Younger Brother: The Tragic Treatment of the Jews by the Christians,* discusses the theology of 'The Land' from a Christian perspective. Firstly, he describes **Replacement Theology,** which has as its core the belief that 'the church' replaced 'the Jews' so that everything that historically and biblically has been applied to the Jewish people in the land of Israel, now applies instead to the church. He contends that this interpretation of scripture fuelled the atmosphere in Europe that enabled the Holocaust to happen. At the Nuremberg trials, some of the worst perpetrators of the Holocaust said they had engaged in the atrocities because of what the great Protestant reformer Martin Luther had told them to do, which relied on this interpretation of the Bible.

A more recent development has been **Remnant Theology.** Advocates of this approach call themselves Christian Zionists and hold to a biblical theology that allows for consistency and continuity between the Hebrew Scriptures and the New Testament. The belief is that Gentile followers of Jesus are grafted into the remnant of Israel, as written by St Paul in Romans 11:17. Israel is depicted here as an olive tree. The Christians are seen as being grafted into that tree, the branches being the faithful remnant from Israel. In verse 19, Paul says something that is totally fundamental to this position: 'Do not boast over the root because you do not support the root—the root supports you.'

The root of Christianity is Judaism. The logic is that if you destroy the root, namely Judaism, you destroy the faith. If you destroy Judaism, there is no real Christianity, so the church is an essential part of the remnant of Israel, as portrayed by St Paul. Adherents to this interpretation of scripture would agree that the modern state of Israel is intrinsically related to the Israel of prophecy and is a direct fulfilment of it. Exponents of Remnant Theology will support Israel politically, usually aligning more with the religious Right-Wing political parties

Other biblical texts that are used to support this approach include Genesis 12:3. 'I will bless them that bless you and curse him that curses you; in you shall all nations of the earth be blessed.' This implies that those nations that bless the Jewish people receive the blessing of God, and the nations that curse the Jewish people will experience the curse of God.

In Romans 15:27 St Paul writes, 'For if the Gentiles have shared in their [the Jews'] spiritual things, they are indebted to minister to them also in material things.' Christians owe a debt of eternal gratitude to the Jewish people for their contributions that gave birth to the Christian faith. So Jesus Christ, a prominent rabbi from Nazareth said, 'Salvation is of the Jews!'

The third theological approach is **Recognition Theology**, which has emerged as a response to the Holocaust. Theologians began asking the question: 'How could this have happened in the midst of Christian Europe?' One of the key arguments is that Judaism was a valid means of salvation. This approach recognises the historic role Judaism has had in the establishment of Christianity. It recognises that at the heart of the Christian faith there was not only Jesus, the Jew, but also thousands of years of salvation history beginning with Abraham. Without Judaism, Christianity in the New

Testament could not be properly understood. It is believed that the 'Logos' in John's Gospel and the Torah (*Shema*) are indeed the same and that salvation could, therefore, be gained either by Jesus or the Torah. The essence of Judaism is seen in the *Shema*. It is the nearest thing that Judaism has to a creed; it's found in Deuteronomy 6:7, and every Jew is obligated to say it morning and night. The *Shema* is an affirmation of Judaism and a declaration of faith in one God. The words are also found on a little scroll within every *mezuzah*, the amulet, which is attached to every doorpost in a Jewish home:

> Hear O Israel the Lord our God, the Lord is one! You shall love the Lord your God with all your heart, with all your soul, and with all your might. And these words which I command you today shall be in your heart; you shall teach them diligently to your children, and shall talk of them when you sit in your house, when you walk by the way, when you lie down, and when you rise up. You shall bind them as a sign of your hand and they shall be as frontlets between your eyes [phylacteries]. You shall write them on the doorposts of your house and on your gates.

The common factor in both the *Shema* and the Christian faith is the love of God. Jesus himself when asked to identify the greatest commandments, referred back to the *Shema*. Those who hold to recognition theology state that both Judaism and Christianity are valid means of salvation. It is a position that has gained support from both Catholic and Protestant theologians and has been accepted by some of the European Protestant churches as their official position.

Resources

Izzeldin Abuelaish, *I Shall Not Hate*, London: Bloomsberry Publishing, 2012.

Ian Bickerton, *The Arab – Israeli Conflict: A Guide for the Perplexed,* New York: Continuum International Publishing Group, 2012.

Martin Buber, *I and Thou,* New York: Martino Publishing, 2010.

Elias Chacour, *Blood Brothers,* Grand Rapids, USA: Baker Publishing Group, Chosen Books, 2003.

Colin Chapman, *Whose Promised Land?: The Continuing Conflict over Israel and Palestine,* Oxford, UK: Lion, 2015.

Viktor E. Frankl, *Man's Search For Meaning*, Boston: Beacon Press, 2006.

Jewish Virtual Library.

Yoram Kaniuk, *Commander of the Exodus,* New York: Grove Press, 1999.

Primo Levi, *If This is a Man/the Truce,* London: Abacus, 2003.

John Lyons, *Balcony Over Jerusalem,* Sydney, NSW: Harper Collins, 2017.

H. V. Morton, *In the Steps of the Master*, Boston: Da Capo Press, 1964.

Benny Morris, *1948: A History of the First Arab-Israeli War,* New Haven and London: Yale University Press, 2008.

Conor Cruise O'Brien, *The Siege: The Saga of Israel and Zionism*, New York: Simon and Schuster, Touchstone, 1987.

Tom Segev, *One Palestine Complete,* London: Abacus, 2001.

Sandy Tolan, *The Lemon Tree,* Cambridge, UK: Black Swan, 2006.

J. Kristen Urban, "Isaac and Ishmael, Opportunities for Peace within Religious Narrative," *Journal of Religion, Conflict and Peace*, Vol 2.

Andrew White, *The Vicar of Bagdad: Fighting For Peace in the Middle East,* Oxford, UK: Monarch Books, 2009.

Andrew White, *Older Younger Brother, The tragic treatment of the Jews by the Christians,* (Self Published) 2014.

Mosab Hassan Yousef, *Son of Hamas*, Pipersville, PA: Tyndale, 2011.

Interviews with Israelis and Palestinians in Israel/Palestine and expatriates living in Australia.

Key Events

2 November 1917: Balfour Declaration—espouses a national home for Jewish people.

7 July 1937: Peel Commission—partition resolution accepted by Britain, Ben-Gurion, Zionist institutions. Rejected by the Arabs.

1934 – 1948: *Aliyah Bet*, 'illegal immigration to Israel'—Holocaust survivors brought to Israel.

22 March 1945: Establishment of the Arab League based in Egypt.

29 November 1947: The UN General Assembly adopted the Partition Plan for Palestine – Resolution 181.

29 November 1947 – 20 July 1949: War of Independence.

14 May 1948: Declaration of the State of Israel by David Ben-Gurion.

15 May – 11 June 1948: Arab invasion of Israel.

1948 – 1967: Jerusalem is divided between Israel and Jordan on the 'green line.' Jordan holds eastern part, Israel the western and southern parts. Jews denied access to the Old City and holy places in contravention of armistice agreement.

1949: Large *aliyah* to Israel from Ethiopia and Arab states; 5 December, David Ben-Gurion declares Jerusalem capital of Israel.

1951: UN Security Council condemns blocking of Suez Canal by Egypt.

29 October – 5 November 1956: The Sinai Campaign. Capture of Sinai Peninsula.

2 June 1956: PLO founded—committed to destroying Israel by armed struggle.

5 – 10 June 1967: The Six Day War. Egypt, Jordan, Syria, Lebanon, and Iraq versus Israel.

29 August 1967: Arab League meets in Khartoum. 'Three Nos': No peace with Israel; no recognition of Israel; no negotiations with Israel.

22 November 1967: UN Security Council calls for 'just and lasting peace'—withdrawal of Israel from lands it conquered in 1967 War, a solution to the refugee problem, and free passage for ships through international lanes.

8 March 1969 – 9 August 1970: War of Attrition—Egyptian bombardment of Israeli troops along Suez Canal.

5 – 6 September 1972: Eleven Israeli athletes murdered at Munich Olympics by Palestinian terrorist organisation Black September.

6 – 24 October 1973: Yom Kippur War—Syria and Egypt versus Israel.

22 October 1973: UN Security Council calls for cease-fire and negotiations.

1977 – 1979: Egyptian-Israeli peace.

17 Sept 1978: Camp David Accords.

26 March 1979: Israeli - Egyptian Peace Treaty signed.

1 April 1982: Completion of Israel's withdrawal from Sinai.

1982: First Lebanon War. Operation Peace for Galilee.

1982: Israel expels PLO from southern Lebanon.

1985: Israel withdraws from Lebanon.

8 December 1987: First Intifada. Yasser Arafat declares Palestinian independence.

17 January 1991: First Gulf War.

30 October 1991: Madrid Conference.

1993: Oslo agreement.

1994: Yitzhak Rabin, Shimon Peres, and Yasser Arafat awarded Nobel Peace Prize.

1995: Yitzhak Rabin assassinated at peace rally in Tel Aviv by right-wing fanatic.

1996: First and only election of the Palestinian Council. Arafat becomes President.

28 September 2000 to 8 February 2005: Second Intifada.

27 March 2002: 'Passover Massacre'—suicide bombing, Park Hotel in Netanya. Leads to Operation Defensive Shield.

2005: Gaza withdrawal—Israel withdraws unilaterally from the Gaza Strip, uprooting thousands of Israeli settlers from their homes.

2006: Lebanon War.

2008: Israel launches Operation Cast Lead against Hamas in Gaza after repeated rocket firing into the south of Israel.

2011: Palestine wins recognition by UNESCO; vote on statehood postponed.

2012: Rate of attacks across Gaza continues to grow; Gaza launches 300 missiles and mortar shells into southern Israel.

2012: Operation Pillar of Defense—Israel Air Force (IAF) kills second in command of Hamas military wing. UN General Assembly updates Palestine to non-member observer state status. In response Israel approves enlarging settlements in the area connecting Jerusalem and Maale Adumim in the West Bank.

2013: Attacks continue on both sides. Benjamin Netanyahu becomes PM for the third time.

Prime Ministers of Israel

David Ben-Gurion (first time, 1948–53)
Moshe Sharett (1953–55)
David Ben-Gurion (second time, 1955–63)
Levi Eshkol (1963–69)
Golda Meir (1969–74)
Yitzhak Rabin (first time, 1974–77)
Menachem Begin (1977–83)
Yitzhak Shamir (first time, 1983–84)
Shimon Peres (first time, 1984–86)
Yitzhak Shamir (second time, 1986–92)
Yitzhak Rabin (second time, 1992–95)
Shimon Peres (second time, 1995–96)
Benjamin Netanyahu (first time, 1996–99)
Ehud Barak (1999–2001)
Ariel Sharon (2001–06)
Ehud Olmert (2006–09)
Benjamin Netanyahu (2009 second time)

Source: Encyclopaedia Britannica

About the Author

David Kerr is a relationship therapist, educator, radio broadcaster, pastor, traveller and artist. He has an M.A. (Theol.) Sydney College of Divinity, majoring in Counselling and Christian Education, and other tertiary qualifications in Counselling, Religious Education, Divinity and Therapy.

David's journey has been shaped by issues of social justice, the impact of clients' experiences and the stories of fellow travellers, which feed his passion for writing. He is ready to leave this planet when he believes he can no longer make a difference.

David's first book was *Out of Latvia: The Son of a Latvian Immigrant Searches for his Roots.*